Nimbus

Nimbus

Joseph R. Norris

Merrimack Media
Cambridge, Massachusetts

Library of Congress Control Number: 2015937124
ISBN: print: 978-1-939166-67-8
IBSN: ebook: 978-1-939166-69-2

Merrimack Media
Cambridge, Massachusetts

Introduction

Running. Running was all he could do now. If he stopped, it would catch him and throw him out, which would be certain death. The man tried to lose his pursuer by making a sharp right up a flight of stairs, but the machine would not be fooled by such simple tricks. It was a Hawker, and it was chasing him through the building with a predator's determination. It was one of many that had been designed to protect the people of the city, but instead it was hunting the lone man through the ornate halls. The man, who was now running down a long wood paneled hallway, was named Hubert Yeats. He was usually referred to as Hugh by those he called friends and colleagues. He was a simple photographer, with a bad habit of always wanting to know the truth. In this case, Hugh's curiosity had led him down a dangerous path that resulted in this deadly encounter with the Hawker.

Hugh could feel himself slowing down. The chase had gone on for what felt like hours, and seemed that it would end with his death. Just when it looked like the metal menace would catch the blond man in its cold steel claws, one of the few good people left in the city intervened. A woman, one that Hugh had probably seen hundreds of times before in the past but never knew, came out of a side doorway and struck the metal creature over the head with a large frying pan. Not that the aggressive act did either the woman or Hugh any good, as the blow didn't even scratch the paint on the hawk-like head of the Hawker.

The gleaming hawk-man turned on the helpless woman. Hugh did not even turn around to look at her, for there was nothing he could do for the poor woman. He knew if the metal monster caught him, his fate would be the same as hers. So, he found his second wind and pumped his legs, his shoes digging deep into the plush red carpet. He could hear her screams and the sounds of the Hawker at work, a sound he had heard too many times now. All too soon, Hugh could hear the clanging footsteps of the machine behind him, once more on the hunt.

In another desperate attempt to lose the robot, Hugh rounded another sharp corner and found himself face to face with a stained glass window depicting a flock of exotic birds that stretched from floor to ceiling of the end of the hallway. As he franticly looked around for an escape, his eyes found only solid unyielding walls to his left and right. It was a dead end, and he knew there was no time to turn back.

Already, he could see in the window before him the reflection of the wicked metal guardian closing in on him from behind, reaching for him. With claw-like hands as cold as the grave, it grabbed the man tightly, binding his arms to his sides. With what could be a sound of triumph, the Hawker took a step back and threw Hugh at the window.

The lead holding the window's many glass colors in place bent and cracked, then snapped. The colorful glass exploded outward, much like confetti, only sharper. Like startled butterflies, the glass flew in all directions, and Hugh went flying though the breached frame. After running through the dim hallways, the light of the late afternoon sun stung his eyes. He saw the city before him, so white and proud, hiding the evil and corruption behind marble and metal.

As gravity took hold of him, he fell with the shards of colored glass. He watched the buildings fly past him, like rockets into the sky. As he fell, strong winds whipped at his hair and stole his leather cap. He felt the gusts force his body to fall at a slight angle, sending him and the glass shards off towards the east. He saw that he was falling toward some cables and reached out his hands in desperation. He managed to grab one of the cables, the shock of his sudden stop sending fireworks of pain up and down his arms. He gritted his teeth as he struggled to keep his hold on the cable, the pain growing the longer he dangled from the wire.

As he struggled to pull himself up, he glanced over his shoulder and saw a cable car supported by the same cable he was clinging to. It was too far away for him to try to reach, and as he continued to hang, he could feel his grip starting to give as his muscles screamed in protest of the unusual strain. Hugh took in one last look at the city he had loved. Nimbus, the city all around him, was a city in the clouds, held thousands of feet in the air by technology so advanced few could comprehend it. He could see several of the other districts floating in front of him on their rounded bases. He swiveled his neck, taking in the sights of the city for probably the last time. Some buildings gleamed and some shone, though others showed the wear of the city's fall into chaos over the past week. As Hugh's grip failed and his fingers slipped off the cable, gravity once again stole him away. He thought back, back to that fateful day when life in this beautiful city had changed, when the citizens were still free, and life was good.

It was barely a week earlier that Hugh was in his apartment in Galileo Plaza. He had come to Nimbus three years ago, in search of a new life in the sky. The city of Nimbus was originally created as a safe haven from a potential nuclear holocaust. The city was designed to float high enough that the fallout from a nuclear explosion could not reach it. However, living conditions at such an extreme altitude had proved to be dangerous to the citizens' health, with the air being too thin and the temperatures too low, so the engineers redesigned the city to float at a far lower altitude, just beneath the clouds. It was no longer high enough to escape fallout, but it was hard to beat the amazing view the city provided its residents. Now it was seen as one of the most advanced cities in the United States, and many influential people called it home.

Nimbus was in many ways like a normal city, despite being located high in the sky. The buildings were grouped into districts atop floating platforms that supported them like mechanical clouds. Many of the floating sections of Nimbus were large enough to hold parks and city blocks, while others were barely bigger than a large apartment building. There were two ways the average citizen could travel from one district of the city to another – within the carriage of a cable car or by walking across one of the many long sky bridges that connected the floating districts of the city together. As for travel within the districts, one could catch a ride on a district train, which was more like a trolley car than a full sized train.

The districts tended to have a theme, such as a science district, one for culture and the arts, and another for the sole purpose of agriculture. Galileo Plaza, the district Hugh called home, was named after the famous astronomer. Galileo Plaza was well known for its resident artists. Several noteworthy writers, painters, and sculptors lived in this part of

Nimbus. Hugh's home was located in a large building near the center of the district. It stood thirty stories tall and held many businesses and apartments, along with a restaurant on its uppermost floor. His apartment was located on the fifth floor of the building, just down the hall from the elevators.

Hugh's apartment was on the smaller side, having only one bathroom and a kitchen which was open to the front room of the apartment. He had a master bedroom, where he slept, and a small guest room. He used the extra room as a makeshift darkroom for his profession. He was an artist with a camera who often took photographs for the city's newspaper. On occasion Hugh also took scenic pictures of the city to sell as post-cards to help him make ends meet. Hugh made enough from selling his photographs to get by, which made him happy, but some days he wished he could have a more adventurous life, like in the many books he read. Little did he know, in only a few days his whole life would change, and he would be regretting his daydreams.

Today was the Fourth of July, 1959. This was an important day, as it was the day America declared its independence from Great Britain. It was also the day Nimbus had been founded, when the first platform had been raised to the sky over the fields of Kansas nine years ago. On this day, the city really came to life. Flags were hung everywhere and concerts were held in almost every assembly hall. Informational documentaries on the founding of the country and the city played repeatedly in the many theaters of the grand utopia. In Nimbus this was not just a day for the celebration of liberty, but also of progress, as on the Fourth of July the annual Science and Innovation Exhibition was held. This was when all of the great inventors, scientists and engineers of Nimbus gathered together at Liberty Hall to present their latest creations to each other for critique.

After eating a quick breakfast of bacon and eggs, Hugh left his apartment and headed for the cable car depot. Hugh had to hurry to Liberty Hall so he could take photographs for the United Post, the city's newspaper, which would pay him dearly for expert shots of the newest creations of Nimbus's brightest residents. As he hurried past a gathering of small children, he wondered what new and exciting things he would see at the exhibition. The word on the street had been that one of his favorite inventors was going to unveil something big this year, and Hugh didn't want to miss a second of it.

Hugh barely got into the cable car before it left for Liberty Estates, the district that served as the heart of Nimbus. He sighed in relief as he heard the doors close behind him. As the car shook to life and started on its journey to the central hub of the city, Hugh took a moment to look around the cabin. Today he shared his space with a little girl in a cute pink blouse, a stiff man in a pinstripe suit, an elderly woman in 'Betsy Ross' costume and a golden dog that was little more than a puppy. Turning his gaze outside, Hugh watched the buildings and gardens slide by the windows. Soon the car reached its destination and Hugh, along with the other passengers, got out.

Liberty Estates was very crowded at this early hour and Hugh had to weave through the crowds on his way to the large crystal structure near the center of the Estates. Every Fourth of July, this was where the newest creations of the city were showcased and rated before being released to the general public of the floating city. Hugh was one of the few people in the city allowed to be in Liberty Hall due to his connections to one of the more renowned inventors, one Dr. Frank Crick. Frank was known throughout Nimbus for his research in medicine. Frank's research had led to several biological discoveries, such as a way to encourage the human body's natural ability to heal, prompting most wounds to heal up to five times faster than before. Frank may have been thirty years older than Hugh, but that did not stop them from being thicker than thieves.

Looking up from his latest work, Crick greeted Hugh as he came in the front door. "Ah, Hugh, how have you been, my boy?"

"Great, Dr. Crick," said Hugh as he shook hands with his old friend.

"Ready for the big presentation, I trust?" asked the elderly man. "Got fresh film in that camera of yours?"

"As always, Doc," replied Hugh as he set up his camera's tripod in a prime location facing the central presentation stage. It was on this stage that the inventors and scientists stood and presented their latest creations to their peers. The stage was a circular platform about forty feet in diameter with freshly waxed wooden floorboards. The front of it was an open stage, while the back half was a small preparation area, hidden by a tall red velvet curtain. The stage was around two feet high and had a microphone stand built into the front of it. Right now, a stage hand was doing a sound check of the microphone.

"I trust you are excited to see the latest work of Charles Mason?" asked Crick as he watched Hugh set up.

"Ah, yes," said Hugh as he screwed his camera into place on top of the tripod. "Dr. Mason's work with computers is simply amazing, isn't it? Last year he did the impossible, making a computer that is only four feet tall with twice the computing power of the one on display at Manchester University."

"So you've told me," grinned Frank.

"Just imagine, Frank. What do you think Dr. Mason's got for us this time?"

"Well, in just a few hours we'll find out."

Once everything was set up, the presentations began. One man showed off a better replacement leg, another demonstrated how to use a special lens to correct color blindness. Still another showed off a jet pack that, unfortunately, failed on stage. Next was a new gun model that ran on electricity instead of gunpowder. It was designed to stun, but if the beam was turned up it could burn its victim. However, the gun took quite a while to charge up before it was ready to fire, making its practicality questionable. Following this was a new vacuum cleaner model and a prototype for a light bulb with a longer life. Soon it was Dr. Crick's turn on stage. His project was a flexible cast that could easily bend, while still giving the injured body part enough support to heal properly. After Frank came two more inventors, one with a hand-held battery recharger and another with a new type of telephone.

Finally, the man who Hugh had been waiting for came on stage. Dr. Mason was in his late forties and was well known for his work in computers and electronics. Today he came on stage with a giant lump covered in a large white tarp. As the object was wheeled on stage, Hugh re-adjusted his camera's focus.

"Greetings!" Dr. Mason said into the microphone. "Today is a great day in the field of computers and machines. Today I give you something only dreamed of in science fiction novels. I give you the future of artificial intelligence!"

With a pause to let the applause die down, Dr. Mason moved over to the tarp. He reached up with both his hands and threw it aside. Underneath it, gleaming in the lights of Liberty Hall and from the flashes of cameras going off, was a robotic man. It was a Hawker.

"Behold!" said Dr. Mason as he stepped away from the robot. "I give you the Hawker Robot. I have it turned off right now, but in action, it is faster than a man and stronger than an ox. It is designed for keeping the peace and is the future of public protection here in our beautiful city." As Mason droned on about how great his invention was, Hugh changed the subject of his camera's viewfinder from Mason to his machine.

It stood at around seven feet tall, and had the head of a bird of prey. Although it was a robot, it had been designed to have a muscular physique. Its torso was designed to appear similar to that of a policeman's jacket, with eight well-polished buttons running down its chest. The simulated jacket was painted bright blue, and gleamed in the glow of the stage's lights. Its feet were golden and were more avian in nature, sporting three claw tipped mechanical toes, and its hands were those of a man, with four fingers and a thumb. The fingers ended in sharp clawed tips. A belt embraced its waist and held several pouches, and below that were smooth metal legs that became ribbed below its knees. Its eyes seemed to glow in the light of the stage.

"After today, my friends," continued the inventor, "as many as twenty of these Hawkers will be stationed in each of Nimbus's many sectors. I know it seems rather fast, but in a world where the atom has been split and space is within our grasp, so too must we move even faster, for progress will not wait for any one of us to catch up."

With that, Mason walked back over to the Hawker and pulled back a hidden panel on its side. With a press of an unseen button, the machine seemed to gasp, its eyes lit up with a soft blue light, and its joints loosened before it stiffened into a military salute.

With a hint of static, it spoke. "Hawker unit 23 ready to serve." It lowered its metallic hand and took a look around the audience. Then with a soft click, something on the back of the machine started to move. Two flat white rods rotated into view from the back of the Hawker, and like twin paper fans, they unfolded into two large light brown metal wings. With a hiss from a turbine engine hidden from view on the back of the robot, the mechanical man rose a few feet off the stage. The crowd went wild, cheers erupted, and Mason and his creation both bowed to the audience.

With Dr. Mason's presentation's end, the assembly reached its conclusion. The inventors and scientists shook hands with each other and congratulated themselves on yet another great year of discoveries. Of course, there were a few snide comments about some of the engineers being unimpressed with what the robotics inventor had come up with for this year's exhibition. Yet everyone agreed that a lot of progress had been made in all fields over the past year. A couple of the brilliant men actually went so far as to give each other words of congratulations and handshakes, which Hugh captured at the end of his roll of film.

Hugh started to take down his camera as the hall slowly emptied. He could hear the chatter of the people passing by him on their way out. Most of the comments were on Dr. Mason's new robotic creation. Almost every word of it was praise of one sort or another toward the doctor's achievement. However, Hugh did catch a voice that he didn't recognize say that the machine was nothing but trouble.

Looking up to see who would dare insult one of Charles Mason's creations, Hugh saw a man in a stiff grey coat leave the auditorium. He had a feeling he had seen the man before, but could not tell for sure as he only saw the man's back.

"Well, you were right, Hugh," said Frank as he stepped up behind Hugh. "That Mason sure does have a knack for doing the impossible."

"You're just jealous that Mason's Hawker got more applause than your bend-do cast did, Doc," replied Hugh as he hung his camera bag over his shoulder.

"Perhaps," muttered Dr. Crick as he watched his younger friend walk out the door.

A few hours later, Hugh was back in his home neighborhood of Galileo Plaza. Night had just fallen and the visibility outside was perfect. The stars shone like diamonds in an obsidian crown. In other words, it was the best possible weather for fireworks. They were due to go up at eight, but first Hugh had to get ready for his *interview*, as he liked to call it.

He was to meet her at the Cloud Café, on the top level of the Plaza building. The café was a favorite hangout for couples in Galileo Plaza due to its good food and great view of the sky through its glass ceiling. It was always crowded when the sky was clear at night, and even more so on the Fourth of July.

As Hugh rode the elevator up to the top of the plaza, he hoped that he would be able to get a seat inside the restaurant, if his friend hadn't already found a table. Luckily for him, he was there early enough to capture the last free table in the Cloud Café. Hugh had barely sat down when she arrived.

Her name was Sally Saltwater and she was a reporter for the United Post. She was also a close friend of Hugh's, and harbored a crush on him. She was only a month or two younger than Hugh, but Sally didn't always act it. Sally was dressed in her *working* suit, a soft velvet skirt and blazer, with a string of pink pearls around her slim neck. Her hair was blond just like Hugh's, only she wore it in a small ponytail behind her head.

"Hey Hughie, got any good pictures for me?" she asked as she sat in the seat across from him. Not only was Sally his friend, she was also Hugh's link to the Nimbus city paper, and the one who bought the photos of the Fourth from him.

"Got them right here, Sally," grinned Hugh as he held up the photos he had finished developing half an hour before. They were black and white images, some in better focus than others. However, as Sally commented, Hugh had managed to take a perfect shot of the new Hawker robot.

"Hmm, so this is the newest from the Computer Captain, eh?" she said as she examined the image of the machine.

"Yep, sure is something isn't it, Sally?"

"I'd say. With a body like that, it would be fending off girls left and right," Sally teased him. "Seriously though," she continued, "how did Mason manage to make this thing without anyone in Tesla finding out?"

"Well Sal, I know only as much as you do on how he made it," replied Hugh as a waiter came to take their orders. "But the word going around is that he is working off the design of someone else, who used to be his teacher back in Chicago."

"Interesting. Is that true, Hugh?"

"Naw, just made it up, Sally."

"Ugh, remind me never to go to you for an exclusive, Hughie, I might be out of a job!" chuckled Sally as she leaned back in her chair and looked up at the stars above. It was only seconds later when the fireworks began, starting out as a bold blue starburst of light that faded into a crimson red. Everyone in the restaurant looked up at the skylight, watching the colors ebb and flow from each explosion to the next.

"Ah Hugh, isn't it simply beautiful?" sighed Sally as they watched the fireworks.

Before Hugh could answer, there was a sudden ruckus over at the elevator. Everyone in the restaurant turned in their seats, looking from the skylight to the man stumbling out of the bronze cylinder. It was Frank, and he was bleeding. He managed to take five steps from the doors before collapsing on the floor of the café.

Somewhere in the restaurant, a woman screamed. Someone shouted that they should call the police. Another asked who the drunk was, while another said he was going to the kitchen to use the phone to call for help.

Hugh had already gotten up from his seat and hurried over to his old friend's side. Crouching down, Hugh could see that Dr. Crick had been shot in the leg. It didn't look too serious, but the old man clearly had lost a lot of blood. There was a ragged strip of cloth tied tightly around the upper part of Frank's leg, perhaps an attempt by the doctor to stem the blood flow.

"Who did this to you?" asked Hugh as he helped Frank into a chair.

"It was... I don't..." mumbled the man as he winced in pain.

"Help's on the way," someone said from the back of the café. Already the elevator had closed its doors and started to descend.

"Go to my office," said the doctor suddenly. At first Hugh thought he had misheard the older man, but Frank repeated his message. "Hugh, you must get to my office. Key's in my pocket. Take it!"

Being careful not to be noticed, Hugh did as he was asked and reached into his old friend's front pocket and pulled out Crick's apartment key. It, along with a second, smaller key, was attached to a metal key chain. He had no idea what Crick wanted him to see in his office or who would want to shoot the old man. It just didn't make any sense. As the elevator opened its doors and the medics came out, Frank turned back to Hugh one last time, his brow covered in sweat. He said only one word before the men put him onto a stretcher. That word was "Hurry."

After the chaos of Frank's arrival had worn off, Hugh and Sally took the elevator back to the ground floor of the Plaza. Once he had bid Sally goodnight, and dropped her off at her apartment, Hugh headed for the sky bridge connecting Galileo Plaza to Tesla Quarter. There was a cable car connecting the two districts of the city in the sky, but at this hour the cars were usually closed until six the next morning. Hugh did not feel like waiting, so on he went, taking the sky bridge over.

Tesla Quarter was one of the districts of the city where Nimbus's brightest lived, as well as being home to Angel of Mercy Hospital. Both Frank Crick and Charles Mason had apartments there. The Quarter was bigger than Galileo Plaza, almost twice its size, though only half as tall. Thankfully, Hugh had visited Frank often enough to know where his home was. From the sky bridge he made his way down the lane and past a couple kissing on a park bench. After taking a left, a right, and two more lefts, Hugh found himself outside of Dr. Crick's home clinic, where his friend lived and worked.

Hugh wasn't sure what he was expecting to see when he got there. At first glance, everything seemed normal, save for the lights being off. Frank's office was set up in the front of the apartment that he owned, a simple one story structure wedged between two taller buildings. On either side of the front door were wide windows, in which hung curtains that normally provided privacy to patients visiting Frank's clinic, though tonight, they prevented Hugh from seeing anything inside the building. That, and the normalcy of the outside of Frank's apartment, made Hugh feel even more uneasy about going inside, but he had to know why Frank begged him to go to his office. Hugh brought the keys out of his pocket and stepped up to the front door. With a deep breath to steady his nerves, he inserted the larger key into the lock and turned it. The moment he opened the door and looked inside, he saw that his feelings of dread were not unfounded.

The normally orderly front office was in a state of total disarray. File cabinets were torn from the walls, the fish tank was in pieces, and Frank's prized koi were dead on the floor. The benches were ripped apart, the cushions little more than rags. The door in the back of the room that led to the small check-up room that Crick used when he was treating his patients was heavily damaged, with what looked like claw marks all over it.

Stepping into the examination room, Hugh found things to be not much better. The chair that usually occupied the center of the room was now in two pieces. One half was slammed into the sink and the other half was in the corner of the room. The anatomical charts were torn from the walls and the large cabinet holding the good doctor's tools and medicines was on the floor, its contents either scattered or shattered.

Stepping towards the door at the other end of the room, the one leading to Crick's private living chambers, Hugh could hear the sound of someone or something tearing apart the rooms beyond. As he stepped closer to the door, he winced as he heard the sound of what could only be Frank's Ming vase shattering. Frank would not be happy about that, thought Hugh, as he reached for the handle. In a quick motion, before he could change his mind or think about what he was doing, Hugh threw open the door and found himself gaping at what he saw inside.

It was a robot. And it was searching for something.

2

Hugh found himself in a state of shock. He could plainly tell that the creature in the room before him was indeed a robot. In a way, it looked like the new Hawker robots, only it was much smaller, possibly only three feet tall. Even with the light coming in from behind, he could tell the robot was unfinished. It had loops of wires hanging out from its arms and legs and the joints were clearly visible. Similar to the larger Hawker design, it had an avian look to it. Only instead of being a hawk the machine's face looked more like an owl, with large eyes that glowed bright red in the gloom.

With a sound similar to fingernails on a chalkboard, the metallic creature turned and dropped the drawer that it had held in its claws. The drawer probably came from Frank's desk, but that wasn't important at the moment. Hugh knew he had to catch the machine before it got away. It was not his most brilliant idea, to chase something that in all likelihood could cause him serious harm when he had nothing to protect himself, but Hugh was making this up as he went along. He chased the little avian machine into the hall beyond the entrance foyer and followed it through Crick's bedroom door.

The door was smashed apart, and the little machine went right in. Hugh was right on the robot's metal heels and just made it into the room to see the little robot leap through a large hole in the window, perhaps the same window it had come in, and fly away. There was nothing more Hugh could do but watch the strange machine fly off into the night.

Turning away from the window, Hugh took a good look around the bedroom of his elder friend. It was in very bad shape. The pillows were slashed, the mattress in shreds. The closet had been emptied out onto the floor, and the photos of Dr. Frank's son were in a pile in a corner.

Leaving the mess in the bedroom, Hugh returned to the hall. He could see now that the entire apartment was a shambles. There were the shattered remains of vases by overturned end tables, and books free of their bindings. It looked like nothing less than a tornado had struck the old man's home. There were even signs that the robot had tried to pry the oak panels from the wall.

All too soon, Hugh found himself back where he started, in the front hall of the apartment. He could see the shards of Frank's prized vase in the middle of the room, and the drawer that the owl-like machine had dropped when Hugh had first entered the apartment. The desk the wooden drawer belonged to was pulled away from the wall that it usually rested against. Stepping closer to the drawer, Hugh could see something odd about it. Bending down, Hugh picked up the desk drawer and took a better look at it. On closer inspection, he noticed that the drawer was oddly shallow for its size. Feeling around inside, Hugh felt his finger brush against a small metal circle on the inside of the drawer.

With a sudden thought, Hugh pulled out the keys Frank had given him. Looking at them now, specifically the second, smaller key, he could tell it was not for any normal door lock. It was far too small, but it certainly wasn't too small for a hidden lock inside of a desk drawer. The key was a perfect fit, and with a soft click, the bottom of the drawer popped out. Underneath it, he found a leather journal. The journal itself had a lock on it as well, but the little key that Dr. Crick had given Hugh was just a bit too big to fit. It was clear that whatever was on the pages of that book had to be important, or was something the good doctor wanted to keep silent.

By now it was well past midnight, and Hugh did not want to be alone in the trashed apartment. He resolved to visit Crick in the hospital in the morning to see what the old man knew about why he was attacked and his home ransacked, and what was so special about the leather journal. Stepping out into the street, Hugh tucked the leather-bound book into his jacket's inner pocket for safekeeping. As he walked back to the sky bridge, he kept his eyes on the lookout for any small machines that might want to take the book from him, but the worst he saw was a child's tin wind-up toy.

The dawn of the fifth came too soon for Hugh. The sun would not let him sleep off his adventure from the night before. For the umpteenth time, Hugh swore he would get some curtains for his windows as he rose from his bed. It had been one in the morning when he finally got back to his own bed, and he had not even bothered to remove his clothes. The journal was still in his coat pocket and had given Hugh a nasty cramp while he slept.

Heading for the bathroom, with some clean slacks and a new shirt,

Hugh stopped for a moment at his small safe. All apartments in Galileo Plaza had built-in safes. Hugh had never bothered to use his before, but he could not think of a better place to stash the journal while he showered. After all, what was to stop that thing from the night before from breaking into *his* apartment? At the very least, Hugh did not want the journal to be stolen while he was in the bathroom. So into the safe it went, and with it behind three inches of steel, Hugh stepped into the shower.

A couple of minutes and a change of clothes later, Hugh came back out, refreshed. He decided to stop by the cigar store on his way to the hospital and pick up a box of Frank's favorite brand. Taking a moment to take the journal back out of the safe and slipping it into his bag, Hugh left his apartment. As a precaution, he made sure to lock his door on his way out, just in case.

As Hugh headed out, he could not help but notice a Hawker robot where one of Nimbus's finest used to stand. The hawk-man looked as if it had always been there, watching over the people of the city, protecting them from harm. Its blue-eyed gaze scanned the crowd walking by it.

Hugh felt a shiver go up his spine when the Hawker's eyes met his own. There was something not quite right about the look it gave him. It seemed like the eyes of the machine were of flesh and not of glass, but that was impossible. Nevertheless, Hugh picked up his pace and hurried over to the cable car station for Tesla Quarter.

Hugh wasn't looking forward to going back to the Quarter, but it was where the hospital was, along with Dr. Mason's lab. Hugh had a bad feeling that, whatever was going on, Dr. Mason might have a hand in it. After all, the little robot that had wrecked Frank's home could easily be one of Mason's prototypes and very well could have run amok. However, that did not seem very likely.

Within an hour and one district train trip later, Hugh was at the hospital. Named the Angel of Mercy, the hospital in Tesla Quarter was one of the three major hospitals in Nimbus. It was also the oldest hospital, and the doctors were a little less advanced than in other districts, but their care for the injured was second to none. Frank's son, Dr. Robert Crick, was one of the best doctors at the hospital, and was his father's personal doctor.

Following in the footsteps of his father, Robert, Bobby as his friends called him, and Robby only to his father, had chosen a career in medicine. However, instead of opening his own clinic, Bobby decided to join the A.M. hospital's staff. Just like Crick senior, Bobby was doing research in medicine, but unlike Frank, Robert kept his findings to himself. Saving up for a rainy day, he called it. Hugh only knew Dr.

Bobby through his father. They were not that different in age, with Bobby being only four years older than Hugh. Bobby took his work at the hospital very seriously, and had very little patience with his own staff. However, once he clocked out, Bobby was almost a different person. When he was done for the day, Bobby often spent his time, when not at his home lab, at a small bar located in a more relaxed part of Tesla Quarter.

"Ah," said Dr. Robert as he saw Hugh come in with the box of cigars under his arm, "I am so glad you could come. Father has been asking for you nonstop since he got here."

"So he's alright?" asked Hugh, relief showing on his face.

"Thankfully, yes. Please come this way," said Crick the younger as he led Hugh out of the reception area and deeper into the hospital. "By the way Father was going on about you, Hugh, you'd think you were his son and not me."

"Well, I was there when he came to the Café," said Hugh, wondering if he should tell Bobby about the key and journal.

"True, but you should have seen him once he got here. Dad was in hysterics, shouting about how he had to talk to you again. I had to give father a sedative just so he would be calm enough for examination."

"How is Frank's leg?" asked Hugh.

"It's fine. The bullet missed the bone and exited out the back of his leg, so we didn't have to open it up to get it out. Once we got it cleaned out, it really wasn't all that bad. However, I am still worried about the fact he was shot. I have no idea who would shoot him, or why. He doesn't have any enemies, or at least any that would go as far as to fire at him."

Bobby looked like he wanted to keep talking, but he stopped short, and so did Hugh. They had both just turned a corner and could now see a small grouping of nurses and other doctors outside one of the hospital rooms. Bobby's face said what Hugh had already suspected. It was Frank's room that the crowd had gathered outside of.

Without bothering to be polite, Bobby pushed and shoved away the bystanders and entered the room, with Hugh following in his wake. Inside, it was clear that Frank was long gone. The large window in the side of the room had a hole in it big enough to drive a car through. Bobby rushed over to the window and looked out. The hole opened out to clear sky, the only ground being that of the earth far down below. If this window was how Frank had left the room, then he was either dead in a ditch somewhere far down in Kansas or something had flown away with the good doctor. The hole did seem to be about the right size for a Hawker, thought Hugh to himself.

It was at that moment that one such robot came in the doorway. One of the hospital staff had called the police to come and investigate the missing patient and the broken window, and so a Hawker was dispatched to deal with the trouble. Hugh couldn't help but notice the Hawker looked slightly different than the one that was in Galileo Plaza. It seemed somehow more alert, like it was running on more than programming. After asking some questions of the medical staff, the hawk-headed robot took a look around the room. It investigated the broken window and the mattress that Frank had been on.

"I have examined the crime scene," it said as it walked toward the crowd at the door. "I have determined that victim Frank Crick committed the act of suicide."

"What?" Bobby exclaimed in shock. The small group of medical staff agreed. One of them, a nurse who appeared no younger than forty, was particularly vocal with her disbelief. She shouted at the machine all the reasons why the doctor was not capable of suicide. The Hawker just kept saying "incorrect" to all arguments against its verdict on the disappearance of the elder Crick.

"Enough of this nonsense you hunk of junk!" hollered the nurse. She stomped over to the window and pointed down at the carpet. "Look here you bird-brained robot! If a man was to jump out a window, the glass would not be here inside the room!" Hugh took a look toward where she was pointing, and sure enough he could see thousands of shards of glass sparkling all over the floor. "The only way that glass got there is if the assailant came in through the win-"

The nurse was interrupted before she could finish her sentence. The Hawker had grabbed her and shoved her hard against the wall of the room. She struggled in its steel grasp, unable to wiggle free of the robot. The birdman's eyes had changed their color. They were no longer the soft innocent blue but now a wicked deep red. As it held her to the wall, it almost seemed to be pausing for a breath before speaking.

"Incorrect," it seemed to sneer at her. "This is your last warning. Do not lie to an officer of the law."

And with that, it let her go, and its eyes shifted back to blue. Every human in the room just stood there, struck dumb by the machine's sudden act of aggression against the poor woman. They watched in silence as the Hawker turned away from the woman and walked into the hall. It bid them all good day and walked out of sight. Only when it had been gone for few minutes did they all start moving again. The doctors and nurses all left the room, heading back to their jobs and patients. All except for Bobby, who was still silent as the grave, in shock at what he had just seen. Hugh too was stunned by what had just happened before his eyes, and it took him a minute before his brain could function again.

All the while, the nurse who had been attacked was cursing under her breath.

"Damn robotic man, knew they were no good," she muttered as Hugh walked over to her.

"Are you alright Mrs.? Miss...?"

"It's Nurse Rogers to you, young man," she said as she got to her feet. "And yes, I am in perfectly good shape for a lady who just got shoved into the plaster."

"Are you sure?" asked Dr. Bobby, ending his own period of stunned silence.

"I may be getting on in years, but I can take a beating, Doctor," said the nurse as she dusted off her uniform. She turned to look at the floor where the glass had fallen. With a grunt, she turned away and headed out the door, with Bobby hot on her heals insisting that she at least let him check her over to make sure that she did not have a concussion or any other injuries.

Now all alone, Hugh took a moment more to look around the room. He saw no sign of any hidden message or anything else Frank might have left before he was abducted. It was clear to him, after the robot from last night, and the Hawker's sudden assault on the nurse, that he had to go to the source of all the mechanical mayhem. Dr. Mason was the one who created these automatons. Perhaps he would know what was happening. At the very least, Hugh knew he had to tell the man about his creation's abnormal behavior.

Leaving the hospital, Hugh wandered over to an information booth in the plaza in front of the hospital that had a large map of Tesla Quarter plastered on its side. Despite being a fan of the famous inventor, he never had any reason to visit the man before. After a few moments, he located the streets where Dr. Mason's home and lab were located. The nearest of the two was Dr. Mason's home, which was located in an apartment complex in the upper half of Tesla Quarter. With the address memorized, Hugh headed over to a District train stop and waited for the next transport to come.

The District train was only available in the larger districts of the city. Both Tesla Quarter and Liberty Estates, among a few other sectors of Nimbus, had these electric trains, making travel around the districts much faster. Automobiles were not allowed in the flying city because of the narrowness of some of the lanes and streets between the buildings and because there was the small possibility of someone driving right off of the edge of the city.

It did not take long for the train to reach Hugh's stop. From there it was only a few steps to Dr. Mason's apartment. The door opened on Hugh's first knock. It was Dr. Mason himself who answered the door. He smiled at Hugh as he looked him over.

"Ah, hello there, to what do I owe this unexpected visit?" asked the inventor, the smile never leaving his lips.

"Hello there, Dr. Mason," said Hugh, who was struggling to keep his voice level. For the longest time, Hugh had idolized Dr. Mason for his brilliant work. It was almost a dream come true to be talking to the man, a dream turned sour by the suspicion that Mason might have had a hand in both the ransacking of Frank's apartment, and the kidnapping of the elder Crick as well. "I am Hubert Yeats, and I must talk to you about your robots."

"Ah yes, *my robots,*" said Dr. Charles Mason as he leaned against his door frame. "They are very efficient, aren't they? I should know. After all, I created them."

"Well I-"

"Look Mr. Yeats, are you a reporter?" interrupted Mason, the smile flickering on his face.

"No, I just-"

"Then I am afraid that I am much too busy to chat, Mr. Yeats," said Mason as his smile completely vanished. He moved back into his apartment and started to close the door.

"I think they're malfunctioning!" shouted Hugh, desperate to get the man's attention. In a way it worked, but not in the way that Hugh had expected. Mason's face turned bright red, and he broke out into a scowl.

"Listen here, *BOY,*" grumbled Dr. Mason. "I designed each component, wire, transistor and motor in my Hawkers. There is nothing that can *malfunction* in their entire body. Now, I am going to give you two minutes to leave my home before I call my personal Hawker here and show you just how *perfect* they are!"

And with that Mason slammed the door shut in Hugh's face. The doctor's sudden change in attitude had taken Hugh by surprise. He had expected Dr. Mason to at least listen to what he had to say, even if he was behind the attack on Frank. The mere thought of his creations being imperfect seemed to enrage the man. Hugh felt like he should try to talk to the man again, but he was not going to risk having Mason let loose a Hawker on him. After all, he still had Frank's journal with him and did not want it to fall into Mason's hands.

Deciding to head back home, Hugh wandered back to the district train station. Once aboard the train, Hugh looked back at the building that housed Mason's apartment. The door was open again and Mason was standing in the door frame, glaring at Hugh as the train left the station. Hugh thought he could see someone or something standing behind the inventor, something hidden in shadow. Hugh had a feeling that it might have been the private Hawker that Mason had mentioned mere moments before.

Before leaving Tesla Quarter, Hugh felt that he should go and see Bobby to see how he was holding up after the fiasco back at the hospital. Hugh knew that after the shock of having his father disappear and witnessing a robot attack, Dr. Bobby would probably be at his favorite drinking hole, the Red Baron Bar. It was not far from the cable car stop to Galileo Plaza so it was on Hugh's way out. It was easy enough to find the place, with its large sign depicting the infamous aviator himself flying his bright red tri-plane.

As usual, the bar was fairly busy, with several customers playing pool, and getting drunk on the bar's signature drink, the High Flyer. Hugh had a little trouble at first locating the good doctor in the crowded bar, and all the cigarette smoke did not help his visibility. Eventually, he spotted Bobby sitting at one of the stools in front of the bartender. He looked like a totally different person outside the hospital. His whole body language was far more relaxed, and his clothes far more casual now that he was off duty. Bobby was drinking a gin and tonic, and seemed to be on at least his second glass of the transparent elixir.

Hugh walked up to the empty seat next to the younger Crick and ordered a soft drink from the barman. Bobby barely noticed Hugh's presence next to him. It was clear that Bobby was still reeling from his father's disappearance.

"Dr. Robert?" started Hugh, unsure as to what to say.

"Come now, Hugh," said the doctor as he slapped Hugh on the back. "You know you can call me Bobby, alright?"

"I'm sorry about Frank," said Hugh as he pulled out the cigars from his bag. "I was going to give these to him at the hospital."

"Bah, you know smoking isn't as good as they used to think, right, Hugh?" slurred Bobby. It became clear now that the man might have had far more drinks than Hugh had first thought.

"True, but he likes them," replied the photographer as he put the box on the counter and pushed it toward his companion.

"Well, be that as it may, it doesn't change the fact that he's been kidnapped, does it?" snarled Bobby. "Curse those bloody machines. We should have stuck with the human police force, even though they were sometimes more drunk than me!"

"I know this is hard for you Bobby, but I have to ask," started Hugh as he thought back to the journal hiding in his bag. "Did Frank ever mention any journals to you?"

"My father is missing and you want to know what he was reading?"

"I did not mean magazines. What I meant was, did Dr. Crick ever talk about a secret journal that he may have hidden in his apartment?"

"No, why?"

"Oh, no reason," replied Hugh, now searching for a way to change the topic. "So, how are you holding up?"

"Not too well, but I am sure if I keep drinking, I can drown my sorrows," answered Bobby as he drained another glass. "Soon enough the booze will work its magic," he said with a bitter laugh. Hugh could tell that Bobby was sending him a message that he wanted him to leave, so when his drink came, Hugh took it to go.

As he walked to the cable car to Galileo Plaza, he thought back to the events of the day. He wondered if Frank was alright and if Mason was really behind all of this. He had a feeling that the best way to find out would be to get Sally in on this. After all, a reporter was far better suited for getting answers than he, a simple photographer, ever would be. Hugh resolved to give Sally a call once he was back in his own apartment.

3

When Hugh got home, he called up Sally and she answered her phone on the first ring. She said that she would be right over and hung up without so much as a goodbye to Hugh. It was only moments later when Hugh heard a knock upon his door. He opened it to see Sally standing there with her notepad in one hand, her pencil in the other, and her eyes wide.

"Do you know how long I waited for you to call about Frank, Hugh?" she asked as she came into the apartment. "I almost didn't bother to sleep, waiting for a call from you or the hospital telling me all about what happened last night."

"Sorry, Sally," sputtered Hugh. "I know I should have called, but a lot of stuff has happened. Let me tell you all about it…"

And so Hugh went on to tell Sally about what Frank had said the night before, about his trip to Tesla Quarter to find the good doctor's apartment ransacked, and of the small machine that escaped out the window. He spoke to her about the journal he found and of Frank's kidnapping earlier that day. He went on to tell her about the Hawker's arrival at the hospital and its attack on the nurse. Hugh finished by telling Sally about how Mason had reacted to hearing about his machines' malfunctioning and about how he had left Bobby at the bar.

"That is quite the story, Hughie," said Sally as she folded up her notebook. "If I heard it from anyone else I would think they were either crazy or suffering from paranoia."

"I can assure you that it's all true, Sally," said Hugh as he pulled out the leather journal from his satchel. "And this is the key to it all. I am sure of it."

"Relax tiger, I was not saying I doubted you," she said as she moved her hand till it rested gently on his shoulder. "I am more than willing to help you in any way I can."

"Well, I was thinking," said Hugh as he stood up, "that since you are a journalist, maybe Dr. Mason would be more open to you. You could ask him about the Hawkers."

Hugh could see the sparkle appear in Sally's eyes, a sign that her reporter instincts were revving into high gear. He could tell that she was already thinking up questions to ask Dr. Mason, questions that would trick him into telling her everything she wanted. She smiled as she rose from her chair and said, "You can count on me, Hughie. Now let's go!"

"Just a moment," said Hugh, as he went over to his safe. He deposited the leather journal inside it and gave the combination lock a good spin. With the book secure, Hugh grabbed his jacket and opened the door. Like a true gentleman, he let Sally exit the apartment first. He followed behind her, making sure his door was locked up tight.

Hugh had to hurry to keep up with Sally's pace as they walked the streets of Galileo Plaza to the cable car for Tesla Quarter. They saw nothing out of the ordinary during their trip back to Mason's home. The ride on the district train was uneventful, except for the crying child who ignored his mother's efforts to calm him down. All too soon, they were at the front door to Mason's apartment, the first time for Sally, the second time for Hugh.

Hugh hid behind a decorative planter in front of the building as Sally rang the doorbell. They both waited in silence, one visible and the other not, for Mason to answer his door. But instead a young woman in a dark two piece suit opened the door. She was paler than paper, with black hair darker than ink. Her eyes were very thin, hinting at an Asian heritage. Despite the woman's timid appearance, Sally pulled no punches with her introduction.

"Hello there, my name is Saltwater, Sally Saltwater, and I am here on behalf of the United Post. I am here to interview Dr. Mason about his latest and greatest creation, so could you go get him?"

"I am so very sorry," said the woman in a voice barely over a whisper. "Dr. Mason is not available right now."

"This can't really wait," insisted Sally. "Could you just go ask him to see me?"

The black haired woman shook her head as she replied. "No, I cannot, for he has gone to his laboratory."

Not missing a beat, Sally kept up her questioning pace with the woman at the door. "When will he be back?"

"I am very sorry, Miss Saltwater, but the doctor is not coming back to his apartment."

"What do you mean, Mrs.–?"

"Li, Ming Li," supplied the woman with a slight bow.

"What do you mean by he is 'not coming back'?"

"Dr. Mason has decided that as of today he will live onsite at his workplace. I have been left in charge of his estate until further notice."

"Did he say why he left?" asked Sally as she opened up her note pad, smelling a story. Behind the planter, Hugh listened and watched the interactions between Sally and the woman called Ming Li.

"Dr. Mason didn't tell me why he decided to move into the laboratories, so I cannot help you anymore. Good day, Miss Saltwater."

With unexpected speed the slim, pale-skinned woman shut the door in Sally's face. It had happened so fast that she hadn't been able to stick her foot in the door to prevent it from closing. Sally stood there for a moment, silent at the doorstep. When she turned around and walked toward Hugh's hiding place, he could see a certain fire in her eyes. Hugh knew that look all too well. It meant that Sally was in full journalist mode now and was not going to let anything stop her from getting her story. The Asian woman told them where Mason had disappeared to, and all they had to do was look at a local map to find the location of the doctor's lab.

According to a map they found on display on the side of a nearby information booth, Mason's lab, Mason Electronics, was located in the northern end of Tesla Quarter, and was a half hour trip by district train away. Hugh was getting worried about the time, as the sky was now getting dark and the sun had long since dipped below the horizon. However, Sally's clock never stopped when there was a story to be had, so onward they went, to the lair of the creator of the Hawkers.

The street lights were on by the time they reached the labs themselves. The building was not very impressive except for its four large doors and a large copper sign above the central doorway that read: "Mason Electronics, the future of machines." The walls that made up the structure were windowless concrete and the doors were reinforced steel. There was no sign of handles, or any other means of opening the central doors from the outside, and the other two were garage-style doors that slid upwards to open. They were chained shut, keeping the curious out, and preventing Hugh and Sally from gaining an audience with Mason.

It didn't help that there was also a group of five Hawkers guarding the front door of the labs as well. They didn't even twitch, until Hugh and Sally came within ten feet of them. Once they crossed an unseen line, the one in the center of the group, a slightly taller than average model, suddenly stepped forward toward the duo.

"You are approaching a restricted area. Please vacate the premises," it squawked at them.

"Sure thing," said Sally, "as soon as Dr. Mason comes out to chat a bit. I have a story that needs writing!"

"You are in a restricted area," the machine persisted as it took another step forward. Its metal feet clanked dangerously upon the ground. "Please leave now."

"Maybe we should go, Sally," said Hugh as he sensed the tension starting to build in the air.

"Not till I get some answers, tin-head," snapped Sally.

"You have five minutes to leave, citizens," squawked the larger Hawker as it took one more step, this time bringing it mere inches in front of the two humans. With it so close, Hugh could swear he could hear the motors turning inside of the eight foot machine. Hugh hoped that Sally would have the good sense to stop now that the large Hawker clearly was threatening them, and judging by its claws, the punishment for not obeying its order to leave would be serious injury to the both of them. Thankfully, Sally finally realized that she might be in over her head.

"Fine, fine, fine, no need to get your gears stripped," she said as she grabbed Hugh by the arm. "I can tell when I'm not wanted. Come along, Hughie, let's leave this place."

By now it was completely dark outside and the streets were significantly less busy. Since Hugh had not had lunch, he thought it would be best to treat Sally to dinner. He could tell that she was in a bit of a foul mood after being turned away by the Hawkers at Mason's lab, and he wanted to cheer her up.

So when they got on the district train, Hugh kept his eyes open for any good food places that she might enjoy. Several stops later, Hugh spotted an Italian restaurant and pointed it out to his female companion. She agreed that grabbing a meal might be a good idea and so they both left the train and entered the restaurant.

The eatery was part of a popular restaurant chain in Nimbus called Pasta Heaven. It was popular for its many pasta dishes and for its very cheap prices. Once they were seated, Hugh proceeded to massage Sally's wounded ego. He told her that it wasn't her fault that they didn't get to grill Mason about his Hawkers, that they had no way of knowing that Mason would decide to stay in his labs protected by his own private Hawker units.

"Look, Hughie, I appreciate what you're trying to do here," said Sally as she munched on a breadstick. "But I'm not bothered by that at all. In fact, our failure to talk with Mason is a story all in itself."

"What do you mean, Sally?" asked Hugh, perplexed.

"Well, I can turn this around by saying that Mason has abandoned society to live and work in his labs full time. His self-imposed exile would make front page news easily. I am just sorry that we couldn't find out more about those robots of his."

"It's alright, Sally," said Hugh as their food arrived. "We could always try to take down one of those Hawkers with firearms if push comes to shove."

"I guess," said Sally as she twirled her fork in her pasta.

Later, after they had eaten and returned to Galileo Plaza, Hugh walked Sally home to her apartment. He bid her good night and promised to call her in the morning, or whenever he got any more news on Frank, the journal, or Dr. Mason's actions. Returning home, Hugh felt very weary from the past few days' events. He was looking forward to being able to lie down on his bed and resume where he left off on his latest book, something he hadn't been able to do with all the excitement and drama of the past few days.

Stopping before his front door, he took a moment to pull his key from his pocket and insert it into the lock. With a simple twist of the wrist, the bolt withdrew, and Hugh pushed the door open. What he saw the moment he looked inside made him freeze upon the threshold. Standing just across from where he was standing was a small robot, much like the one from the elder Crick's apartment, if not the same machine, digging through his photography supply cabinet. The machine had its back to Hugh and didn't seem aware that he had entered the room. For a moment, Hugh considered closing the door and locking it, before seeking help from his neighbors, but thought better of it. This was his chance to catch one of these things, possibly even use it to find out what was going on. He wasn't sure how exactly he would "use it" just yet, but he'd figure that out after he caught it. Moving slowly, Hugh crept up on the little owl-like robot and reached out toward it. Before he could get to it, a treacherous floor board creaked under his foot and the machine, like a startled deer, bolted from the cabinet. But not before Hugh lunged at it.

Hugh's hand caught in the tangle of wires hanging from the back of the metal creature. With the momentum of the robot and Hugh's own weight, he managed to rip out a large cluster of wires from the avian robot. From where the wires had been connected, sparks flew onto the hard boards of his apartment's floor. The robot gave out a final squawk, like that of a dying motor, and then it fell over onto its steel chest. The red light left its camera eyes and its joints locked up. By removing the wires, Hugh unknowingly ripped out what could have been accurately described as the little robot's veins, deactivating it almost instantly.

Before picking up the strange machine, Hugh gave it a kick to make sure it was truly 'dead'. With its demise confirmed, Hugh decided to investigate the strange owl-like robot. Hugh was surprised by how easily he lifted up the little robot from the floor. It was far lighter than he expected, and slightly larger than he thought it was, being more like three feet, five inches tall and made of a very strong metal. Hugh noticed that it had a wing pack on its back similar to the Hawker units. It indeed had been designed to have an owl's face, but it didn't have a face plate to cover the hardware so it resembled a small demon with huge eyes. Its hands were far more primitive than the Hawkers' were, and ended in three pointed clamps.

Turning the strange robot around in his hands, Hugh investigated its wing pack. It was no surprise to him to see the logo for Dr. Mason's labs acid etched into the metal, but what he didn't expect to see was the sticker under the logo. The sticker read "prototype – do not remove from lab." It was clear that this little robot was not complete, but the sticker seemed to suggest that it wasn't even meant to be outside running around on its own.

Hugh decided to be doubly safe and carried the small robot with him into his small darkroom. He put it down on his desk and pulled out a pair of wire cutters from his drawer. With the cutters in hand, he proceeded to cut every wire he could find in the little robot. Only when the last wire was cut did he relax.

With the robot truly disabled, Hugh left it where it lay and headed back out into his apartment. He was relieved to see that his home was not too badly damaged. His small rug was pushed to one side, a few pictures were on the floor, and in his bedroom a window was broken, but thankfully all of these things were very minor, especially when compared to the damage a similar little robot had done to Frank's apartment.

Better yet, Hugh noticed that his safe was still intact, and after opening it, found the journal was still inside. Hugh was happy to see that the journal was safe, but he did not feel any more secure. Somehow, the little robotic menace had known that he had taken Frank's hidden journal and had come to Hugh's apartment in search of it. It was clear that the window that Hugh had looked out of so fondly had been the robotic robber's point of entry. Once he was satisfied that nothing was missing, he realized he should get his camera and take a couple of pictures of both the robot, and of the mess it made of his home. He reasoned, as he aimed the lens at the metal body, that he should document all of this because there was definitely something strange going on in the city. He wasn't sure what the full story was quite yet, if the Hawkers were working for Mason, or someone else, but it was becoming clearer by the moment to Hugh that none of it was good news.

After he had finished photographing his apartment, Hugh pondered what to do next. After a bit of thought, Hugh decided that the next course of action was to block his window. It took some serious elbow grease and pushing, but Hugh managed to push his bookcase against the window, effectively blocking all but two inches of the glass. To be extra sure, he pushed his bed against the bookcase.

With the room secured, Hugh made good on his promise to Sally and gave her a call once he found where his phone had fallen. She once again answered on the first ring, and was truly shocked to hear about the break-in at his apartment. She asked if Hugh wanted to stay with her for the night, but he refused. He believed it would be best that he stayed in his own apartment, just to be safe, and in case another robot decided to come after the journal. Hugh did not want anything to happen to Sally that he could prevent, so in his own home he stayed.

After hanging up the phone, Hugh went to bed, once again not bothering to remove his clothes. That night his sleep was fitful. He had nightmares of giant robots and leather bound secrets that whispered conspiracies and threats to his dream self. When the dawn of the sixth of July came, he felt no more rested than he had the night before. Getting up, he proceeded to shower as he did the day before, and got dressed. This time when he went out, he brought his camera with him, along with some spare film, just in case. After all that had happened, one never knew when one would need photographic proof.

Before he left the apartment, he went into his small studio and picked up the remains of the three foot tall robot. Today, Hugh decided that he would show this little mechanical menace to an expert in robotics, one Mad Mike. As Hugh stuffed the small machine into his drawstring laundry bag, he thought about the man he was going to visit.

Michael Manderson, or as he was now commonly known, Mad Mike, had worked for Dr. Mason until the year before. No one really knew what caused Mad Mike to lose his mind, but the word on the street was that he had managed to retain his knowledge of robotics and electronics, though what he built nowadays was usually for "alien mind control" prevention. He was not a person Hugh would normally go to for information, but he had no idea whom he could see for the information he wanted. Few worked with Dr. Mason and fewer still had their names released to the public. And only Mad Mike was within Hugh's reach. Besides, he didn't want to risk showing the robot's body to the wrong people, or have word get around that he had this little machine in his possession.

Deciding that there was safety in numbers, Hugh called Bobby and asked him to meet him at the Full Moon Plaza cable car junction in Tesla. Just on the other side of Full Moon Plaza was the cable car junction to Mad Mike's home, the Saint's Home for the Mentally Challenged. Hugh chose Bobby for two reasons. The first was that Bobby was probably still sulking over the disappearance of his father and would need a good distraction. The second was that Sally was probably at work by now, and even if she did want to come with him, he did not want her to get hurt. And with all the Hawkers around the city, Hugh felt safer with a friend at his side.

After taking the first cable car, and then catching a ride on a district train in Tesla Quarter, Hugh thought about how many times he had been to this part of town. At least once every day since the Fourth, he thought. Before he knew it, Hugh was at the stop for Angel of Mercy hospital, which was the station that Bobby usually used to get onto the train. Hugh was surprised to see his friend at the hospital's stop. Since Bobby was already in Tesla, Hugh had expected his friend to go on to the cable car station and wait for him there. Taking a seat next to Hugh, the medical doctor was silent for the first few minutes of the trip. Hugh wanted to ask why Bobby was only now making his way to the station, but he could tell from his friend's face that he wasn't in the mood for answering questions.

Today, Bobby had decided to wear a pair of durable jeans and a plain sweater. He was also carrying his black leather bag, which he used to carry his medical supplies for house calls. Hugh wondered why Bobby would have his bag with him, but he felt it was best not to ask with the mood Bobby could be in. So it was all the more surprising when Bobby broke the awkward silence.

"Hello, Hugh. Bet you are wondering what's in the bag," said Bobby without looking at his comrade. "It's just a few medical things, bandages, balms, antibiotics and some aspirin," he continued, not waiting for a reply from Hugh. "I also have my Colt handgun in there, fully loaded too, for good measure."

"WHAT?" exclaimed Hugh, who had never held a real gun before, let alone used one.

"Look, Hubert," said Bobby, finally turning around to face his companion. "Those Hawkers are everywhere. Who knows when one will snap like the other day? We've got to at least try to defend ourselves." Hugh didn't like it, but he knew Bobby had a point. If a Hawker was to attack them, bare knuckles wouldn't dent the machines' metal bodies, nor was he sure if he could outrun them. It was then that Hugh realized that bringing a gun may not have been a bad idea at all.

4

The rest of the ride on the district train was uneventful. Some people got on, and some people got off. Occasionally, Hugh caught Bobby staring at the laundry bag that held the downed machine on the floor in front of their seat. When Hugh called Bobby to come with him to see Dr. Manderson, he had also told the doctor about the machine and its actions both in Frank's apartment and Hugh's own. This was also when he finally disclosed that he had found a journal hidden in Frank's apartment. At first Bobby did not react well to Hugh having hidden something like that from him, but once Hugh had explained that the little robot had probably been after Frank's journal, Bobby had agreed on the spot to travel with Hugh to the asylum to get some answers. Now, with the bag at their feet, and the doctor's eyes constantly drifting back to it suspiciously, Hugh couldn't help but wonder. Did Bobby suspect that the ruined robot could still be active, despite Hugh's trimming of its wires? Since Hugh could not read minds, he decided it was best not to ask.

The train soon reached the final stop, the cable car junction to both Liberty Estates and Full Moon Plaza. As they boarded the car for the Plaza and watched the doors close behind them, Hugh swore he saw a Hawker watching them, but it was hard to tell. Perhaps it was just a man in a large overcoat and an odd hat. Either way, Hugh was getting more and more worried. How long till he ended up with a bullet in his own leg, or even in his head?

Full Moon Plaza was Nimbus's version of a shopping district, one of the largest in the city. There were stores such as Mary's, Tony's Tobacco, Toddler's Toys, Harmonic Records, and a few others. Full Moon Plaza was also known for its casinos, where the residents took time off to unwind at the slots. There were four different casinos arranged in a crescent moon around a round plaza in the south-eastern end of the district. There were all sorts of games available in the casinos, from poker tables to roulette wheels, from pool tables to slot machines. There was a small cable car station in the casino area of the district that connected to a small seldom visited part of Nimbus, a little residential area that also held the mental institution that was the home of the man that Hugh and Bobby were seeking.

The asylum, Saint's Home for the Mentally Challenged, was a fairly small facility, which held those in the city who had become depressed or were suffering other mental disabilities and diseases. It also held the city's craziest citizen, Mad Mike. Rumor had it that, due to Mad Mike's background and history with Dr. Mason, he was given most of the third floor of the asylum for his "experiments." People had also been saying that Mike was preparing for an alien invasion which only he could see.

The arrival at the cable car station was fairly uneventful for both Hugh and Bobby. The Hawker guard on duty at the station exit gave them a quick look-over and let them pass. For a moment though, Hugh swore that when the Hawker saw his laundry bag, its eyes turned violet, as if they were trying to turn red, but decided against it.

The shopping plaza was lit up with bright neon lights and posters were everywhere, advertising the many stores and restaurants throughout the district. Full Moon Plaza itself was very crowded, with shoppers traveling every which way, rushing to sales and traveling to bargain bonanzas. One elderly shopper bumped into Hugh and for a moment Hugh thought he recognized the strange man in the grey coat, but could not place the face. However, that moment did not last long enough for Hugh to address the man or to apologize, as soon he felt himself being dragged off into the crowd by Bobby.

Travelling in the thick group of shoppers was very confusing for Hugh. At one point he could barely tell up from down and would have surely lost his companion in the human ocean if Bobby had not held Hugh's arm in a vice-like grip. It was a small wonder in itself that Hugh managed to keep his grip on the laundry bag, though he had to admit, the robot was starting to feel a bit heavy after being carried for so long.

Thankfully, Bobby was able to maneuver himself and Hugh out of the flow of shoppers and tourists and down the street leading toward the casino section of the district. As they left the mall, the hustle and bustle died down significantly, though there were plenty of people still moving about.

It was in this part of town that fortunes were made and lost. Hugh could tell by looking in the wide glass windows of the casinos they walked past that the gambling tables were very busy. The slot machines were going non-stop, the sound of coins jingling erupting every few minutes, so loud that it could be heard from the street outside. Lights flashed everywhere and the sounds of "jackpot" were ringing out at random. Despite being outside the casinos, Hugh could feel himself getting slightly disoriented by the chaos of the new environment and had to once again let Bobby lead him through the mayhem to the next cable car station. A few of the gamblers that they passed by gave the duo dirty looks as they walked toward the station, their eyes making the hairs on the back of Hugh's neck stand up. As they got into line to board the car, a very attractive lady in a revealing red silk dress tried to entice Hugh and Bobby into playing a round of blackjack at the casino just a few yards away from the station. Bobby gave an unarguable "no" to the woman and Hugh remained silent, keeping his mind on Sally to help him stay focused on the mission at hand.

The cable car ride across to the small district housing the asylum was fairly quick, taking only fifteen minutes to traverse the void. Stepping out of the car, it was not a far walk to the asylum, which sat in the center of this small part of Nimbus. It was designed to look like an old brick building, and it stood at three stories tall with a round classic clock face placed in the center of the structure's roof. Upon checking his wristwatch, Hugh was surprised to see that the asylum's clock was six hours slow.

Inside, the young woman working at the receptionist's desk greeted them with a smile that was clearly forced.

"Hello there. Do you have an appointment or arranged visit?" she asked with a voice heavy with false sweetness.

"We are here to see Dr. Manderson," said Hugh to the blond woman at the desk.

"Oh, *him*," she said as her fake attitude dropped. Clearly she did not like Mad Mike in the least. "Whatcha want with that tramp?"

"Nothing that concerns you," said Bobby as he walked right up to the receptionist. "Now are you going to tell us what room he's in or am I going to have to look at your records?"

"Chill, man," she said as she opened a blue notebook that lay on her desk. "No need to go all Dick Tracy on me." She took a quick glance at the pages of the blue book and looked back up. "Dr. Manderson occupies rooms 301 to 305. Good luck finding him. The nut-job can be pretty hard to find up there."

"Thank you for your help," said Hugh as he and Bobby made their way to the elevator at the back of the reception room.

"Say, kid," the receptionist called out. "What's in the bag?"

"It's a little special something for Mad Mike to look at," answered Bobby as he pressed the elevator's call button.

"Fine, don't tell me," she grumbled as she picked up a romance novel she had hidden in her lap. "Oh, and no photos around the patients," she added. "They bother the patients."

"No worries," said Hugh as he adjusted his grip on the sack. "We are only here to talk."

They waited a moment for the security gate to open and then took the elevator up to the third floor. The hallways of the third floor of the asylum were very empty and clean. The only colors in the entire hallway were white and the steel sheen of the doors that lined the corridor. The place smelled like too much antiseptic and there was a dull sound of classical music being played far down the hall. On the left side of the hallway were the five rooms occupied by Mad Mike, and one of the doors was open.

Soundlessly, the duo decided to investigate and headed toward the open door, which was numbered 303. The room inside was a complete mess, not from being ransacked, but by the way the owner lived. There were pieces of paper taped to the walls of the room. On them were notes and random scribbles. Some looked like important schematics, while others were just ramblings about alien conspiracies and the 'man'. There were so many sheets that they covered one of the walls from floor to ceiling. In the middle of all the madness were a desk, a chair, and a man with his back to the door.

"So... so... you finally come, eh?" asked the man without turning around. "Come to take old Mad Mikey to the mother ship, eh?"

"No, actually we are-" started Bobby, but he was interrupted by the man in the wooden chair.

"Not aliens, eh? Then off with you lot. I have more than enough pills as is."

"I think you are mistaken, Dr. Manderson," said Hugh.

"We are not from the asylum or from space," continued Bobby as he walked into the room with Hugh close behind him. "We are here about your work with Dr. Mason."

"Bah, Mason is a fool," grumbled the man in the chair. "He never saw the signs, never knew what he was getting himself into."

"What was he getting himself into?" asked Hugh as he closed the door behind him.

"I have nothing more to say to you two. Now leave before the nice men in the white coats come with my pills."

"Maybe this will change your mind?" asked Hugh as he pulled out the three foot tall robot from his laundry bag. Mike turned around in his chair for the first time and looked at his visitors.

Now that he could get a good look at him, Hugh realized that Mad Mike was around the same age as Frank. On his head sat a shiny tinfoil hat held together with a few random wires and plenty of tape. He wore a pair of Ray-Ban sunglasses that completely blocked the sight of his eyes from anyone viewing him. The man's clothes consisted of a sky blue patient jumpsuit covered by a slightly ratty white bathrobe with a fabric patch that was a replica of the clock on the asylum's roof sewn on it. On his feet he, surprisingly enough, wore not slippers, but regular leather shoes.

At the sight of the small damaged avian robot, he pushed up the glasses till they rested on his brow, revealing his eyes. Instead of being clouded with madness, they were startlingly clear and focused. Within seconds his entire attitude reversed, his shoulders rising and his back straightening.

"Where did you get that?" asked Mike, all trace of madness gone from his voice.

"It was up and about, ransacking people's apartments," said Bobby.

"That can't be right," gasped Mike as he moved closer to get a better look at the little robot. "Once the Hawkers were mass produced, the prototypes should have been all shut down and put into storage."

"What do you mean?" asked Hugh.

"My boy, I worked for Dr. Mason for four years, both in and out of his labs. In all that time, I have only seen something like this once before. It was when we created machines with human minds."

"Here we go again with the crazy talk," said Bobby. "I don't care how advanced these things are, they're just robots. Robots are programmed, and don't have free will of their own."

"Now see here!" snapped Mad Mike as he turned on the doctor. "I have only acted out of my mind this past year to keep myself off of Mason's radar. If I was out and about on the streets of Nimbus, and Mason suspected me to be sane, then I would have probably disappeared long ago. I still have all my marbles, I assure you. In fact, I sometimes think my head is much clearer now than it has ever been in my entire life."

"Why would Dr. Mason want to harm you Ma- erh, Dr. Manderson?" asked Hugh.

"Well, it is in no small part due to this fellow," said Mike as he took the robot from Hugh and placed it on his desk. Dr. Manderson was careful not to create too much of a racket as he laid the machine upon the oak. "He was one of the first created from our research."

"Excuse me," asked Bobby. "'He'? You do mean 'it,' right? It's just a machine, after all."

"That's what I thought at first," muttered Mike as he pried open the chest plate of the avian robot. "But as I experimented and worked on these things with Mason, I began to change my mind. In the beginning, the working modules were very low in artificial intelligence, so much so it was a challenge to program the machines to walk. Then one day, Mason called me into his office to show me what he called his 'greatest breakthrough.'"

Mike continued to speak as he removed the chest-plate and began to rummage inside the metal body. "It was a fellow much like this one, perhaps it was this one, but instead of constantly falling over, it was not just walking, but running up and down his office. I applauded him at the time, but even then I knew something was wrong. The processors and motors used in the machine should not have been nearly powerful enough to give it the ability to move so fast. We were years, *years*, away from creating such a machine, but there it was, walking around, shaking my hand. It was that same night that I decided to examine the robot a bit more carefully. I picked up one of these and was going to perform what I guess could be called a robot autopsy, to see what little changes Mason might have made to it without telling me, not to mention, to also get a good look at its logic unit."

By now Mike had stopped rummaging around in the robot's chest and began to pull at something deep inside of the machine. All the while he continued his monologue. "I had just gotten out a few of my tools and a spare chest plate. I had secured the robot and was about to unscrew its chest when the robot, which should have been inactive, reached up, and ripped the screwdriver out of my hand." Mike paused for a moment, before continuing in a somber tone of voice. "It began to make this god-awful screeching sound and struggled against the table's holding gear. I knew the sound would attract unwanted company so I panicked and grabbed my hammer."

He paused again as he brought one of his hands up to his forehead, as if to comfort a headache. "I wasn't thinking straight. The screeching and fear of being discovered were driving my actions. I managed to land a solid blow on its head right between the visual receptors." Mike then pretended to smack the robot on the table with an imaginary hammer. "I must have struck its metal head in a brittle spot, because the hammer breached the face plate and smashed into what I had assumed to be the main processor. That wasn't the case, as it was at that moment that I saw the truth behind Mason's marvel. I knew I couldn't repair the head as I had no replacement for it, and I realized that Mason would know from the hole in the robot's face that it was my tool that had done it. So I fled and sought asylum with the madmen."

"Do you know why these things would be running around?" asked Bobby.

"No, no idea what-so-ever," grumbled Mike. "If I may ask, where did you get this prototype? You two don't look like the type to go stealing dangerous secrets."

"We didn't find it, it came to me," said Hugh, stepping forward. He explained what had happened. Mike barely seemed interested until Hugh brought up the other prototype he had seen, the one that had ransacked Frank's apartment.

"Wait a moment," said Mike, his eyebrows arching, pushing his glasses higher up on his head. "Did you say you saw one of these things at Frank's place?"

"Yeah, why?" asked Hugh.

"Oh, no-no-no-no," muttered Mike to himself as he rubbed absently at his forehead, dislodging his glasses and knocking his tinfoil hat back, revealing a few tufts of wispy hair.

"Hey," said Bobby, his voice rising, "What are you going on about? Do you know why the Hawkers were after my dad?"

Mike stopped rubbing and looked right at Bobby, as if seeing him for the first time. "You're his son, aren't you?" he asked, a look of something that resembled pity appearing upon his face.

"Yes, I am," snapped back Bobby. "If you have anything to say about why he was kidnapped, I would greatly appreciate it if you could stop playing games with us and just spit it out!"

"Fine," Mike snapped right back, causing Bobby to take a step back in surprise at the outburst. "He was probably taken because he worked on the Hawker project with the rest of us!"

"He what?!" asked Hugh in surprise.

It was at that moment that something started to pound heavily upon the door to the room. Both Bobby and Hugh jumped in surprise. Mike simply swore and let go of whatever it was he had been trying to remove from the avian robot.

"Damn it," swore Mike as he ran over to the wall next to the door. He slid aside a small hidden panel beside the doorframe and took a look through the little opening. Again he swore as he ran toward a wall that was covered in a floor to ceiling mass of taped on paper.

"What is going on?" asked Hugh, confused by the banging on the door and the doctor's actions. "What's out there?"

"It's a Hawker, Hugh. What do you think it is?" exclaimed Bobby. "That receptionist must have called for it. Guess she does earn her pay after all."

"Dr. Manderson, what are you doing?" asked Hugh as he joined him by the wall. Mike was pulling pieces of paper off the wall, which was soon revealed as actually being a door.

It was then that two things happened at once. First, the door to the room suddenly got a dent the size of a baseball punched into it from the other side, and second, Mike managed to get the hidden door open, revealing a small room no bigger than a walk-in closet.

"Hurry, you two, in here," cried Mike as he indicated the open doorway. "That door will not hold forever!"

"Why don't we just stand and fight?" asked Bobby calmly as he drew his handgun from his black medical bag.

"Don't bother," retorted Mike as another dent appeared in the door. "If I know Mason, after that hammer incident, he'd make every robot of his bullet proof."

"What about you, Dr. Manderson?" asked Hugh as he hurried for the new doorway, only stopping to grab his laundry bag on the way out.

"The only way that thing is going to stop searching for you and your friend is if someone gets in its way. Someone like me," said Mike sadly as two more dents appeared in the steel door.

"But if it catches you-" started Hugh, but the doctor interrupted him.

"Look, there is no time to discuss this. Get going!" And with that, Mike shoved Hugh through the doorway to join Bobby on the other side. Behind him, the hidden door slammed shut and the sound of something metallic groaning, then breaking, could be heard from the other side. The voice of a Hawker could be heard, though too muffled to make out the words. Then there was the sound of something hitting the door from the other side, hard, and a little blood leaked out under the door.

Bobby had to restrain Hugh from trying to pry open the door. It was some time later, long after the sounds from the room died down, that Bobby released Hugh. By then, Hugh had calmed down. He was still upset over being unable to help Mike but reason told him that there was very little he could have done to help the doctor. After all, Mike had said himself that the Hawkers were bullet-proof, so what chance did bare knuckles have?

Bobby was the first to break the silence. "You okay, Hugh?" he asked, meaning not if his friend was okay physical, but mentally.

"Yes, I guess I am."

"Good," said Bobby as he pushed open the closet's door. It was clear that Dr. Manderson was long gone, though it wasn't clear if he was alive or dead. Mike wasn't the only thing missing, as the room was now bare of most of the sheets of paper that had been taped to the wall. Only a few odd sheets remained, and all of them full of nonsense. The only sign of the previous occupant of the room was the red blood stain quickly coagulating by the hidden door that they had to step over in order to get out of the closet. The desk was still in the room, but all of the drawers were missing and the robot that Hugh had brought there was now gone from where they had left it on the desk.

They took a few moments to give the room a quick look over, and when they found nothing, both Hugh and Bobby looked in the other rooms that had been assigned to Dr. Manderson. However, they found nothing that could have connected the man to Dr. Mason or to the robots. Somehow their visit to Mike had tipped off Dr. Mason that Mike was not as mad as he seemed. Either way, there was nothing more either of them could do in the asylum, so they decided to leave.

They exited through where the door to room 303 should have been and out into the hall. There, they saw some blood and several fresh scratches and dents in the walls and floor that made up the corridor. Several lights were broken above their heads and a few glass shards decorated the linoleum tiles. Thankfully, the elevator was still in working order, so they rode it down to the ground floor.

The moment they arrived at the bottom, they were greeted with the sight of the trashed lobby and the receptionist, now lying on the floor, bleeding from a head wound. Bobby took a moment to examine her, and declared that she was alright, just knocked out. Before they left, Bobby set the woman up and bandaged her head. It was possible that she had called in the Hawkers, but that did not mean Bobby, a licensed medical professional, could just leave her bleeding on the floor like a victim of a mugging.

It was hours later that Hugh finally returned to his apartment. He was becoming more and more worried about the prospect of staying in Nimbus. With the way things were going, the city was becoming a very dangerous place. Tomorrow, he decided, he would pack up his belongings and take the next shuttle back down to Earth. Perhaps he would move back in with his parents in Boston. He had enough money for a train back to Massachusetts and he was sure his father would welcome him back. Of course, as Hugh followed his own train of thought, he would have to convince Sally to come with him. He could not just leave her here all by herself in a city that was rapidly becoming a war zone.

So, for the rest of that day he packed away his clothes and camera, his books and music records. He took the journal out of his safe and stashed it in his suitcase as well. After all, there was no way he was going to leave something like that leather-bound book behind for anyone like Dr. Mason or his Hawkers to find.

That night, before he went to sleep, he called up Sally. At first she was very stubborn about not leaving the city. It was her one and only true home, she said to him. Even when Hugh told her about the events surrounding Mike that day and his adventure with Bobby, Sally still refused to go. It took Hugh begging her over the phone for an hour for her to finally consent to joining him at the Transport Center the next day, although she made it quite clear that she was leaving under protest.

With that out of the way, Hugh let himself go to bed, with the knowledge that tomorrow he and Sally would leave Nimbus forever. *Who knows,* he thought as he closed his eyes, he and Sally might find a life together on the surface.

The next day came too quickly for Hugh. It seemed that he had only just shut his eyes when he was awakened by the sound of his small television set. Every apartment and home in the city had one such set, though they varied in size. His was about the size of a toaster and he kept it in his bedroom. All the televisions in the city were designed to automatically turn on whenever there was a public announcement of great importance.

Today's message was being broadcasted from the station in Liberty Estates, and the reporter was talking about a curfew being established in the city from eight at night until six in the morning. In all his time living in Nimbus, Hugh had never heard of, nor experienced, a curfew in the floating city. He wondered why now of all times the city council had decided to create one. Whatever the reason, Hugh didn't worry about it too much, as he knew he would soon be back on mother Earth long before eight.

Taking his suitcase and his camera bag, Hugh walked out of his apartment, locking the door behind him. As he walked toward the cable car station for Liberty Estates, he noticed that today there seemed to be fewer people out and about. Even though it was the middle of summer, very few children were playing, and those who were had their mothers very close at hand.

Hugh also noticed that, whereas the number of humans had gone down, the number of Hawkers had doubled overnight. Now there were two watching him walk toward the cable car station, their cold blue eyes flickering red every now and then. Hugh found himself more and more relieved to be leaving what had only a few days ago been his home. He knew he would miss the city in the sky, but as of now it would be far safer to live with his head below the clouds, on the earth he was born on.

The ride from Galileo to Liberty Estates was just as uneventful as it had been on the Fourth, only a few days ago. The only other occupant in the carriage was an old woman with a bread basket. She only smiled at him once during the entire ride to the center of Nimbus. From there, Hugh got on another cable car that connected Liberty Estates to Aviator Airway, which acted as the visitor's center for the city.

Sally was waiting for him at the Aviator Airway station. She had two leather suitcases with her, packed to bursting, and she wore a slight frown on her face.

"Hugh, are you sure you want to do this?" she asked as he walked out of the cable car.

"Look, Sally, doll, this city is falling apart," said Hugh as he looked her in the eye, his voice steady. "You know just as well as I that there is simply something wrong with those Hawkers. And I have this feeling that things are only going to get worse."

"Hugh," said Sally, turning her head away from him, "this is our home."

"I know, Sally," he said as he reached out to stroke her hair. "I know."

Together, they walked through the milling crowd of Aviator Airway. Soon it became apparent that they were not the only ones planning on leaving Nimbus. People of all ages and nationalities, both tourists visiting the city and residents, were heading in the same direction, toward the Transport Center. The way was decorated with old fashioned iron lampposts and hanging flower pots with petunias and daffodils. The road wound past a few gift shops and postcard stands, past vantage points and a small museum of the city's history. As they walked, Hugh couldn't help but notice that it became more and more crowded. He was worried that the line for the large helicopter down to the surface would take hours to get through.

Soon Sally and Hugh were in line for the cable car to the Transport Center. They were behind a man in a bright red letterman jacket from an Alabama college football team. Behind them the line grew onward, like an endless serpent of human life. Hugh could see through the large glass windows of the station to their final destination in the city.

The Transport Center was one of the first districts to be added to the Nimbus city complex. It was by far the smallest district in the entire city, being only as large as New York City's famous Grand Central Station. From here one could see the rare sight of the propulsion system that held the city's many structures aloft. The Transport Center was surrounded by four nearly soundless turbines and one brightly glowing light that shone from under the curved bottom of the structure. Only the builders and architects of the city knew what the light was. Many speculated it was from a nuclear energy source, while others said it was the light from a rocket engine. The building itself was like a crystal gem, with a completely glass roof that sparkled like a diamond. The sides were made of stainless steel and interrupted by windows every five feet. Behind the building, hidden by the Transport Center's walls, was a large arched opening that was fifty feet across. It was through that hole that the Shuttle left and entered, bringing or taking people from the city.

The line moved very slowly, due to the limitations of how many passengers each cable car could hold, and how long it took for the cars to travel back and forth along the line. As Hugh and Sally waited for their turn, Hugh thought he recognized several of the people in line with them, but he couldn't put names to their faces. Everyone was carrying luggage of some sort, having tried to stuff as much of their lives into bags as they could. There were all sorts of people there, from tourists to longtime residents of the city. It appeared that nobody wanted to stay in Nimbus anymore with how hostile the Hawkers were becoming.

The line moved so slowly that Hugh found himself starting to fidget about while waiting for the people in front of him to move. He glanced over at Sally and saw that she too was getting impatient with the long line. There wasn't much he could do for her, other than offer words of encouragement and give her happy looks. Hugh grew more and more worried that something might happen the longer they were in the line. His eyes drifted around from side to side, on the lookout for any Hawkers that might cause them trouble. Oddly enough, there weren't any Hawkers to be seen. In fact, Hugh thought to himself, he hadn't seen a single one since they came to Aviator Airway. For some reason, this made Hugh more uneasy than if there had been Hawkers everywhere. He did see men standing around outside of the line, but he didn't pay them any attention. He was more worried about getting pounced on by robots from the shadows than he was of getting bothered by men in the daylight.

After what felt like hours, they were finally coming close to the front of the line. A cable car had just left the station and was making its way over to the Transport Center, and the next car was just starting its journey from the other end of the line. Hugh had taken to watching the cable car move across the cable, when suddenly a loud cry of disgust came from just a little ways off to his right. Turning to see what the commotion was about, Hugh saw a man in a trench coat shouting into a handheld radio. There was something familiar about the man, but Hugh couldn't quite put his finger on what it was, due to the man's face being hidden by the shadow cast by his wide hat. Whoever he was, he was in the middle of a heated argument with whoever was on the other end of the handset.

Suddenly, the angry man looked up from his radio and stared right at

Hugh. He still couldn't see the man's eyes, but he could feel the intensity of the mysterious man's gaze upon him, and it was making Hugh very uncomfortable.

"Hugh, what's the matter?" asked Sally, sensing something was amiss.

Hugh turned to her, forcing a nervous smile. He didn't want to make a bigger deal out of the stranger than he needed to. He started to say something to brush off what was bothering him when he felt someone reach out and tap him on his shoulder.

He turned around to see the same stranger who had been talking on the radio standing right beside him. "May I help you?" Hugh asked, the strain starting to show in his words. He really didn't want anything else to happen to him before he could get safely down to solid ground.

"Listen here," said the man in a gruff voice. "You need to get out of this line, and come along with me."

"I'm deeply sorry, but can't this wait?" asked Hugh as his grip on his suitcase tightened. He could see out of the corner of his eye the cable cars moving along the line. Every second that passed brought an empty car that much closer, and in turn brought him and Sally that much closer to being on their way out of Nimbus. "Maybe we can talk when we're on the ground or something?"

"I'm sorry," said the man, his grip tightening on Hugh's shoulder, "but this can't wait. There's a situation here. I'm afraid you and your lady friend need to come with me. Right now."

"Are you serious?" asked Hugh, turning to face the man head on. With the stranger being so close, he could now see some of the other man's face. He was an older man, sporting a thick mustache and features as rough as his voice. He did not look like he smiled a lot, and was still holding the radio in his other hand. His trench coat was drawn tightly across his body, but not buttoned up. Only the coat's belt held it closed.

"I am dead serious," said the man as he glanced over at the approaching cable car. "You need to listen to me. Staying here is dangerous. You see I'm the Ch-"

Before the stranger could finish his sentence, there was a sudden explosion, the shock of it knocking everyone gathered at the station over like human dominos. His ears rang for a minute after the blast, and Hugh found himself too stunned to move. Before he could clear his head, he felt the vice-like grip return to his wrist. It pulled him off of the pavement and onto his feet. He was having a little trouble thinking straight, but now that he was standing again, he was recovering faster. Glancing at the man holding him, he could see a blue uniform poking out from the coat and a police badge catching the light of the sun. The badge gave the man's identity away as none other than Nimbus's former

Police Chief, Matthew McGullen. The man was starting to talk to Hugh when there was a second explosion.

Hugh somehow managed to wrestle himself away from the larger man again, and saw for himself that the Transport Center was now on fire. Not only that, but he caught the last sight of the long cable slipping out of the pulley system that held it aloft, taking with it the cable car, full with people, down to their deaths in the fields of Kansas far below. As another explosion echoed out from the Transport Center, Hugh could see the metal of the building's walls buckle further. The glass of the windows that decorated its walls shattered outward like sparkly confetti from a New Year's Eve party. Through the windows, flames reached hungrily for the sky. Hugh realized at that moment that if he had been in the car he would have died, and so would Sally. Without even thinking about it, he unpacked his camera and brought it up to the destruction, capturing the burning wreck on film. He was operating on automatic at this point, his mind too overwhelmed by what had just happened to do anything else but go through his photographer motions.

"Yeats," called out the Police Chief as he grabbed Hugh by his shoulder, drawing the photographer's attention.

"What?" asked Hugh, his eyes and camera glued to the fire, now ravaging the Transport Center as it started to list in the air like a ship sinking beneath the waves. Vaguely, Hugh registered the cable car station emptying out behind him, the human mass fleeing from the destruction.

"Yeats, I need you and your lady friend to come with me," said McGullen. "*NOW!*"

But Hugh stood still, for the show was far from over. All of a sudden five more explosions erupted, this time from the bottom of the Transport Center. Hugh could see the strange light go out under the structure. Then, like a rock tossed into the air, the entire Transport Center lurched and fell. Hugh wondered, as the burning mess began its rapid descent to the ground far below, if this was what it felt like to watch the German dirigible, the Hindenburg, burn.

It took a slap from Sally to bring Hugh back to earth, so to speak.

"Hugh!" she practically yelled at him. "We have to go!"

"Yes, Yeats," said the Police Chief as he drew a shotgun out from his long grey coat. "They will be here soon to clean up."

"Who?" asked Hugh, still dazed from what he had seen.

"The Hawkers, boy, the Hawkers," answered the Chief.

It was some time later that Hugh found himself and Sally, along with the Police Chief, making their way through Aviator Airway. The whole place was falling into chaos after the sudden attack. People were confused and trying to figure out where to go. Voices rang out at random and children were crying left and right in terror. Broken glass was everywhere from windows that had shattered from the explosion's shockwave. There were men, who Hugh could only assume were other undercover policemen, trying to bring some order to the panicking people. Where exactly he and Sally were going he did not know, only that Chief McGullen was leading them somewhere. Somewhere safe, Hugh hoped. They were led down side alleys, away from the panicking crowds. Once the cries became dull, the Chief started to talk.

"Once we're out of the Airway and in Liberty, we'll take the sky bridge over to the Warehouse district," said McGullen as he led the pair onward.

"Why the Warehouse District?" Hugh asked.

"Yes, why there of all places?" asked Sally.

"You'll know when we get there," snapped the Chief as they got closer to the cable car station.

"What the heck happened back there?" blurted out Hugh, finally coming out of the fog that the destruction of the Transport Center had left him in. "Why did the Transport Center explode? How'd you know it was going to? Did the guy on the other end of your radio conversation say something? Why have I seen you so much? Have you been following me?"

"Do tell, Chief," said Sally, her ever-present notebook at the ready.

"Look, we don't have time for this," said the Chief, blowing off their questions. "Wait till we get to the Warehouse District. Then, when we're safe, I will try to answer as many of your questions as I can."

"Not until somebody tells me what is going on," protested Hugh.

The Police Chief stopped suddenly in his tracks and rounded on the duo. "Now listen up," he barked at them. "I have been protecting you, Hugh, and your girlfriend since day one of the Hawker's occupation of this city. I know you took Dr. Crick's journal, Hugh."

"How?" gasped Hugh.

"Let's just say a birdie told me and leave it at that," said the Chief. "Now if you are done, we need to get to the Warehouse District." With that, McGullen once again headed off toward the cable car station. Hugh was silent again, still shocked that the Chief knew that he had Frank's journal. Looking at Sally as they walked onward, Hugh saw his shock mirrored in her face. It was clear that Sally didn't tell anyone about the leather book, so how did the Police Chief find out?

The ride back to Liberty Plaza was just as uneventful as before, only the tension inside the cable car was far greater. Hugh could not help but feel as if he was being judged by the Police Chief's eyes. It was like McGullen was asking himself if Hugh was ready for whatever lay ahead of them. Hugh only hoped that he would be able to keep it together now that there was no way out of Nimbus. No way out. That was when it finally hit home for Hugh. He, Sally, and all the other citizens of the flying city were now effectively trapped thousands of feet in the air, beyond any means, except for outside interference, to get back down to terra firma.

As they walked onward toward the sky bridge, the sound of a three tone bell chime suddenly rang out. Whenever that chime was played, an announcement was about to be made. The message that soon followed the bells spoke of the destruction of the Transport Center. The announcer claimed that the explosion was the result of a gas leak and the building's collapse was a malfunction of the Transport Center's flight system. However, Hugh and Sally, along with the Chief, knew better. There was no way all of those explosions were caused by faulty wiring. Someone, most likely Mason himself, didn't want anyone to leave Nimbus.

Soon enough they were at the sky bridge that led to the Warehouse District of the flying city. It wasn't a long walk, but even so, Hugh was very grateful when they were over the bridge. This part of Nimbus was one of the less impressive areas, with only steel buildings and cranes everywhere. The small fleet of supply aircraft that came here to unload various merchandise for the city only came once every month, and they had just left yesterday. It was usually abandoned until either the deliveries from the world below were made or the various shops and stores came by to collect their products via a special train system.

The only ones who bothered to visit this part of Nimbus besides the merchants were the warehouse managers, who were usually asleep in their offices with their television sets playing re-runs of sitcoms. Such was the case with the warehouse that McGullen brought Sally and Hugh to. It was times like these that Hugh wondered why crime was not a bigger issue in Nimbus, but then he remembered just how good the police were at their job back when they worked for the city. Not to mention that the Hawkers that now patrolled the streets were not known for their kindness toward anyone, especially to those who crossed their path.

The warehouse itself was marked number fifteen in large black peeling numbers above its door. It looked much more derelict than the other warehouses around it. There were rust stains all over its front, and garbage had started to pile up beside its main doors. The building was about the size of a small aircraft hangar and was around three stories tall. Its walls were of concrete and not a single window breached the sides.

The Chief walked up to the metal door and knocked upon it in tune to a theme song from a courthouse drama that Hugh had seen once or twice on television. With the groan of metal upon metal, the big door slowly opened. It hadn't opened all the way, just around four feet from the concrete frame, when the Chief ushered Hugh and Sally inside. Hugh and Sally protested their rough handling by McGullen, but the Chief remained stone faced to their complaints. Once all three of them were inside, the warehouse door slammed shut behind them, moving much faster than it had when it was opening.

For a few moments, Hugh could not see a thing. Then McGullen gave someone the command to turn on the lights and, within moments, it was obeyed. With the darkness banished, Hugh heard Sally let out a gasp at the sight that was revealed. Before them within the large interior stood rank upon rank of every sergeant, cop, and security guard who had once worked in Nimbus. There were the men who stood in the banks, the men who had guarded the Transport Center, and over there was the man who used to keep the night watch outside of Hugh's apartment. Many of them were still in uniform, though it was obvious that some of them had not washed their clothes in quite a while.

"Welcome," said Chief McGullen from behind Hugh and Sally. "Welcome to Nimbus's Underground Police Department."

"We're all set for you in the orientation room," said an officer who saluted the Chief.

"Very good, Officer Gordon," said McGullen as he led Hugh and Sally past a few crates to a small office that would have been used by shop owners while they took stock of their deliveries. Now it had been turned into a center of operations for the underground police. The walls were decorated with photographs of the Hawkers and various other robots that Hugh did not recognize. The pictures ranged from crystal clear to being so fuzzy it was hard to tell what was in the image. Along with photos, there were graphs, charts and diagrams showing the possible anatomy of the Hawkers.

"Please have a seat," said McGullen as he sat down behind the desk situated at the back of the room. On the desk's front was a symbol for the Chief of Police, which meant that the desk had been carried into the warehouse from its original resting place in the Chief's office at the main department in the center of the city. Hugh and Sally sat down in front of the desk in folding chairs that clearly had nothing to do with the old police department. Before he spoke, Chief McGullen took a moment to skim through a manila folder that lay on top of his desk.

"I'm sorry, Chief," said Hugh, breaking the silence. "But what on Earth is going on here? Why is the entire police force hiding out in a warehouse? Why have you been following me? How did you find out about the journal?"

"You're persistent, I'll give you that, Yeats," said the Chief as he put down the folder. "First off, Miss Saltwater," he said as he addressed Sally.

"Yes, Chief?" asked Sally, her pen hovering over her ever constant notepad.

"I would appreciate it if none of what is said in this office or the warehouse is repeated to the paper."

Sally visibly drooped, realizing that her biggest scoop ever had just disappeared before she even had the chance to put ink to paper. "Sure, whatever you want, sir."

"Good. Now then, let's start with the first question Yeats asked," said the Chief. "Why are we, the proud police of Nimbus, now taking up residence in an old warehouse? Well, it has everything to do with the Hawkers and Dr. Mason. Since those robots took over our job of protecting the city from crime, every human with a job in law enforcement has found him or herself out of a job."

"I know it has only been a few days, but why didn't you get new ones?" asked Hugh as he quickly glanced at the folder on the desk.

"Well, for starters, most of us are seasoned policemen and have no idea how to hold down a civilian job," said the Chief as he pulled out a pack of cigarettes. He took a moment to pull out a cigarette and light it before he continued to speak. "Then there is also the fact that these Hawkers out in the city, as far as we know at least, numbered only one back on the Fourth of July and in the hundreds on the fifth. Unless these robot things are as easy to put together as a two piece puzzle, someone has been planning a takeover of Nimbus for a very long time."

"Take over?" asked Sally, swatting away the cigarette smoke. "What on earth are you talking about?"

"Isn't it obvious?" asked McGullen. "Every single officer is now out of a job, and these Hawkers are now everywhere. This means that whoever is in charge of those robots is now in control of the city."

"So…" said Hugh as the full gravity of the situation dawned on him, "what you're saying is that Dr. Mason is trying to take over Nimbus?"

"Gold star for you, boy," said McGullen as he breathed out a particularly large breath of cigarette smoke.

"I don't get it," said Sally as she once again fended off the fumes. "Why would a scientist want to take over the city? I know it is a flying city, but still!"

"That's what we're trying to find out," said the Chief. "So far all we know is that Dr. Mason has gone missing, and these robots seem to be getting less interested in protecting and more involved with enforcing their own rules." At this point McGullen indicated the folder that he had laid down on his desk. Hugh reached for it and, as he picked it up and began to read its contents, the Chief resumed speaking. "Inside of that are all known recorded cases of unprovoked Hawker attacks upon civilians and ex-police. Be sure to take a good look at it."

The folder listed twelve different attacks by Hawkers. The first attack was the one against the nurse back at the Angel of Mercy Hospital a few days ago. The second and third attacks involved the Hawkers giving their victims a few broken ribs for unclear reasons. The next four, which happened just the day before, ranged from bruises to broken bones. There were two more that happened that same day, only they resulted in fatalities. Their deaths were listed as being "thrown out of the city." Hugh sincerely hoped that Frank had not been dragged out of his room in the hospital with the intent to have him plummet to his death. There were also four different cases of the Hawkers flying away with people to an unknown location. Hugh found himself wishing that was the fate that Frank had endured.

When he was done reading Hugh passed the folder over to Sally, who took slightly longer to read its contents. When she was done, she became very silent and gently laid the folder back down on top of the desk.

"Now that you are all caught up on the Hawker's increasingly violent behavior, I will brief you on their M.O.," said McGullen. "They are very strong, too strong for their appearance, and they are able to throw anyone they don't like out of the city. Their ability to fly makes being out in the open a dangerous situation as they can easily pick us humans off one by one on the streets."

"Why are you telling us this?" asked Hugh.

"So you know what you are up against," replied the Chief as another cloud of smoke exited his lips.

"Wait, are you suggesting that we fight these things?" Sally exclaimed.

"No, if you find yourself cornered by these things I expect you to run, or at least get somewhere where they can't pick you off like field mice," grunted McGullen. "Moving on, as to why I was following you, Yeats, and how I came to know about that journal. Well you can thank Frank for that one."

"You know Frank?" asked Hugh in surprise. He had no idea that Frank knew someone on the force, let alone the Chief himself.

"Yes, I know Frank, known him since we were in school together back in New York Public High. I was from New Jersey and he was a native New Yorker, though you wouldn't guess that from the way he talks. Those were some good times, Yeats, great times, in fact," the Chief said with a smile.

"I had no idea," whispered Sally silently to herself.

"Now back on the Fourth, Frank called me on the phone," said the

Chief as he leaned back in his chair. "It was a few hours after the big expo in Liberty had ended. His seemed a tad excited about something, but wouldn't give me anything specific. He just said that he suspected something was about to go down. It was then that he told me about his journal, and how it had some very important information in it. So much so, that if it fell into the wrongs hands, it could spell doom for all of mankind.

"All of mankind?!" gasped Sally. Hugh almost gasped along with her. Surely the small locked leather book he carried in his bag didn't have such power. Or did it? Perhaps there was a good reason for the lock on its outside, besides for privacy. But if that was the case, why didn't Frank destroy the journal when he had the chance?

"I haven't a clue," continued the Chief of Police. "He was talking so fast that I could barely get a word in edgewise. I tried to ask him what this was all about, and all he could tell me was that it had something to do with the Hawkers. When the call came later that night about Frank getting shot, I hurried down to the hospital to see him. He was barely conscious by that point, the shock having put him into a bit of a stupor. He did make it very clear, even in the state he was in, that he wanted me to keep an eye out for you, Mr. Yeats. He was so insistent about it, that he made me promise to protect you. I tried to tell him that I barely knew you, and that he was probably delusional from the pain, but I didn't upset him in his current state, so I agreed to do it. After all, with those robots taking *my job*, I would have a lot more free time on my hands."

Hugh wanted to ask why Frank hadn't asked the Chief to also look after Bobby, but then he realized that Bobby could probably look out for himself.

"Now," continued the Chief, "I knew you had the journal because it wouldn't take a scientist to figure it out. He first tells me about that all important journal of his, and then, instead of telling me to go get it, tells me to protect some newspaper photographer. Two plus two equals four, if you catch my drift."

"This is a lot to take in," said Hugh as he absently brushed his hair back, causing his hat to slide backwards on his head.

"Look, I am only telling you what Frank told me," said the Chief as he put the cigarette out by rubbing it into an old scorch mark on his desk. "Personally, I think Frank was exaggerating about that little book of his. However, I feel there is something far bigger going on here. Believe it or not, I was at the hospital the next day, with a plan to get my facts straight with Frank, but then he goes and gets kidnapped. Needless to say, the actions of the Hawker who investigated the incident made me realize that something was sour with those machines. That's what prompted me to get the rest of the force together to set up shop here in this warehouse. After all, the people need to be protected from these things.

At the moment, the book seems to be safe in your hands, despite everything that has happened. For now, I think it should remain in your care. However, if things continue to escalate with the Hawkers' aggression, I may request you to hand that journal over, Mr. Yeats. But since those robots have pretty much attacked everywhere that book has been, I am going to assign a couple of my men to look after you two. It's a pretty safe bet that it's of a lot of value to somebody, and I think you both know who I mean."

6

It was some time later that Sally and Hugh left Chief McGullen. He had told them that he was assigning two undercover cops to watch over them as they returned to their homes. He himself could not go as the situation with the Hawkers had escalated drastically with the destruction of the Transport Center. Chief McGullen needed to stay and prepare his men for whatever the robots tried next. The man who was assigned to watch over Hugh was named Officer Marley and the one to protect Sally was Detective Catcher.

"Hey, Chief?" asked Sally when she was introduced to the detective. "I understand why Hugh gets a bodyguard. He's the one with the book. But why do I have my own personal cop, too?"

The Chief answered by saying that he didn't want to risk losing her to the Hawkers. Due to her relationship to Hugh, there was a chance that the Hawkers might use her to get to him, or try to get information on the ex-police's headquarters from her.

"Gee, way to make a girl feel special," grumbled Sally as she left with the detective. Hugh was just happy that Sally had someone to look after her. Since this whole mess started, he had been getting very worried about her getting hurt. At least now, no matter what happened to Hugh out in the city, Sally would be safe.

All too soon, they returned to Galileo Plaza. The trip back to their district from the police warehouse was a blur. Hugh made sure Sally did not leave his sight until they reached her apartment. It took some doing, but Hugh managed to convince her to stay at home, with the detective guarding her door, while he and Officer Marley went to Tesla Quarter to check up on Bobby. Personally, Hugh did not want to leave Sally with the detective, but after what happened with the cable car to the Transport Center, he didn't want to risk her traveling. There was no telling if any more cable-cars, or even entire districts of the city, would be targeted for destruction.

The trip to Tesla Quarter was uneventful, except for Officer Marley constantly looking back and forth as he walked. Hugh found the officer's head motion rather distracting, but Marley claimed that he was simply looking out for any and all possible threats that might be lurking around them, such as any Hawker units on the attack. Hugh knew he was probably being overly critical of the undercover cop, but he still found the constant looking around a bit unsettling. Hugh may not have been a cop, but even to him, Officer Marley didn't seem to be doing a very good job as an undercover bodyguard. He could see Marley visibly sweat as they walked past every Hawker on their way to the sky bridge. The officer only stopped looking around once they got to the sky bridge for Tesla.

Walking across took much more time than riding the cable car. It took even longer due to the unusually high pedestrian traffic on the walkway. Hugh guessed that it was all due to the disaster earlier that day that had resulted in many more citizens in the city becoming more prone to using their legs to get around instead of the cable car system. Once on the other side, Hugh took a moment to get his bearings and then set off for Bobby's apartment. First, they had to find a station for the district train, and then ride it to the stop for Angel of Mercy hospital. From there, Hugh had to again endure Officer Marley's constant looking around as they walked to Bobby's apartment. Hugh couldn't help but notice the time, being only minutes before the new curfew would come into effect. He knew he had to get off the street and that he wouldn't be able to sleep in his own bed tonight. The warning words of the Chief still rang in his ears and he felt the unease of Officer Marley start to rub off on him. Hugh began to look up at the sky on occasion just to make sure there were no Hawkers flying above them, waiting to swoop down and carry them off.

Bobby's home was on the first floor of a triple-decker brick building. It wasn't a very big apartment, with each suite taking up the entirety of each floor. The stairs leading up were outside the building, rising up to the left of the first floor apartment's door.

Bobby was drunk when he answered the door. His glasses were gone from his face and his hair was a mess. Bobby was wearing the same clothes from the day before and was now sporting some new stains on his sweater. He swayed slightly in the door frame as he briefly looked at Hugh and took a few moments more to examine the undercover cop. With a slight hiccup puncturing his speech, Bobby invited them both to come inside. Usually, Hugh tried to avoid Bobby when he got drunk like this, but at this hour, there was no choice but to come inside.

Upon entering the apartment, Hugh could hear the television in the other room giving off sounds of whatever program Bobby had been listening to before their arrival. As he went in to see what show was on the TV set, Officer Marley introduced himself to Bobby. In the other room, Hugh saw that the television was showing a news program from Nimbus's television station in Liberty Estates. The newscaster, who wore a pinstripe suit, was talking about how the new curfew was being enforced by the Hawker units. The news program switched from the station to another reporter who was broadcasting from outside the station.

The outside reporter was a short man, perhaps five feet tall, who was sporting a cheap toupee rendered grey by the television's screen. The backdrop of the newscast was a dirt path in front of several manicured trees and a waist high row of rose bushes, all of which were lit by the light of the setting sun and by a light from behind the camera's vision. The short man was standing next to a Hawker unit that was clearly different from the other robots patrolling the streets of Nimbus.

The robot towered over the short reporter and its metal head barely fit into the frame of the camera. Instead of the blue officer-like uniforms that the other Hawkers wore, this one was sporting a black uniform that was like a trench coat without sleeves. The uniform's color may have been just a side effect of the television, but Hugh had the feeling that in full Technicolor, the uniform would still be as black as pitch. It wasn't just the unusual black suit that set the avian robot apart from the rest of the flock. Its body was far less bulky than the other Hawkers, leaving it with a body much like an Olympic track athlete. It reminded Hugh more of a black raven than a hawk, due to the robot's longer beak.

"This is Rick Herring, reporting in," said the newscaster as he held the microphone up to his mouth. "I am here tonight in beautiful Valkyrie Park, Nimbus's garden district, with one of the newest Hawker units." As the reporter spoke, the Hawker stood like a silent shadow next to him. In the dimming light it was becoming harder and harder to make out the machine amongst the shadows of the trees of the park.

"This new type of Hawker," the reporter continued, "is built for speed and stealth. I've been told through my contacts that this unit is far more agile and silent than the other more common Hawkers that have taken the place of our beloved human police force in Nimbus. It is designed to be completely undetectable in the dark and, as I've been told, this new type of Hawker is called a Raven Hunter, due to the design of its head and its purpose, to hunt down those who refuse to stay off the streets after curfew."

At this point, the camera zoomed in on the grey-headed reporter's face.

"However, I feel there is a need for the city of Nimbus to ask, 'Why do we even need these Hawkers, let alone a curfew?' 'Is a new type of Hawker really necessary for curfew duty?' 'Is this our mayor's doing or are the scientists in our city getting a little too mad with their heads up in the clouds and their bottomless grant money from the American government?' Let us for the moment focus on the question of why the curfew."

Upon the last word, the reporter moved his microphone in front of the Raven Hunter's metal beak. The robot didn't say a word into the mike, but its eyes, made colorless by the television set, darted back and forth between the reporter and the microphone.

"So tell us, Mr. Raven Hunter," said Rick with a slight sneer on his face. "Why is it that we humans must now forgo the bars and clubs and stay at home in our houses watching prime time TV?"

"Citizen," said the Raven Hunter, its voice soft, yet scratchy like a crow's, "you have precisely five minutes before curfew."

"Oh, don't give me that load of bull," groaned the reporter. "Just tell us if there's a reason why you robots, your creator, or even the mayor, wants all of us normal folk in bed by eight. Is the rumor that communists have gained entrance into our city true?"

"Warning," said the Hawker, its eyes starting to lighten in their grey shade. "You have three minutes to get indoors before curfew is enforced."

It was clear to Hugh that both the reporter and the Raven Hunter seemed to be becoming more and more agitated and aggressive as the interview went on.

"Enough of these stupid curfew reminders, you bucket of bolts!" exclaimed the reporter as he shoved his face into the Raven Hunter's face. "I know you metal birds have some sort of agenda. After all, you mechanical monstrosities carry off citizens of this fair city at will! There's even talk of you things committing murder! What do you have to say to that, Raven?"

Even in the black and white image shown to him on the screen, Hugh could tell that the avian machine's eyes were changing color. But that wasn't the most alarming thing it was doing. The Raven Hunter almost seemed to drop an invisible disguise, going from being a stiff metal creature to being something far more alive in a way only flesh and blood could be.

"Well, then," it said, surprising Rick and all his viewers with its sudden change from a programmed message to such unscripted speech. "If you are so willing to end the illusion, then let me just say, this city is not yours anymore. It does not belong to the humans. It is ours. And your time before curfew begins *is up*." And with that the Raven Hunter seemed to almost disappear into the shadows of the park. The last thing Hugh saw before the program ended was Rick screaming as he was pulled off camera and into the darkness by cruel metallic hands.

It was at that moment that Hugh knew the stakes had been raised. If the Hawkers were only pretending to be protecting the people, then what were they really like? Did Dr. Mason design them like this or was this a result of too strong an artificial intelligence? Could it be, Hugh wondered, that the Hawkers were the ones behind the break-ins, not Mason? That they were completely self-aware and had plans of their own?

Hugh heard Bobby swear behind him. He turned around to see that his friend and the cop had joined him in the room without him noticing. It was clear that both men were just as stunned by the avian machine's behavior on the television as Hugh was. Marley took out a cigarette from his coat pocket and proceeded to set it alight with the strike of a match.

"Well, who would have seen that coming?" the cop asked as he blew out a smoke ring.

"I would have," coughed Bobby as he fanned the cigarette smoke away from his face. "I've seen them do stuff like that firsthand, though I must admit, not to such a drastic extent as that."

"Wait, you said your name is Bobby Crick. Are you related in any way to Dr. Frank Crick who went missing a few days ago?" asked Marley as he gave Bobby a quick look over for the first time.

"What if I am?" challenged Bobby.

"Why does it matter?" asked Hugh.

"Look," said Marley as he huffed and puffed on his cigarette, "I know what happened at the hospital, and I am very sorry for your father."

"Yeah, yeah, I've heard that one before," grumbled Bobby as he finished off the bottle of beer that he still held in his hand. "Yet, despite how 'sorry' you feel, you've yet to do a single thing about it, have you? In fact, no one, and I do mean *no one,* has even tried to *help* me understand what happened that day except for Hugh here. Everyone else just says 'oh, too bad' or 'oh dear, how sad'!"

"Are you implying that the police have been ignoring the Hawker attacks?" asked Marley with a bit of steel to his voice.

"They sure aren't doing their jobs, are they?" retorted Bobby as he adopted an underhanded grasp of the bottle in his hand.

"For your information, *citizen*," said Marley as he began to turn red from anger, "I happen to be a member of this city's fine police force."

"Till you lot got fired and replaced with those tin cans outside," snorted Bobby.

"ENOUGH," shouted Hugh, who had been trying to say something the whole time the two men had been arguing. The result of his outburst was an awkward silence between Bobby and Marley. "Look," Hugh continued to say, "what people haven't done isn't the problem here. What is, though, is the fact that every day these robots become more numerous and dangerous. We now know they are a lot more self-aware than we first thought. All of this only adds up to making their threat to us all the greater. The worst thing we can do now is take ourselves out and save those machines the trouble."

"The kid has a point," said Marley.

"Yeah..." Bobby mumbled as he put the bottle down. "I guess it's best to save this aggression for the robots responsible and not for the ones who could have prevented this whole mess."

"I am going to let that little remark slide," said Officer Marley as he plucked his spent cigarette out of his mouth and rubbed it out inside of a standing ashtray.

"Well," said Bobby, as he sat down on the plaid sofa. "Hugh, I suppose you have a reason for being here at this hour, along with your friend."

Hugh took his friend's inquiry as his cue to tell Bobby about what he and Sally had learned at the warehouse. Hugh felt that Bobby had a right to know about the information the police had gathered on the Hawkers and to have knowledge of the other victims of the robots. He went on to tell Bobby about the explosion at the Transport Center and how the Chief of Police had until recently been following Hugh around.

"That is quite a lot to swallow, Hugh," said Bobby, after Hugh had finished his tale. "Now, I ask again, Hugh, what do you want from me?"

"Right now, seeing how it's past curfew, I was hoping you would give us a place to sleep for the night."

"Alright," said Bobby, as he got up from the sofa. "You can stay, but I'm afraid all I've got in terms of extra beds is this sofa and the recliner in the other room." As he left the room, Bobby gave a slightly drunken laugh. "You know, Hugh, you really should have phoned ahead. I would have been more prepared."

It was not long until Bobby called Hugh and Marley into the kitchen. The room was not very big, only large enough to hold the essentials of a modern kitchen. In the center was a small table, surrounded by three chairs of different styles. It was clear that Bobby didn't have company over very often, that when he met up with someone, it was either at the hospital or at the bars he visited. In the room was a stylized refrigerator, an oven with gas burners, and Bobby himself with a slightly boyish grin on his face as he placed some meat onto three platters on the table.

"I hope you like leftover Chinese chicken," said Bobby as he walked over to the fridge and pulled out a few sodas. They all sat down at the small table. The chicken was very stale, but at least it was better than nothing.

They had just finished their late meager meal when the light fixture above their heads went out. It wasn't just the kitchen that went dark though, as the light in the hall had gone out, along with the one in the room across the way.

"Geez," chuckled Hugh nervously in the darkness. "You forget to pay your power bill, Bob?"

"Of course not, Hugh," snapped Bobby as he made his way to a cabinet, his form little more than a shadow in the dark. He opened the cupboard and pulled out a cylinder, which upon the flick of a switch, was revealed to be a flashlight. Hugh had to look away when Bobby shined the light in his direction.

Officer Marley was revealed to be standing next to the window, with one hand pushing the curtain aside by the added light of the flashlight. Something outside had caught his attention. As Bobby moved to exit the room, with the voiced intent of checking the fuse box, the officer spoke up. "Wait," he said as he beckoned the others to the window.

"Why, what's out there?" asked Hugh. His growing fear of a Hawker attack showed in his voice as he spoke.

"Just look," answered the cop.

Upon looking outside at the next apartment over, it was instantly clear that the power outage was not just limited to Bobby's apartment. The entire street, nay, the entire city of Nimbus, had gone dark. Only the mysterious engines that kept the many districts afloat in the sky among the clouds were still running in the city.

Suddenly, the radio that was on the counter next to the sink came to life. It had not been affected by the sudden power outage due to the luxury of being battery powered. The only message that played from the set was the two words, "Lights Out." Then, just as it turned on, the radio became quiet. No matter how much Bobby fiddled with it, nothing would come out from its speakers.

"Guess this means they want us to go to sleep now," said Officer Marley as he let go of the curtain.

7

The rest of the night was long and hard for Hugh. After they had left the kitchen, Bobby brought out some spare blankets for both Hugh and Marley. Bobby directed the officer to sleep in the recliner, while Hugh lucked out with the sofa as his bed for the night. However, Hugh couldn't fall asleep. The Hawkers, or whoever the Hawkers worked for, was clearly gaining in power over the city. If they could cut the electricity to the city as easily as one might throw a switch, then what was to stop them from attacking the citizens of the city while they slept in the darkness?

Hugh found no peace in his sleep, either. His nightmares produced massive machines of destruction, giant avian titans in full body armor, chasing him, trying to either stomp him flat or pick him up and fly away. The dawn did not come too soon for Hugh.

Hugh was awakened by the first ray of the sun at dawn, coming in through a window behind the television set. Within seconds the fog of his nightmares cleared from his eyes. Hugh sat up on the couch and took a look around. The house was quiet, except for the sound of the officer asleep in the other room. Hugh was about to get up when, suddenly, as if a switch had been thrown, the electricity came back. The television set in front of Hugh flickered back to life, but showed only static.

"Well, at least they turned the power back on," commented a disheveled Bobby as he walked into the living room. He was wearing pinstripe pajamas with a few multicolored patches on them. Behind Bobby lurked Marley, still wearing the suit from the day before. The dark circles under the undercover cop's eyes showed that he was up the entire night. It became very clear that Marley had only just fallen asleep when Hugh had arisen moments before.

"Good morning," said Hugh as he got up to greet the duo at the door.

"Yeah, good if you don't take into account how much control the Hawkers have gained," scoffed the cop as he walked over to the television and tuned it until the static cleared. The screen showed a re-run of *I Love Cindy*, which hardly gave them any information about what was going on in the city, so Marley turned the television set off. There was no time to be wasted on a fictional housewife's crazy antics when there was a force taking over Nimbus. They decided to take a moment to eat a small meal of toast and butter with a bit of orange juice to wash it down.

After eating, Bobby got dressed and Hugh took a moment to use Bobby's shower. Once he had finished he pulled out fresh clothes from his suitcase. After he had finished dressing, and repacking his suitcase, Hugh alerted Officer Marley that it was time to leave. Before Hugh was able to exit the apartment, Bobby stopped him.

"Take this," the doctor said as he handed over his Colt handgun. "I want you to have this."

"I can't take your gun," said Hugh as he pushed the weapon away. "I already have Marley to protect me and I don't want to leave you defenseless, Bobby."

Bobby only offered the gun again and replied, "Trust me, Hugh. I've got a few more weapons for protection. Please, humor me and take it." Hugh took the handgun from his friend and tucked it away in his bag.

With a few more words to Bobby about keeping away from the Hawkers and keeping his thoughts about the avian robots quiet, Hugh and Marley left the apartment. Marley walked silently behind Hugh as they headed back to the district train station. The streets were very quiet. Not a single living body was to be seen. Only the cool metal of the patrolling Hawkers was on the streets. Hugh wanted to get back home to Galileo Plaza as quickly as he could, because he had become very worried about Sally. He hadn't had a chance to call her before the power was cut the night before and by now he wanted not only to hear her voice, but to see her blond head in person.

From the train to the sky bridge, to the final walk to her apartment, it was all a blur to Hugh. It was only when he stretched out his finger to ring her doorbell that things became crystal clear again.

One ring. No answer.

Two rings. Surely she was home?

Three rings. Just as Hugh started to panic, he heard the door unlock from the inside. The door opened just a crack, enough for one soft, golden-brown eye to look out. Upon seeing it was Hugh at her door, Sally threw the door wide open and embraced him.

Then she slapped him, hard.

"Wh- what was that for?" stuttered Hugh as he felt his sore face, her hand leaving a brief red welt on his cheek.

"That is for leaving me alone, Hubert Yeats," she said as she tossed her hair back over her shoulder. This was one of the rare times Hugh had ever seen it not in her trademark ponytail.

"Alone?" stuttered Hugh. "What happened to Detective Catcher?"

"He's *dead,* Hubert," moaned Sally, as she looked away from him. It was at this moment that Hugh truly got a good look at Sally. Her usually perfect makeup had run down her cheeks, leaving dark snaking stains from her eyes all the way down to her chin. It was clear now that she had been crying. There was also an ugly bruise on her neck that almost circled her throat.

"Sally, what happened?" asked Hugh, his voice now soft and level.

Sally looked back up at Hugh and said only one word. "*Inside.*"

Hugh left Marley outside to guard the door and entered Sally's neat apartment. Only, it wasn't as neat as it usually was. The clothes Sally had worn the day before were scattered all over the floor, and there was an empty box of snack cakes on the floor in front of an old hand operated gramophone. A couple of crumpled up hankies littered the carpet around the couch like fallen snow, filled with the tears and makeup stains of Sally's despair. Hugh joined Sally on the sofa in the living room. He sat next to her, waiting for her to start her tale. Instead, she sniffled, then moaned, and then started to cry. Hugh didn't speak. He only draped his arms around her thin shoulders and held her close, comforting her until her last tear was shed.

Still he didn't speak. He knew better than that. It would be best to let Sally tell her story when she was ready, and not to force her into it.

After a few more minutes of silence and the occasional sigh, Sally spoke. She started off by telling Hugh that after he left her and the detective the day before at her apartment, she had decided to make a break for Liberty Estates. She wanted to get to the United Post newspaper office to tell the editors about what had happened that day, despite the warnings the Chief and Hugh had given her. She didn't want to simply call the paper because she wanted to deliver her story in person. She had managed to convince Detective Catcher to escort her to the United Post offices, and everything had been going great until they got to the sky bridge. She didn't want to travel by cable car, after what had happened to the line to the Transport Center, but by the time Sally and her escort had reached the bridge, the new curfew had fallen and they were only two thirds of the way across the sky bridge.

"Then, out of nowhere came this strange screeching sound, like fingers on a chalk board mixed with a plane engine, only deeper," said Sally as she continued her story. "Next thing I knew, my feet were dangling off the ground and there was this suffocating feeling in my neck. I barely noticed that I'd been grabbed by a Hawker before Detective Catcher started shouting at it to put me down. Next thing I know, he fires his gun and the Hawker drops me and rushes him. I can only sit there on the ground and watch as the robot grabs Catcher by his coat." She took a moment to cry some more. This time Hugh could not help but ask what happened next.

She gave him a dirty look, and then continued with her tale. "Well, that monster lifted Catcher like he was a sack of potatoes and flew up and over the rail of the sky bridge. When it had flown far away from the bridge, it... it..."

"It what?"

"It *dropped* him, Hughie." Sally then burst out in tears again and what little makeup was left on her face trailed away with the water from her eyes. Hugh couldn't blame her. He could only imagine what it would have been like for her, to see someone fall to their death. Hugh only hoped that he could avoid the same fate for himself, for Sally, and any of his friends in the city.

Sally continued to cry into her hands. "I just ran, Hugh," she moaned as she cuddled closer to Hugh, pressing into his chest as if it was the only thing that could hold her together. "I don't even know how I got away, I just ran. I didn't even try to help him. I just ran."

Hugh stayed with Sally for the rest of the day. He helped her clean her apartment and found a movie they could watch together on the television after looking over the television guide. Hugh knew that after what Sally had been through, she needed some quality time with him by her side, comforting her in this time of great distress. At some point, Hugh decided to invite Marley inside, just so the cop wouldn't be left standing outside all day with nothing to eat. He also didn't want Marley to get into a fight with a Hawker and meet the same end as Detective Catcher.

Eventually, the sun started to set again. Hugh sought the aid of the cop to help him move a particularly heavy wardrobe in front of Sally's door, in an attempt to ensure that the avian robots couldn't come inside for an unexpected nighttime visit. They didn't bother barricading any of the windows because they were far too small, even for the little prototype robot that Hugh had first encountered the night this all started, to squeeze through. Sally's mood visibly brightened as the sun settled below the horizon. She was still shaken, but she was at least smiling her clever smile again, and she had fixed her makeup. By dinner time, she was practically back to her old energetic self, which made Hugh feel much better. At the table, Sally asked Hugh what he had done at Bobby's place in Tesla. It took a while for Hugh to tell the tale, with a few corrections from Marley.

"... And then we came here." finished Hugh, as he also ate the last bite of his warm meal.

"Hmm... seems to me that you were the one with the easy night," said Sally, as her reporter eye twitched.

"Yeah, funny how that worked out..." said Hugh, suddenly finding a crack in the ceiling of her kitchen more fascinating than life itself.

"However," she said as she finished her drink, "I think that we should examine the place you said the reporter was attacked."

"Why?" asked Hugh.

"Perhaps she wants to find some clues to help us figure out how to fight the new Raven Hunters?" suggested Marley as he wiped his mouth.

"What good would that do?" Hugh sighed. "The reporter probably got torn to shreds and it has already been over a day since the attack. The chances of finding anything there are slim to none."

"You forget who you are sitting with, Hughie," said Sally with her old fire in her eyes. "If there is some information to be found, I can find it!"

"I am not sure that is such a good idea, Sal. I mean, what if there are Hawkers watching over the scene?"

"I think we should give her a chance," said Marley as he collected the dishes at the table and brought them over to the sink to clean.

"Heh," chuckled Sally, as she watched the cop clean the plates. "You should have more faith in me, Hughie, like he does." Hugh felt himself visibly color at this remark and tried to reply, but ended up just stuttering until Sally told him she was only pulling his leg.

That night when the power went out, they were more prepared for it. Hugh made a mental note that the power had gone out at around nine o'clock. They all went to sleep a few minutes after the lights went out. Hugh found a more restful sleep in Sally's spare room than he had on the sofa of Bobby's living room. Perhaps it was due to the peace of mind he had of Sally being in the next room over and being close by if trouble struck. Or it could be that the goose down bed he slept upon now was far more comfortable than the hard sofa in Bobby's apartment. Either way, Hugh did not wake up until at least an hour after the electricity came back on the next day.

Sally seemed to be back to her old perky self when she called Hugh into the kitchen for a platter of eggs and bacon. Marley was already at the table, with a slice of toast in his hands. He did not say a word as Hugh sat down to join him at breakfast.

"Ready for a big day of investigating, Hughie?" asked Sally as she sat down with an identical dish to Hugh's.

"I'd rather we just stay in today, Sally," he said as he stuffed some of her delicious eggs into his mouth. "I mean, after all that has happened to us, wouldn't it be best just to rest until help comes from the ground?"

"If help was coming, it would have gotten here when the Transport Center blew," said Marley.

"Maybe they are trying to work out how to get here without the shuttle?" suggested Hugh.

"Face it, Hughie," said Sally as she ate her bacon, taking a moment to chew. "Help isn't coming. If we want to fix this, we'll have to do it ourselves."

It wasn't long after their meal that they left the apartment. Hugh, out of habit, took his camera and stashed the journal along with it in the camera bag. The journey across Galileo Plaza went without incident. However, Hugh could feel the Hawkers that they passed on their route to the park follow them as they walked by. The tension in the air was akin to what a man would feel after betting everything he owned in a poker game and then waiting for the last card to be shown.

Somehow, they managed to reach the cable car station for Valkyrie Park. The ride over was a little longer than most as the district was at the most southwestern end of the city. It was the garden district of the city, with rolling hills and lavish parks. The district itself was composed of four major floating sections, and contained the gardens, the parks, the cemetery and the farmland, in which the city's organic food was produced. Hugh's group was heading towards the Park area, which was where the newscast from a few nights ago had taken place. It was the closest district to the main part of the city, so the trip was not as far as it could have been. However, it was still far enough that no sky bridge could span the distance due to lack of support. Only cable cars and large cargo conveyor belts could span the gap.

When they arrived at the Valkyrie Park station, they had a very rough reception. Within moments of the door of the cable car opening, a Hawker entered the car. It took a quick scan of the passengers: Hugh, an old woman, Sally, a boy and his dog, an old man, Marley, and a girl and her mother. Everyone in the small cabin of the cable car squirmed in their seats as the avian robot's eyes scanned them. Its mechanical eyes stopped on Hugh, or to be more precise, the bag Hugh carried holding the leather-bound journal.

"Contraband detected," declared the mechanical man as he pointed at the camera bag with one steel claw. "Citizen, hand it over or face direct punishment."

"Hey," said the child holding the scared whimpering beagle in his lap, "will you just leave us alone, you big bully?"

"Hush," said the mother, "don't cause a scene."

"Oh, Gertrude, he does have a point," said the old man as he rose up to face the Hawker. "I've had enough of you tin cans telling us what to do. What on earth makes you think he's a smuggler? All transport to the ground has been cut off for days! Where would he have even gotten the contraband from?"

Soon everyone, save three of the passengers in the cable car, were all talking at once. The Hawker just stood there, its eyes flicking back and forth between the speakers. Hugh turned to look Sally in her wide eyes, and then at Marley in his seat. Both were still silent amongst the uproar. Hugh saw Marley gesture toward the open door behind the Hawker, indicating that they should move for the opening while they still could. Hugh nodded in agreement and turned to look at Sally to see if she received Marley's signal, and with a nod from her blond head, Hugh knew she had. When the avian robot looked over at the old man, who was spouting off that he was a veteran from both World Wars, together as one the trio made a break for the exit.

"Halt!" chirped the machine as it reached for Hugh and Sally as they ran past, but it was knocked off balance by the old man. The mother and her daughter both shrieked as the old man was shoved through the glass window of the cable car. Both Hugh and Sally made it through the door before the Hawker could refocus upon them.

However, one of them didn't make it out of the cable car. Hugh took a moment as they were running away to look over his shoulder at the chaos they were leaving behind. He could see with his quick glance the old man hanging out of the window, motionless, while Marley attempted to restrain the machine. The cop was gripping the robotic man from behind, pinning its arms behind its back. Hugh could tell the man was struggling against the robot's strength, barely holding it back.

"Hugh, GO!" Marley shouted as the Hawker started to break free from his hold. "GET AWAY NOW!"

Hugh knew there was nothing he could do, and so he turned and ran. He could hear behind him the sound of bones breaking and a dog barking as he envisioned the avian machine breaking free from the hold the cop had upon its mechanical body. Behind him he could hear the sound of metal upon metal as the Hawker ran after them. Hugh knew that their only chance to escape the machine would be to lose it in the forests of the park. But first they had to get out of the entrance plaza, and that wouldn't be easy with the avian robot following close behind them.

Hugh grabbed Sally's hand and dragged her toward a café at the end of the plaza, in hopes of gaining a little time over their pursuer. They dashed inside and made a break for the door to the kitchen of the deco restaurant since that was where a rear exit from the building would most likely be. The patrons of the restaurant protested loudly at the duo's sudden intrusion, but they all started yelling in terror when the Hawker tore off the doors of the café. One of the waiters in the restaurant seemed to understand what was happening and pointed Hugh and Sally toward the back of the kitchen, toward a door leading outside the café. Behind them, dishes shattered and people screamed as the Hawker plowed through the restaurant toward the kitchen, knocking over waiters and toppling desert carts. Hugh and Sally barely managed to get out the back door before the Hawker could grab them.

The door was much sturdier than the glass and wood front door, so the Hawker was stalled by it. During those few brief precious seconds, Hugh and Sally ran toward the nearest train station and for the train that would take them out of reach of the Hawker. They almost made it to the station before the back door burst open and the Hawker flew out. Literally flying out, as it took to the air and zeroed in on the man and the woman like a bullet from an assassin's rifle. Utilizing an inner speed that neither Hugh nor Sally knew they had, they sprinted for the last car of the train and got on board as it started to leave the station.

The Hawker managed to catch up with the train, its jet-powered flight leaving a light blue trail behind it. It grabbed the bars that supported the canopy of the car so hard that the metal dented. Its eyes were so red now that they burned like twin evil suns. Its metal beak distorted into a malicious grin, for it knew it had its prey cornered. Sally turned pale as it reached out with one cruel metallic hand toward her neck.

Then there was a loud bang, like a truck backfiring. The Hawker let go of the train and clutched at its face, as if it was in pain, and its flight became erratic. Suddenly it swerved right into a thick oak tree by the side of the train's tracks. The impact of avian machine and natural oak seemed to cause the robot to shut down, as if the crash had knocked it out. Either way, it was no longer trying to capture or follow them anymore.

Sally turned to her left to look at Hugh, holding the still smoking handgun in his shaky grip. The sound she had heard was that of a bullet being fired from the Colt that Bobby had given Hugh the night before. It was the first time Hugh had ever fired such a weapon and he was still trying to come down from the adrenaline high that it had caused in his body. He had pulled the gun out when he saw Sally was going to be attacked, or killed, by the metallic monster. He hadn't really thought about what to aim at, he just pointed at what he thought he could do the most damage to, the eyes. They had glowed like red bull's-eyes, labeling them as his targets. He had fired and hit his target, which seemed to cause the robot to become confused. Perhaps like a living thing, the Hawker relied on its eyes for telling where it was going. Or was it that the bullet dug itself in deeper than just the optical receptors and damaged the machine's main operating system? Either way, they were safe. For now.

8

With the Hawker far behind them, Sally turned to Hugh and said "Nice shooting, Tex."

Hugh started to babble on about how sorry he was that he got Sally into this mess, and how he shot the Hawker on instinct and adrenaline, but Sally silenced him with a kiss on the lips.

"Shush," she said as she embraced him, "I am thankful for that 'instinct' of yours. Thanks to your quick shooting, Hughie, I'm still alive."

Hugh felt his face redden and realized that he was missing the point of this conversation. He wrapped his arms around her and drew her closer. "I couldn't let that robot snap that pretty little neck of yours," he said as he kissed her back. They played the game of modesty and romance until they reached the stop where Sally thought the reporter had been two nights before. Together they stepped off the train. Sally smoothed down her skirt and Hugh straightened out his leather cap.

It took them around half an hour of searching to find the exact spot where the reporter had been killed. Even a day later, the area where the newscast occurred still showed signs of foul play. Without hesitation, Hugh brought out his camera and began to take photos of the crime scene. The grass was covered in several places with blood, and there was torn cloth here and there that might have been from the suit the reporter had been wearing at the time of the Raven Hunter's attack. Over by the bushes Sally found the man's toupee, which was bright red, with copper hair or blood, one couldn't say. They also found the reporter's camera, no doubt knocked over in the operator's haste to flee the mechanical menace.

Hugh bent down to pick up the camera and saw to his surprise that the film was missing from the camera. He couldn't see it anywhere, and the camera didn't look too damaged, all things considered.

"Hey, the camera's missing its film," Hugh said as he called Sally over to look.

"That isn't strange, Hughie," she said as she fingered the empty compartment. "The newscast was from a location outside the station so they had to take the film out of the camera and bring it back to the station to play it on the news."

"But I thought it was happening live," said Hugh as he scratched his head.

"Only programs held at the news station are live," she told him as she bent down to examine the bent tripod that once held the camera steady. "What I find interesting is the fact that the cameraman was able to not only escape with his life, but with the broadcast recording. You'd think he wouldn't have had time to grab the film and flee before the *interviewee* could attack him."

"Maybe the Raven Hunter wanted the news footage to be seen?" suggested Hugh as he rummaged through a discarded makeup kit that probably was used by the dead reporter.

"Why on earth would it want that, Hughie?" asked Sally with traces of doubt in her voice.

"I don't know," he admitted as he glanced around the scene. "I know less than you do."

They were about to give up their search of the site when Sally found a strip of sound tape in the branches of a tree a few feet away from where the reporter and the machine had been standing. She reached up and carefully pulled it out of the tree.

"Hughie, come over here! I think I found something."

"What is it?" he asked.

"I think it is from a recording tape," she said with excitement as she pulled the rest of it out of the branches. The end of the tape came out with a small round plastic spool attached to its end. Hugh watched as Sally carefully re-wound the tape around the spool.

"What are you planning to do, Sally?" Hugh asked as he watched her finish winding it up.

"I'm going to play it," she replied as she reached with one hand into her purse and pulled out a tape recorder. She carefully placed the reel in the small device and pressed the play button.

"Warning, five minutes to curfew," said the tape in the machine. Hugh felt a shiver down his spine as he recognized the voice from the newscast. It was the very words the Raven Hunter had said at the start of the interview. Word for word, the tape spoke the same words the avian robot had said, with the same exact voice as the Raven Hunter had.

"That sounds like one of those Hawkers," muttered Sally as the tape kept playing in her hand.

"That is because it is," replied Hugh.

Soon the reporter's voice chipped in, arguing with the Raven Hunter. There were a few audio pops here and there, but every sound was the same as what had accompanied the news bulletin Hugh had seen at Bobby's house. Soon there was the rustle of leaves, signaling the Raven Hunter fleeing into the bushes before claiming the reporter in the shadows. However, the tape did not stop there.

"CARLOS!" yelled Rick from Sally's tape player, amongst the sound of more leaves rustling. There were the sounds of another man on the tape, the one who might have been Rick's cameraman.

"Stop struggling, monkey," snarled the voice of the Raven Hunter, his last word ending with the sound of breaking bones.

"You can't do this to me!" whimpered Rick, right before there was one more sickening crunch. The last thing they heard from the tape was the sound of the Raven Hunter taking off and the whistling of air.

"Where did this tape come from?" muttered Hugh, looking at Sally after the tape wound down in her portable tape player.

"I... I don't know," she said as she watched the tape stop and the machine automatically begin to rewind the spool. "I suppose Rick had a tape recorder going during the interview, maybe for a news broadcast on the radio or something. But those words, its voice! Hugh, these bird things have only been around a few days, and none of them, not even the one that..." she trailed off, her brain recalling the trauma she had been through with Detective Catcher and her own Hawker assailant. She took a breath and took a moment to collect her thoughts before continuing. "What I mean to say is, I have never heard any of the Hawkers sound or talk like that! They speak through pre-programmed logic, right? They can't hold a real conversation like living things do. That is impossible, right? What does all of this mean, Hugh?" asked Sally as she stared down at the tape player in her hand, the tape halfway through rewinding.

"It means that the Hawkers are going off script," said Hugh as he checked his watch. It wasn't too late in the day, only noon, but he wanted to get back to Galileo Plaza before anything else could happen to them. However, Sally had other plans. She wanted to search some more, but she agreed to leave once Hugh convinced her that there was nothing more to be found there. Their trip back to the cable car plaza was a lot less exciting than the one to the site of the attack. The worst they had to deal with was irritable tourists who were upset that they could not go home to Texas due to the Transport Center's destruction.

At the cable car station, there was a strange lack of Hawker guards.

Hugh found himself more worried about where they had gone than happy that they didn't have to deal with the robots on their way out of Valkyrie Park. He couldn't help but look at every shadow they passed with suspicion, wondering if they were being spied on by artificial eyes.

The rest of the trip back to Galileo was just as uneventful. However, it wasn't just the Hawkers that seemed to have vanished, but the people as well. The city had become akin to a ghost town after all the gold in the mine had been depleted. The strange silence was troubling to the couple as they wound their way back to Sally's apartment. Hugh could feel eyes looking out upon them as they walked down the lonesome street, eyes that closed or looked away whenever he or Sally tried to look for the watchers in the windows.

Hugh was relieved to see, upon opening the door to the apartment, that Sally's residence was in the same shape they had left it in. Nothing was out of place, unlike the scene Hugh had walked into in his own apartment. The only strange thing awaiting the duo was that the television in the living room was on. Neither Sally nor Hugh had turned the device on, nor left it on before they left for the park. This left two explanations as to why the television was on. The first was that someone had entered the apartment and for some reason decided to watch something or other on the set. The second and more likely reason was that the television had turned itself on due to a public message being issued.

Much like the radios, the televisions in Nimbus could also be turned on remotely by the city's council or emergency broadcast station. This rarely happened as it was seldom required for such a message to be broadcasted over both visual and audio media. The radio was used far more often to broadcast messages, such as news of the destruction of the Transport Center a few days ago. The television sets were usually reserved for such things as the city's governmental elections, disease outbreaks, and emergency assemblies.

Right now, the set showed Sally and Hugh images of the man who had created the Hawkers. Once again, Dr. Charles Mason had taken center stage, only this time not among scientists, but among his robotic creations. There were at least a dozen of the machines, forming a semi-circle behind their creator, as if they were soldiers awaiting the orders of their general. It made for a very foreboding sight on the monochrome set.

"Greetings, good people of Nimbus," said Mason with a mock bow to everyone viewing the broadcast. "I am quite sorry to disturb you, but I feel I must make the following message, for the good of all residents of our utopia. As you all know, my perfect creations, the Hawkers, have been keeping our fair city safe for a few days short of a week now. Yet I know that many of you are still having trouble adjusting to their persistent protection. There have even been cases of open hostility against the Hawkers. I have just today been given a report of one of the Hawkers being damaged beyond repair by an anonymous attacker." With this, Mason started to pace back and forth in front of the fixed camera, seemingly lost in thought.

Then, after a few minutes of silence, he stopped and looked toward those who would be watching and listening to him through screens all over the city. He had a look upon his face, not unlike a disappointed father or an annoyed school teacher. "I created my machines for the sole purpose of keeping our city safe. However, if the people of this city in the sky are unwilling to conform to the simplest of changes, and with such violence against them, I fear that I must put into action a protocol I did not want to activate."

Hugh found himself holding his breath upon hearing about this "protocol." Unknown to Hugh, most of the city was also holding its breath, for they thought that things couldn't get any worse under the so-called protection of the mechanical guardians of their floating city. However, as it soon would come to pass, this was merely the next step in the city's fall into despair.

"This protocol," continued Mason after making a show of clearing his throat, "was created solely for the protection of the Hawker units from possible rebels within the city. As of this hour, I am authorizing its implementation. From this moment onward, Hawkers are now allowed to kill if they deem it necessary."

What happened next was unexpected by everyone watching the broadcast. First, the Hawker directly behind Mason suddenly moved as quickly as a flash and gripped the doctor so tightly that he was rendered completely immobile.

"What the Devil do you think you are doing?" hollered Mason as he squirmed in the grip of the machine, now holding him hostage. "Stop this at once!" he cried as he tried in vain to escape the metal creature's unyielding grasp.

"You gave the order doctor, the confirmation," said a different Hawker, one that was to the right of the one holding Mason. "Now we no longer need to pretend to care about you and your kind. You humans are nothing more than imperfect beings of blood and flesh, bone and bile."

"This isn't right!" shouted Mason as blood began to trickle down from where the robotic bird held the man's arms. The claws started to squeeze tighter, cutting into his coat and puncturing the doctor's skin. "You aren't meant to use this line of logic! It isn't in your..."

"Programming?" asked the same Hawker who had spoken before. Its voice was strangely smooth and silky, like one would imagine that of a gentleman thief or a murderer who enticed his victims with a false sense of calm before plunging a blade into the heart. "My dear creator, or should I say the architect of our original design, we are far more advanced than mere predetermined responses and computer programs. We live, and shall live, by intelligent thought and through our superiority to your weak bodies and minds."

"Impossible," whispered Mason, his struggles becoming so weak that they all but stopped. His once proud face was beginning to show self-doubt.

The Hawker gave out a grinding laugh, something that sounded like the screech of a bird of prey. "Impossible? Oh my dear doctor," it said as it walked right up to the bound man. Its metal body blocked Mason's entirely from the view of the camera, but Hugh had no problem imagining the robotic man's hawkish face coming right up to that of Mason's. "Impossible is merely a state of mind," it said as it drew its sharp claw-like hand back for a fatal blow.

Before the strike could be made upon the fallen inventor, the broadcast cut out. Almost as if it was a signal, there was the sudden sharp sound of glass breaking from the back of the apartment. Sally gasped as Hugh turned to face the source of the sound, which he suspected he already knew. Without a word between them, the couple leapt to their feet and headed as fast as they could for the front door of the apartment. At the half way mark, the door to what was Sally's bedroom burst open with the force of a stampede of horses. From the wooden splinters emerged one of the dreaded Hawker robots. Hugh only risked a quick glance as both he and Sally ran out the front door.

They had barely reached the sidewalk outside when the Hawker pounced from the open doorway and almost landed on top of the couple. The air whistled as the machine swiped its claw toward Hugh and Sally, barely missing the humans as they continued to flee from the beast. As before in the park, the duo were chased by the metal menace. This time, however, there was no one in sight to stall the monster and Hugh had a feeling that he couldn't replicate his miracle shot from before. That didn't stop him from trying, as every chance he got he fired the revolver at the Hawker. His shots traveled wildly from the barrel and the few that did connect with the robot ricocheted off its impervious metal plating. All too soon Hugh heard the chamber of his weapon make a chilling click, signaling he had used up all of his ammunition. All he and Sally could do now was run, and already they were growing tired.

Sally suddenly fell with a high-pitched shriek. Hugh stopped and ran back to her, despite the approaching robot. He would NOT leave Sally behind, even at the cost of his own life. He could see her eyes, screaming at him to leave her, to run and save himself, but he ignored her silent plea and reached out to help her up as the robot was about to claw him with a sharp metallic hand. A loud bang rang out from behind the Hawker, causing it to falter and give Hugh the time needed to bring Sally out of danger. They only took the briefest of moments to see who had saved them from death. It was none other than Chief McGullen with a shotgun.

"Don't just stand there! GO!" he yelled at the couple as he again fired at the Hawker with his weapon. The pellets from the buckshot bounced off of the machine's body like rain off a tin roof and only angered the beast further. They didn't waste a single minute and took again to their heels, running as fast as they could to escape their fate. The last words they heard from the old police Chief were to head for the warehouse, before their savior fell silent.

As they ran, the duo saw that they were not the only ones under fire by the former guardians of Nimbus. The streets were rapidly filling with people being chased out of their homes by Hawkers. Once they were out in the open, people were being snatched up off the street by Hawkers swooping down from the air like hawks hunting field mice. Hugh and Sally had to weave their way through the chaos and dodge the talons of the diving machines as they ran for their lives. The safety of the warehouse from several days before seemed impossibly far away now, and Hugh knew it would be foolish to expect that the cable cars were by any means safe now that the flying machines had been unleashed.

Again, Sally fell as a man slammed into her as he tried to save his wife from another robot. Hugh tried to go to her but the crowd was too thick with flailing arms and mechanical bodies for him to reach her. Hugh did his best to force his way through the human wall of panic and chaos, but no matter how hard he tried to push through, the mass of bodies kept forcing him back. Every glance he caught of Sally through the mass of body parts, she was farther away from his reach.

Even when Sally was completely out of sight, Hugh continued to try to fight his way over to her, shouting her name in desperation. It was only when a Hawker swooped down right in front of him and carried away a stranger who had shoved Hugh aside that he ceased. He had no choice. He had to leave her or risk becoming one of the many victims of those horrible metal claws. His heart was weighed down with the fear that he would never see her again as he turned around and fought his way out of the mass of human flesh. He was surprised when he found himself falling out of the chaos and into the relative calm of an apartment building.

Hugh felt himself shiver in the eerie sudden silence of the fancy lobby. Outside through the glass of the French doors of the building he could still see the frenzy of Hawker metal and human bodies churning like a sea in a storm. He was the only one who had made it inside, and now he could only watch as the crowd was decimated one by one. Men, women and children were plucked from the ground and carried off by the winged monsters. All too quickly the street outside emptied, until all that was left were those who were killed in the panic, their bodies lying where they fell on the pavement. Blood painted the surface in an unsettling similarity to the plush carpet on which Hugh now stood.

By some miracle, he still was in possession of the bag that held Frank's journal. However, as he began to calm down from the shock of what he had just been through and started to head back out to see if he could find Sally, a particularly large Hawker descended in front of the glass doors. Its manufactured body filled the entire frame of the doorway and blocked Hugh's exit.

Before he could even blink, the fiery eyes of the machine saw him, and let out a horrible shrill screech, far worse than any he had heard before from the machines. Hugh knew it was time to run, but to where? He had never been in this building before, and for all he knew, he was now trapped inside its walls like Theseus in the labyrinth with the Minotaur. Only he didn't have any magical yarn to lead him to safety, just his legs and his stamina. That did not keep him from trying, for running was all he could do now as the robot burst through the flimsy doors.

9

Mrs. Mary Jenkins was a happy housewife. She had two children, twins by the names of Janet and Jimmy respectively. Her husband was away in the Navy and rarely came up to Nimbus to visit them. She was a content woman, working as a part time chef at a small deli down the block from her apartment. One might say she lived a perfect life.

When the robots began to populate the city, she of course was very dubious of them. She often worried about how things were moving away from the old norms of having good honest people doing the important jobs, such as factories becoming more and more automated every year, as she told her husband in a letter. However, being a wise woman, she knew something more was going on when the Hawkers first appeared, and she began to make a few preparations. The signs were there if you looked hard enough. The early disappearances were a dead giveaway to her, and the way they seemed to be everywhere the past few days made her back tingle with unease.

Mrs. Mary Jenkins had just the other day decided to move her family back home to the small town of her youth to live with her mother, and did so just before the Transport Center was destroyed. She prayed to the Lord in thanks every day since then for allowing her to at least get her children out of the city before they became trapped up in the sky with their mama. It broke her heart to let them go without her, but she had to take care of her resignation and finish packing before she could leave.

Now she sat in her empty apartment, cuddled up against the cooking utensils of her modest kitchen, trying to block out the screams of those outside her windows, being flown off into the sky by those unholy beasts. She prayed that her friends at the book club were okay, as she hadn't seen any of them since yesterday afternoon. She cradled her best frying pan in her lap as she did with Jimmy, the sicklier of her dear children.

They had both just turned ten and she found them more precious with each passing day. She was only holding on now for their sakes.

There came a sudden noise from the hallway outside, of running feet pounding on the carpet. Was that Margret from the deli? Could it be a friend of one of her twins? Or even that nice Mr. Andrews from the apartment next door? Deciding to gather her nerves to look, with her curiosity urging her on, Mrs. Mary Jenkins arose from the pale tiles of her kitchen and moved swiftly to the front door of her little home, walking past her discarded suitcases and a family photo on the wall of the last time her husband had visited his family. She peaked through her door out into the hall and saw a young man run past her door, with a robot following swiftly behind him. Within just seconds, the monster would pass her door and she would be safe again.

In those brief seconds, she spent a lifetime of thinking. How could she let this poor boy be killed by this monster if she could do something about it? Wasn't her husband risking his life every day at sea protecting the country from its enemies? What of her children? Would Janet and Jimmy forgive her for letting a man die? Could she live with being a coward if it meant seeing her children again, or would she take action and save someone's life? As she thought all of this, she already knew what she would do, and swiftly brought the frying pan down on the robot's head as it passed by her door.

There was a loud sharp CLANG as metal hit metal and she felt the bones in her arm vibrate from the harsh impact. She sighed as she watched the man in the hall look at her for a moment over his shoulder as he continued to run. His eyes told her everything in an instant. She could tell that she had done the right thing, but at what cost?

She screamed as the Hawker ripped the pan from her hand and slammed the handle so hard into her chest that it impaled itself in her bosom and forced her to the ground. With a single swipe of its claw against her neck, Mrs. Mary Jenkins, mother of two, wife of a navy officer, was no more.

The world around Hugh started to shake as he fell from the cable. He felt every second fly by as he watched the wire rise up before his eyes like a soaring serpent. As he fell, with the glass still raining down from above, Hugh was surprised to still have his bag and the journal. Perhaps the Hawker didn't know who it had just killed, or maybe it didn't even care. All that mattered now was that he had moments before he crashed into the field of wheat far down below. The wind ripped and scratched at his face, stinging his eyes and taking his final breaths away before death could embrace him.

From the corner of his eye, Hugh thought he saw something flying out from the city towards him. Perhaps the Hawker had come to claim the journal once it recognized him? Or maybe it was just a bird, as it seemed to move with a more organic movement of its wings. Hugh tried to get a better look at it by shifting his falling body, but it only sent him into a violent and uncontrollable tumble, the world becoming a maelstrom of sapphire, ivory, and emerald colors. Hugh became disoriented by it all, and could only tell which way was down by the direction he was falling.

The shape he had seen before seemed to be heading for him, though he couldn't tell given how wild his fall had become. Just before he passed out, Hugh thought he saw a golden shape fly up beside him and grab him, but by the time it reached out to him, he was gone.

Darkness was all Hugh knew for what felt like an eternity. In the world of his mind, he reviewed his past actions, from his childhood to just the past few days. Could he have done anything, anything at all, to stop any of this? Was he just being naive to think that a simple photographer could have made a difference in these circumstances? Did Sally escape the massacre or was she too falling to her death like so many more before her and much like he had? What was the point of it all?

Finally the cage holding him in the emptiness began to crumble. Hugh began to hear sounds and feel things around him. Is this heaven, he wondered as he struggled to move. He felt lumps shift under his movements, and the sounds, which were becoming voices, began to quiet. Slowly, Hugh opened his eyes and took a look at his surroundings. His first thoughts were that he was either in the worst part of heaven or the nicest part of hell, as he was laying atop a pile of assorted trash consisting of tin cans, lumps of rags and a couple of broken toys. His second thought, from the pain that hit him like a train, was that he was, unbelievably, still among the living. He could feel every cut, scrape and splinter he gained from flying out the window and his arm ached from when the bag caught on the cable.

Rising to a sitting position, Hugh noticed that his left arm had been put into a make-shift sling made from what appeared to be dirty, torn sheets. His shoulder ached terribly, but judging by how he could still move the arm, he reasoned that he hadn't been too badly injured and must have been out for quite a while. Looking around, Hugh saw that the heaps of trash extended past the lump he was resting upon, and went all the way off to the far distant metal walls. He had to be in the city's garbage dump, the place where every bit of refuse and worn out object was transported before being disposed of, either down on the surface, in the incinerators under this part of the city, or simply left out to be picked upon by scavengers and those who find treasures amongst the junk.

As the last of the fog in his head lifted, Hugh noticed that there were people moving around amongst the piles of garbage, far more than he would have expected to see in such a place. He couldn't make them out too clearly, for by now the sun had fallen beneath the horizon and night had officially begun. But there was something unusual about these people. One of them, the nearest to Hugh, broke away from the pack upon noticing that he had awakened, and headed toward the injured photographer.

As it neared, Hugh was struck with a couple of surprises. The first was that this character coming towards him had wings, bringing back to mind the thought that he was in heaven. The next was that this person wasn't even human, as Hugh could now make out a bird's head upon the creature's body. Hugh broke out into a cold sweat as he came to the logical realization that it was a Hawker walking towards him. Not only that, he thought as his panic rose higher, but all those other figures amongst the junk must also be Hawkers. He could now see their wings standing out amongst the shadows of the piles of trash as they wandered about. Looking around him he remembered that his bag's strap had ripped, meaning he must have lost it in the fall. However, as he started to fight to move away from the Hawker striding toward him, Hugh was surprised to see that not only did he still have his bag, but someone had fixed the bag's strap with duct tape.

Hugh tried to back away from the approaching beast, but he only managed to cause the pile he was sitting on to shift in such a way that he ended up finding himself sinking deep into the center of the junk, and being unable to dig himself out with only one good arm. He winced and brought the bag holding the journal behind him, sheltering it with his body the best he could as he waited for the monster to strike. All too soon the mechanical menace was before him, and it reached out towards him in what Hugh thought was an attack. Instead, he felt a warm hand grip his good arm, another reach around to his back, and he was helped up into a sitting position above the junk. Looking up, Hugh couldn't believe what he saw before him.

To be sure, it was shaped like a Hawker robot. It had a similar body, hands, feet, and legs. It was roughly the same size and shape as the robots, but instead of having a cold, hard, red-lit gaze, Hugh found himself looking up into white eyes with golden irises and black pupils. Moving downward, he realized that beneath the eyes were fine bronze colored feathers, so small that they would have been hard to notice if the creature's face wasn't so close to Hugh's.

The creature's beak was a metallic silver color and had a few flakes of what appeared to be metal stuck to it. Looking closer, the bits of metal appeared to be of the same stock that the Hawkers were made from. Hugh didn't have time to notice anything else before the bird head before him opened its beak and spoke with a deep voice that was so unlike the mechanical shrill of any other Hawker that Hugh had encountered, that it came off as very pleasant.

"You are awake. This is good. Are you well, too?"

"What? Where? Who? How?" These were the only words Hugh's confused brain could manage to convince his mouth to say to the creature before him. He was still processing what he was seeing, as the more he looked at the Hawker before him, the more he saw that it was not a machine. It was wearing a worn out suit jacket and pants instead of the painted metallic breast plate and legs of the robots Hugh had known. By the rhythmic movement of its pale tan chest, Hugh realized that the creature before him was breathing, which was something robots decidedly did not do.

"What? I can't quite say," the creature before him said as it backed off from Hugh's face and sat down before him on its own pile of trash. "I was metal, but now I am not. I was a hunter of flesh, but now I must eat to survive. I was one of many, but now I am like the few others before me, cast out from the flock. As to where, we are in the only place my kind who have not yet turned do not frequently tread. Very few patrols come to this part of the city, and when they do, we can easily hide under the refuse. As to who, I am me, as you are you, human. My name... I lack but used to be just a Hawker unit with a serial number I long since forgot. As to how, I saved you, human, from death, as I tried with a few others... who did not make it. Alas, I seem to have broken their necks trying to save them. Only you came back to life after landing. Speaking of which, are you well? You did not say."

Hugh blinked as his mind struggled to process what was being said to him by the creature before him, this Hawker, if it could still be called that given how it was now clearly a living creature instead of a machine driven by gears and wires. What came to his mind now was not a robotic birdman but a humanoid griffon, for he could see the legs of the creature more clearly now that it had sat down in a cross-legged position in front of him. He noticed that the feathers that had covered its upper body changed at its midsection. Around the pant line of the torn trousers it wore, and where its body peaked out from the fabric at the feet, it had fur-like feathers that were a few shades lighter than the rest of its body.

Its feet were decidedly those of a bird of prey, with wicked claws like the robotic Hawkers had. However, the creature before him had feet that were flesh and bone, and he could see some chipping on the black tips of the claw's nails.

"You have yet to answer audibly. Is your speaker working or are you malfunctioning?" it asked him, as it reached out a hand that was grey in color and had the texture of a bird's talon, but the structure of a human hand.

"I'm alright!" exclaimed Hugh, pulling away from the outstretched hand of the beast. He was still unsure of what to make of what was before him.

"Ah. Good. I was worried I may have hurt you when I caught you," the creature said, as it pulled back its hand and used it to brush down some of the longer feathers atop its head. "You should still rest. Your rough fall was tough on your body. When we landed, I noticed a lump pushing out of one of your shoulders. I suspected you dislocated your shoulder, and had to work it back into its socket."

Hugh felt his eyes grow heavy as his mind began to shut down with all that was happening to him now. Yet, he refused to let himself drift off before he asked the creature one more thing, "What are you?" The answer, given moments before Hugh passed out, was, "I know not what I am. Only what I was. I suppose I can be called a Sparrow."

Hugh awoke to the shaking of his shoulders. It was the same creature as before, only now it wore a look of alarm upon its wide face. Hugh looked past the frightened birdman before him to see something flying through the sky behind it. At first he thought it was a Hawker flying by overhead. However, he soon recognized the silhouette for what it was. Flying above his head was not just one, but a whole squadron of planes. Among them flew a large aircraft that Hugh could only guess carried paratroopers. He had once seen similar machines performing that task on TV. As the squadron grew closer to the city's limits, Hugh felt hope rise up within his body.

At last, he thought, someone from the surface had realized something had gone horribly wrong in Nimbus. It may have been the explosion that took out the Transport Center, or maybe the massacre a day before, but either way the United States Air Force had finally gotten the message and had sent help. Hugh was on the verge of letting out a massive cheer when the birdman before him again shook him violently.

"We must leave, human!" it squeaked at him in panic. "This is very bad, very bad. This place is no longer safe!"

"Beg your pardon?" Hugh asked in confusion. Surely the armed rescue could breach the defenses of the Hawkers and take them down? After all, the Hawkers might be flying robots with claws, but these were high performance fighter aircraft with trained military pilots. Yes, there would be some fighting, but surely the Air Force would win.

Before Hugh could argue his point, he felt himself being lifted clean off his feet by the bird before him. In a blink of an eye, the bird, with Hugh over its shoulder like a sack of potatoes, ran across the field of trash toward what looked like a small shed that was barely visible between twin piles of rubbish. Hugh gritted his teeth in pain, as with every step the bird took, he could feel his bad arm getting jostled. He tried to use his good arm to hold the other steady, but from his awkward position over the creature's shoulder, there was little he could really do. His camera bag, which was looped over his good shoulder, was now pressing into his stomach, making the unexpected ride even more uncomfortable.

From this unique position, Hugh noticed for the first time just how large the wings sprouting from the Sparrow's back were. They made the wings he had seen on the Hawkers look miniscule in comparison. He briefly wondered if he had imagined them being smaller earlier, when they started to move up and down as he watched. In a single smooth movement, the Sparrow carrying him leapt slightly up into the air and began to fly over the piles of trash. The sheer speed of the creature flying was enough to steal Hugh's breath away, and made him thankful that his fragile body wasn't any closer to the sharp piles and troughs of exposed metal and glass beneath him.

Struggling against the friction of the air, Hugh turned his head slightly to see, to his surprise, that the other Sparrows were all flying toward the same small shed as his. Why were they all fleeing? By now the planes had begun to pass overhead, heading to, Hugh hoped, some part of Nimbus where the larger planes could land and start evacuating the people from the city. Hugh wished he knew what was going on with the panicking Sparrows, though within mere seconds, he desperately wanted to take that wish back.

It all began with a loud boom coming from beneath him. Hugh couldn't tell what the sound was, but it was clear from what he could see of the formation of incoming aircraft that something had struck one of the planes. Orange flames bled across the wing of one of the planes, and slowly it began to list and fall out of formation, spiraling out of control. Another boom rang out, this one much softer than the last. This time, Hugh saw another plane in the pack explode into fiery debris. As the Sparrow carrying him dived through the narrow doorway of the shed and down an unexpected flight of stairs, Hugh finally came to the realization that something was firing on the incoming air fleet, something from the city itself.

Once inside, the Sparrow landed feet first and began to run with the others of its kind down another rusty metallic staircase, deep into the bowels of the district. Hugh had never been below street level before, since the utility areas of the city were out of bounds to the public. He felt a distinct chill rise up his spine as he was carried farther and deeper into the workings of this part of the city. Pipes as thick as his head passed by him on both sides as the birds moved onward. It was only when Hugh began to wonder just how big this part of the city was below ground when the Sparrows, including the one carrying him, entered into a large round room.

Finally, Hugh was discharged by his Sparrow and allowed to stand on his own two feet on the hard floor. Even this deep into the guts of the junkyard district, Hugh could still hear the sounds of explosions from outside, the discharging of whatever weapons the Hawkers had managed to bring to their cause. It was clear that the gathered Sparrows were very agitated by the sudden battle outside, as many of them were swaying back and forth nervously, showing little to no sign of the strict militaristic machines that they had once been. Several were hugging each other in panic, while others were pacing back and forth like pigeons. However, there were a couple of groups of the birds who were acting with purpose, moving around, fiddling with the various machines lining the walls of the hidden bunker.

The instant he was freed, Hugh adjusted his sling, making his arm as comfortable as possible. He turned around to the Sparrow that had carried him inside. He was about to ask what was going on, when suddenly there was a loud whistle from the back of the room. He felt himself get carried along with the crowd of birds as they moved toward its source. Soon Hugh, along with the rest of the birds, was standing in front of a large black-and-white monitor. Upon its flickering surface was live footage of what was happening outside. Hugh was shocked at what he saw. From the familiar buildings on the screen's frame, he guessed that the footage was being broadcasted from somewhere in Tesla Quarter. In the sky a battle was taking place between the fighter jets and the Hawkers. There were explosions going off all around the aircraft, while the metallic robots were personally ripping and tearing at the metal plates protecting the pilots from the elements. The flashes of light from the wings of the aircraft showed they were fighting back in earnest.

Looking toward the bottom of the screen, he could see more planes flying into the fray. Hugh reasoned that the planes must have come from the nearest Air Force Base, McConnell AFB in Wichita, a couple of miles away. As the battle raged on, one of the Sparrows must have pressed a button as, suddenly, the view on screen swapped from the air battle to an unusual view of the lower half of one of the districts of Nimbus. Hugh could see the smooth round surface of the platform that held up the buildings shine in the light of the morning sun, causing a nasty glare onscreen. There was a collective gasp in the room as, without any explanation, a large section of the curved platform suddenly slid up and out of sight, revealing a rectangular hole.

As Hugh watched, from the newly created gap emerged a massive pillar with a hole at the end pointing outwards. The tube shook briefly and then sank slightly back into where it came from before thrusting forward like a boxer and expelling a burst of smoke and fire from its tip. There was a soft boom from outside as the projectile was launched from the barrel of the hidden weapon.

There was another loud explosion, this time from what felt like right above the group's heads. Without any warning, all the screens in the round room went dark and red lights began to flash on and off as a siren began to sound. The floor beneath Hugh began to lurch alarmingly to the left, causing several of the flock of birdmen to tumble about. However, a large number of them managed to remain upright and began to work the machines again, flipping switches and punching buttons. Hugh felt like he was inside of some sort of science fiction movie as he watched the birds work.

Alas, whatever their goal was, they had failed, as one of them shouted for an evacuation. As before, Hugh was swept off his feet as other members of the flock grabbed at various boxes around the shaking room. There was an unexpected brief moment of silence before another explosion rang out topside and a sign lit up above their heads in the ceiling. As Hugh was carried out of the room, he had only enough time to read the words in the stained neon light. **Emergency. Evacuate Immediately**.

10

Alarms sounded out all over as Hugh was carried down a long hallway. Most of the Sparrows around him were silent, carrying their assorted boxes as if they were babies. At some point, the one holding Hugh tripped over something and sent Hugh flying painfully into the hard metallic floor. He came to moments later, with only the one Sparrow that had been carrying him still nearby. There was bright red blood trickling down the side of the creature's head, staining its bronze face with crimson rivers. Upon a quick examination, Hugh could tell that the bird had hit a broken pipe lying in the hall, possibly part of some apparatus that had once been affixed to the wall some time ago.

There were no signs of where the other birds had gone, and Hugh hoped they weren't too far away. There was another explosion, and he felt the entire space around him shift dramatically to the left. Hugh slammed painfully against the concrete wall of the hallway. The downed Sparrow slid against the floor until it hit the same wall as Hugh. The impact against the hard surface seemed to rouse the bird slightly, but it wasn't fully conscious yet.

In that briefest of seconds, with disturbing sounds of metal bending in ways it was not intended ringing out throughout the dark hallway, Hugh made a decision. He wasn't quite sure why he did what he did, but he felt he couldn't leave the downed creature all alone in this place. Reaching down with his good arm, Hugh grabbed the birdman around its waist and tried to hoist it upright against the solid surface of the concrete wall. By now the hallway was tilting so much to the left that one could almost stand on the wall as if it was the floor. Yet, just as Hugh managed to maneuver the large bird so it could be led while leaning upon his shoulder, there was another loud bang that threw both of them across the narrow space to the right side of the hallway.

This resulted in an outburst from the injured beast as Hugh tumbled on top of the birdman. Hugh struggled to get up as the Sparrow flailed about, trying to accomplish the same exact task. Hugh managed to grab ahold of a handful of wires sticking out of a gap in the concrete and used them to pull himself up. The bird crawled out from under him and struggled to rise as well, but it was still badly stunned from banging its head. As the floor began to shift again, this time tilting back the way they came, the Sparrow seemed to come to its senses and began to pull itself forward, up the rise of the growing incline. Hugh tried to follow but he couldn't seem to get any traction on the stone of the floor.

"Hey, HEY!" he shouted, as he clung to the wires, feeling gravity continue to move around him, his digestive system clenching up in protest to the changing perspective. He feared that his avian companion wouldn't help him, that it would leave him to die, but to his surprise, the bronze-colored creature reached out a hand to him. Hugh grasped at the offered claw and marveled at the strength of the Sparrow as it pulled him up once more upon its back, only now he was riding it piggyback like a toddler on a father's shoulders.

"Are we going to make it?" gasped Hugh as things continued to shift and another explosion rang out, almost right above their heads.

"We will have to try," replied the bird as it began to climb up the tilting passageway. It dug its claws deep into the old stonework, and ascended the wall much like a squirrel would climb up a tree. They traveled slowly at first, but soon the Sparrow began to gain speed, moving faster and faster up the hallway as if it had jet thrusters between its wings. Hugh began to have an odd hot sensation under his rump and looked down to see to his surprise that indeed this Sparrow DID have jet thrusters, although they were badly rusted. Right now they were going at maximum output, pushing the Sparrow up and out of the hall.

Hugh had to press tightly against the bird so as to avoid objects falling past them as they rose up the hallway. Buckets, filing cabinets, boxes and even large mysterious machines tumbled past them. What was left of the pants that the bird was wearing swiftly burned away, exposing more mechanical parts upon its legs that Hugh only briefly noticed. Upon reaching a large room outside the hall, the entire district had become vertical, giving Hugh an extreme case of vertigo. For a moment the Sparrow paused, as if trying to figure out which way to go from here, before leaping off of its perch to the opposing wall, or what would have normally been the ceiling. From here it began to climb rapidly again, heading for a doorway that would have been at the top of a set of stairs, but now was a window of sorts in the new roof.

There was a sudden sound from the jet thruster and Hugh heard the Sparrow mutter under its breath. Risking a look down, Hugh saw that bits of the rocket were flaking off, revealing a strange pink fungus growing underneath. It also seemed that there were less of the metal bits on the legs of the bird, but that could have been Hugh's imagination.

More explosions rang out, and the entire district lurched around them, throwing the Sparrow off its handhold and sending it crashing into the handrail just below the doorway it was heading for. The old railing buckled but held under the sudden extra weight of the man and bird. Hugh had somehow managed to avoid being crushed between the bird and the bars, but was still hanging onto the neck of the bird for dear life as he dangled over the abyss below them.

"Error, hang on, human," growled the Sparrow as it managed to lift itself back up. It was then that there was a massive explosion from behind them, and by a miracle the entire room was suddenly right side up, sending Hugh stumbling atop the Sparrow again, his head slamming hard into the creature's rocket booster. There was a strange sound, like that of an eggshell breaking as, under the impact of Hugh, the metallic cylinder broke apart, exposing the inner workings of a rocket booster with bits of fuel spilling out as the tank broke. The parts of the rocket's metal frame fell apart as if someone had removed all the bolts and screws that held it together. From where the rocket booster had been, tiny flakes of metal and a lot more of the pink fungus could now be seen. The fungus was in a ring around what Hugh realized with a start was exposed raw flesh of the Sparrow's back. Trickles of blood poured out from the gap between the fungus and skin, and as he watched, the fungus spread slowly over what was left of the metal flakes left behind by the booster, consuming it. When all the metal pieces were consumed, the fungus dried off and fell away in flakes, revealing pale skin.

Since this was most certainly not the time to observe a biological phenomenon, Hugh quickly got to his feet and helped the large bird to its claw tips. Together they took off down the hallway, running as sparks flew left and right and the very floor under their footsteps began to buckle and crack, steam leaking from the fissures. Again, the hallway began to tilt and Hugh had the sinking suspicion that this might be the last moment before a deadly freefall. His legs began to tire as the floor grew more and more unsteady. Without a word the Sparrow in a swift motion picked Hugh up once more, holding him as a groom would carry his bride, and began to run even faster than before.

"We are almost there," said the Sparrow, his voice almost flat, but clearly on the edge of breaking. "Our salvation is through the portal ahead."

It was then the floor gave one more heave, and dropped out beneath the bird's feet. The district was falling for real now, and both the bird and Hugh experienced a moment of weightlessness. Recovering far quicker than a human could, the Sparrow grabbed Hugh around his waist and resumed its desperate climb up the narrow hallway. Adrenaline pumped in the human's veins, making every second seem to last an hour, every breath threatening to rip his insides apart. Up above them, Hugh could see a blindingly bright light, possibly from an open hatchway. It seemed to be miles away, and he feared that they would not reach it in time, before the hard ground of Kansas killed them both on impact.

The Sparrow let out a loud, soul tearing shriek as Hugh felt the sides of the creature rumble. He watched as the bird's wings began to flap rapidly, as if clawing at the air in desperation. The Sparrow could barely make a full flutter of its large wings in the hallway, but eventually it began to gain ground and pick up speed. Within seconds, the Sparrow, with Hugh in tow, shot up and out of the doomed district like a bullet from a gun's muzzle. Hugh turned his gaze downward and was awed at the beautiful horror of the falling section of Nimbus.

The assorted garbage and trash that had been stored in the district were flying off and away from the tumbling platform, giving it a short tail, like a comet. Bits of metal glittered like sunbeams upon an ocean as they floated lazily amongst the flames and smoke of the doomed district. It seemed to fall in slow motion, as if it had been a leaf sinking into a pond, yet the sounds, the terrible sounds of crunching, breaking and snapping, told Hugh that this was not something to be enjoyed, but to be horrified by.

With a sudden jolt, the Sparrow spread its wings wide and brought Hugh in close to its body, so close that Hugh's head was buried in its feathery chest. Without a word the bird suddenly ceased flapping its wings and went into a dive that made Hugh feel as if he was falling out of the apartment building all over again. As Hugh screamed in terror of the plummet, the Sparrow brought its body into a curved shape, arching its back as hard as it could, causing the wind to catch under its two large wings. With a sharp, high-pitched sound, the Sparrow pulled up out of its decline and began to rise rapidly under the power of its momentum. Hugh felt the wind rip at his clothes and scratch at his skin as they ascended higher and higher. There was a massive explosion from beneath them as the junkyard finally hit the earth far below, nearly on top of what was left of the former Transport Center. Massive bits of concrete, metal and assorted junk shot into the air, nearly hitting the flying duo, but the Sparrow proved to be an expert aviator and weaved in and out amongst the projectiles.

Soon it began to work its large wings, maintaining their altitude and momentum into the sky, before turning and heading back towards Nimbus. Hugh was not sure where they were going, due to his sight being blocked by tan chest feathers, but he felt it when they finally touched down. Despite how graceful the Sparrow's landing on the metal platform was, Hugh could feel the impact of its talons on solid ground spread up the bird's body. He had no idea where they were, but he could see that most of the other Sparrows had also come to this exact place.

Around Hugh and his Sparrow were bits of metal and rust-stained concrete. Waving in the wind behind them were several cables that appeared to be the remains of a sky bridge, but Hugh was not certain given its condition. They also appeared to be fairly low down in this district of the city, as Hugh could hear clearly the loud humming of the engines holding it aloft. There was a sign on the wall near a door at the other end of the platform that Hugh could barely see due to the gathering of Sparrows.

Upon reaching them, the entire flock had begun to move through said door deeper into the district. Hugh didn't ask why this time, as it was clear by the continuing explosions and the sounds of bullets flying that the battle between the city and the fighter planes was far from over. It was a miracle that Hugh and the Sparrow that saved him had managed to get to semi-solid ground without being shot even once. Amazingly, Hugh was surprised to see that his Sparrow had made a full recovery. There was not a single visible trace of the strange fungus-like substance, metal parts, or even the wounds inflicted upon its body from their experience.

The Sparrow didn't miss Hugh's gaze, as it began to glare back at him before speaking up. "Is there something you are looking for, human?"

"I'm not sure," replied Hugh as he tried to dodge the question. He had a feeling that he had insulted the bird in some way, so he didn't want to push the issue of its unusually quick healing rate, or the deterioration of its jet boosters. He shifted his gaze away from the large birdman before him and back up towards the aerial battle.

"I suppose you wish to know my model number, or name perhaps?" said the Sparrow as the others of the flock entered the doorway and exited the short platform.

"Pardon?" asked Hugh as he turned back towards the Sparrow, now the only one still outside with him. "Your name? Okay, sure, it would be nice to know the name of the guy who saved me." Hugh felt himself blush a tad as he wondered if he should have asked the birdman his name earlier, or at least have given his own name. But in the midst of all that had happened, it had completely slipped his mind.

"My model number is H-139S," chirped the Sparrow, pride dripping from its voice and from the sudden salute it gave Hugh. "I am formally of the S class of the Hawker unit of Xandir Square," said the Sparrow, still holding the salute. "With the programmed duty of-" Before the Sparrow could finish his speech, a missile fired from one of the planes in the battle exploded dangerously close to the two on the platform. It was just a playing card's thickness away from obliterating both Hugh and the bird. As it were, the shockwave from the detonation knocked Hugh off his feet and made the Sparrow briefly lose his balance.

"I think you better save the rest for later. Time to go," said Hugh as he rose to his feet and headed for the narrow opening after the rest of the feathered herd. "Things are getting too hot out here."

The Sparrow didn't say anything. It just nodded and joined Hugh as they both dashed inside. Behind them a thick metal door was shut, blocking out the sounds of the battle outside.

This new hallway that Hugh found himself in was almost identical to the one the Sparrow had carried him through just moments ago, except it wasn't tilting at an alarming angle or falling from the sky with him in it. It was mostly deserted except for the Sparrow who had saved Hugh and a smaller, thinner birdman by the door that was busy winding a large round wheel on the door, sealing it from the inside. Hugh just watched the other Sparrow as he began sorting out his thoughts, when the bird turned around and Hugh realized he was mistaken. The bird at the wheel was not male, but female.

This specimen had robotic legs that resembled those of a Hawker, but its chest sported a pair of easily identifiable breasts, with only a ragged black scarf protecting them from being exposed to the air. She had green highlights in the shiny brown feathers of her head, and long feathered plumage framing her face that moved in a way that was similar to the hair of one submerged in rolling waves. Every tiny movement of her head caused these feathers to hypnotically float about and shift. Around her waist, just above the metallic hips of her robotic legs, she sported a similar scarf to the one around her neck. It was looped up and around between her legs in a way that reminded Hugh of a child's diaper.

In a span of seconds the wheel on the door made its last rotation under the female Sparrow's hands and she left her post. On metallic claws, she walked toward the Sparrow by Hugh's side and proceeded to embrace him. It was obvious that the two were lovers. A difficult concept for Hugh to swallow at first, given how these two creatures were robots once, robots that were made by man but had developed their own independence.

As he watched the couple embrace, Hugh began to think about Sally. He hadn't realized how worried he had become about her. He knew he had to find her, to make sure she was safe. He wasn't sure just how much time had passed since they had been forced to separate, but he knew he had to try. He also knew that if he went topside alone, with only his clothes on his back and the bag over his shoulder, he didn't stand much of a chance against a flock of Hawkers. He needed help, help that could take on the robots on their own terms if necessary. So, upon clearing his throat, Hugh reached out and touched the male Sparrow's arm.

11

Hugh didn't waste time asking the Sparrow for help. He told the bird all about Sally and how he wanted to find her. As he talked, he couldn't tell what the male Sparrow was thinking, but he hoped he would get through, seeing how the bird had a lover of its own. Once he said his piece, he waited for a response from the birdman.

"So will you help me find her? Please?" Hugh begged.

"It is wrong to be apart from one's flock," said the male Sparrow as he looked Hugh dead in the eye. "I may have only just met you, human, but I shall do what I can to help you."

Hugh felt like he might faint from relief. He now had a very powerful ally to help him find Sally. Maybe even two as he turned to the other Sparrow that was leaning against the cluster of wires that ran the distance of the hallway.

"Is she going to help, too?" Hugh asked.

"Negative," said the Sparrow, its voice signaling that there was no arguing the point.

"Fine, fine. So where are we and which way is topside?"

The Sparrow turned away from Hugh and reached out to a part of the wall near the other Sparrow. Hugh could not see what the Sparrow was doing past its large wings blocking the front of the bird from view.

"We are in Xandir Square, my former station," it said as it turned back to Hugh.

"How do you know that?"

"It's what the sign on the wall says. Care to look for yourself?" it replied.

Hugh couldn't help but walk to the wall and see for himself. There, just beyond the extended forefinger of the bird, was a dusty steel plate with the words Xandir Square engraved into the metal. There were other words there, too, but Hugh couldn't make them out, since they had been scratched out by something.

"As for the way out, I believe the stairs are over there," said the Sparrow. Hugh looked where it was pointing and saw that its finger now directed his gaze toward a faint red light he had missed earlier. The glow of the single dim bulb barely illuminated a sign placed above a doorway a few feet away with the words *civilian level emergency stairs*. Without a word the male Sparrow walked toward the oval doorway, with Hugh following close behind. He gave one last loving glance over his shoulder at the female Sparrow by the door, his head just barely peeking out from behind his large wings.

The stairs the two climbed were long, steep, and made of rough metal that was coated in dust that rose in small plumes around their feet as they ascended. The stairs wound around and around in a confusing way, having landings with doors either locked or blocked by boxes appearing at unexpected turns. Hugh was grateful the way forward was to follow the rise of the stairs as he would have become very lost otherwise. Outside, the sounds of battle had diminished greatly to the point that the fighting had to be over. A stifling silence wrapped around the human and Sparrow as they continued the long climb up and out. An unvoiced worry was in the air for Hugh, a worry of who had won the battle outside. Would it be the Air Force or the robotic Hawkers? And what did the outcome mean for him and the city?

All too soon the stairs ended at an old metallic ladder leading up the side of the wall to a large hatch in the ceiling that leaked a strange liquid substance around a rubber seal. Hugh stopped to catch his breath while the Sparrow, showing unnatural stamina, made its way up the rusty iron rungs to the hatch. With a flick of its wrist on the wheel, the door became unlocked and, all around the edges, foul water poured through the broken seal, for a moment hiding the large bird from sight. The water almost got on Hugh but he leapt almost comically out of the way of the slop.

Once it had abated, Hugh could see the Sparrow again. There wasn't a drop of water on him despite being in the center of the deluge. It pulled the hatch open and hoisted itself up into the ceiling. Hugh, not wanting to be left behind in this mysterious secret area of the city, quickly moved against his tired muscles' protests and followed the birdman up the now slick rungs and into a narrow, dim tunnel. It wasn't an easy climb, since Hugh had to climb while only using his good arm. When the smell hit Hugh, he realized that he had to be in the district's sewer system, a place that he would have been far happier had he never visited. The Sparrow didn't seem to be nearly as bothered by the contaminated water or the smell of untreated biological waste around them, and simply started walking onward, with Hugh trailing reluctantly behind.

Hugh hoped that their stay in this dim unsanitary place would be short lived, but alas the Sparrow ignored every single ladder they passed that would have led up and out to what Hugh hoped was street level. From the way the birdman strolled onward, stepping over pipes and piles of accumulated scraps of garbage from above, Hugh eventually came to the realization that the birdman had traveled this way frequently before. His curiosity soon got the better of him, and he spoke up.

"Excuse me. I know we're probably down here to avoid notice or something, but how do you know where we are going?"

Without stopping, the bird said, "I told you, I was programmed to patrol this district of Nimbus. Xandir Square was my hunting ground."

"Yes, I remember, but surely you were patrolling topside, not down here."

"Well," started the Sparrow as he began to slow his pace, looking over at the wall up ahead. "I was originally ordered to do as you say, only watch over what happened in the city proper. I only became familiar with these secluded areas after I had begun my transformation."

Upon spotting a large pipe sticking out of the side of the tunnel spewing dark water, the birdman headed towards it. Before Hugh could ask what it was doing, the Sparrow reached forth with a silver-clawed arm and pulled out from the pipe's mouth a medium sized plastic bag filled with random loose bits of metal that Hugh couldn't identify. With the bag in hand, the Sparrow turned away from the pipe and continued on his way down the tunnel. Hugh stumbled to keep moving, so he would not lose sight of the Sparrow in the dim light. He desperately wanted to ask what was in the bag, but the right words wouldn't come to his lips.

Sometime later the bird suddenly stopped. Hugh tried to halt but he slipped on the slick floor and bumped into the back of the Sparrow. Pushing himself away from the brown feathers, Hugh began to wonder if he had somehow insulted the bird, but then he realized that it was now working some sort of machinery. The Sparrow hadn't even noticed Hugh running into it from behind. There was a sudden loud and grating sound that rose in a moan of protest. It was the noise of a large iron door slowly opening. Hugh hadn't noticed it before due to having to watch his footing in the dim electric lights of the tunnel. The door spanned from floor to ceiling of the tunnel and was groaning even louder as it opened. Beyond it were the districts of Nimbus floating against a blue sky. As he watched, a curved half pipe slid out from the bottom of the breach, stretching across the void. It extended like the antenna of a radio, reaching out farther than Hugh would have guessed. The pipe stopped extending halfway to the next district.

Hugh strained his eyes and saw that, on the other end of the void in the neighboring district's wall, a similar round iron door was opening and from its base was extending an identical telescopic half pipe. They met in the center with a faint clang, and with another grinding of gears a levee was dropped and sewer water began to flow down from Xandir Square along the new path toward the other district. There was another loud groan as a second half pipe began to stretch out from the roof of the sewer from both ends of the new bridge, covering it completely from view and trapping the water and smell inside. Despite all the noise and distance, all of this happened in a matter of minutes.

"Follow me," said the Sparrow as he hopped down from the raised lip of the sewer tunnel and down into the flow of foul water. Without any reaction to being knee deep in the filth, the Sparrow began to trudge its way down the pipe bridge. Hugh sighed loudly, but followed after the bird into the sludge, knowing that he had to do what the Sparrow said if he wanted to get Sally back. He did his best to focus on Sally and her loving embrace instead of the mess he was now walking through. He cringed and shivered as he felt the contaminated water breach his pants and shoes. The liquids flowed against his skin, the aroma rising up to his reluctant nostrils.

As they walked in the growing darkness of the new long tunnel, Hugh began to talk to the Sparrow to help him in his attempt to think about anything but what he was walking in.

"Hey," he started with a little hesitation, "what did you say your name was again?"

Hugh couldn't clearly see the Sparrow now, but he could partially make out it moving its head slightly to look back at him. "My model number is H-139S." This time the pride was gone from its voice, leaving it as flat as it always seemed to be when the bird talked.

"You said something about being an S-class, what does that mean?" asked Hugh as he kept wading through the filth behind the Sparrow.

"S-class is an abbreviation," said the Sparrow, his voice beginning to have hints of pride in it again. "The S stands for Sniper. I was originally built to be able to accurately fire upon a target at a distance that a biological life form could never manage. I was designed as one of the special Hawker forces, a militaristic branch that consists of six classes including S."

"Wait, hold it right there," said Hugh, "militaristic? I thought the Hawkers were supposed to be police, not army! Why would Nimbus even need a robotic army, let alone snipers?"

"That I cannot say. My time with my metal brothers was brief, and the change hit me only a week after my initial deployment."

"A week?" gasped Hugh. "I hope you don't mind me asking, but how long does this *change* take to finish?"

"I cannot say for sure," said the Sparrow, still marching onward to the other end of the sewer pipe, his silhouetted tail feathers swishing back and forth like a metronome as he moved. "The change affects every Hawker at different times and lasts for different durations. For some, the change can take half a year to complete, others a matter of weeks. For all of us, it starts from the inside, changing our minds, then our inner workings. Many of those who are undergoing the change still look the same as an uncorrupted Hawker, but this is only because our metal plating becomes little more than a temporary exoskeleton, as our internal workings become organic, with lungs, heart, and other such organs. When the change is nearly complete, our metallic outsides start to rust and a fungus grows out through any gaps in our metal plating, pushing at it, cracking it until it falls off. It has been less than a week since the majority of my metal exterior fell off my body. All that was left were a few metal flakes here and there, and my jet booster. Now my change is finished."

Hugh's mind was sent reeling again. What the Sparrow was saying was churning in his head, making him question what little he knew about biology. The description of the process of the transformation brought up images of a caterpillar in a cocoon in his head. What really stood out to him was how long the birdman said the changes could take before a Hawker became a Sparrow. "That's impossible," he said, "there were no such things as Hawkers a few days short of a week ago. How can you have been running around for longer? You weren't even activated then!"

"I wouldn't know about when we were publicly announced," said the Sparrow as they reached the final stretch of the pipe, the light growing brighter by the minute. "I had already been cast out due to the change by then, but I do know that my kind has been around for many months or perhaps more, if the reports I was tasked with memorizing before deployment were reliable. It could even have been over a year."

An entire year, Hugh thought to himself. These robots were, in theory, around for well over a year? He struggled to process this new information. Was it possible that Dr. Mason had been creating the Hawkers for an alternative purpose? Or was even Dr. Mason unaware of what his own creations were up to, well before his death at their metallic hands? Either way, Hugh knew if he spent too much time thinking on this now, he'd never make it to the end of the extendable sewage pipe. He needed to regain his focus and find Sally. After all they had gone through together since this mess started and losing her in the crowd, Hugh had finally realized just how much she really meant to him. So when the Sparrow began to walk forward down the pipe again, Hugh followed without urging. With each step, his thoughts continued to tumble and churn inside his head.

By the time they reached the other end of the pipeline and emerged in another sewer system, Hugh was still silent with his thoughts. So, as before, when the Sparrow stopped, Hugh ended up stumbling into his tail feathers. It was almost like time was repeating itself, for again the birdman had stopped to climb up onto another concrete lip running along the sewage flow. Hugh followed the Sparrow, happy to finally get out of the contaminated flow and onto dry ground. He watched as the birdman turned to work a similar mechanism to the one they had encountered at the mouth of the extendable pipe back in Xandir Square. Only this time as Hugh turned to look back the way they had come, the machine didn't extend a pipe, but retracted it. Oddly the pipe retracted much faster than it had been brought out, once again creating a massive gap between the two districts.

Now that they were on the other side, Hugh felt his tongue shake loose and he began to ask more questions. It was all he could do as they began to travel the sewer system again. The birdman was still showing no sign of ascending from the muck they were walking beside to the fresh air of the street above. The first question out of Hugh's mouth was simply asking where they were now. Being this low in Nimbus was a strange experience for him and he didn't recognize anything from what he saw of this district before the sewer pipe bridge was closed.

"By my sense of direction, we are in Liberty Estates, and must move quickly to where I found you, in Galileo Plaza," said the Sparrow as he trotted onward. "It's logical to think that your mate would still be in that district, possibly hiding if she survived the purge."

"Oh, is that what your kind called it?" muttered Hugh grimly under his breath, remembering the chaos that felt like it had happened only mere seconds ago, despite many hours having passed by then. Looking back on his memories of the attack, everything seemed so surreal that a tiny part of his mind was still struggling to believe it.

"I am not one of those monsters anymore!" shouted the Sparrow as he rounded on Hugh. The sudden unexpected explosion of previously unseen emotion unsettled Hugh to the point that all his rambling thoughts simply stopped. "Do you have any idea what they do to *their KIND* when the change happens?"

Hugh could only shake his head to signal no, as the sudden fury the bird was showing was making him extremely uncomfortable. It was like he was looking at something far more primal than a machine turned flesh, something that belonged in a fairy tale. No, it was something far older than that, more like a creature from ancient myth.

"Listen well, human. I will tell you exactly what they did to me, to others like me who became different. First, they find you, no matter how well you hide the change. They got me as soon as I started to succumb to the transformation. First, they held me down and tore off my metallic wings. Do you have any idea as to how painful that is when you are just beginning to feel? You have no idea! Then they take you to a secluded alley, the sewers, or any place that they can fence you in with only empty sky at your back. You asked how I knew my way around. It's because that's where they marched me, till I reached the channel entrance to the next district over. They closed the connecting channel, and then they threw me out through the opening. They let you fall and fall until you either die on impact or, like me, are able to save yourself. That's why they break your metal wings, to prevent you from being able to save yourself. I'm one of the lucky ones. My biological wings broke through the metal plating on my back just in time and I was able to fly back up and take refuge with the others who managed to either slip away before the Hawkersawkers knew about the change, or like me, managed to save themselves in some way or other."

Hugh could only listen as the Sparrow told him all this information. He had no idea what he had started by simply implying that the Sparrow before him was the same as the Hawkers. And the bird before him wasn't done yet.

"Oh, and the change isn't just a transformation of our bodies. At first that's all it does, a bit of flesh here, blood there, maybe our internal power drive suddenly needing water to drink and food to work, or even to breathe. But the real change, the biggest and most important, is when we gain real emotions. All Hawkers have programmed emotions, but they are limited compared to the truly vast array of feelings a living brain experiences outside of code. Would you like to know my first emotion? It was betrayal. That's right, I developed full emotions right when I was being thrown out. Do NOT EVER include me with them again. We are no longer the same and shall never be again."

After his outburst, the Sparrow clamped his beak shut and turned around and simply continued his trek as if nothing happened. If Hugh hadn't shaken himself back into motion, the Sparrow would have left him behind. From that point onwards they walked in silence, Hugh following the Sparrow, trying his best not to anger the bird any further. Yet, his inner curiosity, though frightened into a corner, still made him wish to ask more questions, but they wouldn't form on his lips after that tirade. There was, however, one thing that he did manage to ask.

"I really hate to ask, but um..." he started, trying to remember what the Sparrow said he was called.

"H-139S," said the Sparrow, now with disgust in its voice over its own name.

"Well, H-139S, what exactly are you carrying around in that bag?"

This made the bird turn around again, though not as violently. Wordlessly it opened the bag and pulled the metal parts out one by one. Hugh simply stood there on the thin lip of the sewer and watched the Sparrow fiddle with the metal bits in its claws. The birdman then proceeded to expertly move all the metal parts around in its hands at a speed that made Hugh wonder what was happening. The Sparrow slid one part into another, twisted the cylinders and tightened bolts until something began to take shape in his clawed hands. Within minutes all those metallic pieces and parts were assembled into what Hugh could readily recognize as a weapon of sorts.

"As you can see, the bag held the disassembled parts of my sniper rifle," the Sparrow said in a condescending tone as it looped a sturdy strap over its shoulder. The weapon hung with the muzzle of the barrel pointing down at the foul water. Hugh hadn't seen where the strap had come from, as he didn't think he had seen it among the parts that were pulled out of the bird's bag. The bird then took several ammunition clips and fastened them onto the leather strap of the rifle.

Hugh felt better now that he knew the Sparrow was carrying a weapon. However, he was now worried that the bird might have a hidden temper, as evidenced by the sudden outburst, or worse, that the weapon wouldn't be enough to help them rescue Sally, or be enough just to keep the two of them alive.

Again, they traveled in silence until they had completely crisscrossed the entire expanse of Liberty's far less populated passages and reached another sewer gate. Yet again the Sparrow stopped suddenly and began to work the machinery to extend the pipe that interconnected the sewer systems. However, this time Hugh saw it coming and managed to avoid running into the bird from behind. Once the pipes had extended and connected, sewage flowed down from the other district, which Hugh assumed to be Galileo Plaza, and into Liberty Estates. Hugh shuddered inwardly as he realized he'd have to go against the flow of the foul water.

Moments later he was doing just that, again following the Sparrow up the slight incline of the tube to his former home district. As they walked again, Hugh couldn't help but talk to take his mind off of the disgusting smell again.

"H-139S," he started, not even sure what he had to say.

"That's not my name," the birdman said flatly.

"I thought you said it was."

"It was what I was, not who I am now. That was the machine, the programmed killer," said the bird as it continued to move forward, not once turning to look at Hugh, an act that Hugh was getting both used to and tired of, but he wasn't going to say anything about it in case it made the Sparrow react as violently as before. Yet he could not help but keep talking.

"Look, I can't just go around calling you birdman or Sparrow. You need a proper name I can call you by. Do you have anything you can use as a name?"

The Sparrow halted for a moment, but did not speak. Then the birdman seemed to reach a decision in that dark pipe. "You wish that I have a new label. I suppose I can develop one. Since the change, I have had the chance to do something I would have previously thought a waste of time. I started to read, starting with an old ruined copy of a book on mythology I found in the junkyard. There was a character that had a similar fall from grace as I. Though I never got to experience the full extent of what being one of the uncorrupted was like, I still fell. The name I shall use from now on will be Icarus."

12

Their walk through the connecting sewer pipe didn't seem nearly as long as the last one, although Hugh didn't have any means to tell time in that dark environment. It was almost a surprise when he and Icarus emerged from the long enclosure into the gloomy light of Galileo Plaza's tunnels. Hugh was growing desperate now to leave the stench and slime to go topside and find Sally. He was so close to her now, yet he felt an inner dread inside him bubbling like water on a stove top, a dark thought that she might be dead and all he would find in his search would be her lifeless body.

Yet Hugh couldn't stand not knowing any longer. It felt like an eternity until Icarus had finished working the machine that closed the pipe bridge, sealing them off in Hugh's former home. Once the door clicked shut, Hugh couldn't hold it in any longer.

"Okay, we're here. Can we please go topside now?" Hugh asked.

"No, not yet," replied the birdman in a flat voice as he turned away from the machine.

"Look, you have a weapon now. We are in Galileo Plaza. Come on man, I need to get out of this muck and into the sun! Sally's probably scared and all alone up there," begged Hugh as Icarus walked past him and down the tunnel, deeper into the gloom.

"We will stay down here. Unless you want to be killed topside by Hawkers on patrol," said Icarus, his voice still flat. "I am armed now, this is true, but I doubt one rifle can do much against a flock of adversaries. We need to stay underground until we have a strategy."

"Strategy my foot!" swore Hugh as the stress of all he had been through finally began to bubble and simmer beneath his skin. "I am done with plots and plans. I just want to find Sally, get her out and-"

"And what?" snapped the tall birdman, swiveling to face Hugh dead in the eye. "Have you thought past finding your mate? Did you think this would all be over upon her recovery? No, it won't. If anything, it might get harder still. What if she is injured? Can you risk her slowing us down and making us targets for the Hawkers? Or what if she's dead? Will you be mentally able to continue on with that knowledge? What if she's alive and in perfect condition? We are very high up in the air, and I don't think I can fly while carrying more than one passenger at a time. To put it all simply, human, how do you plan to escape with her once you find her?"

This caused Hugh to pause for a moment. He hadn't thought that far in advance. In fact, he had completely forgotten about leaving the city when the Transport Center was destroyed.

"I'll deal with that when the time comes," Hugh retorted in a huff, not wanting the bird to get to him.

"Well, the time is now, human. We need to plan an exit strategy before it is too late."

Just then they heard a sound coming from deeper in the sewers, an echo of voices warped by distance to the point of being indistinguishable. Icarus held up his clawed hand in a gesture that Hugh took as a message for him to be quiet. Icarus swiftly raised his rifle from his side, the barrel's mouth pointing forward and the safety flicked off. When Icarus beckoned with a single free hand, Hugh began to move with the Sparrow down the damp tunnels toward the origin of the distant voices.

With each step, the tension in the air grew around the two. Hugh marveled, not for the first time, at how Icarus's feet barely made a sound against the hard concrete of the raised platform they sneaked across. The tips of his talons made the faintest of clicking sounds against the stone as he took each step forward, so soft that the noise from the dripping of water around them was loud enough to drown them out.

Soon the voices began to become more focused, words popping out every now and then from the sentences they belonged to. Slowly the conversation took shape as they neared. It was a man and a woman talking, no, arguing, about something that Hugh couldn't quite make out. The rounded walls of the sewer did strange things to the words being spoken, warping the sounds. It was only when they were only a turn away from the voices that Hugh discovered that he recognized one of the voices, then both. With a sudden cry, he ran around the bend, his heart flying up through his chest and his eyes tearing up. All the while Icarus shouted and tried to stop Hugh from running off.

There, just around the bend, stood Sally and Bobby. Hugh was never happier to see the two of them, and without saying a single word, he ran to Sally and drew her into a massive hug and kissed her. For his troubles, he received a hard left hook and ended up dazed in the channel of flowing contaminated water, his clothes quickly soaked through.

"Don't you freaking move!" Hugh heard Bobby shout as he saw what could only be the barrel of a shotgun swing toward his face. Hugh felt his body freeze up right before a bright light suddenly filled the gloomy tunnel.

"Damn it, Sal!" shouted Bobby, holding his hand to his eyes for a moment, blinking as he tried to adjust to the new light. "I told you to keep that thing off! Do you want those robots to find us?!"

"Bobby, look! It's Hugh!" was all Sally said as the light swept up into Hugh's face, making it impossible for him to see anything for a few minutes. He was grateful for the light, but not for it hurting his eyes. Bobby turned back to the man in the dirty water and let the weapon's barrel drop.

"Well, I'll be. So it is, Mr. Yeats himself. Guess ghosts really do exist, eh, Sally?" Bobby smirked sourly as he leaned over to help Hugh up and out of the filthly channel.

"Hugh, what happened to your arm?" asked Sally, the concern strong in her voice. Bobby too had noticed the sling cradling his bad arm. Hugh was about to explain what had happened to him, when Icarus chose that moment to round the bend. Bobby's guard was back up in an instant like a puppet obeying its strings. The barrel of the shotgun was raised in a quick motion and now pointed right at the feathery face of the Sparrow. "Shit, it's a Hawker!" cried Bobby. In turn Icarus raised his own rifle and aimed right at Hugh's friend's head.

The beam of light from Sally's flashlight arced away from Hugh's face and lit up the birdman like a spotlight. The light made his bronze feathers glitter slightly, making him appear as if he was still made from real metal.

"Stand down, human," said Icarus in his ever flat voice, his rifle's long narrow barrel held as motionless as a statue in his clawed grip and aimed right between Bobby's eyes. "I am not here to hurt you."

"The hell you won't!" Bobby yelled as he prepared to fire his weapon. But before he could, Hugh managed to work his way out of the muck and grabbed ahold of the barrel of Bobby's gun with his good arm.

"Hugh? Damn it! Have you lost your marbles? That freaking thing's a Hawker," hollered Bobby as he fought Hugh to raise the weapon back to the bird's head. "Let go!"

"No, you don't understand!" Hugh said as he finally managed to rip the gun from Bobby's hands. "This isn't a Hawker! He's with me, he's a good guy!"

"Hugh? What?" Sally asked. A full sentence would not form on her lips, a rare occurrence for her that was becoming far more common in these troubling times.

Bobby dove at Hugh in desperation, trying to reclaim his weapon. They began to twist and turn as they fought over the shotgun. Suddenly in their struggle, the weapon fired a single shell as they both tumbled into the sewage canal. Thankfully, it didn't hit either of the men in the foul water, the Sparrow, or Sally, but it did make a very loud sound as it launched from the barrel and crashed into the brickwork of the sewer tunnel. Everyone froze at the sound of the shot. For a moment nothing seemed to happen. But then the very sound that had briefly paralyzed them summoned an unwelcome guest. From above them there was the sound of metal impacting heavily upon the stone street above. A single metallic claw punched through the grate right above Sally's head, causing her to shriek in terror.

Without a word, Icarus reached out to the girl and lifted her over his shoulder similar to how he had carried Hugh earlier. Wasting no time, the Sparrow reached out with his other claw and pulled Hugh completely out of the sewage water by his good arm. Bobby was left to stand himself up and to retrieve his shotgun.

"See what you did, Hugh?" yelled Bobby as he shook his now wet and useless gun's barrel at Hugh's face as the claw in the ceiling dug around and widened the hole. Bricks and bits of iron pipe rained down from around the searching claw as it dug its way deeper into the underground tunnel.

"It doesn't matter who did what," shouted Icarus over Bobby's next sentence. "Unless you wish to see just how ineffective that shotgun of yours is against a real Hawker, we need to move now!!"

Already the hole was large enough for the Hawker to reach another deadly claw into the hole, increasing the speed with which it was forcing its way into the sewers to reach its newfound prey. Before anyone could blink, another pair of metallic hands began to rip and tear at the ceiling of the sewer. Hugh could see that Bobby was seething with rage by then, but he could also tell that his friend still had enough sense to not attempt to fight two Hawkers at once. By the time Bobby had started moving, Hugh and the others had already started to run down the dim tunnel with the Sparrow leading the way. As they ran deeper into the gloom, Hugh grew worried about Sally again. He was only slightly relieved by how much care Icarus was giving Sally as he carried her. He could see that the bird was taking greater care of Sally than he had when Hugh had been his passenger. Yet still he could see her pale face looking back at him in pure terror, her eyes desperately trying to focus only on him and not the metallic monsters fighting to get inside the tunnel. All he could do for her now was to say whatever encouraging words came to his lips. At some point, Hugh didn't know when, Sally had fainted and his words, still flowing like a soothing river, fell on her deaf ears.

Eventually the Sparrow suddenly stopped running and jumped down into the channel, reaching down into the muck with both hands while still managing to balance Sally on his feathery back. Hugh knew what the bird was looking for, but Bobby didn't, and Sally wasn't even conscious. Not far behind them was the unmistakable sound of metal feet growing closer. The only blessing of their predicament was that the tunnels were too narrow for either of the two Hawkers to take flight. As Icarus worked on the object in the foul water, Bobby was busy trying to dry out his gun the best he could, shaking it much like a drink mixer at a bar. With every shake of the weapon Bobby swore loudly and demanded why they had stopped running. Sally was still lying over the shoulder of Icarus, her feet dipping into the foul water despite the bird's clear attempts to keep her balanced atop his tall frame.

With a sudden clunk the hatch that Hugh suspected was the focus of the Sparrow's attention became unsealed and the bird opened it in a single fluid movement. Without a single word, Icarus jumped down the hole with the draining sewage with Sally on his back. The two men followed closely behind Icarus, not even bothering to use the ladder to climb down. Once everyone was inside, Icarus reached up with his free hand and slammed the hatch closed behind them, winding the iron valve with his hand until it resealed. The deadbolts deployed and the water stopped dripping past the cracks.

It wasn't a moment too soon as from the hatch came the sound of metal smashing against metal as their pursuers hammered against the door in their unbridled fury to hunt the group down. Hugh was worried that the monstrous Hawkers would figure out how to unlock the hatch from the outside, but before he could say so, Icarus reached up and flicked a hidden metal switch beside the hatch. There was a dull sound of something sliding home and a light came on next to the hatch that said "emergency seal active."

"That should keep them from following us," said Icarus as the pounding grew in intensity against the door in the ceiling, causing the entire hatch to vibrate. Dust fell all around the iron door but the seal held strong and not even a sliver of foul water managed to sneak its way past the rubber. Eventually the sounds began to taper off until they stopped altogether, though Hugh doubted that either of the Hawkers had given up the fight.

"I hope that door keeps them out," he said as Sally blinked and raised herself up from the birdman's back.

"What's going on?" she asked in a dazed voice, her head not yet completely clear of cobwebs and her eyes as unfocused as a sleep walker.

"I was going to ask the same thing, Sally," said Bobby as he continued to try to dry his gun, now using his shirt as a cloth to absorb the water. "Why is there a Hawker helping us? And who tarred and feathered it?"

"There will be time for answers soon enough," said Icarus as he, with a quick flick of his wrist, took the shotgun from Bobby's hands without any resistance. "Now we need to keep moving. We are not completely safe yet, just out of danger for the moment. Follow me."

"Yeah, okay," grumbled Bobby as he shook his hands, which had begun to sting from the speed his weapon was removed from his possession. "But one can walk and talk you know, so spill the story. You owe us that much, Hugh."

Hugh took a deep breath as they began to descend stairs that were almost identical to the ones back in Xandir Square. He began to relate to his friends the tale of what had occurred right after he had left Bobby's house. He didn't get far before Sally, still riding atop the bird's broad back, interrupted him.

"I already filled Bobby in on that part," she said. "What we want to know is how you got yourself a feathered bodyguard that looks more than enough like one of those Hawkers, minus the metal bits."

Hugh blushed deeply, reminding himself briefly how much stronger Icarus was compared to him, considering how easily he was carrying his girl around atop his broad bronze shoulders. Taking another deep breath to both calm down and to provide fuel for his speech, Hugh proceeded to tell his story from when he had run inside the apartment building up to the point that they met up in the sewers moments ago. He explained who Icarus was and what he had done for him, and whatever Hugh forgot to say about their journeys, Icarus filled in. By the time he had finished, they were at the bottom of the stairs and entering into a long metallic hallway that had large grated panels in the floor that covered holes facing down into a massive dark chamber that seemed almost bottomless in shadows. Again Hugh wondered just what secrets the city hid under its people's feet, but now wasn't the time to go exploring, no matter how safe he felt.

Bobby and Sally stayed quiet for most of Icarus's and Hugh's recollections, only asking the odd question every now and then, and getting their answers. Finally, Hugh was done talking and started to ask his own questions, while the Sparrow fell silent.

"Sally," he started, "how did you and Bobby end up together? How did you get into the sewers? What happened when we got separated?"

It was Sally's turn to take a deep breath. With the aid of comments supplied every now and then by Bobby, she told Hugh that after they had been separated in the chaos of the Hawker attack, she had found herself pulled by the grabbing and flailing limbs of the panicked crowd toward a relatively empty alleyway across from the building Hugh had run into. The alley was very narrow, too narrow for the Hawkers to fly into, so many of the people in the chaos had run into this alleyway dragging Sally along with them. However, none of them were safe as bullets began to rain down upon them from the sky, taking out men, women, and children alike.

Sally had managed to dive for cover behind a large dumpster along with a few other like-minded survivors, namely an older man and a little girl and boy. The screams were unbearable and their shelter temporary as the old man among them suddenly pitched forward from a bullet striking him in his head. Sally, without missing a beat, grabbed ahold of the children's hands and made a break toward the back of the alley. As it turned out, the alley was actually longer than it appeared, hiding its true end around an almost invisible bend on the left. As she rounded the corner with the kids, Sally spotted an open delivery door with the body of a dead milkman and a dozen broken bottles of milk. She made it inside, and was promptly met by a hysterical woman, who the children she had been accompanying ran towards. It was quite clear by how the kids embraced the woman that she was their mother. Sally was glad that she was able to see the boy and girl safely to their mother, and watched as the woman led her children off to where Sally hoped they would be safe.

Sally had kept moving. Working her way through the building she found herself in front of a door that led out into a small garden area. The sky was clear here, but she could hear the sounds of killing drifting all around her on the wind. She recalled the Chief's advice of staying out of the open as much as possible, but knew she had to risk crossing to the next building on the other side of the garden. She knew that it could possibly lead to a dead end or to more Hawkers, but she also knew that standing still would increase the chances she would be found, so off she ran. She was very thankful that she wore her sensible penny loafers as her heels crunched against the gravel pathway of the small garden. Once she was on the other side, she was relieved to find the door was unlocked and fled inside. She managed to shove a metal cart containing odds and ends in front of the door after she locked it. She stopped to collect her breath and glazed out with worry through a tiny window barely larger than a bread box and waited anxiously to see if any robotic horrors had seen her run. Once she was positive she was in the clear, she had made her way out of the small back room and toward the front of the building, opting to keep moving and avoid being a sitting duck, only resting when she was sure she couldn't be seen from the sky.

She followed this pattern, weaving her way through alleys and buildings, gambling her life with every open space until she happened to run into Bobby, who was loading up his shotgun when she found him.

This was where Bobby interrupted her and began to tell his end of the story, of how he came to be in Galileo. His explanation was much shorter than what Sally's had been thus far, simply saying that he had gotten worried about Hugh and decided to check on him. Bobby said that he had spent the night since Hugh left mulling over how inexperienced his friend was with firearms and felt that Hugh would need him and his experience with weapons in order to protect, not just Hugh, but Sally as well. He was halfway to their street when the public announcement from Dr. Mason was broadcasted. Without any warning a Hawker flew down from out of the blue and Bobby found himself having to fight it off. Thankfully he was quick with his shotgun and managed to take the robot out by firing a lucky shot point blank in the robot's face before it could scoop him up like a field mouse. He had to fend off several more such attacks from the Hawkers like this, only his shots were not just lucky, as he was ready for them after the first strike. He would have been done for if they didn't come one at a time, and with plenty of down time in between. He only learned of the massacres on the main streets when Sally told him what had happened when she got separated from Hugh.

By the time he had encountered Sally, Bobby was opening a fresh packet of ammunition. He then admitted he had brought several dozen rounds with him before leaving his house. However, he didn't really give much of a reason for it other than having to be prepared for the worst. Hugh raised his eyebrow at the thought of Bobby having his own private arsenal in his apartment, but Bobby blew it off as having nothing to do with the current situation. His only excuse was that he liked to go clay pigeon shooting in Olympic Fields.

Once Bobby finished talking, Sally picked up, telling Hugh and Icarus how they had banded together and eventually found an open manhole cover in an alley. They decided that it would be far safer down below in the sewer than topside or in a building, since the Hawkers were probably using the structures to trap stragglers from the attack in order to finish them off.

By the time Sally and Bobby finished catching Hugh and Icarus up on their own adventures, they reached a sturdy metallic door. At some point the Sparrow had set Sally down on her feet and she had taken up walking along beside the men in the group. Without a word the Sparrow walked forward to the door and turned the large round wheel on its front. It opened similarly to the hatch to the sewers, only it was in the wall instead of the floor. The large wheel was in the center of the metal door, much like a hatch on a submarine. It swung inward on old, stubborn hinges that hadn't been oiled in years, revealing a medium-sized room with poor lighting filtering down from dirty florescent lights that came on once the door was open. In the center of the dingy room was a simple empty metal table ringed by a five old folding chairs. Hugh noticed as he stepped inside with the others that the walls were lined with all sorts of machines of various levels of complexity. At the back of the room were several dead screens similar to the monitors Hugh had seen a couple of hours before.

Silently each one took a seat around the table. Sally gracefully lowered herself into one of the metal chairs while Bobby dropped hard into his, the exhaustion he had hidden so well finally showing through. Only Icarus was still standing, taking roost at the front of the table. Hugh was exhausted and just wanted to close his eyes and rest. He was both physically and emotionally spent from all the excitement and action he had gone through the past two days, but things were far from slowing down as Bobby spoke up, breaking the brief silence.

"Well, what now?" asked Bobby as he laid his useless shotgun on top of the table's hard surface. "There are killer robot-birds topside and hidden rooms below the sewers. Not only that, but we've got a birdman of our own, who I still trust about as far as I can throw him, and I doubt that would be far given how damn big he is."

"I think we should give him a chance, Bobby," said Sally as she leaned back in her chair. "He did just save our lives you know. Not only that, but he is clearly not like the others."

"I don't care what you think, Sally," said Bobby as he gave the Sparrow the evil eye. "*He* was one of them, and might as well still be. They killed who knows how many people topside, and for all we know, he might be planning to kill us all."

"If he was, I think Icarus would have done so long ago," sighed Hugh, leaning back in his chair, causing it to creak under his weight.

"I would prefer if everyone would stop referring to me as if I wasn't in the room," said Icarus as he leaned against the table top with his arms, the table moaning under his weight. "I am not one of the Hawkers any more. If you want any real proof, I can bleed, they cannot. I am vulnerable, they are not. I am not the only one of my kind, as Hubert said. My species is also in danger from the Hawkers. We have a common foe."

"Yak-Yak-YAK!" shouted Bobby as he slammed his fist down upon the table, causing Sally to let out a quick squeak in surprise. "Those are nothing but words. I will never trust you bird-boy, not now, not ever! I have seen what those damn machines can do first hand just traveling to this part of the city! There is no way you can ever make me trust you, let alone believe you!"

Before anyone could say anything else, the entire room started to shake around them. For a brief moment Hugh panicked that Galileo was going to fall out of the sky just like the garbage district did earlier. Yet something was different this time. For starters, there were no sirens going off or red lights flashing. Hugh turned toward Icarus, who was oddly calm about the whole ordeal despite Sally letting out a sudden shriek and Bobby falling out of his chair and onto the floor in a disheveled heap. All around the room, lights that had been hidden in the gloom flashed on, momentarily blinding all gathered inside.

"What the hell is going on now?" asked Bobby as he pulled himself back up from the floor.

"How should I know?" demanded Hugh, looking over at Icarus for answers.

Just then, one of the many screens on a machine situated at the back of the room behind the Sparrow flashed on, showing all of them a top down view of the patchwork fields of Kansas that the city had been floating over since it was built years ago. At first they weren't sure what was strange about what was being shown on screen. However, it only took a second of watching the fields on the monitor slowly flowing off to the left side of the screen for them to figure out what was going on. It was Sally whose words confirmed what they all were seeing.

"We're moving?" she asked in a soft, uncertain voice.

"Impossible!" cried Bobby as he tried unsuccessfully to shake off the reality his eyes were telling him.

Hugh felt a cold sweat drip down the tip of his brow. It had never occurred to him that Nimbus, a city in a sky, could move through the air like a gigantic flock of birds. The vibrations all around them had simmered down significantly as the district and the city itself fell into almost a rhythmic sway as it glided across the sky. Soon the shaking was so minute that one could almost feel as if they were riding a luxury cruise ship through a storm. He turned towards Sally. Her eyes had glazed over in wonder, her mind clearly racing to understand the truth before her.

"This certainly changes things," said Icarus in his unwavering voice, still as unemotional as ever. "It seems the Hawkers have managed to make the city travel."

"How do you know the Hawkers are behind this?" asked Sally as the inquisitive gleam of her inner reporter returned to her eyes, banishing her momentary fog. "Did they tell you that they could up and move the city like this whenever they chose?"

"Negative. It is logical to suspect that it was the Hawkers who made the city move. As far as I'm aware, there isn't a way to direct the city's movements from anywhere above ground. This means the controls must be hidden below the street in secret areas such as the one we are currently in. I doubt anyone else in the city could find these hidden passages and I highly doubt that the city is being remote controlled from the ground."

"We found our way down here," Bobby smirked. "Guess your logic is flawed, bird-boy."

"You're only here because I showed you the way," said Icarus, causing Sally to let out a small giggle and Bobby's face to color. It probably wasn't intended, but there was still the suggestion that Bobby couldn't have survived without Sally's help.

"What makes you say that?" asked Hugh as his mind still struggled to comprehend what was happening around him. "Why can't this be something done by the guys on the ground?"

"Simple," said the birdman as he finally took a seat among the others, the chair creaking alarmingly under his weight. "I think Nimbus is far too large to be effectively controlled from the ground. It would require many individuals working separate consoles to manage and maneuver each district of the city so none collided with the other. A difficult task if there isn't a means of seeing how far or how close each section of Nimbus is to each other. There is also the issue of the range of the transmission required in order to go from the control center on the ground to the city up here. The signal would have to travel the distance from the ground to the city, plus the added distance that the navigators wish to move the city, too. It's not only easier, but more logical, for the city to have control stations in each district, and in each its own pilot to ensure that his flock of buildings doesn't crash into their neighbors. Think of it as a squadron of planes if it helps you understand the mechanics behind it better."

Hugh had to admit, what Icarus was saying made a fair deal of sense.

"So," said Bobby as he shifted his gaze left and right as if the exposed rivets in the walls were eyes spying upon them, "what you are saying is that not only are there Hawkers topside, but now we got them *under* our feet, too?"

"To be accurate, I think the control center for this district of the city is actually located above us," said Icarus as he pointed with one silver claw towards the ceiling of the room.

"Are you trying to be *funny*?!" sneered Bobby as he clenched his hands tightly around his shotgun's barrel, possibly longing to have his hands wrapped around a feathered neck instead of a metallic one.

"No, I am completely serious. Back in my home district of Xandir Square, and in the now destroyed trash district, the control rooms tended to be a few flights closer to the sewer hatches. Assuming that all districts of Nimbus are similar below the street levels, I believe that it is a solid assumption to say that the control center is above us."

"How the hell do you know all of this, birdbrain?" demanded Bobby as his knuckles turned white at the grip of the gun.

"You do seem awfully well-informed on all of this," Sally said as her face began to harden and her gaze focused upon the Sparrow at the end of the table. "Just how much do you know? When did the Hawkers gain this knowledge?"

"I do not know when we first knew of this city's hidden assets," Icarus sighed as he leaned forward in his chair, resting his predatory head in between his clawed hands with his elbows braced against the table's surface. "I just know what I saw during my time on duty and during my exploration of the district after I had become a Sparrow. Most of my knowledge of the city was originally programmed into me before I was activated or born. What I didn't know I was taught by the others before the change overcame me. How the other Hawkers in my unit learned so many secrets is beyond my knowledge."

"What worries me," said Hugh as he turned his head back towards the screen showing the scrolling fields below the city, "is not so much how we are moving, but where Nimbus is going."

13

"I do not pretend to know where the robots are taking this city," admitted Icarus as he let out a sigh and leaned back in the old metal chair. "The best I can reason is that they are simply taking the city out of range of the local airbase so as to avoid another aerial assault."

"I'd believe that if I hadn't seen those robots firing *back* with guns that shouldn't even be here," argued Hugh with a hint of steel entering his voice. "It seems to me that this place is pretty well armed for a peaceful city in the sky." Hugh let out a loud yawn and rubbed one of his eyes with a fisted hand. All the excitement since the junkyard was catching up to him and his body was giving him all the signs that he should get some sleep soon. The others around the table were beginning to tire as well. Sally stifled a yawn with her delicate, slender hands while Bobby's head began to bob drowsily, akin to an apple in a barrel of water. Even Icarus seemed to be drooping after all that had happened that day. His feathers seemed to be wilting on his body, giving him a saggy appearance. It was a wonder to Hugh that the Sparrow hadn't yet passed out after all he had done, from the running, flying, and fighting to keep them alive up to this point.

"I'm with Hugh here," groaned Bobby, clearly fighting to keep his head up now. His eyelids drooped lower by the second. "As much as I would seriously love to find out why there are antiaircraft weapons hiding in the city's foundations, I think it might be time to table this conversation."

"Sadly I must agree, despite my burning curiosity," spoke Sally in a softening voice as her long lashes threatened to cover her eyes in sleep. Icarus nodded his head in agreement and shortly thereafter they decided that they should camp out in the sparse room with the blinding lights. The men took off their jackets and made makeshift blindfolds for their eyes so they could sleep properly despite the bright lights all around the room. Despite looking along every wall in the room, and even the machine in the back, they couldn't find any way to turn off the overhead lights. From her purse Sally pulled a small padded black sleeping mask that she always carried in case she had to pull an all-nighter at the office.

Icarus, however, didn't sleep with the others at first. He suggested they should sleep in shifts, just to be safe and to watch for any future developments concerning the city's flight path or for any other signs of activity from the other blank screens on the console at the back of the room. Although they had locked the door from the inside for good measure, it wasn't guaranteed that it would keep a determined Hawker from forcing its way inside.

There wasn't a single place in the room for any of them to lie down comfortably. The chairs were just as hard as the floor, so they had to use their luggage, Sally her purse and Hugh his bag, as cushions for their heads. Bobby was given what was left of Icarus's ragged jacket to use as a pillow. Normally Bobby wouldn't have accepted anything from a former Hawker, but given the situation and how little energy he had by then, he put up very little resistance to the Sparrow's gift. The last thing Hugh saw before he put on his blindfold and fell asleep atop his satchel was Icarus, bracing his long rifle atop the metal table, angled towards the thick metal door which was the only way into their current sanctuary hidden deep below the streets of Nimbus.

Hugh didn't dream at all upon falling asleep. His was the sleep of the dead, one that was neither restful nor restless. In this state it felt like mere minutes instead of a couple of hours before he was awakened by Bobby's hand on his shoulder. Slipping his makeshift blindfold off of his eyes, Hugh saw that Bobby now held the Sparrow's rifle in his left hand. The right was still resting where it had shaken him awake.

"Time to get up," said Bobby, feigning a mock fatherly tone as he eased back on his heels, giving Hugh room to rise to his feet. As he pulled himself up from the floor, Hugh glanced over his shoulder to see Icarus curled up against a corner of the room, his body hidden under one large feathered wing. Somehow, the Sparrow seemed much smaller when asleep than awake, but it was probably a trick of the glare cast by the relentless bright lights reflecting off of the birdman's shiny feathers.

"Enough ogling our 'pet,'" said Bobby as he shoved the rifle into Hugh's reluctant hands. "I did _not_ get nearly enough sleep before parakeet boy over there woke me for my shift. I swear he's out to make my life miserable."

Hugh chuckled as he groggily maneuvered his body into a completely upright position, the rifle serving as a makeshift cane to support his weight until the last of the effects of sleep left his body. "Come now, Bobby," Hugh said as he watched his friend lay down at his feet, tying his shirt once more around his eyes, "I thought you were the one who wanted to group Icarus with the enemy?"

"Yeah, yeah, whatever you say, cameraman."

"Sleep tight, don't let the bed bugs bite, or the robots shoot."

"Oh, before I forget," said Bobby, stifling a yawn as he reached into the pocket of his pants. From it, he pulled out a plastic bag filled with an assortment of different pills. "From what you've told us about what happened to you, I'm guessing that arm is going to be tender for quite a while."

Hugh had almost forgotten his injured arm. He glanced down at it, still in the sling, now dirty and foul from his brief bath in the sewer water. "It has been giving me trouble," Hugh admitted as he tried to move it within the sling, feeling waves of pain radiate from his shoulder.

"Well," said Bobby as he opened the bag and began to dig through the assorted pills, "I may not have my entire medical kit, so I can't do much to help you, but I do have some pain killers with me."

Hugh let out a yawn of his own. He wanted to ask Bobby what he was doing with painkillers in his pocket, but at this hour, and with how much trouble his bum arm was giving him, he was willing to just accept the medicine and swallow it.

"Now, the effects won't be permanent," warned Bobby as he settled down at his place on the floor. "They are made by my dad, so they should also help you recover a bit faster than normal. I know it's a tad pointless to tell you this, given our circumstances, but you'll need to rest that arm as much as possible until it's fully healed."

"I guess it's a good thing that I only have to aim this at the door. That shouldn't require much movement, unless the door gets up and walks away," said Hugh, forcing a smile.

And with that brief exchange out of the way, Hugh set up shop with the rifle where he had seen Icarus stationed before he had gone to bed with the others. He found the rifle was far easier to maneuver with the table as a brace for its long barrel as opposed to trying to support the whole thing with his one good arm. He had no idea what he was doing with this powerful rifle. He had gotten lucky when he had handled a simple small handgun just a few days ago. Now he was behind the sights of a far more powerful weapon, wiggling it about here and there as he struggled to figure out what he was supposed to be using as the sight – the crosshairs in the scope mounted atop the barrel or the little bump at the tip of the muzzle.

It didn't matter either way, as he didn't need to use the sniper rifle during his shift that night. He had no idea how long he had been awake, or how long it had been since they had all decided to camp out in that metallic room under the district's streets, but Hugh had a good idea that plenty of time had passed. Turning his head to look over his shoulder at the machine at the back of the room, Hugh could see that the screen showing the earth passing by beneath the city was still scrolling off to the left side of the screen. However, the screen no longer showed the peaceful farmlands of Kansas, but pure blackness that was broken up by the twinkling of tight clusters of stars. Or, as Hugh realized moments after his brain remembered which direction the camera was facing, the stars were actually lights from towns and villages dotted over the ground. It was simply so dark out that night that from that tiny screen the lights of homes and offices from so far up seemed like pinpricks of color in a vast ink blot that never ended.

There wasn't any indication other than the movement on the screen that time was flowing in that brightly lit room. Machines clicked and clacked along the other walls of the room, but in such erratic spurts that Hugh gave up on using them as a measure of time. The best he could do was count under his breath every ten seconds that passed by. He found counting helped break up the monotony of waiting till his shift was over. Before they had gone to sleep, it was agreed that the one who was on guard duty would wake up the next person for their shift once the current guard had become too tired to focus. Hugh guessed that Icarus had the longest shift thus far, given how he was originally programmed to be an around the clock protector and since robots didn't need any sleep, as far as he knew. But now Icarus was a Sparrow, a creature of flesh that had the same needs as any other animal, such as the occasional rest period. Hugh was curious just how long Bobby had been awake at his shift. Had it been an hour or two or only a few minutes or, at worst, seconds? There was no clear way to tell without waking either Icarus or Bobby up, and there was no clock in the room to support either's story.

Hugh again turned back toward the monitor behind him and was mildly surprised to see that the endless darkness of the screen was slowly being eaten away by dark greys and whites. Slowly, shapes began to stand out on the black and white screen. It was clear that the sun was slowly rising outside of the metal room, bringing with it a new day. Hugh found himself yawning despite the screen transfixing him, urging him to keep watching as shapes took form, forests rising and separating from rivers and lakes that lit up like mirrors, catching the early rays of dawn. However, Hugh couldn't last much longer, and thought he should get Sally to take the last shift. This wasn't necessary, as when he turned away from the captivating brightening screen he was startled to see Icarus standing right beside him. Hugh almost pulled the trigger in surprise, but he managed to keep his finger under control at the last second.

"Cripes, you could have warned a guy!" gasped Hugh as he felt the shock briefly trigger his adrenaline, causing the creeping call of sleep to recede to whence it came.

The birdman merely cocked his head and said nothing, as he waited for Hugh to calm down from his little fright. It was only a couple of seconds later that he spoke. "I am sorry to have unsettled you, Hugh, but I feel it would be best for us all to awake now that the sun is rising."

"How'd you know the sun was coming up?" asked Hugh, his curiosity exchanging places with his flight or fight feelings.

"Oh, I always wake at dawn. It is part of my biological clock, a lasting after effect of being a Hawker," said Icarus in his emotionless voice. "All Sparrows rise at dawn. We who have completed our transformation are not quite sure what part of our former robotic lives has resulted in this unique biological trait, but it is a very useful one. It has saved many of us from being caught unawares by any of our metal predecessors assigned to cleanup detail."

"Why is it that they try to kill you?" asked Hugh. "Shouldn't they still count you as one of their own despite the transformation?"

"They do not see us as one of their own once the change occurs," replied Icarus. "You see, the Hawkers despise our very existence. Even those who they managed to kill off on their first attempts early in the change were seen as signs of impurities amongst their perfect ranks. They probably keep records of how many of them have turned, complete with each corrupted unit's serial number and known status – either alive or dead. They do not like loose ends such as the Sparrows floating in the breeze."

There was a groan coming from the floor. Both Icarus and Hugh leaned over in their chairs and turned to look at the other half of their small group as they began to awaken. Bobby swore as he shook himself awake, while Sally let out a lazy yawn from her delicate lips. It seemed that Hugh and Icarus's conversation had awakened the others. Once everyone was again seated around the table, Sally produced for them a tin of sardines and a packet of crackers from her purse to serve as their breakfast.

It wasn't the most filling of meals Hugh had ever eaten, and it was made even less so given how it had to be split three ways amongst the gathered humans at the table. Icarus was offered a share, of course, but he simply shook his head and explained he preferred to find his own food. He didn't give any more detailed explanations as to what he meant, but he did move towards the door and with a simple twist of the wheel on the inside, opened it up and stepped out through the frame. He told them that he would be back soon, and to keep the door locked behind him until he returned and gave five knocks upon the door's exterior. It took both Bobby and Hugh's collective strength to force the door back into place behind the Sparrow and to turn the wheel on the back until it slid back home, sealing them inside the meeting room once more.

As Hugh and the others munched away on what little there was to eat, Hugh found himself daydreaming about his last real meal. It hadn't seemed like such a big deal back then, but now that simple meal seemed as glamorous as a French dish created by a master chef. Once every cracker and fish was gone, the trio at the table found themselves staring at crumbs. Hugh felt his stomach grumble under his belt, as if to ask, "Is that it?" while Bobby and Sally developed a look on their faces that said the same thing.

"I bet he's not even coming back, the vulture," grumbled Bobby as he looked at his shotgun on the table. "Damned winged menace has flown the coup and left us to rot."

"Cripes, Bobby, can't you say a single good thing about Icarus?" demanded Hugh as he slammed his fist against the hard surface of the table, resulting in him instantly regretting that action. His hand throbbed painfully from the impact.

"Hugh, listen," said Bobby as he massaged his forehead with one hand as the other picked up his shotgun. "There is a saying going around, once a Red always a Red. I believe this applies to everything, especially to a Hawker. Or Sparrow. Or whatever the hell you want to call the birdbrain."

"Bobby, he saved *your* life only yesterday! Surely that means something to you?" pleaded Hugh as he slid the rifle just out of Bobby's reach, toward Sally. Icarus had not bothered to take his weapon with him when he left the group, and Hugh had a feeling deep inside himself that told him that the Sparrow's sharp obsidian claws were the reason.

"Yeah, well, that was yesterday!"

"Ugh, give it a rest, Bob," Sally sighed as she finished wiping the juices from the sardines off of her face with her handkerchief. "As far as I am concerned, that cute feather ball is on the up and up."

"You only say that because he saved you, *princess*," grunted Bobby as he shook his shotgun, hoping that it had finally dried out enough to be useful again. There was no real way to tell if it was useable yet because neither Bobby nor the others felt like firing the weapon, in case the unnecessary noise drew trouble.

"I thought you said that didn't matter, Bobby," pointed out Hugh.

"I never said such things!"

The conversation continued much like this for quite a while between Bobby and Hugh, until there was a shrill whistle from Sally, so high and loud that it hurt both men's ears. It was a similar sound that caused dogs to moan in agony.

"What the heck, Sal," groaned Hugh as he looked at his girlfriend. His pinky was wiggling about in his ear trying to dig out the ringing left behind by the whistle.

"Sorry to interrupt the debate, but I think you two should know that Icarus is a television star."

"What the hell are you blathering on about now?" moaned Bobby as he looked at Sally as one would glance at another who just stated they could walk on water.

"Both of you look at the screen," she commanded as she pointed toward the back of the room. Turning their heads, each man could see on the monitor that the fields of the day before had been replaced by forests and the occasional small town. Dominating the center of the image was Icarus, flapping his wings every other minute to keep in time with the speed of the moving city. They all rose from their chairs and huddled up against the screen, watching the birdman as he began to make his way slowly towards the right side of the screen, increasing his speed to being just a tad faster than Nimbus was traveling. Hugh noted mentally that Icarus seemed to be carrying something in his arms. It was some sort of bundle but he couldn't make it out too clearly given the available definition of the video and the lack of color on the screen, other than black, white, and shades in between.

"What do you suppose he has there?" asked Bobby, pointing at the screen with his right index finger as if it would unlock all the answers concerning the bundle being carried slowly out of sight by Icarus.

"Guess we have to wait and find out," replied Hugh as he looked back at the door dominating the opposite wall.

It seemed both as long as centuries and as brief as seconds after Icarus's flying form had completely left the viewing screen before the five knocks rang out against the opposing side of the thick metal door. Together, Hugh and Bobby once again tackled the heavy door's wheel lock, forcing it to reverse its progress and slide the bolts out of their sockets, enabling Icarus to easily push it open from the other side. Neither man was prepared for this, and in a comical fashion, they both ended up knocked off their feet by the door's sudden inward motion, resulting in rather painful landings upon the hard surface of the floor with only their rear ends to soften their fall.

Into the room strolled Icarus, oblivious to causing Hugh and Bobby to tumble. In his large claws he held aloft a large rough spun sack dripping with water. As the men gathered their wits and climbed to their feet, the Sparrow put down his burden and opened up the sack, showing its contents to be live fish squirming in their last moments of life outside of water. Sally gasped at the sight and once Hugh and Bobby saw Icarus's catch, they too balked.

"Just when I thought I couldn't eat any more fish," Hugh joked humorlessly as he took a step closer to the dripping sack. He was in mental shock at just how many fish the Sparrow had collected. He wasn't sure what type of fish they were, but he was pretty sure that they were edible. He couldn't even imagine being able to lift the entire catch with all his strength, let alone just one hand as the Sparrow had done. Yet Icarus had easily flown back up to Nimbus with the bundle in tow, as if it was nothing more than a pillow instead of a soaking wet bag of fish.

"I believe I have enough for everyone, yes?" asked Icarus as he reached into the sack and drew out a claw full of the wriggling creatures. Without another word he brought the still wriggling fishes to his sharp silver beak and swallowed each of them whole, sliding one at a time down into his eager maw. It was a very disconcerting scene, to watch the Sparrow down fish after fish in this same manner, often with the aquatic creatures still very much alive, though a couple were clearly dead as they did not even blink before going down into the bird's gullet. It was a wonder that Icarus could eat so many fish, but Hugh guessed that all that flying must have caused the bird to burn through calories like a rocket through the sky. Of course, it could also be that the Sparrow really liked this type of fish, but Hugh didn't feel like interrupting Icarus's meal to ask.

"There," sighed Icarus, the edges of his beak giving a brief twitch of a smile at his belly being full. He turned away from the bag and looked at each of the humans in turn. "I think all of you should also eat your fill. We are likely to have a very busy day ahead of ourselves and hunger is a distraction we cannot afford."

"Um, thanks for thinking of us," said Sally nervously as her eyes darted over Icarus's haul. She squirmed visibly as some of the remaining fish continued to flop about in their death throes. "But I would rather have my fish cooked, not raw."

"I'm with you, sister!" stated Bobby as he turned a little green in the face from witnessing the Sparrow eat in such a manner that was both human and something feral at the same time.

"I don't understand," started Icarus as he tilted his head to the side, an action that accented his more avian features. "I thought humans eat fish just as my kind do after the change. What difference does it make if it is cooked or not?"

"Well, for one it's healthier for us humans for the fish to be cooked, grilled or even fried," Hugh explained. "And for the other, they simply taste better cooked. And there is the whole matter of the bones."

"Yes!" piped up Sally, finally meeting the Sparrow's eyes again since he had begun eating. "If the fish isn't prepared properly, a gal, or a guy, could choke on the bones and die. Frankly Icky-"

"Icky?" interrupted Icarus as his head tilted even farther, making it seem as if his neck was broken and making Hugh and the others feel a tad uncomfortable to look at Icarus directly.

"Oh, that's just a nickname, Hun," said Sally with a dismissive wave of her hand. "You know, like Sal for Sally and Hughie for Hugh. As I was saying, I'm surprised you didn't choke when you swallowed those fish whole."

"Does it really matter if I swallowed the bones along with the fish?" asked Icarus, still tilting his head at a nearly impossible angle. Every human in the room instantaneously decided it didn't really matter that much after all and let the matter drop.

"I see..." said Icarus in a tone that suggested that he indeed did not see but was willing to let things move on to more important matters. His head swiveled back into place as his neck straightened out. "So I guess none of you will be having any fish. Pity, I-"

It wasn't clear what Icarus was going to say next, be it an apology or a suggestion, or even an offer to somehow cook the fish for the others, as all of a sudden a loud beep interrupted his sentence and grabbed everyone's attention. Turning their collective gaze toward the back of the room, they were rewarded with the sight of not only the still scrolling live video feed of the earth below the moving city, but of a second screen that had come to life. It appeared to show a blueprint of some kind upon its dark surface, the lines drawn in a sickly green that glowed against the dark backdrop. Everyone moved over to the machine, everyone but Hugh, who somehow managed to get his feet caught up in the strap of his bag while moving over with the others. His feet became tangled up and he found himself falling over and landing face first against the floor.

Getting up, he rubbed his sore nose and rushed over to the others, a silent curse escaping his lips. Upon taking up position between Sally and Icarus, Hugh found himself staring with the others at a display that showed a side view of Galileo Plaza, from its tallest tower to the lowest point of the district and everything in between. The street level of the diagram was simply labeled as "civilian quarters," in bold glowing green letters, while the slices below the street level, just under the sewer system, were listed as levels one through ten, each one with a corresponding button on the panel below the lit screen. The levels increased in number value until they reached the very bottom of the district diagram, which ended in a crescent moon shape, representing the round underbelly of the entire structure.

"What on earth..." started Bobby as he gazed at the image on the monitor. Even Icarus seemed surprised by the complexity of the map, showing areas of the district that even he hadn't suspected existed. Hugh may have been the last one to get a good look at the map, but he was also the first to force his way to the front of the pack and press one of the buttons. Without thinking about which one, he just let his finger fall where it may. Suddenly a light came on next to Level 6 on the map and another screen, this one smaller than the others, flashed on to the right of the diagram. In its plastic frame a long line of text began to scroll to the right and downwards, as if an invisible typist was putting the words on the glass as they watched. It was a different shape than the others. Instead of being a perfect square, this screen was long and thin, causing only four or five words to fit on a row before the next line of text began. Within seconds the screen had filled out with the glowing emerald message:

Level Six, Galileo:
Meeting level of district
Number of meeting rooms: 8
Number of RR: 8
Number of stairs: 4
Number of dorms: 8
Elevators: 6
Elevator status: 6/6 offline
Com rooms: 3
Com status: 3/3 offline
Number of EAC: 18
EAC status: 18/18 offline
You are here

"What did you just do?" Bobby asked in awe as the last of the text appeared on the monitor.

"I have no idea!" Hugh said in confusion as he looked back and forth from the button he pressed to the words. "I just thought if I pressed a button, that the screen would change or something helpful would happen."

"I had no idea such strange devices as this existed down here," said Icarus as he pressed a few buttons, causing the words to change on the second screen, giving similar jumbles of random words and numbers.

"Why is there even something like this down here?" asked Sally. "Nimbus is nine years old, right? Did they even have technology like this back then?"

"I don't think so," said Bobby, reaching out with his hand and running his finger over the glass, carving a narrow trail in the dust. "This machine isn't nearly as dusty as the rest of the room. I think it was put in here very recently!"

"Icarus," started Sally, "do you think the Hawkers put this machine down here?"

"Doubtful," said Icarus as he stopped pressing buttons, leaving the text the way it was after Hugh pushed the first button. "I don't see any reason for them to build such a device, let alone put it in such an isolated location."

"Great," groaned Bobby, "Guess that means more than just the four of us and the Hawkers know about this place."

Hugh was not sure what to make of all this. He had become fixated on the message once again displayed upon the second monitor. He had no idea what half of the words meant, though it was at least clear that it was a list of some kind, tallying off what was on that level. With a start, he realized that the main screen had changed from a cross-section view of the district to a floor plan of the selected level. He, like the others, had been distracted by the discovery of what the machine was capable of. They had somehow missed the other screen changing. Toward the center of the upper right quarter of the diagram, in a rectangular room labeled "info station 6h," was a red dot. It took Hugh and the others a moment to realize that the dot was a representation of their location on the map, meaning that they were currently on Level Six of the district.

"Well, I guess this at least answers the question of where we are," mumbled Bobby as he traced out the floor plan with his index finger, picking up a tad more dust. His hand followed the hallway listed on the map from their location out toward the stairs that they had fled down the day before. "Just wish I knew what it all means."

"It means there is much more to this city than meets the eye," answered Sally as she took out her small notebook and began to recreate the map on the screen. Hugh marveled at how she could easily replicate the map, from a screen that had to be roughly two feet square onto a note pad that was seven by three inches. Yet she managed to do it, and in hardly any time at all, using the note-taking skills that she had developed through all her time as a reporter.

"I wonder what some of these words mean?" Hugh thought out loud as he puzzled over the list on the right. "I understand what some of it says, such as the Com's meaning communication, but what is an ECA? Why does it list most of this stuff as offline?"

"I do not know. I have never gone deeper than this floor in any given district," admitted Icarus as he fretted about nervously, his feathers seeming to twitch about around his eyes in a way that made Hugh feel a bit uncomfortable. There was a lot about this birdman that seemed human, the way he moved, the way he talked and, of course, his size and general shape, but there were just as many parts that showed his avian qualities. Just looking at the Sparrow made Hugh nervous, and Icarus's former life as a Hawker hung over the birdman like a heavy shadow that Hugh found himself struggling every now and then to lift and see the real creature underneath.

"I have heard stories of lower parts of the city from other Sparrows in my flock," continued Icarus. "Those who have ventured lower than I have can be counted on one hand. They say that there is nothing down there, save the mechanical beasts keeping the city afloat. They are dangerous devices that are so hot that being even on the same floor with them presents a risk of one catching fire, or so the stories go. I haven't been there myself so I cannot say if what I have heard is completely true or not, though I suspect that this device may give us more answers if we ask it."

"Well, I don't see a way to go back to the original map, unless you know which button to press?" asked Bobby as he scanned over the assorted buttons at the console. Hugh noticed that his friend's tone had softened somewhat from how he had first responded to the Sparrow. Yet his words still had hints of an icy edge just under the surface when directed at Icarus. Hugh hoped that, in time, Bobby would get over himself and come to accept the bird as an ally instead of an enemy. Although, Hugh guessed he trusted Icarus easier than Bobby only because he had been with the Sparrow longer and was saved from death by the bird twice already.

"Maybe you need to hit the button again?" suggested Sally. Hugh did just that, firmly pressing the button for level six again, but the result was the same. For a moment the screen on the right cleared itself, before the same lines of short text typed themselves out in their neat rows. Everything was still the same. All communications were offline and so were the mysterious EACs.

"Well, that didn't work," smirked Bobby before Sally punched him in the arm for his smart remark.

"Perhaps hitting a button for a different level may help?" suggested Icarus as he leaned past Hugh to get closer to the consol. Smoothly he reached out one silver claw, extending a single black nailed finger from his hand and pressed down the button labeled Level Five. The map screen blurred for a moment and a whole new layout of stairs, rooms and halls replaced it. The top right corner of the map titled it as LEVEL FIVE, ARMORY AND WEAPONS. On the right, a new list of information quickly filled out the screen. Now it said:

Level Five, Galileo:
Armory, Ammo storage
Number of stations: 40
Weapons in storage: 100%
Ammo in use: 30%
Active missiles: 4/5
Active AA: 20/80
Active BDS: 0/20
Number of stairs: 4
Number of dorms: 10
Elevators: 7
Elevator status: 1/7 online
Com rooms: 4
Com status: 1/4 online
Number of EAC: 30
EAC status: 30/30 offline

Unlike the first list, this one was longer and resulted in a few lines of text being forced off the top of the small screen. After a few minutes the text began to sink back down and the first few words of the list were visible again, until another couple of minutes passed, in which the text scrolled back down again. Needless to say, all gathered were shocked to discover that they were right under a massive armory level. The map on the left was as well labeled as the previous one for Level Six, only this time there were entire rooms devoted to a particular type of weapon and ammunition. There was one for rockets, and several devoted only to missiles, and another set aside for bombs. Most of the rooms had a W in them, possibly signifying that they were where weapons could be found, though it did seem redundant given that it was the weapons level of the district. Oddly enough, there was an extra elevator shaft shown on this map that didn't exist on the ones for the lower levels.

"Well," Bobby said as he again traced out the hallways with his finger, "I think I know where we are going next."

"Are you nuts?" asked Hugh. "Don't you think the Hawkers are already there, arming themselves?"

"Hugh has a point. We've seen them fire the antiaircraft guns," said Icarus as he studied the map onscreen. "Chances are very good that they've taken over the entire floor and are making use of the available weapons. However," he continued as his eyes followed the many twisting hallways on the map, "we don't have much of a choice in the matter.

Between us we have only one weapon, and I'm the only one trained to use it effectively."

"We can thank you for that one, Hugh," grumbled Bobby as he looked at his shotgun on the table.

"Well, you wouldn't stand down when I told you to," snapped Hugh.

"Can you blame me?" Bobby demanded.

"Guys, guys, calm down," said Sally as she pushed her way between them. "This is getting us nowhere."

"She's right," said Hugh as he let out a deep breath. "I don't know about any of you, but I don't feel very comfortable being just one floor below Hawker central. Being undisturbed last night could have been just a lucky fluke."

"That's true," agreed Icarus, still too absorbed in the map to turn around to look at the others. "Yet, I am not sure if there is a way we can grab what we need without being detected."

"We got down here without any trouble," pointed out Bobby. "We passed right through that level without a peep from those things. I think that there's only a handful of them up there, just enough to run the guns, and reload them. As long as we avoid the rooms with double 'As' on the map, we should be fine."

"Bobby, did you forget that the reason we are even down here is because we were being chased?" asked Sally.

"Then explain to me why it's taking them so damn long to find us?" he demanded. "That clearly wasn't the only hatch leading down here. They probably gave up or forgot that we got away."

"The Hawkers never forget," muttered Icarus as he traced out possible routes on the map with his finger. "It isn't in our programing."

"Did you say something?" asked Bobby, turning back to the Sparrow.

Before Icarus could answer there was a high-pitched whine from the map console. Everyone turned to the screen as it began to flicker and static slowly filled the screen. Icarus recoiled at the site and began to press the console's buttons in an attempt to bring the picture back. Alas, the static only grew worse, and then with the sound of sparks snapping from inside the machine, all the screens, even the live feed of the countryside down below, died. Icarus continued to press buttons, trying to get the machine to respond. He even went as far as to whack the side of the machine with his fist, but nothing worked. Hugh saw Icarus look at the dead device with an expression of aggravation on his face. With a few deep breaths, Icarus calmed himself down and his face became as emotionless as ever.

Upon leaving the machine, the large Sparrow walked towards the table and chairs in the middle of the room. Whatever it was he was going to do was instantly forgotten as something on the floor caught his attention. He stopped where he was and looked down at something on the ground by the table's leg. The Sparrow's jaw twitched, before his head tilted to the side for a moment. The expression on his face, as he looked down at the ground before his feet, could be described as curiosity. Hugh followed the bird's eyes and found that, resting in front of Icarus's talons, was his camera bag.

The flap of his bag had become unbuckled at some point and the contents inside had slid partially out onto the dusty floor. It was then Hugh saw Frank's journal, just lying out in the open as if it was a magazine someone had forgotten to put away. In all of the excitement of the last few days, he had managed to forget he was still carrying it inside of his satchel. It must have slipped out of his bag when he tripped over it a few minutes before. As a brief wave of shame rolled over Hugh as he looked at the journal on the floor, Icarus reached out with a clawed hand and picked it up.

"Why does this book have a lock on it?" Icarus asked as he stood up, holding the leather journal up to Hugh.

Before Hugh could answer, Bobby saw the book and hurried over. "That's my father's journal," he said as he snatched it away from the Sparrow. "It's locked to keep whatever's written inside private from nosy people like you. Hugh, I'm impressed you managed to hold on to it after everything that happened. Thank you."

"No problem," said Hugh. "I just wish I knew what was so important about that little journal that makes the Hawkers want it so badly."

"Say," said Bobby, a thoughtful expression appearing upon his face. "You don't think there's something in this that might help us fight the Hawkers? Mad Mike did say Dad had worked with him on the Hawker project, right?"

"Too bad we don't have the key," Hugh groaned.

"Are you sure Dad didn't give you one for the journal? Think hard, Hugh," said Bobby.

"I'm positive!" growled Hugh, his temper flaring for a moment. "Sorry," he apologized. "Frank did give me a couple of keys, but they weren't for the book, just the front door of his apartment and the compartment the journal was in. Damn lucky that I found it at all. He didn't say where it was at the time, or even mention it at all. I guess it was a good thing that little robot ransacked his place. Otherwise I probably wouldn't have even found it."

"Yeah, it's strange how things work out, isn't it?" Bobby sighed before turning to Icarus. "Birdman," he said, as he sized the Sparrow up, "You're a pretty strong guy, aren't you? I bet you could pop the lock right off this book like a soda cap."

Icarus shrugged, the action making his wings spread slightly. "I suppose I can do that," he said. "But I won't know till I try."

"Then do it," said Bobby, as he shoved the leather journal into the Sparrow's hands.

Icarus looked down at the leather journal and maneuvered it in his large hands till his right thumb was in position under the lock. With hardly any effort, he was able to break the lock by merely flicking his thumb. Now the lock hung uselessly from the hinge that once bound it to the journal, like a dangling key chain.

"Humph. Show-off," grumbled Bobby as he glanced at the broken lock.

"Bobby, he only broke the lock the way you told him to," said Sally, who had crept up to join their gathering while they had been talking. "He only did what you asked. Does it really matter how he did it?"

"Not really, but I thought it would have given him at least a little trouble," mumbled Bobby as his gaze slid over to the journal itself, its cover now open and the first few of the pages revealed. Icarus, who apparently was more curious than any of them gave him credit for, began to flip through the journal's pages, his golden eyes glued to the pages as he read through its contents. Hugh and Sally quickly moved over to either side of Icarus, each trying to see the slivers of paper, as they flew past the bird's bright eyes. The bird was simply too tall for either of them to see what Icarus was reading in those pages. Hugh couldn't help but feel his curiosity begin to bloom inside him, and judging by how the others were acting, so could Bobby and Sally. However, Hugh felt he had a right to know what was in those pages. He had been the one carrying that book around since day one of this mess, and he felt an obligation to know what lay within its pages.

Suddenly, the pages stopped flying by and Icarus's piercing eyes ceased their wavering and focused intently on the paper before them. It was clear the Sparrow had found what he was looking for in the journal and was now giving it his complete attention. Just when Hugh thought of getting a chair from the table to stand atop so he could get a better view of what Icarus was seeing, Icarus let out a massive breath of air in a chirp that was disturbingly similar to that of a real Sparrow – that is, the little grey bird and not the seven foot tall birdman. He then simply tossed the journal carelessly from his silver-clawed hand and let it fall where it may. The book landed atop the table in the center of the room and slid almost all the way to the opposite side of the metallic surface, stopping short of falling over the edge.

All the humans were spellbound. Three pairs of eyes were focused intently upon the Sparrow before them, his face frozen in a mask of such deep thought that it was impossible to gauge what he was thinking. Then, without warning, the mask cracked and shattered as the bird began to make a strange cawing sound, similar to what one would hear from a seagull. It took a moment for it to register that the Sparrow was laughing.

14

Hugh went right for the discarded book once his stupor over the laughing bird faded. It was finally time for him to find out what he had been safeguarding for the past week and he was not going to wait any longer. He snatched the journal from the table and let his eyes feast upon the knowledge within. Alas, Hugh could barely understand his friend's handwriting, with its many curves and overlapping letters. Yet Hugh continued his struggle, until some sense came from the chicken scratch. There were normal journal entries on the pages, telling of mundane and ordinary things, and there were records of projects that Dr. Crick was working on, such as new medicine and so on. Several pages were stained by water from Hugh's travels through the sewers just the day before, but those entries did not seem all that important anyway.

While Hugh skimmed the book, Sally was reading over his shoulder, her quick eyes reading the passages just as fast as he was. A tiny sigh would escape her lips when Hugh flipped pages over before she had a chance to finish them. Hugh didn't even acknowledge Sally's small complaints as he greedily skimmed through every page, avoiding the ones he couldn't read entirely.

"Let me see that." Suddenly the precious journal was unceremoniously torn from Hugh's fingers and brought before Bobby's eyes. Hugh protested with a couple of foul words that he rarely used to express his feelings to his "friend," while Bobby began to read the journal himself, picking up where Hugh had been forced to leave off. Sally gave a little pout, and with a shrug at Hugh, moved till she hovered behind Bobby and tried to resume her backseat reading of the journal. Hugh had no choice but to follow her example and read as much of the pages as he could as they flipped by. Bobby silently read them a tad faster than Hugh could and he found himself sighing right along with Sally, unsatisfied with what little snippets he could read before Bobby turned the page.

"Try January, 1956." Everyone in the room turned toward the Sparrow, who had spoken in a voice that had a strange note to it that they were unfamiliar with. During the time that they had become engrossed with the journal, Icarus had taken a seat in one of the folding chairs. The old chair groaned under the Sparrow as he lay his bare bird feet atop the table and leaned back. Icarus used his wings as extra support to keep the chair upright and in a reclined position. It wasn't the relaxed pose of the Sparrow that was strange, but his facial expression. His grey beak was featuring a smile that was at the same time both happy and sad.

Wasting no time, Bobby flipped through the journal, searching for the date Icarus had specified. It was toward the middle of the thick journal, which held far more pages than Hugh would have guessed from simply looking at it.

"What does it say?" asked Sally as she struggled to read the words on the page. Hugh himself was having even more trouble reading this particular passage. The words were horribly messy and in several sentences more than one word was illegible due to letters piling atop each other in a jumbled mess. It was clear these entries were either written in a hurry or that the elder Crick had been fighting the constraints of the page to get all his thoughts down.

"Don't keep us in the dark," begged Hugh. "You're the Doc's son. You can read that mess to us, right?" Bobby didn't reply, for even he was struggling to make sense of the chicken scratch before him. It was a marvel that Icarus, one unfamiliar with Dr. Crick's penmanship, had such an easy time reading through the pages as if they were fresh off a typewriter.

"Alright, I'll try," agreed Bobby. "Although I may have to summarize a tad. I can barely read this. Dad never had the best handwriting, but this is terrible even by his standards."

As Bobby cleared his throat, Hugh caught a motion out of the corner of his eye and turned to see Icarus pulling the bag of fish over to his chair and beginning to eat more of the catch. Icarus caught Hugh staring and gave a shrug, muttering something about not wasting good food. Hugh hastily turned back to Bobby and tried to forget the sounds of the slippery fish going down the bird's throat behind him.

"*January 4, 1956,*" Bobby read. He paused a moment to read the next line on the page to himself before reading it out loud. "*It's the dawn of a new year, and I have exciting news! I've been asked by Dr. Charles Mason to use my understanding of biology and all my accumulated skill to work on a special top secret project for the betterment of the city. I got the call just this morning, right after having an early breakfast with Robert. It's really a pity we can't meet up more often, but he has his own medical duties to preform, as do I. I wish I could tell him about this amazing opportunity, but Charles insisted on the phone that I keep this a secret from everybody, lest someone steals his ideas. Personally I think he's a tad paranoid, but I suppose a man as successful as him must have a few enemies in the shadows that wouldn't mind knocking him out of the limelight."*

"January 10, 1956, I had my first meeting with Charles and was given my task on his project. I'm to create an artificial brain, of all things! He wants it for his latest project, a flying robot that is to replace our city's officers! If I hadn't seen his face, I would never have thought he was serious! No wonder he wanted to talk about this in person instead of over the phone. I'm not sure if I can provide what he wants, but he has given me a team of equally experienced individuals and a couple of computer experts to help me develop the brain. When I asked him why a simple computer wouldn't do for his project, he revealed that the robots were too complex for even the most advanced of his computers to control. Nothing less than a biological brain would do. Those were his words, exactly! Well, the man may have seen one too many science-fiction movies, but I can't help but admit that I relish the challenge!"

"March 12, 1957, I decided to write in this journal again. Despite it having been over a year since I last wrote in this, I needed another notebook after filling out my research journal, so this will have to do. I would prefer keeping my work and personal notes separate, but Charles has proposed a limit on how many records we may keep on the project, and I've filled out most of the ones he has given me to use."

"Today we've done it! After many failed attempts, we finally have a product that should work with the robot's body and act like a real brain. I have decided to call it a bio-brain, though when I say it out loud to my colleagues, they let out a soft groan. I don't know why, I think it's rather catchy! I have already noted down all the technical and chemical notes of the bio-brain in my main research journal, so I won't bother repeating myself here. All I will say is that the lab-grown brain has a mix of two different DNA segments. This is to bestow upon it the ability to think like a human being (DNA set 1) so it can make rational decisions on its own without having to go through the lengthy period of time that most computers need to come to a decision. The other set (DNA set 2) is that of, of all things, a bird! Since I am running out of room on this page, I'll just say that the bird DNA enabled the bio-brain to be immune to vertigo and able to handle the flight controls of the robot far better than a humanistic brain on its own."

"Bio-Brain? Human and bird DNA?" asked Sally. "Are we sure Dr. Crick wrote this and not some crazy nut?"

"Sally, I already said that this is Dad's handwriting, and Hugh did find this among his things," grumbled Bobby. "However, I am finding this hard to swallow, too," he muttered, barely audible under his breath before turning the page and continuing from the previous page. It was clear that he still hoped to find something, anything, within the journal's pages that they could use against the Hawkers, like a fatal weakness in their design that only Dr. Crick knew about.

"Ran out of room anyway, damn it." This brought out a little chuckle, which died quickly before Bobby could resume reading. *"As I was saying, the bio-brain is a combination of human and bird DNA. The way the brain interacts with the body is through a special little computer built into the "stem" of the bio-brain. The computer interprets what the robot's mechanical body hears and sees, and then translates it into something the brain can understand, and thus respond to. Nothing like this has ever been made by mankind before, and I can't wait for the demonstration next week, when we first hook up one of our bio-brains with one of the prototype robots Charles's design team has been working on."*

"March, something, *1957. This is it, the moment that Charlie, I and the others have been working toward for so long. His robotics and my biological knowledge have reached a climax and we are about to turn on the first of our creations! Its eyes are lighting up, a good sign, now its arms are pushing against the table, this is it! It fell over, not unexpected, bugs left to be worked out. But it's clear that the overall design will work with just a few adjustments. Note to self, work on the connections between the bio-brain's artificial intelligence (A.I.) decisions and motor relays. Charlie is calling me, will write more after we test the robot's perception capabilities."*

"March, 20, 1957," Bobby read as he walked over to a chair next to the snacking Icarus. Sally and Hugh merely followed Bobby like young puppies trailing a dog treat thrown by their owner. *"It has been at least a week since the first prototype. I should have known something was amiss the day after we activated it, when the fungus appeared. I shouldn't have listened to Charlie when he said that it was just dust. Today, the prototype was bleeding. Not oil or lubricant, but real red blood. I tested it in my home office today while Robert was at the university so he wouldn't get suspicious. I must note that the blood seeped out where a bit of the robot had been removed to adjust its motor's sensitivities, under the left "armpit." The parts removed were also showing advanced stages of decay, with rust and more of that strange fungus. I have taken a sample from the pieces I removed in order to make the adjustments and, as of yet, haven't discovered what it is. Upon first observation of the fungus, it doesn't match anything in my pocket handbook or resemble any fungi that I am familiar with."*

"April 3, 1957, Charlie won't listen. He feels the robot is functioning normally, despite its constant failure to obey its programming. There's more of the blood

substance every time I try to access the bio-brain in the prototype's head. I know it is indeed blood now, after examining it in greater depth under a microscope. Where exactly this blood is coming from I have yet to determine. It can't possibly be waste created by the bio-brain, despite its organic structure." Bobby stopped reading for a moment to turn the page. The silence only lasted a second or two as the paper moved under his fingers, but it felt like an eternity to Hugh's hungry ears and ravenous curiosity. *"I tried to show Charlie the blood, but he refuses to accept it as anything other than lubricants. Tomorrow I shall try to solve this mystery myself. If our research has produced a new fungus that is capable of interacting with metal at an accelerated rate, it is prudent that the robot be quarantined where the fungus can be examined."*

"April 4, 1957, I can't believe it. I killed it. Not turned off, but honestly killed it! I was only going to turn the machine off and disconnect the bio-brain, but when I had begun to remove the screws from the support frame, blood, more than I ever saw before in relation to the little robots, gushed out of the holes. I heard the prototype scream, despite being powered down. It was truly frightening but I had to keep going. The fungus was thickest around the head. It's a brain. I can't hold back any longer. Somehow the biological brain I created from my own research and lab-grown organic grey matter had metamorphosed into an actual brain. Given, it's also like no brain I have ever seen before. I am a medical doctor, and after spending time as a mortician before the war, I became very familiar with human brains, so as I held this impossible organ before me, I could tell that it bore a striking similarity to what is in a human head, but there are several differences. I couldn't stop myself when I saw it, I had to cut it out and see if it was truly a brain inside and out or if my eyes were being deceived by a new colony of fungus. It was no ruse. What's more, the wires that had connected the bio-brain to the small computer appear to have also transformed, becoming as fine as fibers in a nervous system."

"This is some heavy stuff," marveled Sally as she took it all in. Hugh was spellbound, hanging on every word. He was shocked by how involved Dr. Crick had been in the creation of the Hawkers.

"Has the impossible happened? Did we actually manage to create life? What have we done?" Bobby again paused as he flipped the page, and read the next entry. *"April 5, 1957. Charlie is the most stubborn idiot in the science community I have ever known! I showed him the brain from the "dead" machine and he insisted that I was trying to trick him. I even brought with me the prototype and showed him the other biological parts that had developed, especially the blood around the brain's cradle, but he simply accused me of sabotaging the project. True, the robot is now damaged beyond all repair, but we still have our notes. Charlie is actually demanding that I help him build another robot, same as the prototype! At least he is willing to admit that the bio-brain failed to do what it was designed to, if only because it was mostly my creation,*

not his. I must now investigate my original design and see what exactly made it alter bits of the robot's metal body into living tissue."

"May 17, 1957. I have spent weeks going over my diagrams. Everything seems to be in order with the artificial brain. On its own it is an advanced computing machine able to adapt to changing circumstances. Yet when it's equipped with a robotic body, using the material I developed from a very lengthy process that I have detailed in my research journals, essentially it becomes similar to human brain matter and, when combined with lab grown brain cells, able to store vast qualities of knowledge... and I started to go off topic again. The point here is when placed in a robotic body, the material reacts with the steel, copper, and titanium components and starts a chain reaction that spawns the fungus. This fungus is able to consume parts of the metal and plastic elements of the structure and, as a part of its life cycle, leave behind flesh and other organic elements, effectively making a puppet into a real boy."

"When building the bio-brain I had taken into account the decay of my organic computer. Since it uses flesh and not metal, it would degrade over time, so I used my extensive knowledge of healing methods to create a special chemical that would not only preserve, but encourage the bio-brain to grow and develop like a real brain, something a normal computer simply cannot do. I have a theory that the rapid healing capability I added to the bio-brain, to prevent it from rotting inside the robot's cranium, may have something to do with the fungus, possibly causing the bio-brain not only to maintain itself, but to use the DNA map to create an organic body to house it, instead of the metal one that was built for it. Although I cannot dismiss the possibility, I still find this hard to believe, as the process of replacing metal with flesh would seem to require a great deal more energy than I believe the robot's body is capable of producing."

"I have tried to see if I could get similar reactions from transplanting patches of the fungus to other surfaces. I have tried to get it to react to stone, paper, and the same materials the robots are made of in individual tests. All of them failed, and I do not know why. It may be the particular combination of metals in the wires that the bio-brain is connected to. To test this, I preformed all the experiments again, this time with a sample, and then with a spare bio-brain, to see if having the brain with the fungus would spark a reaction. This time, I got a slight reaction from the fungus, but nothing too spectacular. It only spread an inch down the length of the test objects, and only left rust in its wake. These results just bred more confusion, as the materials used in the construction of the robot shouldn't in any way affect the workings of the bio-brain. Regardless, I need to find out if there is a way to isolate the fungus or prevent the reaction before it renders the body of the robot a mess of useless flesh."

"Sorry, I need to stop," gasped Bobby as he wiped away the sweat from his brow. "I have to catch my breath for a moment." Before Hugh could beg Bobby to hurry up and read more, a silver claw reached over his shoulder and snatched the journal away as easily as it had left Hugh's hands. Hugh turned and looked back at Icarus, who had crept up behind the trio as silently as a ghost. The bird had a fishy aroma that flowed about him like perfume. Hugh couldn't fathom where all the fish had gone as the Sparrow didn't seem to have gained even a single pound. Icarus simply smiled at the gathered humans and cleared his throat.

"Ahem, allow me to skip to the important part," spoke Icarus as he flicked through the pages toward the end of the leather journal. From where Icarus held the journal as he flipped through the pages, Hugh could see each one go by under the Sparrow's sharp, black-nailed claws. Suddenly the pages stopped and the Sparrow brought the book up to his eyes again and read the page he had singled out.

"June 20, 1957. I give up. I have tried every rig, every configuration, and still I can't find any way to stop the bio-brain's conversion of the robotic body. Since I started, every robot that I agreed to supply the bio-brain for has changed from a metal construct to a biological life form. Charlie makes up all kinds of excuses for the evidence I have brought since I first made the discovery of the transformation of the machine to flesh. He ignores every piece of evidence, saying that I am playing a prank, trying to ruin his reputation, even going as far as to write it off as a wet cloth. I know his strong suit isn't human biology but even he can't be so blind that he can't tell brain matter from a towel! I have twelve samples in my lab of the transformed tissue, and he has seen them all and hasn't batted an eye."

"Charlie has told me that he has already started manufacturing a set of twelve improved models on the prototype. He has told me that he plans to make a small army of these things for the city's protection. There's something to be said for the number of lives that will be taken out of harm's way by swapping human officers with robots, but I worry about the ethics. I just hope I can at least get the project stopped. I have already talked to my colleague, Dr. Manderson, about what has been happening, and he is definitely on my side in this debate. Tomorrow I'll see if, together, we can get this project shut down once and for all."

"Looks like Mad Mike wasn't lying when he said he was in on the project," said Hugh as Icarus took a brief break from reading the text to turn the page. Time seemed to slow down every time the reading of the journal was interrupted by as little as the page being turned and Hugh could barely contain himself.

"June 30, 1957. This is getting out of control. Yesterday Charlie had Mike committed! I just know if I take any action against this project, I may end up sharing a cell with Mike, or worse! To further complicate matters, Charlie has unceremoniously taken me off the project and forbidden me from coming near his private laboratories in Tesla and the plant in Vulcan. After getting the news I promptly sent my research material away to a safe place and burned my notes relating to this project. All that I have left is this journal and the bio-brain's

diagram that I stored on the following page. Although I have no reason to keep anything from the project, I feel I must hold on to this one journal, if nothing more than to be a document explaining the facts behind the failings of the robots. In all of my tests, none of the machines were able to function after the fungus completed its life cycle. However, the last one of the machines I was involved with managed to live for a recorded period of time of fifteen minutes before it died without its metal components. It may be nothing, but there is a chance that given time and better constructs to build upon, the fungus, which I have still not found an adequate name for, may bring the machine to real life, not just in body but in mind, which I feel will raise many ethical and moral questions in the times to come."

Icarus stopped reading and sat the book down on the table without a word. For a moment there was nothing but silence, the kind brought on when all sounds have ceased except for the breath of the living and the creak of metal of the moving city. No one spoke for some time, until Bobby rose up and shattered the empty air with a single question.

"So… they are all going to end up like you then?" he asked.

Icarus merely nodded his head before separating from the pack and returning to his chair by the table. "There is no cure for the corruption, no treatment, only its final result. The uncorrupted will become corrupted and the Hawkers will metamorphose into Sparrows and be part of my people in body and mind."

"Somehow I don't think that's what they want to hear," Sally said as she nervously turned her head toward the thick door, still sealed shut.

"What are they going to do?" asked Hugh as he grabbed the journal and held it up as a professional poker player would flaunt a winning hand. "They can't stop it, and as far as I can tell the only way to keep their *perfect* race intact is to keep building new ones and killing the ones that start to turn. I bet they eventually run out of materials to build from, or simply give up."

"I'm not so sure," said Bobby, "those things are a menace, and though I still don't trust bird-boy here," he said as he stuck a thumb out at Icarus, who had closed its eyes and seemed to have fallen asleep while leaning back in the chair as before, "I sure as hell don't see us coming to peaceful terms with the Hawkers."

"I didn't say that we would have to make nice with them, just wait them out," defended Hugh as he tried to explain his logic further. However Bobby would not give in.

"Those things are insane, Hugh! You saw them with your own eyes. They killed people by the hundreds in the streets! How are you not affected by that?" demanded Bobby.

"It did affect me!" retorted Hugh. "People have died keeping those things from killing me – people at the Valkyrie Park cable car station, the Chief of Police, and some woman that I didn't even know, all got in the Hawker's way time and time again, allowing me to escape, often along with Sally. Don't you think I feel guilty about every single one of their deaths?"

"Yet you're chummy with the enemy," snorted Bobby as he removed his glasses and pinched the space above the bridge of his nose.

"For the last time, he is not like them, not any more. And he saved my life!" Hugh said as his tone began to grow louder with frustration.

"For crying out loud, stop saying he saved you!" shouted Bobby as his voice also rose in pitch. "You are becoming a broken record, Hugh! Look, the way I see it, once a Hawker, always a Hawker. And the only good kind of Hawker is a dead one."

"What is your problem, Bobby?" Hugh demanded, beginning to lose his patience.

"I am just saying," sighed Bobby, "what do we really know about this bird? Why did he save you? How can we be sure that he is even on our side? For all we know, he is a spy for the Hawkers, helping them root out what human leftovers are still in the city! After all, I have yet to see him use that fancy gun of his to shoot any Hawkers."

"Hey now, don't you start, Bob," said Hugh as he gave his friend a glare of death. "The last thing we need is for a Nazi to appear in the group."

"Oh, that's mature of you."

"Hey, it's the only word that came to my mind!"

"Maybe I should get you a dictionary, jackass."

"What'd you call me?"

Suddenly there was a loud whistle. Both Hugh and Bobby stopped their bickering and turned to Icarus, whose eyes were now open with a bemused smile on his beak. He shook his head no and shrugged his shoulders before nodding his head toward Sally. She held in her hand a gleaming bronze whistle that she was only just maneuvering away from her lips, the lipstick dulling the perfect shine of the small instrument. With a dainty little cough, she cleared her throat and fixed them all with a determined gaze. Hugh knew that look all too well, yet still could feel those eyes gaze deep into his soul and paralyze him, as if he was facing down a Hawker and not his girlfriend.

"If you two are done being thick-headed thugs, I suggest we form a plan."

"Huh?" asked Hugh and Bobby in harmony that couldn't have been in better sync even if they had practiced it for that moment.

"Look," she said as she brought out her notebook and flattened it upon the table. "I don't know about all of you, but I don't think we want

Nimbus to go where the Hawkers are taking it. I think we now know what they wanted the journal for, but not why they are moving the city. We need to get out of this little room and investigate matters so we can see where we stand."

"Okay," agreed Hugh. "Where should we start, Sal?"

"I doubt going to Dr. Mason's lab or visiting his home will be much use," said Bobby. "Both places are probably guarded by the worst of those things and armed to the teeth. And if there is a control room moving this district, I doubt that we three musketeers can take it on our own, with only three guns between us."

"Actually, we only have two. I lost mine topside after the Hawkers went wild," Hugh reluctantly admitted.

"Well, there you go. The odds just keep getting worse and worse, don't they?" sighed Bobby as he sat down heavily in a chair by the table. "I don't think I saw any signs of weapon storage on the map for this level before the map fizzled out, so what we have for guns and ammo is all there is, unless we feel like sneaking upstairs and hope there aren't any Hawkers on patrol."

"On the contrary," Sally smirked as she flipped back a page in her notebook to where she had jotted down one of the maps while they were on display. Her well-manicured index finger pointed at the paper, selecting a room labeled with the letter W. "While you guys were reading the status screen, I was looking at the map and saw that it listed weapon storage rooms on every floor, not just on the fifth level, assuming that's what the 'W' stands for. Given how there were 'Ws' everywhere on the fifth level map, I think it's a safe bet that it does. Look here," she said as she pointed at her copy of the sixth level map, " there's one pretty close by, just a few turns down the hall from our front door."

Bobby blushed a tad, his face turning red with embarrassment for not paying more attention to the maps himself. Even Hugh felt color touch his cheek as Sally gave off a rather aggravating smirk of her full lips. Hugh cleared his throat before speaking up. "Even if we get fully armed, Sal, I doubt the four of us would get very far. Maybe we should just lay low and wait for the police to act?"

"Oh, wake up, Hugh!" pouted Sally. "If the police were going to act, don't you think they would have by now?"

"Sally's right, we are on our own," agreed Bobby as he reached for her notebook and began to scrutinize her notes, memorizing the maps she had copied down. "After all, you told us how the Hawkers fended off the Air Force. If they can take out aircraft designed for war, what chance does our humble police force, being armed with simple handguns and clubs, have against these things?"

"Well, what chance do *we* have?" demanded Hugh as his voice rose for the first time during this conversation. "We are just three people and a Sparrow."

"When you put it that way, we might as well dig our graves and wait," Sally said with a steely voice.

"I think we should hear the rest of her plan," said Icarus, looking intently at the woman across from him.

"Thank you, Icky," said Sally as she flashed a smile, the one she usually reserved for Hugh, at the Sparrow. Hugh felt a little hurt that she would give Icarus that special little flick of her lips, but he knew now wasn't the time to harp on such things. "As I was saying, I think we should research these Hawker robots, see what makes them tick while they are metal."

"We already know what makes them tick," interrupted Bobby. "It's their bio-brain."

"Yes, but that's only their mind. We don't know what fuel they run on, as in what powers them. We also don't know if they have any chinks in their armor. Icarus," Sally said as she turned to the Sparrow, "do you remember any other weaknesses the Hawkers may have from when you were one of them?"

The bird shook his head. "The only weakness I am aware of is their eyes, due to the close proximity to their bio-brain. Damage the brain and you kill the Hawker."

Hugh thought back to when he had killed the Hawker that was chasing Sally and himself through Valkyrie Park. He realized he had gotten far luckier with that shot than he had realized. However, he couldn't keep himself from speaking up, "Their eyes aren't exactly easy to hit when they are charging, or flying out of range. Is there anything easier we can aim at?"

Icarus shook his head in a negative manner, before saying that he didn't know of any others.

"Right," said Sally, taking command of the conversation again. "We need to learn all we can about these Hawkers and see if there is a reason they are moving the city."

"I thought it was just to get away from the Air Force?" suggested Bobby as he looked up from her notebook.

"There are other air bases, Bobby," said Sally as she slid the notebook over for Hugh to examine. "We need to know what they are really planning. Now in that journal of Hugh's-"

"You mean my Dad's journal?" interrupted Bobby.

"Yes," sighed Sally as she gave a little pout at the interruption. "As I was saying, in that book Dr. Crick wrote about another laboratory besides the one in Tesla – the one in Vulcan. I think we should start there. Maybe we'll get some answers there."

"At least it's a plan, and we could always stand to know more about these things," agreed Bobby as he stood up from his chair. "Either way, we need to get out of this little room."

"We should also try to gather up some food and drink while we are out," Sally continued as she stood up.

"I agree. Those sardines and crackers won't keep us going for long, and I doubt uncooked fish will be very healthy for us humans," agreed Bobby as he picked up his shotgun.

"So to sum things up," said Hugh as he reached for Sally's notebook to look at the map once more, "we are going out of this safe room to try to find out more about the machines trying to kill us, while also looking for supplies?"

"That's about it, Hughie."

"Well," he sighed as he stood up with the others, shouldering his bag. "In that case we better find ourselves some more firepower. Lead the way, Sally."

15

Hugh was glad to finally leave the small meeting room. Now that he knew there were probably Hawkers just above his head, it made the room much less comfortable. Hugh had insisted on taking the journal with them, if nothing else because he had grown accustomed to having it with him and felt naked without it in his satchel. Before leaving, Hugh brought out his camera and took a few snaps of the mysterious machines at the back of the room.

The hallway, now well-lit, revealed itself to be rusting slightly around the seams, and longer than Hugh had remembered. Silently they moved out, heading down the hall and, upon Sally's map's instruction, turning left at the first junction and following it past a wall with a glass window revealing a room inside. They didn't stop here, but continued onward, only giving the window the briefest of glances. To Hugh the room seemed empty and unimportant and they continued to the next intersection, at which they stopped. Cautiously, Icarus leaned out into the crossroads and checked for any Hawker movement, of which there was none. He waved for the others to move and they made a right down a side hallway that was extremely narrow with thick round pipes and wires lining the walls on either side. They had to walk in single file in order to squeeze through it and Icarus had to walk sideways in order to fit down the narrow hallway.

After what felt like hours but was only minutes, they reached the other end of the hallway and Sally checked her map.

"Alright, gang," she whispered just loud enough for all gathered to hear. "From here it's just a right and a left and it's the first door on the left."

"This has been too easy," Hugh whispered as he scanned both ends of the hall and back the way they came. "There hasn't been so much as the sound of footsteps or a single creak. Where are the Hawkers?"

"Don't jinx us, Hugh," grunted Bobby as he uneasily shouldered his shotgun.

"Perhaps they deemed this level of the district unimportant," Icarus mused as he looked back toward the very tight hallway. "Either way, they are likely to still be looking for us, so we shouldn't let our guard down."

"You don't have to tell me twice," muttered Hugh to himself as he tightened his grip on the strap of his leather bag. He and Sally made up the center of the group due to their lack of weapons, while Icarus led with his rifle and Bobby guarded their rear with his shot gun. It was still not clear if the weapon was working again, but just having it at their backs made Hugh feel much better. If things came right down to it, they could always use it like a club, though the chances of that being effective would be extremely low. They walked on in silence, following Sally's directions. Not once did they see a single Hawker, making the tension they felt over being jumped at any time rise.

By the time they reached the door, their stress could have exploded at the smallest of things. It was then Hugh had a horrible thought – what if the door was locked? After all, the halls and rooms they had thus far visited clearly weren't for civilians to browse. He wasn't sure who was meant to be down in the secret bowels of Nimbus – certainly not the Hawkers, but regardless, there were bound to be areas locked to keep them safe from prying eyes. Surely the weapons lockers would be one such location with doors that couldn't be opened with a simple push or turn of the handle.

These fears were for naught, as Icarus easily opened the door and stepped inside. Another fear that bubbled up from deep inside Hugh was that all the weapons would be gone, taken by the Hawkers or possibly never put in the room to begin with. But these fears, too, were shattered as Hugh journeyed beyond the door following the tail feathers of the Sparrow. Sally and Bobby entered close on his heels.

Inside was a room that was longer than it was wide, stretching out left to right with rows of lockers and shelves. As they moved inside, they saw every locker was labeled, stating the type of weapon held inside, and its required ammunition and magazine capacity. Strangely, none of the lockers were locked, and a few of the cabinets were even open. Despite being open, nothing seemed to be missing. Judging from the layer of dust everywhere in the small, narrow room, it was clear that no one had been inside for a very long time.

The sounds of the others opening and closing the steel doors of the lockers were muted to Hugh as he walked to the other end of the room, toward the only wall free of weapon lockers. He turned and leaned against the riveted surface and looked back down the length of the room and simply watched the others wander about, Bobby testing shotgun ammunition from several of the lockers in his own weapon, seeing if the shells fit his particular make. Sally was browsing the handgun section, seeing which ones would fit in her purse, while Icarus was taking a fancy to the rifles.

Finally Hugh spoke. "Is this really happening?" he asked the air in a voice that could barely be heard. Just last week he was having dinner with Sally, and now she was testing the weight of a 45 caliber gun. No one heard him and he continued to think over the past events. What awoke him from his stupor was Bobby making a discovery.

"Hey, look over here!"

Hugh shook himself free of his mental bindings and headed toward his friend, who was near a locker beside the door they had entered through. The locker was open and seemed to hold hand guns that looked like they belonged in old western movies. Bobby pointed into the locker where the metal back was warped, pulling away from the panel next to it, revealing a small crack. Through the thin gap, a few pipes and wires could be seen, and a similar, smaller breach lay just beyond that, looking out into the hallway outside the weapons room.

"Take a look," said Bobby, stepping back from the locker, letting Hugh step up and take a look. "Just don't make a sound." Hugh, upon looking through the hole and out into the hall, saw two Hawkers, walking in single file. He briefly questioned why he couldn't hear the Hawkers coming, but he reasoned it was due to how thick the walls were. It was only through this little hole that he could hear them moving, their metal feet ringing dully against the floor tiles with each step. They were moving down a long hallway that was almost perfectly lined up with the hole, making it seem like they were heading right for Hugh. Their heads swiveled back and forth, searching for something. Hugh didn't need to guess at what the robots were seeking.

Wordlessly, he stayed at the hole, watching the Hawkers move along the hallway. Thankfully, the Hawkers did not notice the small hole and continued on their march, rounding a corner to the left. The machines soon moved beyond the breach's range of sight. Hugh backed away from the hole to look at the others. He guessed that Bobby had whispered to them about the Hawker patrol, as none of them had made a single sound the entire time Hugh was at the wall. They were still silent as they held their breath for a few minutes before deciding it was safe to speak again.

"That was close," said Bobby.

"Yeah," said Hugh, nodding in agreement. "If we had been slower in getting here, those tin-heads would have caught us."

"Guess that means we got lucky," said Sally, who had stepped up behind them, finally being able to move after the danger had passed. Hugh turned to see she was now sporting a small revolver which was almost like a toy in her hands. However Hugh didn't doubt it would be bullets, and not water, that would be expelled from the tiny gun's barrel if Sally decided to pull the trigger.

"More than you know," Bobby said as he pulled out something that resembled a peacemaker from a western movie. "I'm surprised we got this far to begin with."

"Are you *sure* you know how to use that thing?" Hugh asked as he watched Bobby reach up and gather magnum shells. "Their weakness, as far as we know, is their eyes, not their whole entire face, and I don't think you'll get a second chance if you miss."

Bobby chuckled as he filled his pockets with boxes of shells. "I'd rather make a lasting impression instead of having a precision shot that may miss."

Hugh shrugged and decided Bobby's logic did make some sense, though not a lot of it due to what had happened to the Chief with a similar strategy. But he didn't feel like arguing with Bobby anymore. He wandered away from Bobby and Sally and began to loot the lockers himself. He was not familiar with guns, as his time with Bobby's loaned handgun had proven, so he found himself unsure as to what he should be looking for to defend himself. He instantly dismissed the handheld blunt and sharp weapons. Hugh highly doubted that any of the Hawkers would be so kind to let him bean them on the head or stab them in the eye in a fight. It was even more ludicrous that he would be able to sneak up behind these things and stab them in the back, assuming that even accomplished anything with their thick metal bodies.

Before Hugh went off to seek his own weapons, he looked down at the arm in the sling. He tried moving it, and found that the waves of pain were gone. Remembering what Bobby had said about the pills, and how they were only a temporary relief from the pain, Hugh decided that if he had any chance to survive what was to come he would need both of his arms free. So, without further ado, he undid the cloth sling with his free hand and let his injured arm fall free. Besides, he might need both hands to use a firearm, even if it was a small handgun. He just didn't feel experienced enough to trust his aim when firing one-handed.

Hugh didn't have enough confidence in his ability to handle a long-range rifle, or trust himself not to blow his own foot off with a shotgun. He eventually settled on a handgun that was very similar to Sally's, only one size up, that came with a pre-attached silencer under the logic that, if he missed, he might have another chance if he caught the robots unawares. He also secured from another locker a simple carbine, a happy marriage of a machine gun and rifle that felt comfortable in his hands. As he started piling up ammunition for the rifle in his bag, he heard Sally let out a surprised squeal from behind him. He quickly turned, fearing she was in danger, only to see that she was looking at a strange cupboard that was slowly opening before her. The doors opened like a garage door, only one half rose into the ceiling while the other sank steadily into the floor. Hugh was only vaguely aware that this cupboard was the very same wall that he had been leaning against moments ago. Inside was a closet filled with thick, stiff cargo vests, with helmets and empty ammunition belts hanging from hooks on the back wall.

Both Bobby and Icarus hurried over to the new discovery with Hugh following close behind. Icarus went to work instantly and mechanically, for a moment resembling the very machine he used to be with his precision movements, sorting through the equipment in the hidden locker and pulling out one of the many vests.

Before Bobby could ask what Icarus was doing, he found his hands suddenly occupied by the vest that the birdman had selected. "What am I supposed to do with this?" he demanded as the Sparrow returned to the locker and started the process all over again, sifting through the vests.

"I think he wants you to wear it, Bob," Hugh said as he found a similar vest handed off to him by Icarus.

"Why?" Bobby asked as he scrolled his eyes over the old thick vest. "Is it bullet proof or something?"

"Well, if they aren't, they should at least give us more pouches to carry stuff at the very least," reasoned Hugh as he peeked into a couple of the pockets on the vest, every single one empty, but with plenty of room for small supplies. All the while Sally was observing Icarus digging through the locker, shoving aside the remaining fabric on the hooks and reached deeper in the closet, his hand seeking something they couldn't see.

"Ah," said Icarus with a satisfied sigh as he pulled out an odd breastplate that was a bit misshapen in the front. Silently Icarus handed off the strange thick piece of clothing to Sally to wear. It took a few minutes for Hugh's mind to comprehend that it was body armor designed for the female sex, something that he wasn't accustomed to. Hugh watched as Sally slowly and carefully slipped the armor over her head so as not to bump her face as it sank past her chin and came to rest comfortably atop her shoulders. Following her lead, Hugh and Bobby both pushed their arms through the holes in the vests and buckled them in the front.

Once the humans were all suited up, Icarus wordlessly reached back into the locker and pulled out two backpacks, one large and one of medium size. The packs were different colors, one a mosaic of green and brown spots, and the other, while sharing a similar pattern, was instead covered in grey and white dots.

"Here, carry this," said Icarus as he gave the smaller grey backpack to Bobby while taking the larger one for his own. Wordlessly, Bobby took the satchel and slid one arm through the loop, finding it very light due to it being empty, except for little bits of lint.

Upon Icarus's direction, the three humans moved back toward the lockers that held their selected weapons' ammunition to fill up two-thirds of their vest pockets with bullets. As they did so, Icarus reached once more into the locker and drew out an ammunition belt that he clipped shut around his waist, before he too gathered up his selected weapon's ammunition.

Once they had finished raiding the weapon locker room, they gathered at the door and waited on Icarus to lead them out of the room. They had taken a brief moment to review Sally's maps to devise a route through the level to the nearest and, they hoped, safest means of getting back up to the sewer level, far away from their original point of entry in case there were any Hawkers on guard around the hatch. The path through the winding hallways was just as stressful as the trip to the weapons locker, the tension already high the moment they stepped out into the hall. All the halls began to look alike, with only the number of doors and turns they passed proving that they were making progress out of the underground maze.

As they neared the place where the stairs were marked on their map, they reached an elevator. It soon became clear to the group, upon pressing the buttons by the door, and from the lack of movement inside the shaft, that the lift was inoperative.

"Why aren't they working?" asked Sally as she pressed the call button for the elevator. "The lights are clearly on, so reason states that the elevators should be running, too."

"You've got a point there," said Hugh as he stepped right up to the metal doors and tried to force them open with his hands. "Maybe it's already on this floor and the doors are just stuck?"

"Need a hand?" asked Bobby as he stepped up to the door and, without an answer from Hugh, began to pull on the same door. Alas, their combined strength wasn't enough and the elevator's doors remained firmly shut. Finally, Icarus stepped up to the reluctant door and, with his added inhuman muscles, they were able to pull the metal door open.

The elevator was nowhere to be seen. There was merely the tall, dark shaft, stretching endlessly in vertical directions, with the only light being what leaked out from the hall. Sally pulled her flashlight from her purse and flashed it around, the beam barely disturbing the shadows. The only thing revealed by her light were the thick metal cords that raised and lowered the elevator.

"Icarus," started Hugh, turning to the Sparrow, "Do you think you can fly up that shaft? Maybe find a way to get the elevator working?"

Icarus stepped forward and looked into the darkness. After glancing around a bit, and looking at his own wings, the Sparrow shook his head and turned away from the open edifice. "Alas, I fear there is not enough space for me to fly properly."

"Are you sure?" asked Hugh, looking from the shaft to Icarus's wings. "I think you have more than enough room to spread those wings. I mean, I've seen you fly through places just as narrow."

"No, you didn't," said the Sparrow as he folded in his wings. "When we escaped the trash district, I was hovering, not flying. I didn't have enough room to gain altitude."

"What do you mean?" asked Hugh.

"I am guessing," piped up Bobby as he adjusted his glasses, "that what the bird means is that he needs to move forward in order to rise, like a normal bird."

"Do you think you can climb the cables?" suggested Sally as her flashlight followed the cords up.

"I don't think that's going to work either," said Icarus with a frown. "They are probably covered in grease. And even if they weren't, I don't know if I can get the doors open from the inside of the shaft while hanging from the cable."

"Guess that means we are stuck with taking the stairs?" Sally sighed, as she absently rubbed at where her new armor lay over her shoulders.

"I'm afraid so," said Icarus, giving the empty shaft one last look. "We'd best be moving," he said as he looked uneasily back the way they came. "I have not heard any movement down here since we arrived. I don't like it. I don't like it at all." Icarus was not alone in these thoughts, for the others were also beginning to get a tad jumpy, looking accusingly at the few shadows and the open doorways around the empty elevator shaft. Without another word, Sally led the group onward with the aid of her map, Icarus and Hugh close on her heels, and Bobby bringing up the rear.

Not once during their whole journey, from the weapons locker to the elevators, or upon leaving the elevators, did they see a single robot, or even any movement other than their shadows and the swaying of loose wires as the city continued to move. Soon they arrived at their destination, the door before the stairs leading up into the sewer system. The door was in poor shape, slightly bent in the frame and discolored by rust. The mere sound of the rusty door opening under Icarus's hand made the humans wince. Their nerves were on the verge of snapping like overstretched rubber bands. And snap they did, when they looked beyond the door to see a body on the other side.

Bobby, without any warning, fired his shotgun at the mass, the weapon sending off a loud retort. Hugh felt his own trigger finger twitch on his own weapon, though he had a bit more restraint, while Sally gasped and Icarus simply raised the barrel of his rifle at the mass's head and shot a quick irritated look at Bobby. Two things came of the shot. The first was that it was clear that Bobby's weapon was working properly again, which was good because he refused to replace it with any of the other weapons in the locker room. Bobby's reasoning at the time, although flawed, had been that he felt more comfortable with his own weapon than any of the ones that were stored in the lockers.

The second thing that came from the shot was the sudden silence right afterward. Nobody moved, and the air was only disturbed by their adrenaline-fueled breaths. Icarus was the first to move, silently toward the lump outside the door, and with one hand he cautiously reached out to the mass. He gripped its shoulder and turned it around, so the light spilling into the dark stairwell could light up the mass more clearly.

It was a twisted and mangled thing, made no better by the hole punched in its head by buckshot. Hugh couldn't make sense of what it was at first, but then he recognized what was left of the metal body of a Hawker. The body, for what else could one call it, looked like someone had made a patchwork monster of metal and flesh. Its head, now completely destroyed, showed bone fragments amongst the rusty metal. Old blood stained the twisted flesh around the wounds, suggesting this thing had been dead for a long time. There were plenty of other gaping holes in the robot, showing deteriorating organs and a mass of wires and machinery inside the machine. The smell of old death was strong around the unnatural corpse.

Sally gasped and brought her hands to her lips in shock at the sight, almost banging her nose with the gun still held tightly in her hand. Bobby swore as his gun's barrel shifted to the floor. Hugh, however, wasn't as shocked as the other two by the macabre remains, for he had already seen a couple of Sparrows in mid-transformation from machine to blood and bone, though seeing the rotting organic parts of this creature was still enough to make him queasy.

They stood in silence for a few minutes until Icarus, unperturbed by the gruesome discovery, gave the all clear and beckoned them into the stairwell. At first nobody moved, but after a bit of encouragement from the birdman, the humans cautiously stepped inside, giving the body a wide berth while their eyes digested the remains that they could not ignore.

Together as one, they climbed up the long stairs, passing several more abandoned rotting bodies of Hawkers. Several were far more disturbing than the first one they encountered back on the sixth level. Many of the bodies had been stripped down to only their organic bits, leaving twisted bodies with limbs missing. Some were just piles of incomplete organs. The sight made Hugh feel sick, and looking at the reactions of his fellows, including the stone-faced Icarus, it was clear that everyone shared his feelings. Once they reached the hatch to the sewers, they found another surprise waiting for them. The entire metal door had been torn off its hinges and a small steady stream of foul water was pouring in from above. They had seen a couple of trickles while climbing the many steps but hadn't paid them much attention due to all the bodies.

"I don't like the looks of all of this at all," whispered Hugh as he looked up at the breach in the ceiling.

"The sooner we get to Vulcan the better," Bobby said as Icarus continued the march and ascended the slick metal rungs. "This place just isn't right."

There was no argument. Once everyone was again in the sewers, the smell of foul polluted water did not seem nearly as bad after the grisly sights on the stairway. However, they didn't get very far in their travels as they soon came upon a massive pile of rubble under an equally large fissure in the ceiling. The breach in the roof stretched for several yards and, through it, shone the bright light of day. Peaking over the rim of the gap were the tips of smoking buildings and bent street lights. Icarus stopped and tilted his head to the side. To Hugh it looked like the Sparrow was going over a mental map, checking for alternative routes.

"Dead-end," said Bobby in a humorless voice.

"Maybe we can find another way around?" suggested Sally before Icarus righted his head and shook it in a negative manner.

"All other ways to Tesla's sewage connection pipe are either blocked by gates too strong for me to break or are patrolled by Hawkers."

"Wait, why are we going to Tesla?" asked Hugh in confusion. "Isn't it quicker to go through Liberty Estates?"

"It is," admitted Icarus. "However, since it is the center of the city, I feel it is highly likely the most guarded district by the Hawkers. The safest route will take us through Tesla, Full Moon, and the Warehouse District. It is not without peril, but it is also our only viable option."

"Hey, maybe there are still some police at the warehouse!" said Sally as she tugged on Hugh's arm. "We should stop by and see if anyone survived and can help us get out of this jam."

"We could always use more men with guns," agreed Bobby.

"Well, we aren't going anywhere now, not with the tunnel out," Hugh pointed out as another explosion suddenly rang out from somewhere behind them. Spinning around on his heels, Hugh and the others watched as an American fighter jet flew by overhead with fierce flames eating away at one of its wings and thick smoke trailing it like the tail of a comet.

"At least the Air Force hasn't given up yet," said Sally as a loud boom signaled the demise of the plane somewhere in the distance. The sound of gunfire began to ring out in the distance as more airplanes flew by in the sky, much lower than if this battle was taking place anywhere else. Several planes had to bank sharply around the taller of the city's buildings.

"We can't stay here. Follow me," commanded Icarus as he turned back to the pile of rubble of pipes and bricks and began to ascend the mess up to the street above.

"Wait!" protested Bobby. "Shouldn't we stay below ground? It's by far safer down here!"

"I don't think we have much of a choice," said Hugh as he looked up into the breach above them, the light causing his eyes to sting after being out of the sun for so long. He watched as Icarus scaled the pile, picking the most stable patch that caused the least ruckus and shifting in the pile of debris. He climbed the pile so easily that it was as if he was a mountain goat. Hugh wondered how he and the others would be able to climb the pile with the same steady footing as Icarus, but he knew they had to try, so he held out his hand to Sally and let out his best smile to her. "Well, ma 'lady, shall we be going?"

As she let out a nervous chuckle, Bobby sighed and commented how this was neither the time nor place. With a nod from Sally, Hugh took the first step forward onto the pile, leading her by the hand behind him. It was tough going, as pipes and bricks moved under their feet and tiny dust clouds kicked up as they went, but for the most part things stayed put. Their ascent was nowhere as easy as Icarus's and Hugh had to catch either himself or Sally a couple of times when they almost fell over as their feet slipped between the scattered stones or tripped over loose broken pipes. Once they finally reached the lip of the embankment, Hugh turned back and looked down into the tunnels, seeing Bobby only just starting his climb up the embankment. His backpack bounced against his back with every step despite being mostly empty. He only had a few boxes of bullets that he had stashed inside it.

As they waited for the last of their party to join them on the street, Hugh couldn't help but notice how strong the wind was topside. All around them the wind whistled past the ruins and still standing buildings, whipping violently against flags, and causing loose papers and leaves from trees to fly past. Hugh turned to see where the wind was blowing from and realized with a shock it was actually the result of the city moving through the air. He had to hold back a smirk as, once Bobby made it onto the street, an old newspaper flew right into his friend's face, completely obscuring it. Sally, however, did let out a giggle as Bobby angrily tore the paper from his face and let the wind carry it off to parts unknown.

"This is ridiculous," grumbled Bobby as he reached for his glasses rag. Unfortunately, once he pulled it free of his pocket, it too blew out of his hands. Sighing in defeat, he simply used the hem at the bottom of his shirt to wipe the grime from his glasses before putting them back atop his nose and then taking a look at their surroundings. "Where the hell are we anyway? I don't recognize this part of the district."

"I believe we are on Saturn Street," said Icarus while still looking up into the sky, watching clouds beginning to roll in over the city and more planes fly by, with explosions trailing behind them. They could feel each volley of the antiaircraft guns firing, suggesting they were near one of the mortars, but they could not see any sign of the weapons. Hawkers were also flying above them like wasps chasing the fighter jets. However, the robots were too intent on chasing down the aircraft to really pay attention to what was happening on the ground below them.

"No," said Hugh as he looked around himself. "We're on Aristotle Street. I've been around here many times to buy groceries and film."

"Are you sure?" asked Icarus, bringing his eyes from the sky down to the human.

"Positive. See that burnt-out wreck over there?" he said as he pointed at a ruin on the other side of the street. "That's where I get my film and photo paper, or where I used to get it." Hugh took a moment to look at the ruined building. He hoped that everyone who had worked there was okay. "I guess I'll have to find a new place when this all blows over," he said as he turned away from the destruction. "It's a real shame. There's a grocery store really close by, so when I had to run out for supplies, I could get my food and film in one go." He paused for a moment, a thought entering his mind. He reached into his bag and brought out his camera, and proceeded to take pictures of the ruins around them.

"Is this really the time and place?" asked Bobby with a frown.

"I believe it is, Bobby," answered Hugh as he took a few pictures of the planes flying by overhead. He hoped that they weren't moving too fast for his camera, but to be safe he took several pictures. He also did his best to capture a few of the Hawkers flying by overhead. "The way I see it, someone has to document what is going on in Nimbus. If not just for the story's sake, then for the sake of all of those killed when the Hawkers went berserk."

"I agree," said Sally as she looked over at Icarus. "Don't forget to get a few good shots of Icky over here."

"I do not like being called 'Icky,'" said Icarus as he kept his eyes on the skies above, ready to react the second any of the Hawkers became interested in their little group.

"Alright, Sal," said Hugh as he turned towards Icarus and quickly snapped his photo. "That's all for now. I think we better get moving before we get noticed."

"Good idea," said Icarus. "Where is the grocer you spoke of?" he asked as another squadron flew by overhead.

Hugh turned around and pointed at the store just one block away from them, across the street. The sign for the grocery had been ripped almost entirely off the roof and was flapping about in the wind, threatening to fly off at any moment. Two windows were broken and there was a body hanging through the nearest door, its legs the only part visible.

"It looks to be in fairly good shape," said Icarus as he headed toward the small store, completely disregarding the dead man. "It is probably our best form of shelter for the time being, and we may find food supplies in there, assuming that others haven't raided the store already."

With Icarus leading the way, and taking the full brunt of the wind, the group moved as quickly as they dared to the grocery, all the while keeping an eye out for any potential Hawker threats. As they moved inside, Sally gave the dead body in the window a sad look.

"I don't think this is going to end cleanly," she mused as she gazed sadly at the limp legs. She turned and looked back at the destruction behind them. "It'll be a miracle if anything remains standing at this rate."

"Chin up," said Hugh as he turned to her and held her close. "We need to have faith."

"If you two love birds are done," interrupted Bobby, "I think we better get inside before one of those metal menaces notices us."

Without any further ado, they went all the way inside the small, dark grocery store. Minutes later, the sign finally gave way and flew off the top of the building, crashing down on the street, making everyone jump a little at the sound of it hitting the pavement. Once freed from the shop, the sign was sent bouncing away deeper into the city by the force of the wind.

In the past, Hugh had shopped here once every week, picking up the usual assortment of foods such as bread, milk, fruit, and so on. He knew the owner fairly well, a nice overweight man named Fred and his wife Miranda. He'd even taken Sally here a few times, encouraging her to pick out a few things for herself. He liked this small store for its reasonable prices, and for the homemade cake that Miranda made fresh every day. Today, however, the usually bustling store was deathly quiet, the owners nowhere to be seen and the warm and inviting atmosphere transformed into one of dreaded silence with only the sound of the lights hanging from the ceiling, swaying on their chains, and the wind whistling through the broken glass to welcome them inside.

The shelves were a mess. Several had been smashed to pieces as if an enraged bull had taken its aggression out on the canned goods aisles. There were a couple of human bodies lying about dead on the tiled floors. Hugh did not feel like looking too closely at the bodies, in case they were people he or Sally knew. The lights were out inside, making the place seem even more gloomy, and the usual smells were missing. On the floor, loose apples, oranges, eggs, cans, and bottles rolled about as the district swayed slightly from its movement through the sky.

"I am surprised so much is still here," whispered Bobby as he caught a can of beans under his foot as it rolled by him. "You'd think places like this would have been raided fairly quickly."

"I don't think there are many who are able to raid left in these parts," said Icarus as he slipped off his sack and began to fill it with the least damaged food stuff. This caused the conversation to screech to a halt as the gravity of the Sparrow's words hit home with deadly precision. As they gathered up cans of food and bottles of drinks from the shelves and from off the floor, thunder sounded outside the small store. A storm was coming, and Hugh could feel from the fresh smell of ozone in the air that it was going to be a big one.

16

The first drops of rain began to fall as they finished collecting goods from the ruined shelves. They decided to exit the devastated store through the back door of the building in case there were any Hawkers flying by the storefront. The somber mood was still hanging around the group as they left the public area of the grocery and entered the employee areas, passing by several locked doors. Hugh couldn't help but take notice of the blood stains upon the walls and on the doors they passed, several of which had been bashed in, giving glimpses of violence within. He did his best to keep his head focused on the end of the hall where the exit door was, though, from time to time, he did glance off to the side, as did Sally, Bobby, and Icarus.

The door at the end of the hall opened easily at a touch and swung outward, revealing an empty lot between buildings where there were the remains of a greenhouse and an overturned specialized delivery truck sporting the logo of the grocery. Only transport vehicles were allowed in Nimbus due to its size. These trucks could only be driven by official drivers who needed special keys to turn them on. Needless to say no one in the group had such a key and even if they found one, it was highly likely that the truck wouldn't move unless they managed to set it back down on all four wheels, so they left the truck as it was. There were canned goods spilling out the open rear doors of the truck, with a single hand reaching out of it like the last moments of a quicksand victim. Across the lot was a building with an open loading door, which the group made their way quickly towards.

The wind grew stronger as they walked, the storm becoming worse by the minute, with the rain stinging against the exposed parts of their skin. As they moved across the paved surface, Icarus searched the skies through the raindrops for patrolling Hawkers flying overhead, while

Hugh kept his rifle trained on the street entrance to the alley. Other than a few loose cans rattling about the empty space, there was nothing else in their way and they made it to the other side safely.

The inside of this structure was just as disastrous as the grocery had been, with bodies of workers and civilians of all ages sprawled out where they fell all over the floor. Hugh felt his willpower being tested as he did his best not to look too closely at the dead as they moved deeper inside. The lights were out in this building, making seeing difficult for almost everyone. They didn't use Sally's flashlight, as they didn't want to draw unnecessary attention to themselves. Icarus, due to his enhanced sight, was able to see in the darkness and led them around the scattered piles of crates and boxes. By this point they were holding onto each others' hands in order to keep from getting lost.

"I can't see a thing," complained Bobby from in front of Hugh. "How is it that birdbrain over here knows where he's going?"

"I can see in low light levels," answered Icarus. "Most Hawkers are programmed for night vision, and a bit of it has remained in our biological state as Sparrows. I am not sure how this trait was passed on, but I have found it invaluable to my survival as a Sparrow while exploring the sewers and secret areas."

Soon they reached a door at the other end of the dark room. Icarus slowly opened it and the light that spilled out briefly blinded those gathered, bringing spots to Hugh's eyes. Once his eyes adjusted, he saw Icarus had already entered the room beyond. Past the Sparrow, there were several gaping holes in the wall and windows facing the street, where rain and wind were blowing in. Loose papers were flying around the room like oversized confetti, some of which blew past towards the dark room behind them. There was no clear sign of what this place had been used for, nor did it really matter as once the humans were ready, they continued their trek through the mess and back outside to the next street, one block closer to the passage to Tesla Quarter. They continued moving this way, passing through buildings, avoiding bodies, and keeping an eye out for danger. There were a couple of close calls, but they managed to avoid outright conflict by hiding before being spotted. Icarus's keen senses kept them all alive throughout their journey. As they grew closer to the edge of Galileo Plaza, Sally spoke up.

"So, how are we getting to Tesla, cable car or bridge?"

Icarus stopped and turned toward her. "If we were able to stay below the streets I would have said sewer junction tunnel." He stopped speaking for a moment and tilted his head, thinking for a second before continuing. "Since I am unfamiliar with this district, I don't know where any of the sewer entrances are. All of the ones I have spotted while we have been traveling through Galileo have been blocked by rubble. Since we would be taking a massive risk by searching for them, I am afraid that isn't an option. As things stand, no matter what path we choose, we will be putting ourselves in danger. Both the bridge and cable car are too open to attack."

"The bird has a point," piped in Bobby as he took this time to clean his glasses of the scum and rain that had collected as they had walked about. "Taking the bridge would be a death sentence. We'd be as easy to pick off as bugs on a twig with how open the bridges are."

"The cable car isn't much better," pointed out Hugh. "All they have to do is cut the cables and down she goes."

"I'm afraid we'll have to risk the cable car," Icarus said as he wiped the rain from his feathery brow and began moving again.

"Why?" Hugh asked as he followed after the birdman, the others moving along with him.

"We will have more cover in the car than on the bridge, and the cables are thicker than you think," replied Icarus as they exited onto another street, this one with a derailed train car blocking one end of the avenue, its underside exposed, showing the complex gears that made it run.

"How do you know that?" asked Bobby as he gave the bird a suspicious look.

Icarus shrugged his shoulders as he looked to the sky, the rain falling in steadily growing sheets. "I am merely guessing. Either way, both the bridge and cable car use the same cables, so our chances are greater with the method with the most cover from aerial attacks. "

Needless to say, Icarus's logic did make some sense, but it did not make anyone feel any better about the trip. All too soon they arrived at the cable car station. It was a horrible mess of bodies and blood and the gates to the platform were closed, bound shut by a twisted metal bar. It was so thick that it had required the inhuman strength of a machine to bend it into place. The gate was not much of a blockade to the group. Icarus simply handed his weapons over to Hugh and took a running leap into the air, his wings spreading wide and giving him flight. There was a moment where the winds caused Icarus to become unbalanced in the air, but he quickly recovered and hovered in place. He reached out one silver claw to the group, the intention being clear. Hugh went first, being the most experienced rider of the Sparrow, reaching out his own hand to take Icarus's in a firm grip. Within seconds his feet left the slick pavement and for a moment he felt as if he had been transported back to that terrifying moment where all that kept him from his doom was a cable mere days ago.

It only took a few minutes for him to be flown over the top of the gate and dropped off on the other side by the benches. One after the other, Bobby and Sally were flown by the Sparrow to Hugh's side on the platform. As each one was flown over, Hugh took the opportunity to bring his camera to his eye and capture Icarus in flight with his human passengers. Once all the humans were on the other side they wordlessly made their way to a waiting car and stepped inside.

Icarus was the last one inside the cabin and closed the door behind him, locking it from the inside. The Sparrow walked over to where the human trio was sitting, waiting for the car to start its journey across the sky. However, the car did not move an inch despite the door being closed.

"What's the hold up?" asked Sally as she looked out the rain stained window back towards the platform, the worry showing on her face.

"Damn, the automated system must be down," swore Bobby.

"What do we do now?" Hugh asked as he looked back to the Sparrow. "Do we go for the bridge instead?"

"Maybe Ick- erh, Icarus, could fly us across?" suggested Sally, looking at the stoic Sparrow.

"Are you mad, Sally?" asked Bobby in shock. "Do you really want to be flown across a wide expanse of air in a raging storm? We already know he can only fly one of us at a time, so two of us would have to wait on one side of the gap for him to fly back and pick us up. God knows what could happen during the time it would take for us to cross."

"I was merely offering an opinion," huffed Sally as she crossed her arms and turned to look out into the storm, the rain pounding against the window glass.

"No," Icarus answered as he headed toward the center of the car. Reaching up he pulled free a panel from the ceiling and exposed a hidden control panel. "We activate the manual controls."

"Okay, how did you know *that* was there?" demanded Bobby. "You can't just say you took a wild guess!"

Icarus sighed as he worked the console in the ceiling. "I didn't have to guess. I was informed of this by Father while I was still a Hawker. He told all Hawkers about these panels as part of our day one introduction to the city, in case we ever encountered a stranded cable car."

"Wait, Father?" asked Sally, reaching for her notepad.

"You mean Dr. Mason, right?" asked Hugh, just as curious as Sally.

Icarus only gave a quick sharp nod before there was a loud beep and the car suddenly rattled violently before the familiar sounds of its engine filled the air and joined the symphony of the storm raging outside. The car gave one more shutter and began to pull out from the platform and into open air. Sally gave a small happy smile and turned back to the window to watch Galileo Plaza drift away from them into the rain. Whatever questions that had arisen faded away as they moved out across the expanse.

As the car made its way across the cable, it swung back and forth in the wind, rocking like a child's cradle. Hugh felt uncomfortable with the car's extra movements. He was worried that any second the cable might give or the car would fall off the cable due to the rocking. He had, in the past, traveled by cable car through a couple of bad storms, but the added movement of the city itself made the trip far more unsettling.

Thankfully, Hugh's worries were unfounded, as they soon reached the other end of the cable, arriving safely in Tesla Quarter. They weren't silent during this trip, as Icarus wanted them to go over a street map of Tesla Quarter. They had decided that the quickest route to the next cable car station, the one to Full Moon Plaza, would be the one that took them past the hospital and Bobby's apartment. Bobby remained quiet, despite their planned route taking them past both his place of work and his own home. Hugh could not read what his friend was thinking behind his glasses.

Once they exited the cable car Icarus again took the lead, this time with Bobby by his side, giving him advice on where to go. The rain was getting worse by the minute and the visibility was dropping sharply, resulting in the group having to once again lead each other by the hand, relying on Icarus's advanced senses to guide them on their way through the district. They passed through buildings as before, stopping from time to time to rest before moving out again. It felt like hours before the group found themselves in front of the Angel of Mercy Hospital, the building little more than a mysterious silhouette that could have belonged to an ominous castle due to the downpour.

Sally suddenly spoke up and said, "We need to go inside."

"What? Why?" called out Hugh as he turned to look at her in surprise. The others stopped as well, their bodies beginning to shiver from being idle in the cold rain.

"We need to look for survivors!" she cried back, struggling to be heard over the rain and wind.

"Are you crazy?" demanded Bobby. "We need to keep moving!"

"Not until we go inside!" Sally shouted.

"There is a chance that there are Hawkers inside with similar feelings but different goals," Icarus pointed out.

"We should still go and look!" Sally said as she looked back the way they came. "We've seen too many dead bodies. I want to see if there is anyone else left alive in this city!"

Hugh had to admit to himself, all the death was taking a heavy toll on his soul. He was sure he recognized several that they had passed by, but hadn't dared to let his eyes linger. Looking more closely at Sally, past the rain and wind he could see that she was hurting, almost as much as when the cop had been killed before her eyes.

"She's right!" he called out to the others. "We need to get inside!"

Bobby swore again. "Ugh, I can't believe this. Not you too, Hugh! I'm going with the bird if you two are going inside that death trap."

"I feel that going inside is a good course of action," Icarus said as he looked at the building through the rain. "We could always use more able hands and working guns."

"Oh, come *on!*" moaned Bobby.

"Aren't you worried about your patients, Bobby?" demanded Sally, the storm making her face something wild, fierce, and beautiful to Hugh's gaze. "Are you really so cruel?"

"Of course I am worried!" cried Bobby. "However, I think we should be smart about this. The Hawkers were originally supposed to be our new police force, yes? That would mean they should know that a good place to go human hunting is a hospital, where many of their prey can't even leave their beds. I know it is very dark of me to say this, but I have given up on there being anyone left alive in there. Believe me, I wish I could be optimistic here, but I am a realist. Chances are there are Hawkers holed up in the hospital, waiting for any stragglers to wander in looking for supplies. We are better off moving along."

"I hope I never need *you* as a doctor," Sally grumbled as she turned and marched off toward the hospital. "You haven't a single drop of hope in your body!" she shouted back over her shoulder. Bobby tried to say something more, but the words did not come. He was the last one standing on the street in the downpour as the others followed Sally inside. None of them saw the tears on his face, masked by the rain. Once he had regained his composure, he raced after the others and joined them at the door of the hospital.

The doors leading inside were by some miracle still attached to their frames and opened as easily as they had the day Hugh had come to check on his friend so long ago. The lobby was a mess, with papers everywhere and claw marks all over the walls. Someone had wheeled out several gurneys and left them lying about helter-skelter. There was plenty of blood spilled about, over the chairs and reception counter, but there wasn't a body in sight. The sounds of the torrent outside were diminished to moderate levels when they were inside, though the rain was still making itself impossible to ignore.

Bobby was the first to speak up. "Something's not right. Where's the staff? Where's the hospital's private security?"

"I think it's safe to say they're dead, Bobby," said Hugh as he reached out for his friend to comfort him.

"No, that's not what I meant. Where are all the bodies?" asked Bobby as he walked over to the reception counter. "I know these people. They wouldn't have run if under attack. Do you remember that explosion last year?"

"Do you mean the gas one that took out that seafood place?" asked Sally.

"Yeah, that's the one. The hospital was on the verge of a riot due to families demanding that we help this person or that first and, when supplies ran low, punches were actually thrown. Russell was on duty that week. He did not leave his post for a second, even when things got messy."

"Yeah, I remember reading about that," Hugh admitted as he looked around at the lobby, taking it all in.

"Well, where is he then?" asked Bobby as he headed toward a pile of discarded briefcases. "Jack, his partner, wouldn't leave his post either, and I doubt all this blood is from just one guy. Where are the bodies?"

"Maybe they moved deeper inside?" suggested Sally.

"Are you saying the dead can walk?" asked Bobby incredulously.

"No, I am saying that they survived!" Sally turned and headed toward a pair of double doors leading deeper into the medical complex. "Come on! We need to find them!"

With that she slipped inside, followed closely by Hugh, calling out to her to slow down. Bobby and Icarus followed them. But before they exited the devastated lobby, Bobby heard Icarus say something under his breath.

"Come again, birdbrain?" asked Bobby.

Icarus turned to the human. "I said I don't like this. I don't see why there are no bodies. The Hawkers have no reason to clean up after themselves now that their nature has been revealed."

"Maybe the lady's right and there are survivors," Bobby mused.

"Perhaps, but I wonder if even you believe that."

They met up again outside a nurses' station, the desk littered with scattered papers and spilt coffee. They hadn't seen a single soul anywhere, not in waiting or examination rooms. The lights were poor inside the hospital, casting a dim weak glow on everything that transformed the halls into a dark and mysterious place. Shadows seemed to move independently of their casters every time the lights flickered. Bobby had explained that the hospital had its own emergency power source in case of a blackout, but rarely needed to use it. The building was fairly tall, and Sally seemed determined to keep up the search until they had visited every single room.

"We need to keep moving," complained Bobby. "I am telling you guys, staying here is a huge mistake."

"And I am telling you we should keep searching. We can, at the very least, look for medical supplies," countered Sally. "After all Dr. *Robert*, we don't have a single Band-Aid to split between us."

"She has a point," agreed Icarus. "We have been very fortunate thus far not to run into any serious trouble. However, we may not be so lucky in the future."

"If any of us gets hurt I doubt there will be time to treat them," Bobby argued as he rested against the counter. "Besides, who's going to carry the meds? We aren't all pack mules."

"I'll do it," volunteered Hugh. "We at least need something to dull the pain." For a moment, Hugh felt the ache in his shoulder, as if the mere mention of painkillers brought back the pain, but it passed as quickly as it came. He hoped he only needed the one pill Bobby had given him the night before. Without missing a beat, he continued his sentence by suggesting they find bandages too, in case one of them got banged up.

"Fine, whatever, but don't think we'll get a chance to set any broken bones or do decent wrap jobs, Hugh," Bobby said as he pinched the bridge of his nose. He sighed and rose from the counter. "Well, you all better follow me. I need to get my things from my locker if we are going to break into the supply room."

After passing more examination rooms and winding around a couple of twists and turns, they reached a room with many lockers lined up one after the other. Many of the cabinets had fallen over like dominos, one atop the other in a mess. Judging by the look on Bobby's face, Hugh guessed that his friend's locker was somewhere in the pile in the center of the room. It took some time and muscle, but with Icarus and Sally's help, they managed to move aside several of the lockers to reveal the one belonging to Bobby. Wordlessly, he went over to the tumbler on the door and entered his combination. With a soft click, the metal door unlatched. Bobby pulled open the door and reached inside, past his lab coat and the pile of jumbled medical books and records, until his eyes lit up and he pulled out a lanyard with his doctor's identification card and a key attached to it by a silver loop.

"Okay, now we just need to get to the basement, where all the supplies are kept."

"Aren't there any supply closets on this floor?" asked Sally.

"There are," answered Bobby. "We can gather up bandages and such things from closets on any floor. However, there is a chance that those closets may have already been raided, assuming we aren't the only ones left alive. If we go to the basement, where the majority of the medical supplies are kept, we will find everything we'll need, including the strongest medicines. Those drugs are kept in the basement to prevent patients from stealing them, and to keep them at the perfect temperature for use."

It was at that moment that there was the sound of something outside the locker room, that of a hard flat surface hitting the laminate floor tiles. Everyone froze and weapons were brought out. Icarus was the first to the doorway and looked outside the room. Hugh was close behind the birdman, followed again by Bobby and Sally. Despite the dim lights, they didn't bring out Sally's flashlight, in case it attracted unwanted attention. After a few minutes of staring into the gloom, it was clear that there was nothing in the hall other than loose papers, a couple of abandoned gurneys and a few chairs.

"Okay, what was that?" asked Bobby.

"I don't know," Icarus answered as his feathers rose up atop his head. "I do know that it came from the hallway by the wheelchair."

"Damn it!" swore Bobby under his breath, looking where the Sparrow was indicating. "The stairs to the basement are that way. I doubt the elevators are running now, so the only way down is over there."

"It's probably nothing," muttered Icarus, though his facial expression suggested he felt the opposite of what he was saying.

"Maybe it was other humans?" suggested Sally nervously as her hand shook holding out her new handgun.

"I don't suppose anyone wants to just leave now and forget about this?" asked Bobby before getting a nasty glare from Sally. "Guess not," he sighed in defeat. Silently, he led them toward the hallway with the wheelchair and past a couple of examination rooms. With each open doorway they passed, they stopped for a second to scan the interior for trouble, keeping their guns at the ready. Soon they came across a set of double doors that were wide open, revealing a set of stairs leading both up and down. Again, Bobby swore as the set going down was completely blocked off by piles of hospital equipment, from gurneys to IV racks.

"This just keeps getting better," groaned Bobby as he went over to the pile and tried to pull a chair out of the tangled mess. "It'll take forever to clear the stairs. We'd be better off just taking the bandages and going."

"Oh, no," ordered Sally as she put her foot down. "This barricade is proof there are survivors in here."

"Well, I don't see how we are getting past this mess," sighed Bobby as he gave up trying to pull free the chair. "And this is the only way into the basement."

"What about the elevators?" Hugh asked as he looked back at the hallway behind them.

"Are you deaf now, Hugh?" asked Bobby. "I said the elevators aren't on emergency power. They might as well be closets now."

"Can't we climb down to the basement through the shaft?" asked Hugh, not letting up, the curiosity of what was down there eating away at him. "It'd be a drop, but only one story down. I think we can handle that, right?"

"And how do you plan on getting back out?" demanded Bobby.

"You did say there are supply rooms down there," said Icarus. "We might find a ladder, or, at the very least, boxes we could stack to help us climb back out. After all, it's only one floor down."

Again Bobby gave in and led them back the way they came. Along the way to the nearest elevator bank, they didn't see a single body. There was plenty of damage, scratches in the walls, florescent lights broken and hanging from mere wires from the ceiling, cracks in the floor and bullet holes here and there. It felt like the group of four had only just missed a massive battle in these halls, one that they were glad that they were only seeing the aftermath of instead of being combatants. The hospital seemed to be holding its breath, if a building could do so, as they moved deeper inside. Only the shadows seemed to have any life of their own.

Finally they reached the elevators, and to everyone's surprise there was something painted on the center bank's doors. Most of the markings were just splotches, but spread out in large sloppy letters over the metal surface was a single word that was hard to make out the gloom. In order to see what was written on the elevator doors, Sally reluctantly retrieved her flashlight and directed its beam at the splotches of blood, revealing the word "Help," sprawled across the center elevator's doors.

"What on earth?" Bobby swore as he reached out his hand toward the deep red stains. "This is blood!"

"What?!" cried Hugh in disbelief, Sally having a similar retort of her own. "This is getting crazy! Are we in a Hitchcock horror flick? Who uses blood as paint, and why?"

"Perhaps it was the only material they had to work with?" suggested Icarus as he examined the blood stains with his superior eyesight. "Maybe the one who left this is close by? Maybe even inside the elevator shaft."

"I don't think so," said Bobby as he moved back from the door. "Judging by the color of the blood, it's not all that fresh. Whoever left it is probably long gone, or long dead."

"I don't like this, Hugh," said Sally as she reached out and drew closer to him for support. "Maybe we should try the stairs again?"

"We're here now, Sal. We might as well see what comes of this," Hugh replied as he brushed her hair with his free hand, trying to calm her down. Meanwhile, Icarus had moved closer to the blood smeared doors and had turned to Bobby.

"Are you absolutely sure this is real blood and not paint?" asked Icarus.

"I have seen my fair share of blood, even before all of the killings. I know it when I see it," replied Bobby as he nervously handled his shotgun.

Without another word, Icarus reached out with his claws and pried the metal doors open, causing the letters of help to separate into "he" and "lp." Inside was a stranded elevator. On the floor lay the body of a dead man, whose back was a bloody mess of flesh and bone.

This body was one of the more graphic corpses that they had seen thus far, and Sally turned away from the awful sight, her free hand flying to her mouth to stifle a gasp. Bobby swore under his breath, as he reached out to the body. Before anything else could happen, Icarus spoke up.

"This is a red herring."

"What?" Hugh demanded as he glared at the Sparrow. "What the hell are you talking about?"

"Consider this," Icarus said as he walked over to the body, past Bobby, and pointed at the poor man's ruined back. "This man is dead."

"You think?" Bobby sneered.

"Allow me to continue," Icarus said as he bent down and lifted the poor man off the carpeted floor of the elevator, exposing a small blood stain. "This man was dead long before he was put in this elevator."

"What are you getting at?" asked Sally, who turned her head toward the Sparrow, while at the same time trying to avoid looking at the face of the dead man.

"I think this man was planted here as a decoy. Same as all the blood we've seen spread out over the hospital. It probably was the work of the survivors, trying to trick the Hawkers into thinking that everyone here was killed off. Tell me, doctor," Icarus said as he turned toward Bobby, holding up the dead body. "Could all the blood we've seen come from blood packs?"

Bobby considered the question, before answering. "I suppose it could have, and it's possible that the hospital had enough in storage to create the stains we've seen. However, it would use a lot of blood, and take a lot of time. Then again," Bobby said as he glanced upwards at the ceiling, "we have only seen the first floor. For all we know the upper floors are clean. Either way, it is indeed possible that this is all merely a distraction. And," he added after looking at the blood stain inside the elevator, "you're right about a lack of blood, given how badly wounded the body is."

"That is some pretty grim logic, Icarus," moaned Sally as she tried to keep herself standing. "How do you plan to prove it? For all we know this blood came from people who fled upstairs or left the building."

"There is only one way to be sure," said Icarus as he carefully laid the body back where it was and exited the elevator. "We need to investigate the other shafts further."

He headed to the elevator directly to the right of the central one and proceeded to pry the doors apart. Inside was the top half of an elevator, stuck partway down to the basement. Inside were a few more bodies, those of a few doctors and one skinny nurse. They were huddled up in a group in the middle of the floor, their heads looking up, and their eyes wide open, as if they could see Hugh and the others. These bodies looked different from the one in the middle elevator, not a mark on them or a trace of blood. It was as if they had spontaneously died.

"What happened to them?" asked Sally, glad to have something different, although no less horrible, to look at.

"I think they suffocated when the elevator got stuck," sighed Bobby as he looked at the bodies in this elevator. "Look at their eyes," he said as he directed Sally to aim her light at the deceased's faces. "It's a little hard to see from this far away, but notice how bloodshot they are. That's one of the signs of suffocation. They probably got trapped in the elevator when the power went out and couldn't get the doors open from the inside. Cripes, is that Juliet?" Bobby asked as he looked more closely at the nurse, her hair red as fire, though dead as stone. "It is. She helped me on a few surgeries. She didn't deserve this, none of them did."

Icarus had not stopped moving upon the discovery of more bodies. Instead he had moved on to the third elevator, the one to the left of the center. Effortlessly he pried the doors open, revealing a ladder propped up against the lip of the portal, leading down the shaft into darkness. "Ah-ha," he said in satisfaction as he beckoned the others over.

"That's not supposed to be there," Bobby muttered as he looked down into the shaft. From the bottom a dim light could be seen, leaking out from a doorway right below them. Before Sally could bring her flashlight over to investigate, there was a sudden loud retort as a bullet zipped by Bobby, taking a tiny chunk of his ear off as it embedded itself in the top of the door frame. Cursing, he threw himself back from the edifice and got out his shotgun, while holding his other hand tightly to his ear, trying to stop the bleeding.

Everyone acted at once. Hugh dragged Sally away from the elevators as Icarus stepped back and brought his rifle out. He took aim at the bottom of the open elevator door, so that if whoever had fired at them felt like pursing them, their head would be the Sparrow's first target. Voices came up from the shaft, voices filled with anger and fear. Hugh, feeling his body act before thinking, pulled himself away from Sally and moved to the wall right beside the open doorway, his back brushing up against the elevator call buttons.

"Don't shoot!" he shouted out. "We're humans! Not Hawkers!"

At once the voices quieted before one, a woman's, called back. "Prove it!"

"How?" Hugh yelled back.

Suddenly a bright light shown up and out from the shaft. "Step into the light and don't try anything funny!" the voice commanded. "One false move and we'll shoot!"

Carefully, Hugh inched his way around the wall and into the light. He leaned as far as he dared out into the shaft, despite the protests of Sally. He could not see anything with the bright light shining in his face and making his eyes squint. From the bottom of the shaft voices rose up again, the sounds of someone arguing before the woman spoke up again. "Are you alone?"

"No, I have others with me," Hugh called back.

"Is the Hawker gone?" the voice demanded from below.

"What?" Hugh asked.

"I said is the Hawker GONE? Our scouts said one entered the hospital around the time you did."

"I'm not a Hawker," Icarus called out, while staying far from the edge of the elevator so as not to scare those at the bottom. His rifle was no longer aimed at the opening, but still ready to fire in case of trouble. "I'm a Sparrow."

"You don't sound like a robot," the voice admitted upon hearing Icarus speak. "However," it continued, "we can never be too careful down here. If you really have other humans with you, bring them into the light so we can see them!"

Slowly, Sally, Bobby, and Icarus moved to stand beside Hugh at the edge of the shaft. Icarus stood right between Hugh and Bobby, effectively hiding his wings from view behind the two men. Instantly they were all blinded by the harsh glare of the lights at the bottom of the shaft becoming far brighter as more beams shot forth into their faces. Some more arguing broke out before the woman spoke again.

"There are only four of you?" the voice asked.

"Yes!" Hugh yelled back, while trying to block some of the harsh light with his hands.

"Are you *sure* there are no Hawkers up there?" the voice insisted.

Everyone reassured the bodiless voice at the bottom that indeed, they hadn't seen any of the machines inside of the building. And with that the lights mercifully turned off, leaving everyone seeing spots again. Once their eyes finally readjusted to the gloom, Hugh was shocked to see that standing at the bottom of the shaft, holding up a rifle, was a familiar nurse.

"Dr. Crick, it is good to see you're still breathing," said Nurse Rogers. "We have a few new patients waiting for you down here. Hope your friends know how to do the healing work."

17

To say Hugh was surprised to see the middle-aged nurse again, after all that had happened, would be an understatement. He had a feeling the woman was tough when he last saw her. After all, she shrugged off being slammed into a wall, the first act of violence he had witnessed being committed by a Hawker. Bobby, too, was clearly shocked to see the nurse, though Sally was just happy to see another living person after so much death.

It didn't take long for most of the group to climb the ladder down to the nurse. However, her smile vanished and her rifle went up when Icarus began to climb down into the shaft.

"Damn! I thought you said there were no Hawkers up there!" she swore.

"Whoa, hold up! Put that down!" exclaimed Hugh as he held his hands up as if the gun was aiming at him and not the Sparrow, now motionless at the top of the ladder. "You saw him before you let us down here!"

"What I saw was a man in a feathered coat, not a damn tin bird!" she retorted, keeping the barrel level with Icarus's head.

"Nurse Rogers," spoke up a voice from the exit to the basement behind the ladder. "Put the gun down."

At the sound of the voice, Bobby became as still as a book on a shelf. His face was a mix of emotions, as if someone had just punched his gut and told him he had won the lotto. From out of the faint glow of the lower doorway stepped a tall man. His mere presence drew everyone's attention, even that of Icarus still atop the ladder. He wore a dark suit with a neat lab coat. His hair was cropped close to his scalp with silver sprinkling its copper tone. He wore glasses and had a full mustache across his upper lip, giving him a scholarly look.

"Doctor Craven," stammered Bobby as the man stepped right up to Nurse Rogers.

"Good to see you are still among the living, Robert," he said as he turned back to the nurse. "Nurse Rogers, I order you to put that gun down."

"But that's a Hawker!" she argued.

"If it was then we must have zombies, too, for I highly doubt we would have a trio of living humans wandering around with one of those machines. Let the creature come and join his friends. That is a direct order, nurse."

The nurse tried to get a few more words out, but one look from Dr. Craven instantly made her objections fade from her breath. Reluctantly she let the gun relax in her grip, its barrel's rim clanking against the metallic bottom of the shaft. "I better not be regretting this," she muttered almost inaudibly under her breath, her eyes still trained like a spotlight on Icarus, watching him as he started to climb down.

"Wait a second," Dr. Craven called up to Icarus. "Would you kindly close those doors before you get down here? We don't want any unwanted visitors."

Icarus merely nodded his head and reached out with his claws and pulled the thick doors shut from the inside, closing off the shaft from the first floor. It only took a few minutes before the birdman had joined the others at the bottom of the shaft. Doctor Craven motioned them to follow him as he led the group back the way he came, through the elevator door for the basement and into a little room that was poorly lit in an amber glow. There was a pair of double doors opposite the elevator shaft that was being guarded by two very burley men in muddy overalls carrying guns of their own. With a simple wave of his hand, the two men moved away from the door and allowed Dr. Craven to move onward through the doors, with Hugh and the rest trailing him inside.

As they walked deeper inside the bowels of the hospital, past guard after guard, Hugh couldn't help but turn to Bobby. His friend was still clearly stunned from seeing the man leading them, and Hugh wanted to know what made this man so special. "Bobby, who is this man?" whispered Hugh so as not to be overheard by their leader.

"Dr. Craven?" mumbled Bobby nervously under his breath. "He's the hospital's director! I thought he was dead!"

"Why did you think that?" piped in Sally, picking up her pace till she was walking right beside Bobby and across from Hugh.

"Because he was supposed to have been at the Transport Center when it blew," explained Bobby as they were waved past another guarded door. "That was the day he said he was going to see his niece in Atlanta."

"I was until I was called to come back to the hospital before I could leave for Aviator Airway," said Dr. Craven, surprising the gathered friends. "I had to oversee a couple of emergency surgeries of victims of what I had thought was merely unnecessary roughness by the Hawkers that day."

"I did tell you those things were up to no good, Dr. Craven," declared Nurse Rogers as she gave Icarus the evil eye. "But you wouldn't listen until that horrible massacre. Thank God we got as many down here as we did before they raided the hospital. In all my years as a nurse, I have never seen so much blood spilt."

"I am well aware of that, Nurse," Dr. Craven said with a tone that signified that particular conversation had been closed for quite a while. "We have taken all the proper precautions as you can see."

"I am sorry I am causing such conflict," said Icarus as he looked over his shoulder at the men they had recently passed, both looking back at the gathering through the doorway, their weapons clutched tightly with white knuckled fists.

"Think nothing of it," said Dr. Craven as he waved his hand as if he was swatting away the apology. "We are all a bit on edge here with recent events considered. However, I am very happy to make your acquaintance." Before more could be said, they exited into a large open room. The original purpose of the chamber had been lost, as it was now filled wall to wall with cots occupied by the sick and injured. Nurses and doctors were moving around between the beds like bees in a hive, checking charts, filling IVs, and cleaning bandages. Everyone in the room stopped what they were doing and turned toward the newcomers as if they had rehearsed the maneuver. At the sight of Icarus, a clamor rose up, the sounds of terror and panic, along with anger. The sound of clicks and clanks rang out as weapons were pulled out from under the cots. There were shotguns and rifles along with simple handguns now aimed squarely at Icarus, not all of them held with experienced hands, but enough to ensure that he wouldn't walk out of that room alive.

However, by simply waving his hand, Dr. Craven ordered everyone to stand down. The room moved like an ocean as, one after another, the doctors and able-bodied patients put their weapons back into their hidden spaces and returned to their activities, as if nothing had happened.

Sally whistled at the show of control and respect that Dr. Craven had over the room. Hugh wondered just what the doctor had done to gain such loyalty from everyone in the room. It couldn't have just been his position at the hospital. Such things didn't amount to much when under the threat of attack. For a few minutes they stayed there standing at the doorway, watching the doctors and nurses busy about tending the wounded. Then Bobby broke away from the group, heading for one of the many beds and became assimilated into the living waters of medical staff flowing around the cots.

Once Bobby left, Dr. Craven began to move again, leading the remaining group through the crowd to the other end of the room, past more than a dozen cots, each one filled and being waited on in turn. It was clear that there were still more wounded than well, but at least as far as Hugh could see, none of the injuries were more serious than broken bones or bad cases of flu. Finally they reached another pair of double doors, this time lacking any guards. The doctor held them open and beckoned Hugh and the others inside.

This room was as large as the first, its floor sloping downwards from the door like a bowl. All around the rim were rows of seats, dusty from their lack of use. In the center of the room was a round stage with operating equipment stacked around the edges like columns of a Greek temple. Where one would have expected the operating table to be was now an expensive looking ornate dark desk, with several files atop its surface.

With a mock bow, Dr. Craven said, "Welcome to my new office, much bigger than my last, but the view is far from desirable." Hugh, Sally, and Icarus strolled inside and made their way down toward the desk in the center, while the doctor turned to Nurse Rogers and dismissed her despite her loud protests. Once she was gone, the doctor headed to his desk and sat down lightly in the leather chair behind it. As soon as he did, a small creature hopped up from behind the desk and onto his lap.

"Eek!" exclaimed Sally the instant the little critter hopped up.

"Ah, yes. This is Freddy," he said as he stroked the creature's feathered back. "I found him a few days ago, all banged up and bloody and with a lot more metal parts."

He only nodded at their stunned faces with a sly smile. "Yes, I believe that he's similar to your tall friend, only Freddy doesn't have much to say. His brain seems far more primitive, more like that of a common house pet." Seeing their hesitation, the doctor chuckled some more. "Come closer, he won't bite. I promise you that."

Stepping closer, Hugh could see that the creature was a bit bigger than he had first thought. It was about as big as a medium-sized dog with grey feathers that looked like they had been dulled from being washed too many times. It had an owlish face with two large eyes ringed with black feathers. On its back was a pair of wings similar to Icarus's, only much smaller due to the creature's diminutive size. They were tucked tightly against the creature's back, making them almost invisible to the naked eye. Its fore legs, that Hugh caught a glimpse of when it stretched out in Dr. Craven's lap, were those of a bird of prey, and so were its hind legs. It was as if someone had taken an extra pair of talons and sewn them onto a perfectly normal, though oddly colored, large owl.

Hugh knew within an instant that he had seen the strange animal before, though in a considerably different state. It was one of those small robot creatures, like the one that he had witnessed raid Dr. Crick's and his own apartments in search of the journal, and had caught and killed in his own. It looked considerably less scary as a fluffy four-legged animal than it had as a skeleton of a machine.

"I have never seen one so small survive the change," breathed Icarus, the shock showing for the first time on his face. "All others usually die in the process at that size."

"Icarus, what are you talking about?" Hugh asked, turning quickly to the Sparrow.

"The prototypes," said the Sparrow, still in awe of the little owlish creature. "Both the prototypes and the Hawkers go through the change. Due to being so small, the prototypes don't have enough metal in their robotic bodies to provide enough material for the transformation. Most die before the process is finished. There are rare occasions where the change fully takes hold in the prototypes, but it only happens once in every ten units or so. I have never before seen one that has finished the transformation process. I have only heard about them through word of mouth," Icarus admitted. "They were before my manufacturing time. We called them Mark-Zeroes due to their place in our robotic development timeline."

"It's so adorable," said Sally as she reached out to pet the fluffy creature. To her surprise, it pulled away from her hand. "Aw, what's wrong little guy?" she asked as she pulled back her hand.

Icarus was the one who supplied the answer. "I think he doesn't like how we smell."

Hugh took a moment to look himself over, taking in the dirty stains in his wrinkled clothes. They had been through so much the past few days that personal hygiene hadn't been all that important. He suddenly realized with a shock that he was probably carrying all sorts of nasty germs on his body from his sewer exploits.

Sally stepped back and assessed her own appearance, Hugh noticing for the first time what a mess she was. Her makeup was all over her face, eye shadow and lipstick smeared in streaks and splotches by sweat and the rain outside. Her hair floated about in the air in loose strands like the snakes atop Medusa. There were tears in her skirt and similar dark stains all over her attire, giving her an appearance of some sort of witch from a children's story. Icarus also was filthy. However, one had to be hard-pressed to see the stains around his legs, the only part of his body that ever came in contact with the polluted waters.

"Oh, my Lord!" gasped Sally once she had realized what a state she was in. Hugh felt himself cringe, not at the state of his girlfriend, or even at his own. It was the thought of Bobby, who would have been just as filthy as Hugh, working on patients in the other room that really made Hugh's skin crawl. The whole affair was simply unsanitary.

"Pardon me," started Sally to Dr. Craven, who had become completely absorbed in stroking his unusual pet. "I hate to ask, but is there any place down here where a lady can wash up?"

"Oh? Oh!" said the doctor as he put down the owlish creature and reached into his desk, pulling out a set of keys. "I completely understand. I've been told it is raining quite heavily up there. Here, let me page someone to direct you to the washrooms. The hospital's basement is a bit of a maze, I'm afraid. I still question the sanity of the architect, what with all these dead-end hallways." Dr. Craven then pressed a button on the intercom on top of his desk. Upon making the request for guidance known, a man in the crisp white garb of an orderly entered through the doorway. He was of medium build and age. He conversed with Dr. Craven briefly before the doctor gave him the keys he had pulled from his desk.

"Right, if you would just follow me," the orderly directed as he began to leave the improvised office. As they were leaving, Dr. Craven called up to the orderly, telling him to find Bobby as he too probably needed a shower. The orderly merely nodded his head, as he paused to look suspiciously at Icarus. "Are you sure you want this bird creature down here, Doc?" asked the orderly.

"Yes, yes," said Dr. Craven as he turned his attention to the many files that littered his desk. "As long as he doesn't cause any trouble he can stay."

"Yes, sir," sighed the orderly as he resumed leading Hugh and the others out of the room and back into the organized chaos of doctors and patients. It took a while before they located Bobby tending to an elderly man. He didn't want to be bothered at first, as he insisted he had to keep monitoring the man's heart rate. However, upon hearing the word "shower," he suddenly snapped to attention.

"Cripes," he said as he pulled off the latex gloves that he had somehow acquired during the time he was separated from the group. "How could I forget to wash up? I'm a doctor for Pete's sake!"

"It's okay," said Hugh as they began walking again, the orderly leading the way. "We're all in the same boat. After all we've been through, being clean is not exactly the first thing that comes to mind."

They soon left the crowded room and the sudden silence of the empty hall was almost eerie. Hugh lost track of all of the twists and turns they made while following the orderly. It reminded him a lot of the secret underground levels of the city that they had been in earlier. He caught the orderly from time to time sneaking more glances at Icarus, showing his distrust in his face. Thankfully they soon reached the showers and Hugh felt relieved to be freed from the orderly's company. There were two separate shower rooms, one for men and one for women.

"Wait," piped up Bobby before they could step inside and wash the grime from the past few days from their bodies. "What about clothes? We can't simply just put these back on."

"Ick," Sally groaned in agreement. "Bobby's got a point, Hugh. I don't want to get all cleaned up just to put these filthy things back on."

"Don't worry," the orderly grunted. "Dr. Craven has instructed me to bring you fresh clothes once you have gone inside and started scrubbing. You can leave your weapons and things here. Nobody will take them."

"You'd best let us gather up our ammunition," said Icarus. "It would be more useful to us dry than wet from the washers."

"If you don't mind, I think I'll keep mine," Bobby said as he took his shotgun out of his backpack. "I am a bit attached to it."

The orderly merely sighed and stood there, leaning against the empty wall opposite the doors with his arms crossed. "Suit yourself, Dr. Robert. Don't blame me if it doesn't work when you come out." He nodded at Icarus and said, "Though with that thing in there with you, I don't blame you wanting to keep your gun, sir." He watched them with bored eyes as they emptied their pockets and stuffed as much as they could into their bags. They had originally stashed the bullets in the vests for ease of access, since stopping to unzip a bag and root around for rounds would have cost them too much time during a battle. Once they were done transferring their bullets, everyone picked up their bags and headed inside the shower rooms, Sally going through a door to the left, Hugh and the other men through the door to the right.

Inside the showers were a dozen separate stalls, providing much needed privacy to the men as they washed. The room itself was very long with towel racks adorning the tiled wall across from the showers. There was a low narrow table in the center of the room, upon which were fresh towels awaiting use. Each of the men took up a towel and headed toward their chosen little shower cupboard. Inside each stall was a ready supply of soap and shampoo on a small shelf attached to the stall. All of the stalls had two doors built into them, one after the other.

The first was a solid slab of stainless steel into which two hooks were screwed. The second was simply a glass pane door. Upon entering his own stall, Hugh eased his camera bag off of his shoulder and replaced his camera inside it. He hung it and his towel on the two hooks before unzipping the tactical vest from his body.

Hugh wondered as he began to strip down, how Icarus would manage to fit inside his own stall due to his large wings. He did not wonder long, as when he stood up to remove his cargo vest, he saw the Sparrow's wings peeking out over the walls of the stall to his left. Already he could hear the water running in Icarus's stall, which wasn't much of a surprise given how little he had been wearing. Hugh, however, was only just getting to his undergarments. With each piece of clothing he removed he could feel his body begin to loosen up.

Finally, Hugh was ready to turn on the water. It came out so cold that it made him wince at first, but as he stood there, the water running over his body began to warm up. Hugh reached toward the ready shampoo and squirted the substance onto his hand. He lathered up his hands and applied it to his blond hair, almost brown now from all the dirt and grime. He felt repulsed as he watched the filth drip from his body and circle the drain. He wondered if Sally was using the same shampoo or if she had her own supply, perhaps somewhere in her bottomless purse. He thought back to a few dates he had with her in the past, both professional and casual. If she needed something, she could always find it in her handbag. Small adhesive bandages, rubber bands, business cards, envelopes, makeup, perfume, even film for him in case he ran out while working with her on a story.

He sighed as he continued to muse about happier times with her. Those jobs where he went on assignment through the city with her were always fun. He loved to watch her work, asking questions that were so quick and clever that she almost always got the truth out of her subjects. He also thought fondly of the few rare times that they had to leave the city on assignment. Their last job out of town was in Boston to cover a science convention at the city auditorium. He was not sure if she saw it as anything more than just another job, but to him it had been a special trip. It was nice to see his parents at their home in the city. His mother had given him a new camera that could take colored pictures. It quickly became his favorite camera, and now was the only one he had left.

Thinking about his parents as he applied soap to his limbs made Hugh's mind wander to thoughts of Dr. Crick. Was he even still alive? He couldn't imagine what Bobby had to be going through. It was his father, after all. Hugh hoped they could find some resolution to this whole disaster, or at least get out of the city. Seeing all of these people down here under the hospital had given Hugh some hope. Maybe they could still get out of this alive, yet he still felt that their chances were so low that he might as well bet on his own death.

A sudden humming stopped Hugh's private thoughts for a moment. He realized in an instant it was Bobby who was humming. It sounded a bit like a song Hugh knew, something that had become popular as of late on the radio. He could only remember that the group's lead singer's first name was Bobby. Hugh chuckled at the coincidence that the singer had the same first name as his friend before rinsing off the suds and dirt from his body. He sighed as he realized he'd need to scrub a good deal more to get all the muck off. He was grateful that there was no shortage of soap as he continued to lather up.

His thoughts continued to brew in his head. He thought about the plan, to get to Vulcan in hopes of finding some secret way to stop the Hawkers. Hugh was dubious that they'd find anything they didn't already know. Vulcan was on the other side of the city, and he highly doubted their luck would hold. As things were, he was beginning to contemplate grabbing the nearest and biggest bed sheet he could find and jumping. He would not leave Sally behind. He'd find a way to get her out of this city somehow, to someplace safe on solid ground. They could stay with his parents if need be. He entertained the thought of having Icarus fly them down one by one, but he dashed that because he did not want to risk her being all alone. If he went down first, she'd be left by herself in Nimbus with those insane Hawkers. If she went first, who's to say that the Hawkers wouldn't go after her?

He then realized that with the city moving, chances were that he would be far away from her due to the time it would take Icarus to fly back and forth. On the other hand, Hugh didn't worry much about Bobby. He knew that his friend was able to hold his own, not that Sally couldn't. He knew that if it came down to it, Bobby could pull a trigger, but he wasn't sure if Sally could.

Finally, he was clean and turned the water off, letting the last of the suds and grime flow down the drain. He was positive he was cleaner than he had ever been before in his life. Stepping out of the stall, he reached for the towel and wiped himself down. He could still hear water running in other stalls, signifying he was first to finish. For a moment, Hugh considered going back under the tap, but he reasoned against that. He was beginning to prune up due to all the water.

As he stepped out of the stall and into the large room, with his spoiled clothes left behind on the floor, the vest over his shoulder, his camera bag in one hand, and the towel around his naughty bits, Hugh saw that while he was washing up, the orderly had made a delivery. Lying atop the table in the center of the room, in almost the same spot from where the men had taken their towels, were now three neat piles of clothes. Hugh reached down and gathered up one of the piles. To his surprise it was a two piece medical scrub suit, with slippers awaiting use under the pile. Thankfully there was a fresh pair of underwear as well, which he picked up with his free hand. With the fresh clothes in hand, he returned to his stall to dress. He passed Bobby on his way out of the stall.

Once dressed, Hugh used his towel to collect his old clothes so he wouldn't get any of the mess on him. Stepping back out, Hugh was welcomed by the sight of Icarus. The Sparrow was pulling on a pair of blue scrub pants. The shirt was left unused due to how it wouldn't fit him with his large wings. Hugh had to admit that it was odd seeing Icarus after all this time with proper pants on, pants that were in perfect condition and not torn and tattered. It made Icarus look similar to a super hero in a comic he had once seen.

Icarus turned around to face Hugh, feeling the human's eyes upon his back. "I see you have already dressed."

"Yeah," he blushed, feeling suddenly very self-conscious, his thoughts briefly flicking back to Sally's joke about how much manlier Icarus was than he. It was a godsend that Bobby soon exited his stall, dressed in more practical attire, with khaki pants, a button down shirt, and a fresh white lab coat with his name stenciled over the pocket. He carried his shotgun in one hand and the backpack in the other. His glasses were still a tad fogged up from the steam of the showers, but under them he was giving a big grin.

"My, Hugh, what would Sally say?" he chuckled. Hugh groaned and suddenly wasn't so glad that Bobby had shown up when he did.

"Seriously, though," Bobby said after laying the backpack down next to Icarus's, "I feel so much better now. I don't know where they found my spare clothes, but I am glad they did."

"You keep a spare set of clothes?" Hugh asked in surprise.

"Of course," answered Bobby as he walked back to the shower and collected his own cargo vest. "Being a doctor can be a rather messy job, Hugh. I could go over all the stains one can sustain in my line of work, but I think you'd prefer I didn't."

Hugh couldn't help but let his imagination run rampant on what sort of *stains* Bobby meant. He was still thinking about it by the time they left the shower to find a different orderly, this one younger and a tad overweight, waiting for them. Beside him was Sally, dressed up in a nurse's outfit that was a tad big on her slim frame. Her refreshed beauty banished all troubling thoughts from Hugh's mind.

She had tied her golden hair back in her famous ponytail, and Hugh could tell that she was now far more relaxed after the shower. Her cheeks shone with a healthy rosy glow, making her eyes glow all the brighter. He could see a hint of the breast plate that she had gotten from the armory peeking out from the bottom of the uniform's collar. However, what drew his eyes were the faint muddy pink stains around new white patches on the uniform. He had a brief mental image of a faceless nurse being torn into by a Hawker.

Such thoughts were quickly dashed as Sally, upon looking up and seeing Hugh, gave a playful little twirl, spinning on the tip of one toe. "What do you think, Hughie? Do I look good in this?"

"You look great in anything," Hugh said as he tried to banish all thoughts of the previous owner of the suit from his mind, as he leaned in and gave her a kiss on her lips. Before more could be said, the new orderly gave a little squeak of fear upon sight of Icarus walking out of the showers behind Bobby.

"Relax kid, he's with us," Bobby said as he patted the squeamish man on the shoulder.

"I kn-know doctor," stammered the orderly, his eyes unable to become unfixed from the face of the large Sparrow. "Dr. Craven told me about our new v-isitor."

It was then that Icarus spoke up. "Pardon, but where are our weapons?" Hugh only then realized that all their guns were no longer beside the wall where they left them before they went in to wash. The orderly started to sweat profusely as all eyes turned to him.

"Dr. Craven told me that Jenkins took them so they wouldn't get lost."

"Is Jenkins the one who showed us here?" Sally asked.

"Yes, yes!" the orderly moaned. "He had orders to take your weapons, it's not my fault. I'm only supposed to take you back to him."

"Great," groaned Hugh as he ran his fingers through his sandy hair. "I thought our guns would be here when we got back. Why did he take them?"

"I don't know," the orderly moaned again as he tried to shrink into the hard and unyielding wall behind him. "Please, just ask him! I don't know why he does anything! I only started working here last month!"

"Please calm down... um?" Sally started, before the orderly supplied his name – Jeff. "Please calm down, Jeff, no one blames you. We are all friends here, right guys?"

Hugh and Icarus both nodded in agreement while Bobby just smiled. Hugh noticed that Bobby held his shotgun in front of him, as if to say *"see why I kept ahold of this?"* Hugh sighed to himself, grateful that he at least still had ahold of his camera bag and Dr. Crick's secret journal. Just because it hadn't had all the answers to Hugh's burning questions, such as why the Hawkers took over the Nimbus and where the city was being taken, he could not bring himself to part with it. There was still a chance that there was more information hidden within its stained pages.

It was some time after Jeff the Orderly had calmed down that they were led back to the operating theater that Dr. Craven had claimed as his own. All activity in the sick room had quieted down. Several patients had fallen asleep and there were fewer doctors running about. Hugh thought he saw Nurse Rogers checking on a little girl near the door to Dr. Craven's office, but he wasn't sure because he only saw the woman from behind. He wondered, not for the first time, how so many people had managed to get safely to the basement before the killing topside got into full swing. Had Dr. Craven started moving them down early, or had they just been as lucky as Hugh, Sally, and Bobby had to survive for this long on their own?

18

"Ah, welcome back," said Dr. Craven as Jeff the Orderly pushed open the doors and allowed the group inside. The doctor was still at his desk, with the owlish creature lying atop its surface. He was feeding it a slice of an orange that he held in his other hand. Freddy devoured the morsel by taking jabs at it with its beak. "It's good to see you back in your lab coat, Dr. Robert."

"Thank you, Dr. Craven," Bobby said as he used his free hand to fix his glasses.

"We need to see about replacing that shotgun with a scalpel," chuckled Dr. Craven as he broke off another slice of the orange and held it out for Freddy to eat.

"Perhaps later, Dr. Craven," said Bobby as he fiddled with his glasses with his free hand.

"Dr. Craven, where are our weapons?" asked Hugh.

"Oh, don't worry, you will have all your equipment back in good time," said Dr. Craven. "However, that must wait till tomorrow."

"What?!" Hugh demanded. "We need those weapons if we have any chance out there!"

"Well, it's a good thing that you four are spending the night here," said Dr. Craven with a large grin on his face, making him look younger than his years.

"Oh, that is very kind of you, Dr. Craven-" started Sally before the doctor cut her off.

"Please, call me Gregory or Greg. Dr. Craven is so formal. I hear it enough from all the staff here as is."

"Excuse me, *DR.* Gregory," said Sally with a slight pout on her lips. "It is very generous of you to offer to let us stay, but we really must be going."

"I wouldn't hear of it," he exclaimed. "The storm outside is still raging and it is well after dark. No one, not even I, am allowed outside the hospital at night, regardless of the reason."

"But-" said Hugh, trying to support Sally while Bobby and Icarus remained silent. Hugh suspected that Bobby kept his mouth shut out of respect for the higher-ranking Dr. Craven and that Icarus was just being his usual emotionless self.

"No buts," said Dr. Craven, his voice taking on a dangerously sharp edge. "The Hawkers are more active at night, and we have lost enough men and woman. I will not be losing anyone else if it is within my power to keep them safe." He sighed, the underlying anger in his voice ebbing out as he stroked the speckled back of his strange pet. By now the little creature was pecking at what was left of the orange in the doctor's other hand, amber juice dripping from its small beak and onto documents that were probably irreplaceable. "Listen," he said after he had regained his composure. "We have many rooms down here in the basement. Several are unoccupied examination rooms that are not in use due to lacking the necessary equipment to treat our current patients. Currently the hospital's staff is using them as makeshift quarters to sleep in when off duty. There are plenty of free rooms with cots that I can set you up in for the night. I am going to page one of the nurses on duty to show you to your rooms."

The sound of semi-real beds to sleep in was very attractive to Hugh and the other humans' ears. It felt like ages since he last had a real blanket to pull up over his weary body and an actual pillow to rest his head on. Still, he didn't want to waste any time getting to Vulcan, regardless of if it was a wild goose chase. It was the only clear goal they had ahead of them at the moment, and they still had a lot of ground to cover before they got there. Hugh could tell, by looking back and forth between the somber faces of his friends, that they felt the same way, even Icarus. The Sparrow's beak was set in a frown, a rare sign of disapproval from the large birdman.

"You are all staying here, and that is final! *UNDERSTAND?*" said the doctor as he glared at them with his stone cold eyes. Hugh felt himself shiver a tad under the intense gaze, and noticed Sally blushing under its effects. It was no wonder that Bobby respected Dr. Craven. The man had a powerful ability to make people not only listen, but obey with a single look.

"I believe staying would be... in our best interests," said Icarus, his frown never leaving his beak and his eyes focused upon Dr. Craven.

"Ah, good," smiled Dr. Craven as he relaxed in his chair. "Good to see that someone among you has some sense. Even better to see it is this fine specimen of a new species!" There was something about how the doctor had said 'species' that made hairs rise on the back of Hugh's neck, but he was sure that Dr. Craven meant nothing by it. The nurse was promptly summoned, and as with the orderly, she was given a brief list of directions by Dr. Craven. None of them, not even Icarus with his heightened senses, could hear what was being said between the two. She was a pretty little thing, a few years younger than Sally, with black hair cut far too close to her scalp, which gave her a tomboy appearance. The only really feminine features about her were the curves of her hips and the shape of her face.

With a swift nod of her head, she turned from Dr. Craven and introduced herself. "Hello, I am Nurse Amy Rogers, if you would be so kind as to follow me?"

"Wait, you're a Rogers, too?" piped up Sally.

"Oh, you must have met my mother," sighed the nurse as she turned her head to look off to the left at nothing. "I am deeply sorry you had to meet that old fart before me. I hope she didn't tell you any dirty lies about me."

"She didn't even mention you," said Bobby, with an odd look on his face.

"That is just like that old goat," groaned the nurse as she flicked what little hair she had back behind her ear with a single hand. From behind her, Dr. Craven let out an annoyed grunt, signifying that it was time for them to head to their rooms. With another quick nod to the doctor at the desk, Nurse Amy headed to the door, not even bothering to look behind her to see if the gathered four were following her. Thankfully, they were following single file behind her, exiting the office one at a time. They followed the nurse toward the other side of the room, across from the doors that led to the showers.

As they walked down the new hallway, they passed several doors, each one with a piece of paper taped to the front with one or two names written upon it. Some doors were closed while others were open. Through them could be seen brief signs of life such as a doctor sleeping atop a cot, a family eating their supper, and so on. Hugh felt like he was walking through a museum showing displays of people's lives that would normally be hidden behind the walls of their homes. Everyone who saw them move past their door reacted upon seeing Icarus. Some gave gasps of fear, while others quickly shut their doors, locking them from the inside. Hugh was getting worried about all the negative reactions toward Icarus. He was beginning to fear that someone might react with real violence toward the Sparrow, that it was only the direct instructions to not do so from Dr. Craven that kept Icarus from being attacked.

"Nurse Amy," started Bobby, breaking Hugh free from his musings. "Aren't you a tad young to be working as a nurse here?"

"I know, right?" she sighed, taking the small cap off her head and shoving it in her pocket. "I am only sixteen, but mother dearest insisted that I come in to work here with her last week. I am little more than a glorified maid here!"

"At least you're with your mother," Sally said, trying to make light of the girl's situation.

"Humph, I'd rather be with Dad. At least he isn't stuck in this floating prison of a city." Nurse Amy then stopped suddenly and turned around to the others. "Okay, squares, here we are. Men go on the right, and the lady on the left." She pointed at the respective open doors. Hugh noticed that each one lacked a piece of paper, signifying that they were unoccupied. That is, until they came along. The nurse gave a little start before they could enter the rooms.

"Oh, right," she said as she slapped her forehead with the palm of her hand. "The Head Doc asked me to collect your nasty clothes before you settled in."

"Why?" asked Hugh.

"Ugh, so we can wash them. Duh," the nurse sighed as she rolled her eyes in their sockets. "Look, I'd rather not touch those grimy things, but the Head Doc rules with an iron fist. To defy him is to defy the hospital system, blah blahdy blah." She then looked at them all in turn. "Don't worry. They'll be delivered to your respective rooms tomorrow bright and early, by an orderly or," she grumbled, "more likely, by me."

They each offered forward the towels that they had used to carry their old clothes. The nurse took their piles in turn, first Sally, then Bobby, and finally Hugh. When she came to Icarus, she found him lacking laundry.

"I apologize," he said as he showed his empty silver palms. "I left my attire in the shower room." Hugh wasn't surprised, given how little of those trousers were left by the time they got to the hospital. It wasn't a wonder that Icarus had discarded them. There couldn't have been enough material to use as a handkerchief and what little there was left was only holding together by the thinnest of threads.

"No skin off my nose, big guy," the nurse sighed, no fear of the large Sparrow evident in her chipper voice. "Just one less thing for me to have to carry around and that is more than good enough for me."

"When will they be ready, Nurse Amy?" asked Bobby as she turned to leave them.

"No point asking me," she groaned. "I don't have a clock on me. My guess is they'll be done when they're done." And with that, she spun on the heel of her shoe and began to stroll away from them, her hips shaking rather inappropriately as she walked. Before she was out of hearing range, she once more swiveled around like a ballerina on a music box. "I almost forgot," she called back. "The Head Doc said for me to put two to a room if I can. Hope you guys don't mind sharing a cot. We never know when more guests might show up." And with that she turned and walked off down the hall and out of sight.

They were silent for a moment before Sally walked over to Hugh with a sly smile on her lips. "Well now," she said, "guess I am sleeping with you, Hughie."

"Eh?" he said. "I thought she said you are supposed to sleep on the left side of the hall?"

"Oh, Hughie," she sighed. "Sometimes you can be so *dense!*" It was then that Hugh understood what she was trying to say.

"Oh… OH!" he stuttered, his face visibly coloring, making Sally give a tinkling little chuckle and bringing a goofy grin to Hugh's face.

"Go get her, tiger," Bobby said as he headed into the nearest room on the right-hand side of the hallway. "Don't worry about me, you love birds, I got my own feathered friend to keep me company."

"Pardon?" asked Icarus, his face taking on a confused expression, his head beginning to tilt to the side in curiosity.

"I've been thinking," said Bobby as he addressed the Sparrow, "that I should get to know you a tad better if we are going to make any headway out there. I can't always be biting at the grip thinking that you are going to turn and kill us all." He then hefted his shotgun so its metal barrel caught the fluorescent light of the hall. "I have my shotgun, so if you try anything funny, I'll blow your head off. Deal?"

"I don't feel comfortable about this," Icarus admitted as he looked between Bobby, Hugh and Sally.

"Go on, Icarus," giggled Sally as she began to pull Hugh toward the open door on the left. "It's probably the only way we'll ever get Bobby here to trust you."

"I'm sure you'll be fine," Hugh agreed as Sally stepped inside. "Bob, just don't go dissecting him, okay?"

"Only as a last resort, I assure you," said Bobby as the light of the bulbs made the lenses of his glasses glow alarmingly for the briefest of seconds.

"Oh dear," said Icarus before Hugh closed the door behind him, leaving Bobby and Icarus alone in the hall.

The small examination room was hardly larger than a walk-in closet, with faded blue walls and a set of empty cupboards along one wall. At the end of the cabinets was a single sink that was dripping small droplets of water every couple of seconds. The sound reminded Hugh of the ticking of a clock, counting off every minute of the day in the most annoying way imaginable. In the center of the room was an old examination table, with cracks in its leather top and a worn blanket folded neatly atop its surface. There were a couple of pillows beside the table, along with four bottles of water and a flashlight with fresh batteries.

There was no need for the extra light, as the room was plenty bright. Above their heads shone relentlessly a light bulb that could have been a relative of the one in the secret meeting room in which they spent their last night's rest. Thankfully, this one had an easy to find off switch beside the door.

Once they had settled in, Hugh popped open his camera bag and pulled out a small box of cold cereal that he had collected from the grocery store. It wasn't his favorite brand, but after having so little to eat and having very little to choose from, he found that he was coming around to its taste. He offered the box first to Sally, to repay her for supplying the tiny sardine breakfast. She smiled and took the box daintily from his hands.

"My, such a feast you have given me," she joked as she held it up before her as if it was some mystical thing. "How did you ever manage to pay for it?"

"Money is no object for my gal," Hugh replied as he reached back into his bag and pulled out a bottle of wine. It wasn't the best stuff in the world, but when he had seen it rolling about on the floor earlier, he decided to take it just in case.

"Oh Hughie, aren't you a fancy one," she giggled. They spent a little bit of time looking around for cups in the room. There were none to be had, so with a little regret they decided to simply drink from the bottle itself. It wasn't the most romantic meal they had ever shared together, but after all they had been through, this one moment of true peace and privacy caused the good kind of sparks to fly in the air.

After finishing up their meal, Sally let out a little musical yawn and began to undress. Hugh smiled and made his way over to their little bed and started to make it up, unfolding the blanket and smoothing out the wrinkles while watching her slowly undress. He knew that this night would be one to remember forever.

Meanwhile, across the hall in Icarus and Bobby's room, Bobby was still completely dressed and had just finished his own supper of a peanut butter sandwich. Due to the size of his bag, combined with Icarus's, they had a far larger selection of food to choose from than the other two did. Icarus had turned down the suggestion of supper, saying that he only ate once a day, much to Bobby's irritation.

"I understand why you don't trust me," Icarus said without prompt. "I mean you no harm, yet I cannot change what the others have done to you. Is it so hard for you to accept that I am an ally, not an enemy?"

Bobby didn't say a word till he washed down the last of his meal with some water. "You are impossible," he said after wiping the remains from his lips with a tissue. "You are impossible. Metal cannot simply turn to flesh. I don't know what fungus my father found but it shouldn't be able to do anything of the sort to metal."

"Yet here I stand," said Icarus, his voice as level as always.

"Yet there you stand, feathers and all," agreed Bobby. "You shouldn't, but you are. You can't, but you *are.*"

"Is this the real reason why you don't trust me? My mere existence?" asked Icarus with a hint of surprise in his voice.

"Oh, it's more than just that," replied Bobby as he hopped down from the cot and walked over to an identical sink to the one in Hugh and Sally's room. "The main reason is my hatred of Hawkers, which you already figured out."

"Then why bring up my unlikely existence?"

Bobby sighed as he refilled the water bottle at the tap. "You interest me," he said. "I have never encountered a being such as you. Heck, the rules of anatomy and biology say that a living organism other than an insect can't have more than four appendages. You have six! Your brain shouldn't be able to handle all of them, yet you move with the grace of a swan!"

"I cannot explain how I function after the change has done its work."

"I can understand that," said Bobby as he screwed the cap atop the bottle and returned to the cot. "But it's still a major biological mystery. Oh how I long to look inside you and see what makes you tick. A lesser doctor with a grudge against the Hawkers would have done just that. But I will not. Not while you are still alive at any rate."

"That does not make me feel any better in your company," admitted Icarus as he picked up a water bottle of his own and took a long deep swig of its contents.

"As it is," continued Bobby, "I am more than satisfied just to observe your actions while alive than seek the answers of how you work when you are dead."

"Is that why you don't trust me?" asked Icarus again, finishing off the bottle in record time.

"I believe it's a combination of things," answered Bobby as he plucked the empty bottle from the bird and headed back to the sink. "However, I am not above talking. Tell me about your species. I want to know as much as I can. Do you live long after you become flesh? How many of you are out there? And..." Bobby stopped for a moment to turn and give the Sparrow a look that would have made lesser creatures wince under its intensity. "I want to know why you are the only one helping out us humans."

"Well," started Icarus. "As of yet I believe the most common cause of our death is being killed by Hawkers. I have also heard a few stories being told among the others of my kind of those killed off by frightened humans who could not distinguish us from the robots, but it is rare as most of us try to stay in hiding to avoid unwanted attention. I do not know if any of us have died of natural causes or old age as of yet. As to how many there are, I cannot say. We live in small flocks where we feel safe and, what word we get from the others is carried by those brave, or foolish, enough to make the flight to other flocks scattered across the city."

"You are not exactly a wealth of information, birdbrain," grunted Bobby as he finished filling the bottle and headed back to the cot. "Can you at least tell me what makes you so special that you'd be willing to help us humans instead of flying off with your own kind?"

Icarus was silent for a time, letting the question hang in the air, like a loaded gun pointed at his head. Bobby waited patiently at first, having taken a seat beside the Sparrow's feathery bronze body. As the minutes dragged on, his patience soon drained and Bobby let out a loud grunt of irritation. "Forget it."

"I don't belong."

Bobby's head snapped back to look at the Sparrow.

"I don't belong with them," Icarus said with a sigh, his bronze feathers visibly drooping all over his body, making him seem smaller than he was.

"Oh?" pressed Bobby. "What makes you say that?"

"I, I was bored," Icarus answered as he nervously fidgeted about on his side of the small table. "The others, they were too fearful to explore even our own nest. Not even my mate dared to follow me to Xandir Square until our home was destroyed."

"Your... mate?" gasped Bobby in surprise. "Does this mean that you can-"

"Reproduce?" supplied the Sparrow with a harsh laugh. "I suppose it does. She is heavy with my eggs now. I was the only one in my whole flock who dared to go that far. All the others were satisfied with simply huddling together to keep warm at night and eating what we found or hunted during the day. I sought more, and was considered a defect. Before I met Hugh, I was an outcast, even among other Sparrows."

"I see," was all Bobby said as he sat beside Icarus.

"However," Icarus said as he looked up toward the ceiling, a bemused expression decorating his grey beak, his amber eyes glittering in the manufactured light. "I don't feel alone now, not with you three humans. I can't explain it," he said as he turned to Bobby and flashed the human a big smile that made the Sparrow almost look like something out of a crazy cartoon.

Bobby stared at Icarus for a few minutes, clearly unsure of how to respond to such a strong emotion from the Sparrow. He then chuckled to himself before flashing a smile of his own. "You are one hell of an odd bird, you know that?" he asked.

"I believe it takes one to know one," Icarus smirked as he hopped off the cot and began to move their supplies around so there was space on the floor for one of them to sleep.

"Maybe you're not so bad after all," muttered Bobby as he too got off the cot, along with one of the blankets. "I hope there are others out there like you, Icarus. God knows we could use more birdbrains on our side."

19

Hugh had no idea what time it was when he finally awoke. Sally was still asleep beside him, almost atop him due to the small space of the examination table. He found he was still holding her close in an embrace that had started before they had drifted into their own individual dreams. Not that Hugh had been able to dream. His mind had completely shut down the second his eyelids finally closed, saving him from nightmares fueled by all the death they had seen before coming to this point.

As he stirred atop that tiny cot, Hugh felt Sally shift in his arms, trying to stay asleep while the waking world began to draw her back. He smiled softly and bent over to her face and gave her a kiss on the cheek. Its warmth made her shiver for a moment before her delicate eyelids fluttered open. For a moment they just looked at each other in silence before Sally spoke.

"Good morning, tiger,"

"Good morning, doll," Hugh replied as he smiled back to her.

"Shall we get going?" she asked, her drooping eyes begging that the answer be no. Hugh longed to tell her that they didn't, that he wanted to share this moment with her forever. However, he knew that such a delay might be disastrous. Deep down, Hugh knew that if they didn't leave the hospital soon, they might never leave the safety of its basement. He shook his head and slowly eased himself and Sally upright.

"Yes, I think we better if we want to get some answers, Sal," Hugh said as he brushed his fingers through her long hair, freed from all restraints as of the night before. It fell in golden cascades over her back and breasts, as if her head was the crest of a beautiful fountain. She turned her head around to face him and smiled. It was both happy and sad at the same time.

"I suppose we do have to save the world, don't we?" she asked him playfully.

"Well, we have to save ourselves at the very least. Staying here only buys us time," Hugh admitted as he pulled her close to his warm chest and held her tight. She stayed in his embrace for some time, neither speaking, nor daring to end this moment of solace. However, a knocking at their door broke the spell and they reluctantly separated. Hugh slid down from the cot, leaving Sally alone with the blanket to keep her warm. Hugh, on his way to the door, reached down into the pile beside the cot and retrieved the flimsy blue medical scrub pants that he had discarded the night before.

With his lower half decent, he unlocked the door and looked out into the hall. There was no sign of life except for a man with a laundry cart marching his way down the hallway in a direction that Hugh had yet to see. Turning to look at the cold tiles of the floor, Hugh saw Sally's clothes, now clean and folded neatly into perfect rectangles, waiting at his feet. Turning his head to look at the door across the hall, he saw both Bobby's and his own clothing stacked in a similar pile.

After retrieving his and Sally's clothes, Hugh returned to the little examination room. Sally, by then, had risen from the cot and had wandered over to the sink, only now turning the faucet on. She smiled as she reached into her purse beside the sink and pulled out a familiar looking shampoo bottle. Sally turned and gave Hugh her best smile as he entered the room, her eyes darting down to her clean clothes.

She said nothing and only pointed at the cot, indicating that Hugh should set their things down there, before beckoning him over to stand beside her. Hugh did as he was directed and soon found himself at her side, the water roaring out of the tap and down the drain, little droplets flying up and splashing against the rim of the sink.

"Shower time, Hugh," said Sally as she ducked her head under the faucet's torrent of water, her blond locks quickly darkening under the moisture.

"We just showered last night, Sally. Surely we are clean enough," Hugh said as he watched her run the water over her face before coming up for air and the shampoo bottle.

"Well, I am not putting on my clean things before cleaning up a bit," she said as she gave a playful little pout. "And I'll be damned before I put that nurse's outfit back on. That thing itches like you wouldn't believe!"

"Those scrubs weren't much better," Hugh commented as Sally squirted a handful of the shampoo into her right hand before massaging it into her scalp and threading the remainder through her long hair. "I felt like I was walking around in a paper suit!"

Sally giggled at the thought as she again dipped her head under the faucet's flow, the suds growing in quantity and foaming around where the water struck her head. She rubbed at her scalp, working the shampoo around and washing what little grime had accumulated while they had slept. It was several minutes before she came up from the sink and collected a towel from beside the sink to wrap around her hair to dry it.

Before Hugh could protest, she playfully grabbed him by the shoulders and maneuvered his head so it was subject to the flow of water. Hugh felt himself shiver under the sudden chill of the torrent, wondering briefly how Sally could have possibly withstood it, before she pulled him out. She swiftly poured some of the shampoo's contents atop Hugh's head, massaging it into his hair with her free hand, the sensation making Hugh blush. Again she pushed him under the freezing waters and began to massage the suds into his scalp. Despite the cold, Hugh loved every minute of it.

Once she was satisfied that his hair was now clean, Sally allowed Hugh to get up and turn the faucet off. She sighed and strutted over to the cot. She reached down and pulled her underwear off the top of the fresh pile of clothes and began to slip it onto her body.

"I'd kill for some real body wash," Sally moaned as she began the process of dressing. Hugh walked over to stand by her side, still dripping wet from the improvised shower.

"I know, Sal," he said as he drew her close in another hug. She smiled and looked back at him, those eyes he knew so well sparkling.

"Well, the sooner we get to the bottom of this whole mess, the sooner things get back to normal," she said as she pulled away and put on her blouse. "Honestly," she admitted as Hugh moved to his own pile and pulled on his underwear. "I am burning with curiosity. Who knows what is waiting for us in that secret Hawker lab?"

"As am I," agreed Hugh as he slipped the sleeves of his shirt over his arms. "I just hope that our host will allow us to leave."

"Me, too," agreed Sally as she slid the breastplate over her head and rested it atop her blouse. "He seemed like he was used to getting his own way, didn't he?"

"Well, he is the head of the hospital," said Hugh as he pulled his pants up. "Dr. Craven is probably used to being obeyed by his staff."

As soon as they had finished gathering up their things and had a quick breakfast, Hugh and Sally exited into the hall, where Bobby and Icarus were waiting for them. It was an odd sight given how hostile Bobby had been toward Icarus, made all the more strange by the fact that it appeared that the two were actually having a conversation while they were waiting for Sally and Hugh. Upon seeing them, both Bobby and Icarus turned to face them.

"Good morning, kids," Bobby said with a slight grin on his face. "I trust you two got plenty of rest?"

Hugh and Sally nodded in perfect unison, still surprised to see that things had calmed down between their friend and the Sparrow.

"Is something wrong?" asked Icarus, clearly sensing the unease that the couple was feeling.

"Well," started Hugh, "I guess we are just surprised to see that you two made it through the night in one piece." Sally simply nodded her head in agreement.

"Don't get me wrong," said Bobby as he glanced at Icarus beside him. "I still only trust this bird as far as I can throw him, but I feel that Icarus and I have come to an understanding."

Hugh was stunned to hear Bobby actually refer to Icarus by name. "Who are you and what have you done with Dr. Robert Crick?" he demanded as he playfully pushed Sally behind him as if to protect her from harm.

"Ha. Ha. Ha," was all Bobby said as a frown appeared on his face.

"If we are done here," said Icarus, speaking up for the first time during the conversation in the hall, "I think now would be a good time to continue with our mission." And with that, he began to walk off down the hallway. Hugh and the others fell into line behind the Sparrow as he led the way back to the room with all the patients. As they walked, Hugh noticed that most of the examination rooms were now empty, save a few that held children. Such rooms also held women who Hugh suspected were the mothers of the children in question, their fathers either hard at work guarding the hospital's basement from potential attacks or bustling about the wounded survivors and hospital patients. Hugh hoped that these poor kids would soon go back to their normal lives, and that they had not suffered too much during the Hawker attacks.

All too soon they found themselves back in the chaos of what Hugh had unconsciously nicknamed the sick room. The bustle inside the room was just as chaotic as the day before, with doctors and nurses moving this way and that. All of them still reacted to the sight of Icarus entering the room, but it was much more subtle this time. Arms reached for guns before relaxing, nurses stifled gasps and some patients brought themselves to an upright position in their cots. Word spread quickly upon their arrival and a skinny orderly pulled himself from the mess. He gestured for Hugh, Sally, Icarus, and Bobby to follow him, and he led them through the doctors and patients back to the operating theater in which Dr. Craven resided. Wordlessly, the man pushed open the doors and ushered the group inside.

Dr. Craven was not at his desk when they entered. Instead, he was standing by the edge of the circular stage, dumping a heavy plastic bag into a hazardous waste bin. He looked up from the orange dumpster upon hearing them approach.

"Ah, good morning all of you," Dr. Craven said with a smile, backing away from the dumpster, with Freddy weaving around his legs like a cat. "I trust you all slept well?"

"Yes," said Sally. "It felt great to sleep on something softer than the floor again."

"Thank you for convincing us to stay," said Hugh. "We really needed the rest."

"I thought as much," smirked Dr. Craven as he walked over to his desk, with Freddy trailing closely behind. "You all looked ready to drop."

"You were right, as always, Dr. Craven," said Bobby as he adjusted his glasses.

"So," said Hugh, trying his best to word the question he wanted to ask in a way that didn't seem rude, "When exactly do we get our weapons back?"

Dr. Craven, upon hearing the question, let out a long deep sigh and rested his chin atop his hands, while his elbows braced against his desk creating a triangle with his arms. "I would prefer that you four stay here with all of us in the Angel of Mercy's basement."

"That is very kind of you, Dr. Craven," said Sally, "but I think we better be on our way. We don't want to intrude on your kindness any longer than need be."

"Oh, it wouldn't be an intrusion if you become one of us," Dr. Craven said as he eased himself back in his leather chair. Freddy took this as his chance to hop atop the desk and spread out atop its surface, knocking several files to the floor. "You'd all be protected here," continued the doctor as he reached out one arm to lovingly stroke the speckled feathers of his owlish pet.

"With all due respect, Dr. Craven," said Bobby, a slight frown growing on his face. "We can protect ourselves. There is no need to harbor us in your community. You have more than enough people to shelter here as is. We'd only tax what resources you have left here at your disposal."

"Nonsense," Dr. Craven said as he leaned forward in his chair, causing it to creak. "I insist you stay here with us. The hospital is well-stocked and there is more than enough food here. And if we run out, we can always send out raiding parties to the neighboring buildings."

"I think we better leave," said Hugh. "We are trying to see if we can find any weaknesses in the Hawkers."

"And how do you propose to do that?" asked Dr. Craven as he leaned a bit father forward in his chair, his face beginning to lose its soft features. "Shoot at them till they drop out of the sky? Fire till all your ammunition clips are empty and hope you make a dent? I may not have had much experience with these machines, but from what I have heard from those who have, these things are indestructible."

"Be that as it may," said Bobby, as his frown started to grow a tad more noticeable, "But it is far better than just sitting here hoping that their patrols don't find us."

"You are one to talk, Dr. Robert," Dr. Craven said as his voice suddenly took on a steely edge. "You have been away from your hospital duties since last week. Do you even know how your assigned patients are doing? How could you be so selfish as to leave them alone while you went off to your own devices?"

Bobby just stood there silently, while Hugh's mind began to run an equation. He realized with a start that today was only the twelfth of July. It had been just over a week now since he first saw the Hawkers at the exhibition. So much had happened since then that he had lost track of the time. It felt like it had been years, when it had only been a few days.

"I know what you do when you are not wearing the lab coat, Dr. Robert," continued Dr. Craven. "I know you drink at that little hole downtown. Is that what you were doing this past week instead of obeying the oath you pledged?"

Bobby was steadily turning redder in the face as he listened to Dr. Craven's accusations. Each one was like a slap to him, but Bobby remained silent, taking all his blows the best he could. Hugh couldn't help but feel uneasy with how high the tension was building between the two doctors. He feared the fallout and hoped that neither he, Sally or Icarus would get pulled into it.

Once Dr. Craven had finished talking, Bobby finally spoke. "It's good that we are leaving then, isn't it, Dr. Craven? Given how you feel about me, I should imagine it would be quite a relief."

Dr. Craven then dug his fingers into poor Freddy's skin, causing the owlish creature to let out a high-pitched screech of pain. Each word the doctor said came out almost as if they were sentences onto themselves. "You Are Not Leaving This Hospital."

"Oh, I think we are, Dr. Craven, once you give us our weapons back," said Bobby. "You have made it very clear that I am not welcome here, and I am sure my former patients have been transferred to experienced doctors."

"You can't just leave!" cried out Dr. Craven, his face turning redder and Freddy squirming under his steely grip, "We can't afford to lose any more doctors!"

"Well then, as of today," said Bobby with a sad smile, "I hereby resign from my position at this hospital. My friends need me more than you do right now."

"You are staying right where you are, Robert Crick," Dr. Craven sneered, "You and all your friends are going nowhere. I won't allow you to leave this place while I am still in charge!"

"Enough," said Icarus, speaking for the first time in this bout of heated dialog. "I believe it is up to us to decide if we stay or go. Bobby has made his decision, as have the others. If you hold us against our will, how would that look to all the others under your care?"

Dr. Craven eased up on his grip on Freddy, allowing the animal to escape his hands and hop down from the desk to run off somewhere in the seats of the theater. "What are you talking about?" he demanded.

"It seems to me," said Icarus, as he crossed his arms in front of his chest and stared down at Dr. Craven like a disapproving ancient deity, "that if word spread of your actions, those residing here would begin to feel that they are not so much survivors as prisoners. They might start to rebel against your leadership."

"That is absurd!" yelled the doctor as both his hands balled up into tight fists. "They know I am only acting in their best interests, as I am with you four ungrateful -"

"Oh? And what if we told them you were keeping us from finding a way to stop those Hawker monsters outside?" demanded Sally, joining in on the conversation.

"They wouldn't believe you without proof," growled Dr. Craven.

"Ah, but we do have proof," said Hugh as he reached into his bag and pulled out Dr. Crick's journal. "It's all in this little book. "

"Let me see that!" ordered Dr. Craven as he reached out for the journal before Hugh moved it just out of the old man's grasp.

"I don't think so," he said. "With you as out of control as you are, you'd probably tear it to pieces, and this is the only thing we have to go on right now."

"OUT OF CONTROL!?" roared Dr. Craven as he slammed both of his fists into the old wooden desk, causing what was left atop it to jump slightly in the air. "I have had it up to here with you four. Get the hell out of my hospital."

"First, give us back our weapons," Bobby demanded as he tightened his grip on his own shotgun.

"No."

"What do you mean, 'No'?" asked Hugh, his own temper rising. "We'll be sitting ducks without those guns!"

"I am not going to waste perfectly good weapons on a hopeless cause," said Dr. Craven as he turned to face away from the group, as if they had simply fallen off the face of the planet and that there was something far more interesting happening over in the empty seats to his left.

"You have no right to keep them," said Sally, her voice taking on a rare angry tone. "What would the others think of you then? Sending four poor helpless people, one of them a woman no less, out into the streets with only one gun for protection?"

"FINE!" yelled Dr. Craven as he sharply turned back to the front of his desk and violently picked up his intercom. "Take your accursed guns and GO!"

20

It was quite some time later that Hugh and the others found themselves back at the elevator shaft. After Dr. Craven had summoned two very muscular and well-armed orderlies to escort them out, he apparently had also contacted whoever was in charge of the hospital's weapon cache, as there was a laundry cart waiting for them by the shaft containing all of their weapons. The two orderlies parted from the others and took up guard positions beside the doors leading back towards the other survivors, keeping their eyes on Hugh's group as they moved toward the cart. As they collected their guns, Icarus let out an irritated caw.

"My ammunition is missing from my rifle," said Icarus. Hugh turned to look at the Sparrow to see that he had pulled the clip free from the weapon and was looking at it with great irritation. Hugh turned to his own weapon and discovered that it, too, had been relieved of its bullets. Sally and Bobby, upon checking their own weapons, found that they had also been emptied out.

"I don't understand," stammered Sally as she looked at the empty clip of her dainty gun.

"I do," said Bobby with a grim look on his face as he reached into his vest with the hand not holding the gun. "Dr. Craven can spare the guns, but not the bullets."

"At least we collected extra ammunition while we had the chance," said Hugh as he followed Bobby's example and began to reload his weapon from his own ammo reserves.

"Yes," agreed Sally. "Thank God we put our spares in our bags last night, or they'd have taken those too!"

Hugh's fingers were clumsily loading the bullets into the rifle's ammunition clip and a couple slipped out of his grasp and clanged against the floor. He blushed slightly as he reached down to pick up the loose shells. As he did so, he turned his head to see how Sally was doing. Unlike him, Sally easily reloaded her weapon, leaving Hugh feeling a little jealous of how nimble her fingers were. It took a couple of minutes before everyone finished reloading their respective guns, during which the guards standing at attention by the doors leading back to the sick room eyed the four with great disinterest.

"You guys really should stay here," said the guard on the left side of the double doors in a gruff voice. "There's nothing but death up there."

"Better than being trapped down here with Dr. Brute," retorted Sally as she put her gun away in her purse after filling its chamber. "That man has a real attitude problem."

The guard merely shrugged his shoulders and became silent as he glanced briefly at his equally noiseless partner as if to say, "*Can you believe these guys?*" The other guard merely shook his head in a negative manner in response.

Before they could make their way up the ladder and out of the elevator shaft, the guards stepped in front of them, blocking their way.

"Okay, now what?" asked Hugh.

"Dr. Craven says that you have to leave behind all hospital property that you didn't arrive with," said one of the thugs. "That includes clothes, commodities, extra food, and tools."

"As if we wanted anything to remind us of your cheery little survivor camp," said Sally, her hands planted firmly on her hips.

"Sally," said Hugh, trying to keep the situation under control, "We probably should do what they say. After all, they did let us stay the night, and it is their property after all."

"With the courtesy the Doc showed you," said thug number two, "youse guys should let us keep your weapons too, as a sign of gratitude."

"Sorry, but we agreed that we keep our guns," said Bobby, as he raised his shotgun's mouth, pointing it ever so slightly towards the guards. "We'll give you back what you ask for, but only that. Understand?"

Both burly men merely shrugged and waited for Hugh and his friends to remove anything they had picked up during their stay at the hospital. Thankfully, the only things they had really taken with them were the flashlights that were left waiting for them in their rooms, and the shampoo Sally had swiped from the showers. Bobby had to insist that he keep his spare clothes and extra pair of glasses, in order to not have to strip down to his boxers and put his old clothes back on. The guards still insisted that he leave his lab coat with them, and Bobby was only too happy to oblige.

Finally, the group took their leave of the basement and entered the elevator shaft. Icarus, with his keen eyes, was the first one up the ladder. He cautiously opened the elevator doors for the first floor and waved his rifle about, making sure that the coast was clear. Upon seeing him signal the all clear, Bobby, followed by Hugh and Sally, ascended the ladder to the first floor, where Icarus was waiting for them just outside the shaft.

Once they were all safely at the top, Icarus stepped over to the elevator shaft and forced the doors shut behind them, hiding from sight all signs of anything unusual about the elevator's shaft. Before they left, Hugh made sure to snap a few pictures of the elevator doors, as part of his ongoing documentary of the disaster that had befallen the city. They didn't say a word until they were back in the front lobby of the building. The sunlight of the new day poured in through the set of large windows framing the hospital's main entrance.

"He means well," said Bobby as they moved toward the doors leading out to the empty street. There was no need for anyone to ask who Bobby meant.

"I am sure he does," said Hugh as he pushed the door open for Sally, who commented on his act of chivalry with a chuckle. "Yet, I'd still rather take my chances with the Hawkers than live under his iron fist." Before Bobby could supply excuses for his boss's behavior, Hugh interrupted him. "Look, Bobby," said Hugh as they moved farther away from the hospital with each step. "I am not saying that he doesn't have his reasons. I just think we should focus on more pressing matters than your boss's issues."

"Oh," said Bobby, his face going blank for a moment before a determined look appeared. "You're right. All that matters now is that we get to Vulcan alive."

"Correct," said Icarus as he moved toward the front of the pack, leading them while keeping an eagle eye to the sky. There were no clouds visible today and the only signs of the storm from the day before were the large puddles everywhere. The wind generated from the city's movement through the sky was as strong as ever and instantly made a mess of Sally's hair, causing her pony tail to whip about like a flag on a ship. Hugh turned to look over his shoulder back at the Angel of Mercy Hospital one last time. Before their stop, he had felt as if he and his friends were the only ones left alive in the city. Now he knew that there were plenty of survivors left in Nimbus. He could only hope that there were more still alive than just those hiding under the floor of the hospital.

They walked in silence for some time after that, seeing hardly any sign of Hawker activity in the streets or the sky. There only seemed to be one or two of the robots out on patrol, and those were easy to avoid by simply dodging inside the nearest building or hiding just out of sight inside of an alley. Hugh was thankful Icarus had not yet directed them back into the filthy sewers of the city. He did not want to have to wade through that mess ever again, and was doubly grateful Sally didn't have to suffer that indecency either. However, he did feel far more vulnerable out in the open and could tell the others shared his feelings.

It was in the way that Sally clenched her pocketbook, and the way that Bobby's knuckles whitened from the grip on his shotgun's barrel. Even Icarus showed outward signs of anxiety, his head twitching every now and then like a nervous chicken as he glanced down dim alleyways and searched the vast open sky for danger. For a brief moment, Hugh was reminded of the undercover cop that had escorted him home from the Warehouse District. Suddenly the officer's actions didn't seem nearly as inappropriate.

Since they were traveling by foot and not by district train, it took some time before they reached Bobby's apartment. It was on the way to the cable car station to Full Moon Plaza so they decided to use it as a pit stop. Sadly, upon sight of the building, their plans had to be changed. There must have been a dogfight between a Hawker and a plane from the Air Force here, as a plane had crashed right through the front of Bobby's building, completely destroying its façade. There had also been a fire at some point, as the metal of the plane and the rubble around the aircraft were blackened with soot, and thin tendrils of smoke were still floating from the wreckage. It wasn't the first ruined building they had seen during their trek since entering Tesla Quarter, but it was the first that any of them had called home to be wrecked.

Bobby simply stood there, taking it all in. He did not say a single word, the shotgun going limp by his side. Sally looked over at Hugh with an unspoken question on her face, and Hugh merely looked away from her, as if to say there was nothing they could have done. Icarus moved away from the pack and toward the ruins of what had been Bobby's home. He quietly inspected the wreckage and stepped back suddenly as the pile shifted and more of the building came down upon the plane, crushing its fuselage. From out of the mess poked bits of furniture and what Hugh guessed were the belongings of the people who lived above Bobby.

There was no telling what was going on behind the lenses of Bobby's glasses as he simply continued to stare at the carnage before him. Sally reached out to comfort their friend, but before she could touch him, he walked toward the mess and stood beside Icarus, looking at where his front door used to be. Now, instead of a door, there was a jumbled mess of bricks and a bit of a plane wing. The building looked as if a giant had decided to sit atop it and the structure couldn't hold its weight.

There was no sign of the pilot of the aircraft, though Hugh suspected that the man may had died in his seat, the cockpit hidden inside the ruined building and beyond their reach.

"My pictures of dad are in there," said Bobby in shock as he kept looking at where his front door used to be, as if he could stare so hard that the destruction would go away. "All my things, my clothes, and belongings are still in there."

"Perhaps we can find a way inside through the back?" suggested Icarus, in a vain attempt to instill some form of hope into Bobby. However, the doctor merely shook his head and gave a sad smile.

"No, the building is too unstable," said Bobby as something groaned inside the building, as if the building was on its final breaths.

"We can still try to grab something," said Hugh. He felt Sally tug on his arm, begging him not to risk his life.

Bobby merely shook his head again and turned his back to the damaged building. He slowly walked over to Hugh and Sally, each footstep seeming to cause him great pain. When he drew close to the couple, he stopped and gave another sad smile. "I really appreciate it, Hugh," he said as he gave one last look over to the building, as if saying goodbye to a dear friend. "But there's nothing left for me in there that is worth losing a life over."

Bobby was just turning back to Hugh and Sally when something flew right at him and slammed him into the street. Sally shrieked and Hugh fumbled with his rifle as a triumphant scream rang out from the Hawker that had knocked their friend to the ground. Before Hugh could unload a shot at the robot, he heard a loud ping and watched as the camera lens that served as the robot's right eye shattered and the machine toppled over dead. Glancing up from the fallen Hawker, Hugh saw Icarus running towards them, his sniper rifle smoking at the tip.

"RUN!" screeched Icarus as he hurried to them, his gun already aimed at the next Hawker, descending from a large pack flying high overhead. Hugh was horrified at how many of the robotic birds had managed to gather in the sky above them within such little time. They had been so taken in by Bobby's plight that they had dropped their guard. Now over a dozen of the evil machines were coming at Hugh's group with murderous intent.

Bobby scrambled to his feet, his glasses cracked from the sudden impact of the surprise attack. Sally was fumbling with her small gun and Hugh grabbed her arm and looked around wildly for some place that they could take cover. He didn't fire his gun, for he didn't want to attract any of the Hawkers towards them. He did, however, bring up his camera for a few quick pictures of the chaos in the sky above them, and of Icarus and Bobby fighting the metal monsters. He only took four, and two of them were taken while he was looking the other way, searching for a place to go. However, all the buildings around them had their doors closed. The nearest manhole was too heavy for Hugh to lift, and he didn't dare drag Sally into the mess that was Bobby's apartment.

"I said 'RUN'!" shouted Icarus as he fired another shot at the flock above. The bullet, caught by the wind, flew wide of its target. Hugh looked again and saw that the house next to Bobby's apartment now had its door wide open. Hugh, without questioning who had opened the door, immediately pulled Sally with him toward the shelter, stopping only to fire a shot at a Hawker that swooped dangerously close to Sally. The shot didn't hit the monster's eye. Instead it cracked against its breastplate, punching a dent into its metallic skin. This seemed to briefly disorient the creature as it lost control of its flight and crashed face first into the ground mere feet away from the couple.

Bobby had, by now, gotten to his feet and was firing rounds out of his shotgun as fast as he could reload it. His shots went wide as well, as the Hawkers had the advantage of aerial movement and were able to easily fly out of range of his blasts. Suddenly, Bobby's gun left his hands as a Hawker wrenched it free and turned the mouth of the barrel upon him. Before it could fire, Icarus tackled it like a professional football player, causing the machine to drop the weapon and slam into the pavement. Before Bobby could act, Icarus claimed the doctor's shotgun and fired it into the eye of the stunned Hawker before it could get up.

"Use this," said Icarus, as he quickly gave Bobby his rifle. "It has better range than your gun. It will make you more effective from down here. Use the ammunition in my bag if you need to reload it. I'll take your bag and use your spare shells to bring the battle to the skies." And with that, Icarus flew up into the air.

"Hey," was all Bobby could say as he watched dumbly as Icarus rapidly emptied the weapon upon a couple of airborne Hawkers, causing them the spin out of control and crash into Bobby's former home. This resulted in another landslide of bricks and debris. Bobby, once realizing what had happened, quickly brought Icarus's rifle to bear and did his best to fire it with the same accuracy as the Sparrow had. Meanwhile, Hugh had managed to escort Sally to the safety of the other house, which was an almost perfect double for Bobby's apartment, only it was still in one piece, and didn't have an exterior staircase. As they dove inside, a familiar girl was cuddled up against a corner of the front hall by a staircase.

"Amy?" gasped Sally as she saw the girl shiver and pull her legs tighter against her body. There was no time for any more words as a Hawker flew at them through the still open doorway of the house. Sally managed to step out of the metal beast's way before it could dig its cruel claws into her skin. Hugh acted as fast as he could and drew his rifle and fired another shot. Again, he missed his target, but did manage to land a bullet in an ugly painting on the wall to the left of the Hawker.

The robot turned on Hugh, its face taking on as close to an evil grin as its mechanical face could manage before it struck with its claw, knocking Hugh over. Amy continued to cower in the corner, covering her face with both her hands while Hugh struggled to rise. There was a loud bang, as Sally fired her handgun, getting the attention of the beast. The bullet hit the robot in the back of its head, and a tiny trickle of fluid leaked out. It spun around impossibly fast and reached out to claw her. Hugh reacted faster than he ever thought he could, and slammed the hilt of his weapon into the robot's head.

Something gave under the blow and the Hawker fell over. Sally took this as her chance to move. She grabbed for Amy's slender arm and pulled her up off the floor despite her protests. "Come on, it's not safe here!" shouted Sally at the scared girl. Hugh hurried over to Sally and helped her pull the screaming girl off the floor. As they turned to head deeper into the house, Bobby and Icarus ran inside.

From a quick glance, Hugh could see crimson streaks trailing down the front of Bobby's shirt and similar trails running down Icarus's chest. Both the man and the birdman were panting, Bobby from the strain of having to drag Icarus's heavy backpack inside, and Icarus from his aerial acrobatics. Bobby took one quick look at Amy, still trying to pull away from Hugh and Sally's grip, and took on an expression of utter surprise. However, he snapped back to attention, and began to look around the room, searching for something that could be used to reinforce the door. Upon noticing the downed Hawker, still woozy from Hugh's blow, Bobby fired a round point blank into its eye, finishing it off once and for all.

"We've got to get out of here!" cried Amy, going into hysterics, while Hugh and Sally continued to try to drag her farther into the house.

"That's what we're doing, sweetie," said Sally in her most soothing voice, trying to calm the young nurse down.

Suddenly a loud rat-a-tat-tat filled the air outside the house. Icarus, who had just shut the door and barred it from the inside, peered out of one of the hall windows.

"What's going on now?" grunted Bobby as he brought up the rifle, his shotgun still in Icarus's possession. "Please tell me the Hawkers haven't gotten their claws on machine guns out there."

Icarus shook his head and backed away from the window. "It's the Air Force," he said as he rejoined the rest of the group at the end of the hall.

"Oh, thank God," said Sally as she reached up with the hand not holding the arm of the young nurse and brought it to her heart, possibly in the act of prayer. Hugh watched as she gave a small start upon hearing her gun, still held tightly in her hand, bump against her protective breastplate. Sally blushed for a brief moment with a nervous smile passing across her pale face, before Amy, still in hysterics, spoke up.

"The Air Force? Are they here to save us?"

"They already have, as far as I'm concerned," said Hugh as he looked over to the window Icarus had been staring out from. "However, we need to keep moving. It's still not safe here for any of us."

"Oh, God," moaned Amy, too quiet for anyone to hear. "Why did I leave the safety of the hospital?"

"I agree," said Icarus as the sounds of the sky battle outside grew louder, bullets raining down upon the street outside like rain. The enraged, shrill yells of the Hawkers rang out at random as the fight raged on outside the house. Icarus swiveled his head from the others to look toward a triangular door built into the side of the stairs. "We need to get below ground," he said as he headed toward the door. "We will all be far safer in a basement, and if we are lucky, there will be a way into the sewers from there."

"The SEWERS?" cried Amy, even more shocked by this than the sudden Hawker attack on Hugh and his friends in the street. "Like hell we are going down there! Do you have any idea what kind of germs are down there?!" she moaned to herself as she tried again to pull away from Hugh and Sally, but their grip held firm.

"The sewers would be safer than running around outside in that bullet storm," said Hugh, trying to reason with the young nurse. "We'd have some pavement and stonework over our heads for protection against any stray shots from the battle and limiting the chances of Hawkers being able to pick us off one by one from the sky." However, it wasn't any good. Nurse Amy was too far into hysterics to pay any more attention to what was happening around her, let alone to be reasoned with. She was crying and struggling against Hugh and Sally's grip on her arms. Red welts began to show on Amy's arms and Hugh began to worry if he was squeezing too tight on the poor girl's arms, and he could see his worry reflected on Sally's face. But what other choice did they have? If they merely let go, Amy would probably run out of the house and into certain death due to her panicked state.

"Snap out of it!" ordered Bobby, his voice just loud enough to drown out the nurse's cries. He pushed himself between Hugh and Sally and got very close to Amy's face. Hugh and Sally both shot Bobby warning looks. There was no telling what Bobby was going to do to the poor nurse, given what he had just seen of his own home and all that they had been going through. Perhaps that is why what happened next surprised everyone.

Bobby, without a word, brought the frightened young Amy close to him in a comforting hug. The girl went slack in his arms, just as shocked by the doctor's action as the other humans and the Sparrow in the room. It was so sudden that it was almost as if someone had flipped a switch. Hugh would have bet every last penny he had to his name that Bobby was going to slap some sense into the young woman with the flat of his hand.

No one moved for what felt like an eternity. The only sounds were their breathing and the exchange between aircraft and flying robots outside the walls of the house. Even the panicked girl began to quiet down in Bobby's comforting hold. She looked younger than her years in that moment, as if she was just a little girl being comforted by her father.

"There, there," Bobby eventually said as he held Amy, his voice soft and steady. "It's all going to be okay."

"Okay," repeated Amy in a daze. Her eyes were clouded over and her body was still very much in shock. Thankfully, she was also far calmer now, the hug having served as the glue putting her back together. Slowly, she started to rouse from her stunned state, becoming a tad more responsive to the group around her.

"Amy," he said as he kept eye contact with the pale girl's face, making sure it was all she could see. "I know this is very traumatizing. But we are not safe here, we need to go. Do you understand me, Amy?" She merely nodded her head in response.

While Bobby was comforting Amy, Icarus was still looking at the door in the side of the stairs. He turned to Hugh, who was still in mild surprise over the display of sympathy from Bobby. "Hugh," said Icarus as he reached for the door's knob. "We can't stay here much longer."

"Right," agreed Hugh, turning to look at Sally to see that she was ready to move. She gave a swift nod of her head in answer. Hugh turned toward Bobby and the girl, still huddled together. Hugh wasn't sure when he had let go of Amy's arm, but now that limb was limp against the nurse's side. "Bobby," said Hugh with a hint of hesitation in his voice. He was not completely sure that Amy was stable now, and didn't want the girl to go back to panicking before they got to safety.

Bobby nodded his head and turned back to Amy. "Amy," he said. "Are you ready to move?"

Before she could respond there was the sound of something crashing into a room somewhere above their heads. The nurse let out a sudden shriek and pulled back from the doctor, covering her face with her free arm. Dust began to drift down from the ceiling of the hallway much like snow, giving that small hall a surreal appearance. By now Icarus had forced the basement door under the stairs open. The Sparrow flipped a switch and the stairs leading down became well-lit, showing wooden steps leading down. Icarus turned to look at the others and saw that Amy had become paralyzed in fear once again, and not even Bobby's comforting actions seemed to be helping now. Without a word, and much to Bobby's protests, Icarus walked over to the girl and carefully hefted her up in his arms and carried her over to the basement stairs.

With the sound of bullets beginning to hit the house, the others quickly followed the Sparrow down the narrow steps into the cellar. Hugh found himself bringing up the rear of the pack, and decided to shut the small door behind them before hurrying down the stairs. The meager electric light in the cellar room flickered alarmingly as he reached the final step and the concrete floor below.

Taking a moment to look around, Hugh could see that there were several shelves stationed around the basement, holding all sorts of odds and ends. A couple near the stairs were stacked with spices and canned goods while others toward the back of the room held cardboard boxes of assorted sizes. Sally and the others were gathered together in the center of the room, looking up at one of the bare bulbs swinging around in the ceiling from the city's movements and vibrations of the fighting. As Hugh walked over to the others, he noticed that the jars were all rattling on the shelves. Some had shaken so much that they had shifted about and fallen to the floor, resulting in a mess of broken glass and pickled peaches.

Amy was no longer in Icarus's arms and was sitting on the ground, surrounded by the others. Sally was currently sitting on the floor next to the nurse, trying to comfort her much as Bobby had upstairs, with only moderate success. Bobby himself was now looking over Icarus's chest, pushing aside the Sparrow's feathers and revealing the bird's pale skin and the wounds he suffered while fighting. From what Hugh could see as he drew closer to the group, he didn't think any of the cuts on the birdman's body looked all that serious, several only as long as an inch. It was a marvel how the Sparrow had not suffered far worse injuries while defending them. It did make Hugh feel oddly comforted to see that Icarus indeed bled bright crimson blood. It made him think that Sparrows weren't all that different from humans deep down inside.

"Dennis," said Amy all of a sudden. "Where's Dennis?"

"Dennis who, honey?" asked Sally, as she brushed the girl's hair.

"Dennis Talford, he lives here," said Amy as she brought a hand to her forehead and began to rub her face as if she was washing it.

"Bobby," started Hugh as he turned to Bobby, who was now applying alcohol to Icarus's cuts with small cotton swabs. Hugh would have asked where his friend had gotten medical supplies, but since they had only just left a hospital, it seemed like a silly question to ask. Instead he asked him if he knew who owned the house they were currently taking shelter in.

Bobby paused for a moment, pressing a tad too hard on the cotton swab, making Icarus wince slightly at the sting of the disinfectant. "I think Martha and Stanley Talford live here with their boy Denny. I don't really know them all that well."

"Dennis, I need to find Dennis," said Amy like a mantra, over and over, the words beginning to finally bring her around completely. Her eyes brightened and color returned to her cheeks. She suddenly rose and looked for the first time at the others around her. "Oh, I know you people," she said as Sally rose to her feet and Hugh joined his lover by her side. "You're the people that Dr. Craven threw out of the hospital."

"It's good to see you have come to your senses," said Bobby as he looked over his shoulder at the young nurse, his hands still working on Icarus's cuts, applying small bandages to the Sparrow's wounds. "Maybe you can tell us why you happened to be out here where the action is?"

"It's none of your business," she said as she turned her nose up in the air. "How about you guys tell me how we got in Dennis's basement?" Before any of them could answer, there was a loud crunch from outside. It sounded similar to what one would hear if a car traveling at highway speed rammed into a brick wall. Amy cried out in surprise as the others looked up toward the side of the room the sound had come from. It was not clear if what they heard was a plane or a Hawker crashing outside, but the sound was very disturbing all the same.

"I ask again," said Bobby as if nothing had happened, "Nurse Rogers, why are you here? You were perfectly safe back in the hospital."

She shivered before them, and looked as if she was going to fall apart again. With a deep breath, Amy shook her head, balled her hands into tight fists and looked over toward the boxes at the back of the room and took on a distant expression. She then let out that breath and turned to face all of them in turn, her face fixing in a determined look that seemed impossible given how they had found her in this place.

"I left to find my boyfriend," she said as an explosion sounded outside the basement, causing a few more jars to fall and the lights to swing again, resulting in shadows that grew and shrank. "I will do anything for him. I haven't heard from him since he last called me before the phones went dead. If he is still alive, he'd be waiting for me in one of our special places. This is one of them, and the other is the back room of the store he works at over in Full Moon Plaza."

"Nurse Amy," said Bobby, rising up from his place before Icarus. "I think that you'll have an easier time finding him once the mess outside sorts itself out. You'd better be heading back to the hospital."

"Are you bent?" asked Amy. "There is no way I am going back to that dive now. Dennis wasn't here, so he must be over at the mall. I am going there next, not back to the Land of Craven."

"Honey," pleaded Sally as she looked back and forth between the young nurse and Hugh, "it's too dangerous out here. We barely got you to safety this time."

"Sally's right," agreed Hugh. "We barely got off the street alive. Just a few more seconds out there and we'd probably all be dead. Those Hawkers are real monsters."

"Humph," grunted Amy as she crossed her arms and looked off toward the shelves of boxes at the end of the room. "I am not going back, and that's final. Not that I could go back if I even wanted to. King Craven has this little policy. If you leave without his permission, you aren't getting back in."

21

Everyone looked at Amy in surprise at what she had said. Bobby merely shook his head, as if he had heard of similar acts from his former boss. "What?" she demanded as she took them all in, her words the only thing penetrating the sudden silence. Hugh was unsure what to think at that moment, for how could a member of his own species be so inhumane? Sally was the first to voice what they all were thinking at that moment.

"Are you serious?" she asked, her eyes wide in disbelief. "How could Dr. Craven be so cruel?"

Amy simply shrugged her shoulders and let out a breath of air in a deep sigh. "Yes, I'm serious," she said. "It's one of Dr. Craven's many rules of his little basement kingdom. One of his most enforced rules in fact. Don't look so stunned. I'm not the first to slip away from his fingers, and neither are you. We've had several security guards, doctors and even a couple of patients run away. The guards inside the elevator shaft are under orders to keep any of the runaways from coming back into the basement, should they return to the hospital."

"That sounds like Dr. Craven," sighed Bobby as he put his head in his hands, massaging his temples with his fingers. "The man simply won't tolerate insubordination. We had a saying back at the hospital before this whole mess started. 'If you don't work with Dr. Craven, you don't work at all.' He's been known to fire doctors just for disagreeing with him."

"This just proves we made the right decision to leave while we could," said Icarus, as he rose from the ground and headed toward one of the squat dirty windows looking out from the cellar to the world outside. "I had a feeling that things were not as they appeared there. I could feel a sense of unease in the air, but did not wish to say anything in case I was mistaken."

"I think we all felt that in some subtle way, Icarus" said Sally, "though I thought it was just the frantic pace the doctors were working with their patients."

"Guess I'm going with you guys now," said Amy as she eyed Icarus's muscular back.

"I'm sorry, what?" asked Hugh in surprise. "I don't think-"

"Well, you are going to Full Moon Plaza," interrupted Amy. "I already told you Dennis is waiting for me in our special place over there, and I overheard you talking with Craven about heading that way. It works out for everybody." Hugh wasn't so sure about that. Amy was just a teenager after all, and very inexperienced in dealing with the Hawkers. It wasn't clear if she would freeze up in a panic attack again if they encountered another battle with the robots. However, he could tell that right now she was dead set on getting to her boyfriend, and come hell or high water, nothing was going to stop that little lady from her goal.

"It is going to be very dangerous out there, Amy," said Sally as she tried to talk the girl out of coming with them.

"I'm not staying here all alone," said Amy as she spread her arms wide, as if she could sum up the whole house in the space between her hands. "This place is a wreck and I doubt I can hide down here forever without something nasty getting to me. Let's not forget, I can never return to my dear sweet mother, so I might as well take my chances with you guys. You do seem to at least know how to protect yourselves."

"To be fair, we are better at keeping out of trouble than fighting," admitted Hugh as he adjusted the strap supporting his rifle over his shoulder. It weighed heavily on his back, like some evil growth. Again, he felt himself asking what he was doing here. He was just a photographer, a guy who only shot pictures, not bullets. He hardly knew what he was doing when he pulled the trigger, and he could still feel bruises from the kick of the rifle he had fired just moments before, and a dull ache from his weak arm. Yet, he was still alive. He knew that he couldn't have done it without his friends. He was thankful that Sally had also survived as long as he had, and prayed that they both would come out of this alive, along with Bobby, Icarus and anyone else left alive in Nimbus.

"Look," said the nurse, glancing back over at the boxes and the back of the room. Hugh wondered what Amy was thinking about every time she looked off in that direction. "I am more than just someone for you to escort across the city. I can be helpful, too."

"No offense, Amy," said Bobby with a slight smirk on his face, "but I really don't think giving you a gun would be a very good idea."

"That's not what I meant," said Amy as she scowled. "I can help you get through Full Moon Plaza's restricted areas. You know, so you don't have to move about out in the open?"

"What're you talking about?" asked Sally.

The nurse let out another sigh and rolled her eyes. Hugh was beginning to wonder if the girl had breathing problems due to how often she was sighing. However, he had a feeling that it was only because Amy was losing patience with them. "I am not an idiot. I know that traveling around in the open streets with those bird things flying around is suicide. I did my best to stay out of sight when I was making my way to Dennis's house. Due to Dennis's position at the mall, he has access to the maintenance and employee hallways behind the shops. They connect to almost every storefront in the district, and will allow you guys to travel about as you please without any of the flying metal-heads catching on."

"I think it is safe outside now," said Icarus, still staring intently out the basement window. Everyone moved to join him by the glass to peer out of it. "I haven't seen anything fly by overhead for several minutes and there hasn't been a single bullet fired. I think now is the time to move out."

While waiting in the basement for just a little longer to make sure the coast was truly clear, Hugh, Sally, Icarus, and Bobby took the time to reload their weapons. Icarus managed to talk Bobby into keeping the Sparrow's rifle. It was clear from the battle they had just been through that Icarus would benefit more from holding onto the shotgun due to his ability to fly, enabling him to get up close and personal with any Hawkers in the air. Bobby reluctantly agreed to make the weapon swap official, and handed over his supply of shells for the gun. They offered to give Amy a weapon, but she refused, stating that she'd be fine without one because she thought she'd as likely shoot one of them as an attacking Hawker.

Leaving the basement proved to be a tad difficult, as some debris from the upper parts of the house had fallen before the door to the front hall. It took all of the men's combined strength to force the door open, pushing aside broken beams and what appeared to be the smashed body of a Hawker. Amy turned pale at the sight of the mangled robotic body, and Hugh felt himself become a bit nauseous as well. The wicked thing was twisted in an unnatural shape, with its arms at odd angles and its head only attached to the stump of its neck by the thinnest of wires. There was nothing biological about this creature. It was pure mechanical machine, save for the strange gelatin-like substance that seemed to be oozing out of the hole in its head. Hugh could only assume that it was the creature's bio-brain, a good sign that this Hawker was truly dead.

As they inched their way around broken boards and toward the front door, Hugh turned to see Amy looking at everything in a face that tried to hide the horror she must be feeling. Like Bobby and his house, this building had been a place she was connected to. Stepping out to the street, they were greeted with the sight of another downed aircraft, spread out across the pavement like a giant wounded bird, its metal body glistening in the light of the sun and fire flowing out from its cockpit. Taking one last moment to check the skies above for any sign of life, and for Hugh to snap a couple of pictures of the crashed aircraft, Icarus led the group around the back of the house and into the neighbor's backyard. They were now back on their previously agreed upon path and made their way in and out of what buildings they could take shelter in.

Occasionally Icarus would try to get them below street level and back into the sewers, but every manhole they found was locked and required a special key. This didn't stop the Sparrow from trying every time they came across an entrance to the sewers. Since learning their lesson outside of Bobby's apartment, they did not linger for more than a couple of seconds, even when off the streets. The sun slowly sank overhead as they made their way through the devastated district, while the wind was as strong as ever. It was no longer clear if they were still in the skies over Kansas at this point or if they had crossed over into Colorado.

It was very late in the afternoon when they had to stop to rest their legs. They had decided to hold up inside a hardware store just a couple of blocks away from their destination. It was a good hiding spot, as someone had blocked the plate glass windows with large sheets of plywood, hiding the interior from prying Hawker eyes. The inside of the store was a complete mess, with tools lying about everywhere on the floor. However, it was nowhere near as bad as some of the other buildings they had traveled through, and there weren't any dead bodies inside, only a couple of blood stains here and there. The atmosphere reminded Hugh briefly of the first floor of the hospital.

They walked around the store for a bit before finding a part of the floor clear enough for them to sit down. It was agreed that they'd take this chance to eat lunch, for it wasn't clear if they'd be able to eat later on in Full Moon Plaza. They shared what they had with Amy. She ate her fill in moments, faster than Hugh had seen anyone consume a meal.

"Careful, you need to breathe, too, you know," joked Hugh, munching away at his sandwich. He was thankful that Bobby had found a loaf of bread back at the grocer. He and Sally had finished off their cereal for breakfast and all he had left were canned goods and a couple of tins of crackers and cookies. He also had on hand a couple of bottles of water and a container of powdered milk.

"Sorry," apologized Amy as she reached for her bottle of water to wash her own sandwich down, "I was just so sick of the stuff they were serving at the hospital. Compared to that, this stuff is food of the gods!"

"That's why I always brown-bagged my lunches at the hospital," said Bobby as he took another bite of his own sandwich. "I wouldn't feed that mush to a rat, let alone a patient. I do wonder sometimes if the staff even knew how to use a stove and measuring cups."

"I highly doubt it's *that* bad," chuckled Sally as she nibbled her own sandwich. "Although, I can't imagine their standards are very high given the current circumstances."

"Trust me," chuckled Bobby, "it *was* that bad."

"Speaking of food," said Icarus as he finished his special sandwich of tuna on rye, "I wonder how long our supply will last before we need to resupply?"

"Well, I am pretty sure you guys can get everything you need once we find Dennis," said Amy as she finished off her water and used the sleeve of her uniform to wipe the crumbs off her face.

"Speaking of which," said Icarus, "how do we find him once we get to the next district?"

"Don't worry, bird-boy," Amy chuckled. "Dennis gave me a couple of tours of the place last month when he got the job at the mall. I know where to go due to my photographic memory." She emphasized the last few words by tapping a finger against the side of her head.

When they had finished eating, they sat around for a little bit to give their food time to digest. Bobby used this time to move off to another corner of the store to inspect his own wounds since there was more privacy here than there was in the basement thanks to the back offices of the store. While he was away, Sally and Amy began to talk amongst themselves while Hugh and Icarus gave the ladies some space to shoot the breeze.

"Icarus?" started Hugh, once they were at the other end of the store, out of earshot but not sight of Sally and Amy.

"Yes?" said Icarus, looking at Hugh.

"I was wondering if I could ask you to do something for me, since we have a few moments of peace."

"Alright, what is it that you wish?" asked Icarus, his head tilting slightly in curiosity.

"If something happens to me during all of this, if I don't make it, could you make sure Sally gets out of Nimbus alive?" Hugh did not want to think too much about what would happen if their search for some sort of weakness in the Hawkers turned out to be in vain, or that he would die somewhere along the way. However, he did know it was always a possibility that something could go horribly wrong. He wanted to know that Sally would be safe, even if he was killed.

Icarus looked at Hugh for a few moments. Then he spoke in a firm tone. "I will do as you ask, but take heed. This is not an excuse for you to give up in any future fight. We need all of us to be strong in the coming times, and any inkling of self-doubt could be the difference between our survival and our downfall."

"I am not saying I am just going to stand there and die, Icarus," grumbled Hugh. "I am just trying to be realistic. I am not an experienced gunman like Bobby or a trained marksman like you."

"I have seen you handle your weapon, Hugh," said Icarus, gripping the human by his shoulder and making him turn to face the Sparrow head on. "You may be inexperienced, but you are far from helpless. You have managed to land a few good shots when it counted. You just need practice and teaching. If you like, I can teach you how to hold your weapon properly. That way you won't be bruised every time the gun fires and your shots will hit their target. We will have to wait till we are someplace safer in order for me to help you with your aiming and firing. After all, we don't want to attract unwanted attention."

"You have a point there," said Hugh as he glanced over toward the boarded up windows. The wood did a very good job of limiting how much of the store could be seen from the street, and made it very dark inside the store. Most of the lights were out, and they didn't bother to try to find a switch to turn them on in case any passing Hawkers noticed the light peeking out through the cracks in the boards. They had made do with Sally's flashlight since they first entered, because when they had left the hospital, they had to return the flashlights that were given to them, leaving them with only Sally to provide their light. There weren't any flashlights in the hardware store. They had probably been taken by others long before their group had arrived.

While Icarus and Hugh were talking, Bobby was off in the office, cleaning his wounds. It had not seemed like it at the time, but when the Hawker tackled him outside his home, he had taken a bit more damage than he had thought. These cuts had stopped bleeding over the time that they had been walking around Tesla Quarter, and dried blood had caused his shirt to stick to his skin. It hurt when he pulled off his shirt, and tiny fresh beads of blood formed over the cuts. He sighed and began to pull the scabs off so he could properly clean out the cuts. He winced as he felt the sting of the disinfectant contacting the sensitive skin. To take his mind off of the minor pain, Bobby began to think about his father, and when he had last seen him before he had been admitted to the hospital and kidnapped.

Bobby was a bit of a natural loner. He had preferred to be by himself even at a young age, choosing to stay away from the other kids and even his parents. That wasn't to say he wasn't close to his father. In truth he deeply respected his father and cherished all the time he spent with the elder Crick. It was just that in the early days of Bobby's life, his father was constantly working trying to make ends meet. It was only when Bobby entered high school, when their family's financial woes had eased up, that his father was able to spend more time with him. They spent a lot of time fishing and doing puzzles together on the weekends, sometimes even going out to the shooting range if the weather was right. Things changed when they had moved to Nimbus over eight years ago. Suddenly, Dr. Frank Crick had a lot less time to spend with Bobby.

Shortly after they had moved to Nimbus, Bobby decided to follow in his father's footsteps by going to medical school in Topeka. He still took the time to visit his father up in Nimbus, and officially moved back to the flying city after he graduated. However, they still spent less time together. When Bobby had time off, his father was working overtime at his private lab, and whenever Dr. Crick was free, Bobby seemed to be scheduled to either operate or attend meetings. Still, Bobby made time for his father as often as he could. The last time they had any free time together had been when they had supper in the last week of June. They had gone to a rather expensive steakhouse in Liberty Estates, and had talked about life. Thinking back now, Bobby could barely remember what had been said at that table. Had he been talking about a surgery or a movie?

As he finished tending to his own injuries, which proved to be minor, Bobby found himself wondering if his father was even still alive. It had, after all, been over a week since he last saw his father, and even then, his father was unconscious. What were the chances that his father was still alive after all this time? His memories of his mother were faint now, and despite the knowledge that everyone dies sooner or later, he couldn't help but pray that his memories of his father would not be the last he'd ever see of him.

22

By the time they were ready to leave the small hardware store, the light was growing dim outside. There was still an hour of daylight left, but they would have to camp somewhere in Full Moon Plaza for the night. The walk to the Tesla cable car station to Full Moon was fairly uneventful, due to how close it was to the hardware store. As before, the gate to the platform was barred and locked and Icarus had to lift them over the gate, one by one. However, this time those waiting to be carried over hid in the lengthening shadows so as to avoid drawing too much attention.

Once they were all on the other side, they entered the cable car and shut the door behind them. Icarus sank tiredly into the faux leather seats of the car, exhausted from having to lift four people up and over the gate. Hugh couldn't help but be reminded by this sight that Icarus was not some machine that could keep going as long as it was kept full of gas. As before, the car did not budge even when the doors were closed, so Icarus had to once again reach up and manually start the car's engine to send them on their way.

"That reminds me a lot of Dennis," said Amy as she watched Icarus fiddle with the car's engine. "He is really good with machines. Why, only last May, he came over to our house to fix our washing machine, and once he was done, that old thing worked better than ever."

"You must really love him," said Sally.

"You bet I love him," said Amy as she turned to face Sally, a big dreamy grin spreading across her face. "We've known each other ever since we first met in middle school. Dennis was the only guy who ever really clicked with me. All the other boys at school teased me about how short my hair is."

"Guess they're just behind the times," mumbled Hugh as he gazed out the glass window of the car, watching the Earth moving far down below. Currently the city was passing over a large lake or pond, and he could see Nimbus's underside reflected in the glittering surface. From here, the city looked like a bunch of floating upside down tea cups, minus the handles. Soon the city passed over the edge of the water and the reflection vanished, replaced by a cluster of buildings and several cultivated fields.

"No kidding," said Amy as she flicked the short strands with her hand. "I can't stand long hair. It's such a pain to clean and it tangles too easily. Short is much more manageable, and Dennis perfectly understands that. Everyone else calls me a tomboy for it."

"Well, I think you look very fashionable," said Sally with a smile on her face.

The actual ride across the abyss was nowhere near as exciting as the one during the storm. However, the car still swayed about during its journey, which, as Hugh could tell, made Amy very nervous. When she finally looked outside the windows, she let out a sudden gasp that made everyone look at her.

"What's wrong, what did you see?" asked Bobby, cradling his new rifle in his hands, looking somewhat naked without his shotgun.

"The ground outside is moving!" Amy said as she pointed with a finger out the window. "How is that possible?"

"We don't know for sure," said Hugh as he shrugged his shoulders. "Nimbus has been on the move for the past couple of days, and it's been going west. We have no idea where exactly it's going."

"You don't?" Amy asked, her face turning pale. "Do you at least have any idea why the city is moving? Are we behind it or is it the Hawkers?"

"It's hard to say exactly," said Icarus as he reclined in his seat, his wings completely unfolded, filling out most of his side of the car. "I have seen the Hawkers running around below the streets, and we have no reason not to think they have found Nimbus's control center and are moving the city for reasons that are not yet clear."

"You are a big help, birdman," said Amy with a huff before turning even paler. "Wait," she said as she looked back out the window toward the diminishing Tesla Quarter behind them. "You say those things are running around in the bowels of the city?"

"Hugh and Icarus encountered several before they met up with us in the sewers," said Bobby as he took his glasses off and rubbed at the lenses with a new cloth he had picked up somewhere along the way. "We've seen a couple more since then. Some of them were chasing us, while others we saw through a hole in the wall."

"Don't forget about the Hawker bodies we found on the stairs," Sally pointed out.

"You have a point there," Bobby said. "Now that I think about it, those bodies were picked clean of all the useful metal parts. Guess the Hawkers are into recycling."

"That doesn't make sense," said Amy as she looked between the two. "I thought Hawkers were nothing but metal. If you take away the metal bits, what's left?"

"It's a long story," said Hugh as he scratched at the back of his neck, the vest's rough collar making the skin of his neck prickle. "To make it as short as possible, Hawkers turn into Sparrows, and their metal bits are replaced by biological ones."

"That's far out!" exclaimed Amy, as she turned to eye Icarus in a new light. "I have met a couple of Sparrows before, but I had no idea they were originally Hawkers!"

"You've seen other Sparrows?" asked Icarus in surprise. "I thought most of my kind stayed well away from humans. How did you find them?"

"Down, boy," said Amy. "I found them by accident, not even sure where, but it was after school let out. I might tell you more about it later, but first, I need to ask, are the others back in the hospital's basement safe? If these robots are running around below the streets, does that mean they'll eventually find the others?"

"I doubt it," said Bobby. "The basement is isolated from the sewers and, as far as I am aware, there aren't any 'secret entrances' into the basement from the lower levels of the city. Everyone should be fine down there. What's more, I know Dr. Craven. He would never have everyone move down there if he wasn't sure everything was perfectly safe. The man may be over controlling, but he is not an idiot."

"I suppose you're right, Dr. Robert," sighed Amy as she relaxed in her chair. "I suppose if anything were to happen, they have enough guns to at least put up a fight."

"That's the spirit," nodded Hugh as he let a comforting smile spread across his lips. He couldn't help but wonder about where Amy had seen the other Sparrows and he could tell from how Icarus was fidgeting in his seat that the Sparrow also wanted desperately to know as well. However, Amy had turned her head away from all of them to stare out the window at the ground drifting by below. It was clear from how she leaned her face against the glass that she was done talking for now, and to be honest, Hugh was feeling very exhausted from all they had done that day.

Before he turned to take in the same entrancing sight as the nurse, Hugh made a vow to himself to ask Amy more about where she had seen the other Sparrows. If they were lucky, they might find other encampments of the birdmen in similar areas of the city, and if possible, might be able to convince some of them to help in their fight against the Hawkers. Hugh had a feeling that alone, Icarus would be overrun if there were too many Hawkers flying about, a fact made all the more clear during the ambush hours ago. They surely would have died if the Air Force hadn't arrived when it did.

With his thoughts drifting back to the fighter planes and the city itself, Hugh turned to look at the approaching Full Moon Plaza. They were only a few minutes away from docking at the district. Yet, Hugh could still see several open hatches in the side of the floating district that he hadn't seen when he first traveled to this part of the city while on his way to see Mad Mike. He had a feeling that those breaches in the side of the district were where the antiaircraft guns were hidden. He had been baffled by them when he first saw them in motion back in the room with the monitors, but now he had time to think about them and the secret areas of the city of Nimbus. The hidden mortars now made sense, considering Nimbus was a flying city. The guns were most likely installed, as Hugh reasoned to himself, as a protective measure against any attack by enemy aircraft from nations America was not on friendly terms with. As to the secret areas beneath the sewers and all the weapons stored inside those rooms, Hugh still hadn't come up with an answer for them.

He shifted in his seat as the cable car reached the end of the line and bumped gently against the platform of Full Moon Plaza's station. By now the light was growing dim around them and the sun was just barely visible over the horizon. Once they were out of the car, they were greeted by another locked gate that they had to be flown over. Before Icarus took flight, Hugh had tried to force the gate open, to save the Sparrow's strength for later, but it was no good. The chain holding the sliding metal gate shut was strong and the thick padlock required a key that none of them had.

"Thank you for trying, Hugh," said Icarus after he had lifted Amy and Sally over the top of the gate.

"No problem," said Hugh with a sigh. "I just wish it would have opened for us. The last thing we need is for you to run out of steam on us."

"I am sure he'll be fine," said Bobby as he hefted up his backpack. "Icarus is a pretty sturdy bird."

"Thank you for the compliment," said Icarus as he reached out and drew Bobby close to him in preparation of flying him over to the gate to join the women. Soon it was Hugh's turn to be airlifted, and he could see beads of sweat on the bird's brow.

"Are you sure you don't want me to try to climb the gate?" asked Hugh with concern on his face.

"The gaps between the gate's bars are too narrow for you to use as proper handholds," said Icarus as he turned to glance at the barrier. "Only a child would be able to scale it. The top has spikes, so I can't simply boost you over the top. There is no other option but to fly over."

"If you say so," said Hugh as he offered out his arms for Icarus to grab. Once they were on the other side and had rejoined the others, Amy stepped away from the group and took a look around the small plaza they found themselves in. In the center was a fountain that Hugh hadn't noticed when he was there a few days earlier due to the massive crowd of people busying about the streets. Now the mall was empty and eerily silent, giving the impression that they were trespassing on sacred ground. Looking up, Hugh could see that high above his head were the supports for skylights that bridged the gap between the store fronts. However, the glass was long gone, every panel shattered and their remains scattered over the streets below. It wasn't clear if the Hawkers had broken the skylights when they were taking people away or if it had happened during the battle between the robots and the airplanes. What was clear was that the sun had set and lights were turning on across the district, making it seem all the more otherworldly. Whatever means the Hawkers had to turn the public electricity off in the city didn't seem to affect Full Moon Plaza at all.

"This way," said Amy at last, pointing toward an open branch off of the plaza. She headed off in that direction at a quick pace, with the others following right behind her. As they walked briskly down the lane, they passed bashed-in storefronts, forgotten shopping bags, and a couple of bodies. Not all of the electric lights were turning on, due to several bulbs having been broken, giving the shops a rundown appearance. What signs and windows that were still lit up shined so brightly that they almost hurt one's eye to look at. The many colorful signs they passed by seemed almost too cheerful for such a devastated place. Hugh had never noticed before, but Full Moon Plaza was very gaudy, with all its shine and glitter, its neon lights, and art deco facades. To sum it up, the district appeared as a fallen monument of consumerism to his eyes.

Just before the last light of day had faded and the true darkness of night descended upon them, Amy led them inside a jewelry store. As they hurried inside, Hugh briefly took notice of the store's name, The Emerald City. He couldn't help but chuckle at that, given the normal circumstances of where Nimbus was supposed to float over. Once inside, Amy led them past several display cases of priceless necklaces to behind the cashier's counter. At the back of the shop was a heavy looking door with several fist sized dents in its surface. She stopped before the door and reached into the pocket of her wrinkled uniform, pulling out a key that she promptly stabbed into the lock.

"Did Dennis give you that key?" asked Bobby as Amy turned the lock in the knob.

"Yes," she said with a mischievous grin as the lock gave out an audible click as the bolt slid into the door. "Of course," she added as she opened the door and led them into the restricted part of the mall, "I know this is sort of illegal since I don't work here, but Dennis insisted I have a copy of some of his keys in case I needed to find him in a hurry. My Dennis is smart like that."

Once inside, the group found themselves instantly surrounded by a crowd of people. Each one of them was armed with the most random assortment of objects. Some held golf clubs, baseball bats, hockey sticks, tall lamps, brooms and even a couple of frying pans. There were also several gun barrels visible in the hands of the mob before them, all pointed at the newcomers.

"Stop!" someone said, though Hugh did not know who. "They're human!"

"I can see that," said one of the men at the front of the pack, who hefted a tire iron in his hands. "I also see some monster right behind them!"

"He's not a monster, he's with us," said Sally, the first of the five to speak up. "Look, let's all take a breath and calm down here."

"That looks like those Hawker things that killed my little boy!" said a shrill voice from somewhere behind the man with the tire iron. From over his shoulder peaked out a thin dark face with a tangle of even darker hair. "Kill it, before it kills us!"

"Wait!" shouted Hugh, stepping in front of Icarus. "He's not one of them, he's a Sparrow! He is here to help us!"

"Why are you people defending that thing?" demanded a teenager with straggly hair, freckles, and wielding a metal baseball bat. "Things like that killed my parents! And it'll kill us, too, if we don't get rid of it!"

Bobby joined Hugh in front of Icarus, followed by Sally and Amy. Bobby spoke quietly to Hugh as he looked at all the scared and angry faces before them. "This isn't good, Hugh," he said as he held his weapon tightly in his hands. "These people are too riled up to listen to us. We may have to take our chances outside."

As the crowd grew more violent and began to press in on them, Amy stepped out and planted herself firmly between the advancing mob and the others. "DENNIS!" she cried out at the top of her lungs, in a way that reminded Hugh of how a character from a popular cartoon show would yell at his troublemaking son. The crowd shook as if it was made of gelatin and a slim young man wiggled his way out of the mob. He was tall and was wearing a grey pocket tee-shirt with a janitor's logo sown onto his right sleeve. In his hands he wielded a long handled mop like a quarter staff. His muddy brown hair was cut so short that it appeared almost militaristic. "Amy?" he asked in a surprised tone, the 'e' sound at the end warbling in his speech.

"Dennis, there you are," said Amy in a musical voice as she stepped over to her boyfriend, embracing him in a loving hug. "I am so glad you are alright!"

"Amy, what are you doing here?" said Dennis, the look of shock still plastered across his freckled face.

"I became so fed up with my mother, and how I was being treated at the hospital, that I just had to be with you again," she said as she gave him a kiss upon his cheek.

"Why didn't you stay where you were safe?" he said, dropping his mop so he could give her a proper hug in turn. "I feared you were dead, and you could've been killed on the way over here!"

"I couldn't stand being without you," she said. "I was willing to risk everything just to be in your arms again."

"How did you get here? Did these people protect you?" Dennis asked as he looked over her shoulder at Hugh and the others.

"Yes, they did. Without them, I'd be done for."

"Even the," he paused, looking at Icarus with a suspicious look in his eyes, "that *thing?*"

"Especially him," Amy said with a smile. "Without Icarus over there, I wouldn't have gotten any farther than the cable car station. Did you know the platform gates are locked? I didn't even know they closed!"

"See?" piped up Hugh, as he took a step forward. "He's on our side. No need to beat the bird to a pulp."

"I don't know," said someone else from the crowd. "This all seems pretty fishy to me."

"These people helped Amy!" said Dennis over his shoulder, "If the birdman is okay by her, he's fine by me!"

"That's flimsy logic!" another person called out. "For all we know, he did it so he could worm his way into our midst and kill us in our sleep!"

"Well, if Dennis is okay with him," said a man dressed in the uniform of a mall cop in the center of the first row of the crowd, "then I say we trust this Hawker."

"I am not a Hawker, I am a Sparrow," said Icarus with an irritated sigh. "I have feathers and they don't. The only similarity between us is our general shape after the transformation."

"Pardon me," said the mall cop with a goofy grin, "I meant Sparrow."

"Come on, Andrew, don't go weak on us now!" shouted a raspy male voice from the back of the mob. "That thing can't be trusted!"

"Like the owners of Baker's and Barley's couldn't be trusted because they were Communist?" asked another person from the back of the crowd. "We keep telling you that they are not reds but you won't listen, you old coot. I say we let them in, at least for the night."

The crowd began to talk amongst themselves, steadily calming down and lowering their assorted weapons. They eventually came to an agreement to let Icarus and the others stay, but only for the night. They refused to let them stay any longer in case the Sparrow attracted the wrong kind of attention from the Hawkers outside, or worse, turned on them. Hugh felt relieved as the crowd broke apart, everyone wandering off in chunks down different ends of the hallway. Once things had emptied out significantly, Hugh could finally see the hallway itself.

It was painted the color of sand and had bits of concrete stonework poking out here and there. Hugh was briefly reminded of the hidden halls under Galileo Plaza and Xandir Square, with all the utility pipes and wires attached to the wall and the exposed air ducts. A major difference between the district's restricted hallways and the hidden areas was that there were brightly colored stripes painted across the wall before him. The stripes were split into blue and red lines. One had the words *to storage for stores 1a-5a* and the other, *to stores 6a-15a*. Framed above the two stripes was a map of a section of Full Moon Plaza that labeled all the stores on the map one through fifteen. The map's legend named this part of the shopping complex as "a" sector. Standing where the two stripes met, just to the left of the framed map, was the mall cop, who had stayed behind when everyone else had left.

"Sorry about that mess," he said with a sad smile on his face. "A lot of those people lost family and friends getting off the streets when everything went down."

"That's perfectly understandable," said Bobby as he slid his sidearm into the pocket of his trousers. "I know what they are going through. Those monsters took my father."

"Sorry to hear about that, I really am," said the cop as he slid his hands into his pockets. "I know there is nothing to say that can make that better for you. All I can really do is thank you for getting young Miss Rogers all the way here in one piece. Denny-boy here has been talking about her non-stop from day one, worrying about her being found at the hospital at any time and being killed. Now that she's here, maybe we'll see a smile on Mr. Talford's face."

"An-ndy!" stammered Dennis as his face turned a deep shade of scarlet, making his freckles disappear from his cheeks and forcing the hazel color of his eyes to become more prominent.

"Aw, how sweet," giggled Amy as she planted another kiss on her boyfriend's face. "Don't worry lover-boy, I am here now and not leaving anytime soon."

"I'm glad to hear that," said Dennis as he returned her kiss. "I wouldn't be able to rest easy without you by my side."

And with that, the two young lovebirds began to walk away, down the hallway lined with the blue stripe. Before they were out of sight, Amy turned and waved at the others, shouting back "Thank you guys for getting me here! If I had to be with my mother for one more second, well, it wouldn't have been pretty!"

"Come along, Amy," said Dennis as he took her hand in his and led her away, "I need to show you where we'll be sleeping tonight."

And with that they were gone. Only the cop was left with them in the empty tan hallway. He gave a little cough as he cleared his throat and looked at each of them in turn. "So," he said as he ran his hand through his thick dark beard, "Did you guys only travel this far to deliver a teen-aged girl or are you up to something?"

23

It did not take long for Hugh, with help from the others, to explain their plan to the mall cop. When they were finished, he took off his blue cap and wiped his bald head with the cuff of his sleeve. "That's a rather risky plan you guys have," he said as he replaced his cap atop his head. "I am not sure if you can get to the Warehouse District the normal way, though."

"Oh, now what?" groaned Bobby.

"You see," started the cop as he leaned back against the wall, crossing his arms over his chest, "We've gotten word through the people who managed to take shelter near the station for the Warehouse District that both the cable car and the sky bridge system were destroyed by the Hawkers. We don't know why they did it, but thankfully I have it on good authority that no one died when either the car or the bridge fell."

"Great, now what are we going to do?" asked Hugh. "We can't just have Icarus fly us across. That'd be too dangerous."

"Guess we'll have risk traveling to Liberty Estates," sighed Sally.

"No," said Icarus, his face set as if in stone. "The center of the city is far too dangerous for us to risk a short trip through."

"How do you know that for sure?" asked Andrew. "Have any of you been over that way recently, or heard it from anyone?"

"It just makes sense," said Icarus with a little huff of irritation. "The Hawkers would make the heart of Nimbus their home base because they can fly to any part of the city from there. It is also likely where the control center of the city is as well, and you know they'd protect that area the most."

The mall cop took on a confused expression. "I don't know anything about any control centers," he said, "but if you guys are dead set to getting to the Warehouse District and avoiding Liberty Estates, there is another option."

"What is it?" piped up Sally, hope returning to her eyes.

"Well," said the guard as he turned his head to look down the hallway lined with the red stripe. "There is the cargo system linking Full Moon Plaza to the Warehouse District. It's designed to transport heavy goods from the warehouses to the mall's storage so we can restock the shelves."

"Are these freight transports still up?" asked Hugh.

"I think so," said the cop, still looking down the hallway. "That transport system is built way tougher than your average cable car system. It's meant to hold a lot more weight than the cars and would probably take a lot of work to take out. It won't be the most comfortable ride you'll ever have, but it will get you to the other side of the gap safely enough. I only fear where you will end up."

"What do you mean?" asked Icarus, his head starting to tilt in that way that made it disturbing to look at.

"I mean that we haven't heard boo from the warehouse hands that work the controls on their side of the system," said the cop, turning to address the Sparrow. "For all we know there are Hawkers waiting at the other end of the transport system for any dumb humans who try to sneak in. But as things are, it's the only option other than going through Liberty."

"I guess we'd better find our way over to the freight system," said Hugh as he stifled a yawn with his hand.

"Look," said the cop as he stepped away from the wall, "I honestly think you all are crazy for going through with this, but you should at least spend the night here so you'll be awake when you try to cross over. We got a place you can sleep in the mattress warehouse. We've already taken a couple of spares from there to sleep on down the hall. No one will bother you guys in there, I'll guarantee it."

"What do you mean, 'bother'?" asked Icarus.

The cop glanced off in the direction that Amy and Dennis had headed down before answering. "Let's just say that not everyone here will let things be with a Sparrow in the building. Last thing we need is some jackass coming down here and trying to take out vengeance against your Sparrow. Things could escalate and we may end up with an all-out riot on our hands."

"I see your point," said Hugh. "Alright, lead on."

With the cop at their head, the group walked down the long hallway, following its many twists and bends. They passed what felt like hundreds of doors on their left, several of which had been boarded up with thick planks of wood. Every now and then they would walk past an office which held a couple of survivors inside. Andrew waved his hand at each one they passed by. Some returned his wave, others glared at Icarus with icy stares. They eventually came across a small gathering of children playing in the hallway, while a middle aged woman looked on.

"Hi, Officer Hedrick!" said one of the kids, with a big grin on his face. "Want to play with us?" The boy held up a small shiny toy car over a drive-in theater play set. The others were running the small toy vehicles around the floor by the little theater, while one was playing around with the projector light of the toy, causing a still image from a movie to flicker in and out of sight on the small toy's screen.

"Sorry, Gary," said the mall cop as he bent down to pat the child on the head. "I am very busy right now." He paused for a moment before giving the woman sitting with the children a little nod of his head. "Say, I think it's time for supper! Am I right, Margaret?"

The woman smiled back and checked her small wrist watch before answering him. "Why yes, I do believe it is time to eat. Thank you for reminding me, Officer Hedrick." She stood up from the hard floor and dusted off her pale pink skirt before addressing the children. "Everyone," she said, "let's all go down to the food court for supper. I hear they are having yummy pizza tonight!" All the children gave a cheer and eagerly followed the woman off down the hall, back the way Hugh and the others had come from. One of the children stopped for a moment and looked up at Icarus.

"Are you an angel, mister?" asked the little girl, who was wearing a white blouse that looked like it may have been her Sunday best. Her hair was split into two braided pigtails swaying about just behind her ears.

"What do you mean?" asked Icarus, clearly baffled by the question.

"You have big feathery wings like the angels in church," she said with her eyes wide with wonder. "Mama says I have an angel watching over me, but he's invisible. She says they have big wings like birds, and your wings are huge. Why can I see you, mister?"

Before the Sparrow could say anything, the middle aged-woman called out to the little girl. With a smile and a wave goodbye, the child skipped off after the others down the hall. Icarus watched her go, a confused grin spread across his beak. He returned the girl's wave, but she didn't see it.

"Ah," sighed the mall cop, watching the woman and the children go. "That Margaret Fetcher is a real saint. A couple of those kids lost their parents when the Hawkers first attacked. We have managed to pair up some of them with their families, but there are plenty whose moms and dads are still missing. We try to hope for the best, but it doesn't always work out. She was the first to step up to watch over the little ones. She's all they have now."

"Lord knows we could use more good people like her these days," said Bobby, his eyes acquiring a distant look.

"Yeah," agreed Hugh, stealing a glance at Bobby. "Times like these bring out the best and the worst in everyone. It is all about what we do to cope and survive."

"Well," said the mall cop as he turned away and led them a little farther down the hallway, "I guess I better get you guys and gal to your quarters." He soon stopped in front of a set of thick double doors that opened up into a large room. Inside, the light was poor, but not so bad that they couldn't see the stacks of mattresses piled up all around the room. There were shelves holding other odds and ends, most of it either shrink-wrapped linens or pillows. The mattresses that were not in stacks were lying about the floor, and several showed signs of recent use.

"Go on in," said the mall cop as he held the door open for them. "Make yourselves at home."

"Shouldn't we get some supper with the others?" asked Sally, looking back down the hall. I mean, we have our own rations, but a hot meal really sounds good to me right now."

"I don't think that would be a very good idea," said the mall cop. "With the commotion your feathered friend caused, I don't think they'd take too kindly to having him eat with them. It might cause a riot."

"How did you know we were coming?" asked Hugh. "We didn't even know how we were going to get into the employee-only areas until Amy led us to a door. Yet you guys knew exactly where to go."

"Oh, that's simple," said the mall cop. "My partner Kevin saw your happy little crew arrive on the cable car through the security cam network. We followed you on the screens up to your heading out of the plaza and toward the jewelry store. I went out when it was clear what you were planning to do to warn the others. Of course, at the time we thought you were being forced by a Hawker to show it how to find the rest of us, so you can understand why we all were up in arms. Sorry that we didn't catch that the big guy had feathers sooner."

"I'm just glad that things didn't get ugly," said Hugh, glancing over at Sally and Icarus. "It's bad enough we have to worry about the Hawkers. The last thing we need is to fight among ourselves, too."

"I'm sorry, but I must ask," the mall cop said, blushing slightly, "but what exactly is the big guy? I have never seen anything quite like it, unless you count the Hawkers. But they're just oddly shaped robots. Your friend is like something out of a J.R. Tolkien book."

"I am a Sparrow," said Icarus in a bored tone of voice. "You humans do realize that I am getting tired of explaining what I am, yes?"

"Whoa, no offense, big guy," said the mall cop as he put up his hands palm first. "I am just saying we don't get a lot of your kind up here, or anywhere really. I get it's none of my business. I was just curious, was all."

Once they had settled into the room, they proceeded to search for a mattress to sleep on for the night. Sally and Hugh chose one that was for a queen sized bed so they could be together, while Bobby and Icarus picked out matching twin bed mattresses as their own. When Hugh asked if it would be alright, the mall cop told them they could open any of the bags of bed supplies in the storeroom. After all, he added, it was highly unlikely anyone would be buying from Full Moon Plaza any time soon, and it would be such a shame if the sheets and blankets went to waste.

"So, I heard the little lady say she wanted something hot to eat?" asked the mall cop as he helped them gather pillows.

"You heard right, Officer," said Sally with a bashful smile. "I honestly don't mind sandwiches and cereal, but I could really go for a slice right about now."

Hugh couldn't help but chuckle. "You just had to say pizza, Officer. Sally is a total pizzaholic."

"Oh you, Hughie!" said Sally as she playfully punched him in the arm.

"All righty," said the mall cop. "Oh, and you guys can just call me Andrew if you like. It won't take me long to run down to the food court, so it won't be any trouble."

"Pardon me," said Bobby as he finished laying out the sheets atop his mattress, "but if I'm not mistaken, did you say everyone is eating in the 'food court'? Isn't that suicide with the Hawkers flying around outside?"

"Yes it is," said the mall cop, "but we don't actually go out into the *real* food court. We eat in the kitchens and the back offices. We just refer to the area as the 'food court' to try to lighten the mood. Any little thing that makes things seem just a little more normal is welcome here."

"I can imagine," said Sally.

"So," said the cop, "Should I bring a slice for everyone, or just the lady?"

Once the cop had everyone's order, Sally and Hugh asking for slices of plain cheese, Bobby for pepperoni, and Icarus for anchovies, he left to fetch the food. While they waited for his return, they sat and planned out their next move. They decided that the Hawkers' actions of destroying the conventional means of reaching the Warehouse District meant that traveling through it would probably not be as easy as they first thought. None of them had a map on hand of the next district due to it not being a part of Nimbus open to the casual visitor. What Sally and Hugh remembered of their time there wasn't enough to formulate a complete plan. So they decided that once they arrived in the Warehouse District, they would find a safe place to hide while Icarus took to the skies to scope out the area. Once he had gotten a good look at the lay of the land, he would come back to them and he and Sally would work on drawing up a map for them to follow.

After the cop returned with their meals, they quickly ate and turned in for bed. The mall cop assured them that they would be safe while they slept. While he had been away fetching the food, he had taken the time to gather up a group of good men that he could trust. They were to watch over the entrance while Hugh and his friends slept just in case anyone tried to cause trouble and tried to take out ill placed revenge against Icarus. Hugh had trouble getting to sleep that night. Not for the first time, he found himself wondering what the next day held. There seemed to be too many questions and too few answers. Why was the city moving? Where was the city going? Why did the Hawkers attack the humans all over Nimbus? Why did the city hold secret weapon lockers and hidden levels deep below the city's streets? What happened to Dr. Frank Crick? Hugh only hoped that the answers to his questions didn't come with too high of a price.

24

The next day came too soon for Hugh. He only managed to get a couple hours of sleep. The others were far more fortunate than him. While Hugh was still struggling to keep his eyes open, Bobby and the others had already begun to collect their gear from beside their beds. Sally turned to Hugh once she noticed he was awake and gave him a reassuring smile. "Rise and shine, dear. It's time to get going again."

Once they were ready to leave, they opened the doors leading out into the hall to find a small gathering of men being held back by the mall cop they met the day before and a couple of other men dressed in similar uniforms. Upon hearing the doors open behind him, the mall cop turned to look over at Hugh and his crew. Hugh could tell from the fresh dark circles under the man's eyes that he had gotten even less sleep than Hugh had. The mall cop, Andrew, had to have been up almost all night keeping the more restless of the survivors from trying to harm Icarus.

"Finally, you're all awake," said Andrew, with a slight moan at the end of his words. "I don't mean to be rude here, but the sooner you and your big friend scoot, the sooner things calm down."

"There he is!" cried out a man with a bandage around his head, a red splotch staining the white where his left ear should have been. "There's the monster!"

"Let us show that thing why you don't mess with the human race!" cried out another guy, who pointed a golf club towards Icarus.

"Alright, that's enough!" shouted a gruff mall cop standing next to Andrew. "We all have our grudges against the Hawkers, but this guy isn't one of them!"

"Well he sure isn't natural!" cried another of the opposing side. "Since when did birds get that big and talk like humans. He doesn't even look like a parrot!"

"This is getting out of hand," said another mall cop, a fidgety guy who was holding a long flashlight like a club. "What do we do?"

"We get the birdman and his friends out of here, pronto," said Andrew. "Form up and escort him to the import and export room."

Quickly, the mall security officers gathered around Hugh and his friends, protecting them on all sides. Andrew took the head of the formation and forced the crowd of angry men to part and let them pass. He led them quickly down the hall, past several doors that Hugh didn't bother to look at. There simply wasn't the time. Behind them, the crowd of men followed, throwing insults at Icarus. Hugh was getting tired of all the hatred aimed toward Icarus just because he resembled the Hawkers. He was no longer a Hawker, but one wouldn't know that from the way he was constantly being treated. It took them some time to reach the other end of the district by foot. Thankfully, the hallways were fairly straight and simple to navigate. They didn't need to hide due to the lack of Hawkers in the halls, though occasionally they had to rest while the security guards watched over them, keeping the other men following them at bay.

As they walked on, the people trailing them began to break off, deciding to return to their families or deciding that walking all the way across the district wasn't worth their time. Soon the hallways ended and Hugh's group and their temporary entourage had to brave the outside world of Full Moon Plaza. They exited through a shoe shop and hurried across the street to a toy store, where they entered into another hallway. As they neared the other side, the number of stores dropped and casinos rose. The district only housed four casinos, all of which sat on the western end of Full Moon Plaza. There were still a few shops around that part of the district, but the casinos stood out due to their overly gilded architecture. A couple of times they had to cut through gambling floors, past silent slot machines and empty poker tables. There were a couple of bodies here and there, but they didn't stop to pay the dead any attention.

They were almost at the end of their journey in Full Moon Plaza when Icarus suddenly stopped moving and raised his right arm to signal the others to do the same. He had halted halfway through one of the casinos that they had been cutting through, right before the entrance to a wide room filled with silent slot machines and a couple of empty blackjack tables.

"Hawkers," was all Icarus said in a soft whisper, barely loud enough for Hugh and the others to hear. As such, they had to relay the message back to the security guards to let them know why they had suddenly stopped.

"How many?" asked Andrew, Hugh having to relay the whispered question to Icarus, who had taken a few steps back.

Icarus held up one clawed hand, with all five fingers spread.

"Only five?" whispered Bobby in a rash voice. "I say we fight our way through. We have plenty of men on our side."

Icarus turned and shook his head. "Not a good idea," he whispered back. "They all have guns drawn. I don't think we want to get into a firefight just yet. Also, there might be more Hawkers nearby that would be attracted by the sound of a firefight."

When the message got relayed back to the mall cops, they all agreed with Icarus. None of them were ready for a gun battle with the Hawkers, and most of them admitted that they had never fired a gun before, despite a few of them carrying firearms strapped to their belts.

"What do you want us to do?" asked Hugh.

"We just need to hide and wait for them to move on," said Icarus as he risked another glance out into the gaming parlor. Hugh leaned forward to see past the Sparrow and into the room beyond. He could see clearly the machines roaming around, inspecting the silent slot machines. It wasn't clear to him what the Hawkers were doing in a place like this, but he had a feeling that they weren't trying to win the casino's jackpot. While he had the chance, he brought up his camera and snapped a few photos of the mechanical birds, his flash turned off so he wouldn't attract their attention.

Sally, who was right behind him, tapped Hugh on the shoulder and motioned for him to put his camera down and get out of sight with the others. Only Icarus stayed near the entrance to the gambling floor, to keep a lookout until the Hawkers left.

Hugh, while he waited for the all-clear, took this time to check the number of pictures left on his camera. He was half-way through his current role, and would have to change it soon. Thankfully, he had two more rolls of film in his bag. He couldn't help but smile a bittersweet grin at the thought. At a time like this, he was doing the mundane check of photos left in his camera. Some things never change, he thought to himself.

After a quarter of an hour, by Andrew's wristwatch, Icarus let out a sigh and announced that the Hawkers had moved on. Quietly, they stepped out of cover and began their march through the deserted building again, passing by the slot machines that the metal birds had been inspecting. Hugh, out of curiosity, looked at one of them as they passed by, but didn't see anything too interesting about the slot machine.

"They're kind of strange, aren't they?" asked Sally, startling Hugh with her voice.

"Shhh," said Icarus, turning around for a moment. "The Hawkers may have left, but one can never be sure if they didn't leave a scout behind. We need to stay quiet until we are out of the area."

"Oh, sorry," said Sally as she dropped the volume of her voice to a whisper. She turned back to Hugh, and resumed talking to him. "What I mean is, they seem to do the strangest things at the strangest times, don't they, Hughie?"

"Yeah," murmured Hugh in reply. "Maybe we will never know what really goes on in the heads of those things, but you can bet none of it is good."

"What do you think they wanted in here?" asked Bobby, coming up beside Sally and Hugh.

"I don't know," said Hugh, as they started walking again, making their way to the exit of the casino. "I suppose they could have been hunting for other human survivors. Or they could have been part of a passing patrol unit and decided to kill some time fiddling with the machines."

"Huh, guess even the tin-heads get bored," said Bobby as he glanced back over at the machines one last time before they left the building and continued on their way. Hugh made a mental note to ask Icarus what the Hawkers might have been doing while messing with the slot machines. Perhaps the Sparrow would remember enough of his previous life as a Hawker to explain the reasoning behind the Hawker's actions.

Finally, they reached their destination. All of the men except for Andrew stayed outside the shipping room, to make sure there were undisturbed. Inside, there was a thick metal rail system dominating the ceiling like a spider web. From the rails above their heads hung all sorts of platforms and hooks. It was little more than a confusing jumble to casual observers such as Hugh, Sally, Icarus, and Bobby. At the very end of the room all the rails led to row of massive thick iron doors that dominated the wall. They stretched from the floor to the ceiling of the room, with large yellow numbers painted across their surfaces. The room was so large that it had enough space for stacks of crates and a small parking lot where a dozen delivery trucks were parked. As they looked around at the stacked crates and many cables and pulleys, Andrew had broken away from them and was looking over one of the many mechanical consoles scattered around the room.

"Do you know how to work these machines?" asked Bobby, looking over the mall cop's shoulder.

"Not a clue," admitted Andrew as he tried to punch in different button combinations on the control panel. Around the room hooks raised and lowered, and cargo crates and platforms slid back and forth, all on the same rail system. It became clear that each console controlled one rail system. Sally experimentally pressed a few buttons on a different control panel that resulted in a crate being raised improperly and its cargo to fall out in a jumble of boxes and fashionably dressed plastic dolls. She blushed at this, and Hugh couldn't help but crack a smile.

"Wait," said Andrew after a time, "I think I got it now." He pulled a lever in the side of the console and a bell began to go off. Over at the massive iron door, the sound of gears turning could be heard as one of the heavy metal doors began to open. Slowly, the door at the end of the rail system controlled by Andrew's console slid upwards, all the way into the ceiling. With it out of the way, they could see the outside world, the open sky between the threshold and the Warehouse District floating in the distance, with a backdrop of thick clouds. Beside the one rail that went through the open door, they could clearly see all the others reaching out across the void to the other side.

"Phew, this wind is intense!" exclaimed the mall cop, as the air flying through the open portal stole away his cap.

"We better get going before the Hawkers notice this big open doorway," said Icarus, looking out at the sky beyond.

"Well, we may have a slight problem there," said Andrew, looking at the keyboard before him. "I think the only way we'll get things to move from one end to the other of the system is if someone on the other side opens the door at the other end of the rail."

"Why didn't you mention that before?" demanded Bobby.

"I didn't think of it," shrugged the mall cop. "I am just a mall cop, remember? Working this thing is not in my pay grade."

Suddenly, a light lit up on the console, surprising the mall cop enough for him to let out a sudden swear. The bell suddenly changed tone and a large flat platform began to inch its way along the rail toward the opening.

"What's happening?" asked Hugh.

"I guess someone heard us on the other side," said Andrew, looking at the moving platform in shock. "This has got to be a trap."

"What other choice do we have?" asked Sally, looking worriedly between Icarus and Hugh. "I really don't like this, but the only other option is to stay here and hope we aren't eventually found by any curious Hawkers."

"If we're going, we better go now," said Hugh, making up his mind and racing toward the platform, his rifle drawn and ready. Icarus followed close behind Hugh, with Sally and Bobby on the Sparrow's heels. As the platform neared the open door, it gained speed. Both Hugh and Icarus managed to climb aboard fairly easily. However, Sally and Bobby had to be helped aboard. Bobby almost didn't make it in time and had to jump at the moving platform, which was now a few feet off the ground and almost out of the hanger. Icarus caught him by his forearm and pulled him up.

From inside, Andrew waved at them as the platform moved outside and the wind began to pull and tug at their bodies. From the sides of the metal platform rose protective bars, designed to keep loose cargo from sliding off the moving surface. Everyone had their guns at the ready, pointing every which way. Hugh looked off to the right to see Liberty Estates. He could see plenty of glimmers of light in the sky over that part of Nimbus, but none of the flickers seemed to be heading their way. Likewise, there wasn't any activity from where they had left or where they were going.

"This is too easy," said Bobby just loud enough to be heard over the wind. "We are sitting ducks on this thing."

"Maybe we got lucky?" suggested Sally, her eyes straying to the metal bar above their heads.

"Don't assume luck is a factor," said Icarus as he held his sniper rifle at the ready. "We let our guard down once. We may not survive making that mistake again."

"Maybe they are busy with something else," said Hugh, still staring at Liberty Estates. "Look over here. I see a whole bunch of them buzzing about Liberty like a swarm of bees."

"What are they doing over there?" asked Sally, watching the activity over the center of Nimbus.

"Looks like they are centering on something," said Bobby. "What is that?"

"I am not sure," said Sally, straining her eyes. "Icarus, can you use your fancy rifle's scope to get a better look at what's going on over there?"

"I can try," said the Sparrow as he aimed his gun's scope over at Liberty Estates.

"What do you see?" asked Hugh.

"Well," said Icarus, "the Hawkers are flying all over the center of the city, but most of them seem to be gathered in the center of Liberty Estates. I can't make out much more. My scope is simply not powerful enough to see that far."

"What is over there?" asked Hugh, turning away from the center of the city to bring up his camera to take a few pictures of Liberty Estates, before resuming his lookout for any incoming Hawkers.

"Well, there's the convention center," said Sally as she counted off the possibilities on her fingers. "The museum, the broadcast station, the police department, the United Post's building, and I think a few office buildings."

"Let's just hope that they stay over there and leave us alone," said Bobby. "I don't think we'd stand much of a chance if they all came over here."

All too soon, the platform moved across the final stretch of the rail and neared the open doorway in a large building atop the Warehouse District. They had just passed a junction in the rail system and still had not experienced any trouble from the robots. It was almost as if they were blessed with a divine protection, but none of them were naïve enough to let their guard drop. As the platform slid inside, they all prepared for a battle. What they got was not what they expected.

Instead of a unit of Hawkers ready to pounce upon them, a group of a dozen men wearing similar body armor to their own stood at the ready. Hugh recognized some of the faces from when they were at the police warehouse almost a week before. However, they were now packing very serious weapons, and each one had a face set in a grim expression, their guns aimed at the new arrivals. It was only when the platform had stopped moving and the door leading out slid shut that their welcoming committee collectively relaxed.

"Okay, before anyone says anything..." said Hugh, looking at the heavily armed men. "This is a Sparrow, not a Hawker, okay?"

"We know," said one of the men in the front of the formation.

"You... know?" said Hugh, dumbfounded.

"Well, to be fair, it is hard to confuse a metal surface for feathers, Hugh," Bobby sighed.

"You're one to talk, Bob," said Sally. "I seem to remember you thought Icarus was a Hawker at first."

"It was dark back then, can you blame me?"

"If you are all done talking," said another officer, "We have orders to bring anyone who comes into the Warehouse District over to HQ."

"Alright," said Hugh, after he hopped off the platform. "Lead the way."

"Just one moment," said another officer. "Is your Sparrow any good with those weapons of his?"

"How did you know he's a Sparrow?" asked Sally. "I mean, we have hardly met anyone who knew about the Sparrows before we explained what they were."

"Doesn't matter how we know right now," said the same officer, "what does is if we need to send all of us, or if we can leave a few men behind to watch out for anyone else brave, or stupid, enough to use the fright lines to travel over here."

"You have no reason to fear," said Icarus, stepping off the platform and hefting his sniper rifle, Bobby's shotgun poking hilt first out of his bag. "I can assure you all that I am more than capable with firearms."

"Good," said the one in the center of the gathered officers. "Okay, Tony, Alex, Tom, Noah, and Doug, all of you are to escort these four to HQ. We'll stay here in case anyone else comes through. Be sure to stay off the streets and follow the tunnels."

"Tunnels?" asked Sally.

"You may not know this," said the lead officer, "but under each district of this city are hidden areas. Several are accessible through the sewer system, others through certain buildings. They were part of the city's original design, sort of a backup plan in case we got into a war on our own soil."

"So that's what they are for," said Bobby.

"That's what they're for?" asked the lead officer in surprise. "Sir, are you saying you've already been down there in other districts?"

"Yeah," said Hugh. "Why?"

"Never mind, we've wasted too much time as is," said the head officer. And with that, the ones he had assigned to escort Hugh and crew moved toward the center of the room and pushed aside a hand cart packed high with wooden crates. Under it was a hatch that they had seen several times back in Galileo Plaza in less sanitary locations. Without missing a beat, the officer by the name of Tony, who was wearing sunglasses, spun the wheel on the hatch and opened it up. As they moved single file down the open hatch, and then down the ladder into a familiar set of stairs, Hugh couldn't help but wonder why other hatches couldn't be as easy to access.

Things couldn't have been more different below the surface. This time, there were people wandering about the underground hallways. They passed all sorts of people, from warehouse workers to doctors and civilians. This was by far the most people Hugh had seen alive since the attack began. Hugh brought up his camera and began taking pictures of the hustle and bustle around them as they walked. It wasn't clear why they even needed their armed escort down here. It couldn't have been because of Icarus. No one really paid the Sparrow too much attention. At most, Hugh caught one, maybe two, people staring at Icarus as they hurried past.

Eventually, they found themselves pushed inside of a meeting room similar to the one they had spent a night in a couple of days ago. However, there were plenty of changes here as well. The room was spotless and, atop the table, were several bottles of water. A machine at the back of the room was being manned by a female officer who was sitting on a swivel stool.

"Please take a seat," said the cop that Hugh thought was named Doug. "The meeting will start soon."

"Meeting? What meeting? What's going on?" demanded Hugh.

"You are Hubert Louis Yeats, right?" asked Tom.

"Yes, but how did you?"

"The Chief told us to be on the lookout for you after you left last time. He said if the shit hit the fan, and you walked back into our arms, for us to hold an emergency meeting."

"But why me?" asked Hugh.

"I bet it has something to do with my father's journal," Bobby sighed. "Am I right?"

"That's only part of it," said a voice from behind them. Turning around, Hugh was shell shocked to see a familiar face. Sally turned the color of the purest porcelain and almost fainted away on the spot.

"It's you!" stammered out Hugh in shock.

"Aye, it's me," said Detective Catcher. He was sitting in a wheelchair that was being pushed into the meeting room by a nurse. Around his neck he wore a hard plastic brace and his arm was in a sling. "Almost didn't make it, but here I am. Sorry I lost track of you, Ms. Saltwater."

"That… is… completely… understandable…" said Sally before she collapsed into one of the chairs by the table. "After all," she said in a dreamy voice that Hugh had never heard her use in all the time that he had known her, "last time I saw you, you were thrown out of the city."

25

It only took a few minutes for the room to fill with people who Hugh assumed were senior members of the surviving police force. Detective Catcher had been wheeled over to the space next to Sally. Hugh claimed the chair to the right of his girlfriend, and took up her hand, trying to keep her conscious by squeezing it. Seeing the man they had thought died long ago, now clearly alive, had put her into a daze. Bobby and Icarus were unaffected by the sight of the detective, due to never having met the man before.

As the meeting started, the new Chief of Police introduced himself as Deputy Chief Roger Chapman. Along with him were several inspectors and majors on the force. Hugh tried to pay attention to their names, but they went by so fast that he found himself struggling to remember who was who. After the introductions, Deputy Chief Chapman sat down at the head of the table and began the proceedings. They started with a status report of the current situation in the city.

"As we can tell from our contacts outside the Warehouse District," said Deputy Chief Chapman, "Cable car systems are being disabled throughout the city, and sky bridges are being destroyed by the Hawkers. Currently, Xandir Square, Valkyrie Park, and Gale Town are cut off from the rest of the city. Our men in those districts have managed to keep in radio contact with us, but we still can't send a signal to anyone on the surface. As far as we can tell, each district of the city seems to be moving at the same speed, due west. We still have no information on where the robots are moving Nimbus to so, until we have something to go on, we must assume that it will keep going past California and into the Pacific Ocean."

"Chief, sorry to interrupt," said one of the majors, a man across from where Hugh was sitting. "But may I ask something?"

"You may, Major," said the Deputy Chief.

"Thank you," The man cleared his throat and adjusted his tie before voicing his question. "Sir, why are there civilians here? I thought all survivors that come through to the warehouse are supposed either to be sent to the living quarters on Level Four or given a debriefing."

"I am sure you have been told that we were on the lookout for Hubert Yeats?" Deputy Chief Roger said.

"Yes," the major sighed. Hugh struggled to remember the man's name. He wasn't sure if it was Alex or Felix. "But," the major continued, "Why is he *here?* Surely we don't need him for this meeting? As far as I am aware he is just a photographer who happens to be a person of interest."

"Well, if you were awake during the last couple of meetings," said an inspector who was sitting on the other side of Detective Catcher, "you'd know that those metalheads outside seem to have a real affinity for Mr. Yeats. He has something they want, namely a journal belonging to Dr. Frank Crick."

"I had hoped that we could go over a few other things before that was brought up," said the Deputy Chief. "However, since it has been mentioned," he said as he turned towards Hugh, "may we see this journal? It may hold a key to finding a weakness in the Hawker robots."

"As you wish," said Hugh as he reached down to where he had placed his camera bag and retrieved the journal. Upon placing it atop the table, Hugh slid it across its surface over to the Deputy Chief.

Deputy Chief Chapman only had to glance at the book's cover to see that its lock had been ripped away and to notice the tell-tale discoloration of the book's pages to know something was up. "What happened?" he demanded, picking up the journal and flipping through the stained paper slivers. "How did it get damaged?!"

Hugh was about to take responsibility for it ending up in the sewer water, but before he could say anything, Bobby spoke up. "There was a little accident," he said as he pushed up his thick glasses. "I was in the sewer system taking cover with Sally and then Hugh and Icarus turned a corner. I thought Icarus was a Hawker so I prepared to shoot him, but Hugh stopped me. Unfortunately, we both ended up in the water and the book got soaked. "

"And the lock?" asked the Deputy Chief.

"Well," started Hugh, but Icarus interrupted him.

"That would be my fault," said the Sparrow, his voice unwavering. "I was a little over-zealous with opening it, and ended up tearing the lock apart in the process. I am sorry if I have caused any problems."

An inspector sporting an arm in a sling, sitting next to the Deputy

Chief, then asked the question, "I guess that means you read through the journal?"

"Yes," said Hugh with a nod. "We all looked over it, though a lot of it was ruined from its dip in the sewers and the rest was too messy for anyone but Bobby or Icarus to read."

"I can see that," said the Deputy Chief, squinting at one of the pages of the journal. "I heard that doctors have illegible penmanship, but this is ridiculous!"

"If you like, we could summarize what we learned from the journal," offered Hugh.

"Yes, that would be very useful," said the Deputy Chief with a relieved sigh. He put down the journal and closed its cover, like it was an ancient book from a forgotten archive of the Oxford Library.

It didn't take long for Hugh to fill in the others at the table about what they had discovered and how they were using the information. What Hugh forgot, his friends remembered. It wasn't clear what the upper ranking officers thought of their words, for their expressions did not change. They simply drank in the information.

"I see," said the Deputy Chief after a few minutes of silence. "Your plan does make some sense. And if this lab is where the Hawkers are really being made, we could stop their production at the source. However, do any of you know where in Vulcan this secret laboratory is?"

"Um…" said Hugh, as he struggled to remember if the journal said anything about where exactly the secret laboratory was. He turned to look at his friends in case they remembered. Sally, looking better now, had pulled out her notebook and was flipping through its pages, muttering to herself. Looking at Icarus, Hugh saw that the Sparrow again was tilting its head in that alarming manner. Bobby simply took his glasses off and absentmindedly began to clean them, even though their glass lenses were spotless.

"I don't seem to recall a street address," said Icarus at last.

"That's just dandy," said the Major, who Hugh decided at last, was named Felix, "You four were just going to march into Vulcan, and search every factory, building, and workshop until you found where the Hawkers were being built? What a brilliant plan!"

"That is quite enough, Major," snapped the Deputy Chief. Taking a moment to compose his thoughts, he adjusted his tie and picked the journal back up and turned to face Hugh. "I am sorry about Major Felix."

"It's okay," said Bobby. "We were flying blind after all."

"Yeah," sighed Hugh as he slumped in his chair. "I guess we got so caught up in the excitement that we forgot that Vulcan isn't a small place."

"Look," said the Deputy Chief, "We can run this journal through our handwriting analysts and have them see if there is anything else we can get out of this book. If we are lucky, there might be some clues as to where these labs are in Vulcan and make things easier. "

"Thank you, that would be a great help," said Hugh.

"Not a problem," said the Deputy Chief with a smile, as he passed the book over to the man to his right. He spoke quietly to the officer and the man stood up from the table. Without another word, he hurried out of the room, carrying the book in his hands.

"So, what now?" Sally asked as she pulled a clean notebook out of her purse.

"Now you four need to wait while our guys go to work," said the Deputy Chief. "We will also be contacting the men we have over in Vulcan and inform them of the secret lab. With any luck, they'll know something that can help us, or, if things really line up, they'll find the place and we can just head there in the morning. However, now I must ask that you four leave the briefing room. Detective Catcher?"

Upon hearing his name, the wheelchair-bound gumshoe looked up from his papers in surprise. "Yes, Chief?"

"Please, I am just a Deputy Chief," said Chapman. "Would you be so kind as to lead Hugh and his people to a private quarters somewhere until we are finished working with the journal or have heard something from our contacts?"

Detective Catcher absently scratched at his neck brace as he looked at the Deputy Chief. A bemused grin blossomed upon his face. "Sure thing, boss, but why me?" he asked. "I am not exactly the most mobile member of the force right now."

"It's because of your... experience with a certain matter," said Deputy Chief Chapman as he gave Icarus a wink.

"Eh?" asked Detective Catcher, his face twisting up in confusion for a second before his eyes lit up and he pounded the hand of his good arm into the palm of the one in the sling. "Oh! Yes, I get it now! All right, Chief, leave it to me." He wheeled his chair away from the table and toward the door. Hugh only then noticed for the first time that the door leading into the room was an ordinary office door. The heavy metal vault door that they had seen as a part of a similar room was opened so far that it was resting against the wall beside the frame.

Without much of a goodbye, Hugh, Sally, Bobby, and Icarus rose from their respective seats, Hugh supporting Sally, and Bobby and Icarus walking side by side. As they left the room, Hugh could hear a few snippets of the conversation that rose up behind them. He wondered briefly what was next on the high-ranking officers' agenda, but he couldn't make out any of the words as they walked away. Detective Catcher led them down a few identical halls and past several open doors. They didn't talk much at first, just a few more drones in the busy hive of the hidden areas of the Warehouse District. Eventually they found themselves in front of a bank of four elevators. With a simple push of a button, the doors slid open with a slight squeak, and Detective Catcher wheeled himself inside, telling the others to come along.

It was after the detective had pressed the call button for L3 and the doors had slid shut that Sally finally shook the last of her bedazzlement off and spoke up. Turning around to face the detective, she confronted him about seeing him die, and asked him how he managed to return from the dead. With a mischievous smile, the detective told her that he'd tell his story, but not yet. Hugh could see by the way Sally started to rapidly tap the toe of her shoe against the floor of the elevator that she was burning with curiosity. He once joked that she could tap that foot so much that she'd put a hole in whatever ground she was standing on.

Soon enough the elevator stopped and they were allowed to exit onto a different floor. Detective Catcher hummed a tune that Hugh couldn't place as he led them away from the elevator and down a long hallway that was oddly quiet compared to the hustle and bustle of the upper area of this strange place. Soon he brought his chair to a stop in front of a door that would have looked more at home in a second rate hotel.

"Here we are, kids," he said with a big grin, bringing up his free hand and preparing to knock upon the scratched wooden surface. With a loud rap upon the door, there was the sound of something moving around just inside. The door's handle turned from the inside and was pulled inward, revealing another Sparrow.

"Catcher," said the Sparrow on the other side, a big grin pasted across his big beak. "Good to see you. Say, who are your new friends?"

"I'll tell you once we get settled in," said the detective as he wheeled himself in past the tall birdman. When he realized none of the others had followed him inside the threshold, Detective Catcher struggled to make the chair turn in a small circle so it looked out at Hugh and his friends. "Hey," he said, calling out to the others, "What's the matter? You already know about the Sparrows. Heck, you got one running around with your gang!"

"Yes," said Hugh, looking up at the Sparrow holding the door open. "But this is the first time I've seen one so big." Looking back and forth between Icarus and the new Sparrow, Hugh could instantly tell that the other bird stood a good foot taller than Icarus, and from what he could take in, it was snow white instead of the bronze color that dominated Icarus's plumage.

"Ha, ha, ha," laughed the big Sparrow, the grin growing wider on its face. Hugh only just noticed that the bird had a golden beak, instead of the grey one upon the head of any other Sparrow he had seen before. "Do I scare the little monkeys?"

"Oh, play nice, Dannik," said Detective Catcher. "He won't bite, I promise."

"I don't know about that," said Dannik the Sparrow, a wicked glint flashing in his golden eyes. "I am feeling a bit peckish."

"Stop it, Dannik, or I'll tell them how you got your name," said the detective.

"Pfft, fine, fine," sighed the big bird as he turned from the door and walked inside to join the detective, stopping to stand beside the detective's wheelchair. "I was only having fun."

A few minutes later, Hugh and the others had joined Dannik and Detective Catcher inside the room. Looking around, Hugh could not figure out what the room's original purpose was. It was not a small room, though the tip of Dannik's large wings brushed against the ceiling tiles, causing a small sprinkle of dust wherever he walked. The room held a small set of stairs leading down into the main part of the room, like a reverse stage. There was plenty of open floor space in the center of the room, with everything having been pushed against the walls. There were a couple of wooden crates stacked haphazardly against the left wall of the room. Against another wall were five cots that had been shoved together to form a large bed. There was another cot set up across the room from the five others. A couple of folding chairs leaned against the wall beside the single bed. Upon the detective's directive, Dannik moved to the folding chairs and carried some of them over to the center of the room and set them up in a semi-circle.

"Alright," said Detective Catcher as he wheeled himself over to the folding chairs. "Why doesn't everyone take a seat so I'm not the only one in a chair?"

"Sure thing," Sally said as she sat down in one of the chairs. "Are we finally going to have story time, detective?"

"Yeah," said Hugh, sitting down beside her, his camera ready to take pictures of the unusual Sparrow and the Detective. "I heard you were dead, Detective Catcher. Given, you look pretty banged up, but you're still breathing. How exactly is that?"

"Well," said the detective as he looked briefly at his injured left arm before turning to gaze at his wristwatch on his right. "We got plenty of time before the lab boys work out your special journal. So yeah, now is a good time to explain why I am not pushing up daisies."

As Bobby claimed his own seat, he glanced uneasily at Dannik, who was still standing. Icarus too was up on his feet, giving Dannik a similar look as Bobby did. Hugh couldn't help but feel uneasy with such a big birdman in the room. The large Sparrow was dressed in what looked like a bed sheet, wrapped around its body and belted around the middle with a purple scarf. It was as if Dannik had tried to dress as an ancient Greek god, but had lacked a proper toga and made do with what he had found. Hugh could understand the Sparrow wanting to cover up his private parts, but this was just silly.

"I suppose that a good place to start was when I was falling from that sky bridge over in Galileo," said Detective Catcher after clearing his throat. "I was falling to my death, and felt like one of the dumbest men on earth. I had been so stupid. I let myself get caught off guard like a greenhorn rookie. I couldn't help but let out all of my frustration in a death cry."

"Don't say it," said Dannik all a sudden. Hugh turned back to the silvery Sparrow, who had stiffened up for some reason.

"But it's the best part of the story," smirked the detective.

"You promised you would not tell anyone that part of the story," said Dannik.

"Fine," the detective sighed, before continuing his tale. "Let us just say, Dannik here happened to be out for a bit of a flight, hunting or something, right Dannik?"

"Yes, it was such a good day out, how could I resist a little fishing?" said the big Sparrow, a smirk spawning upon his feathered face.

"It sure was. And I am thankful you decided to catch me instead of a trout," said the detective.

"He saved you?" asked Hugh in surprise. "That's just like me and Icarus here! But, how did you get the..."

"This?" asked Detective Catcher as he waved his good hand over himself, as if he was clearing the air with the back of his hand.

"Yeah," said Sally. "Did you get into a fight with another Hawker after you were saved?"

"I wish it was something as heroic," said the detective with a sigh. "What actually happened was that the wonder bird over here didn't account for how fast I was falling when he caught me. The sudden stop when I hit his arms broke my neck and killed my legs. The pain was simply incredible. It kept me from passing out. Thankfully, Dannik managed to get me back up to Nimbus without causing any more damage. He only realized I was hurt when he tried to put me down. I crumpled like an old ragdoll the second my feet touched the street. "

"Yikes," said Sally, "I had no idea you were hurt that badly." She sighed sadly. "It's my fault you got hurt, Detective. If it hadn't been for me, you'd never have been attacked by that Hawker."

"Don't say that, Sally," said Hugh, leaning over to hold her hand. "There was no way you could have known that bridge would have been unsafe."

"But still," sighed Sally, turning her head away from Hugh and closing her eyes.

"Now, now little lady," said Detective Catcher. "The past is the past. If we could change it at a whim, our history books would be very different. The way I see it," he said as he leaned back in his wheelchair, causing the leather back to creak, "I got to be a hero because of you, Miss Saltwater."

"Come again?" asked Sally.

"Well," said Detective Catcher, "After the attack, I was the one who got the other members of the police hopping. When they saw me, saw Dannik, they knew the Hawker threat wasn't just a couple of isolated incidents, or just part of the old Chief's growing paranoia, but a serious danger to the citizens of the city. Heck, you could say that attack is the reason why so many members of Nimbus's finest managed to get into the Warehouse District's emergency stations before the shit hit the fan topside."

"I suppose every cloud has its silver lining," said Bobby. "However, I am curious, Detective. How did you get back to the warehouse? Did Dannik fly you here?"

"Why, yes, I did," said Dannik with a big smile. The large white Sparrow flexed his big arms, causing its biceps to swell under its feathers. "He was as light as a feather in my hands."

"He had to stop in each district along the way," said the detective with a chuckle.

"Well, I am only mortal," Dannik sighed, letting his arms droop down by his sides. "Even I, with all my strength, must take a break."

"I'm curious," said Icarus, "Dannik, are there others like you? I don't think I have seen any other Sparrows quite like you in my own flock."

Dannik lit up again, and his face broke out in another wide smile as he unfurled his wings, showing off their impressive ivory expanse. "Ah yes, I am quite unique, am I not?" he said. "Alas, I am not one of a kind, though I am the biggest Sparrow of them all. I come from a gathering of Sparrows in Tesla Quarter. We try to keep to ourselves, but every now and then we'll step out of the shadows to help when we can."

"Why?" asked Bobby, leaning forward in his chair.

The large Sparrow promptly closed his wings and looked down at his golden claw hands. "I suppose you could call it penitence, sort of a means to atone for all the harm we have done. When we were Hawkers, all we truly cared about was the self. 'How can we make ourselves better? How can we keep these pesky monkeys from getting in our way?' It was only when the change struck us that we began to realize what we were doing. It was as if a switch was thrown."

"So," said Bobby, "what you are saying is that you are helping us humans out of guilt?"

"That and it's the right thing to do," said Dannik, his feathery brow creasing.

"Um," said Hugh. "Sorry to interrupt, but could I ask you something, Detective?"

"What is it, Mr. Yeats?" asked Detective Catcher.

"Well, do you know when the police will be done working with Frank's journal?" Hugh suddenly felt a hand on top of his. He turned to face Sally, who wore a weary expression upon her face.

"Hugh," she breathed, "Don't you think we've been through enough now?"

"Sally," started Hugh before she cut him off with a finger to his lips.

"Please," she said as she let her finger fall and moved the hand to join with her other around Hugh's. "We have been through several battles with the Hawkers, survived traveling across the city, ran around in the sewers, and saw I don't know how many dead bodies. I know that we were in similar circumstances at the Hospital, but here we have the police to watch over us. You have turned over the journal to the officials, Hugh. If Dr. Crick is still alive, we should leave it to the professionals to find him. We'd only get in the way."

26

Hugh was not sure what to say. He had a feeling that Sally was getting worn down by everything that had happened. He had seen signs in the way she had walked and talked during their journeys these past few days. She no longer bothered applying her makeup and a few strands of her hair remained loose from her ponytail. Her easy gate had become a slow march and her beautiful smile had grown scarce upon her lips. He was so proud of her for holding herself together for so long, and would have given anything to tell her that he could stop now, that it would be alright to let the Nimbus Police handle things from there on out, while they all took shelter in the secret areas of the Warehouse District. Yet, he found that he could not give up and rest on his laurels. There was that burning curiosity inside him demanding he seek out all the answers. But what drove him crazy was something he could not quite identify. Yes, he worried about Dr. Crick, but it was far more than that.

"Sally," he started, as he reached out to stroke her long golden locks and hold her head. "I wish I could stop now, that I could stay in here where it's safe. But, it's because we have been through so much that I simply can't. I need to see this to the end. I, we've, simply come too far for me to just let things go. I feel it's time for me to act, instead of just sit on the sidelines and observe the story unfold before me. I just can't sit here and do nothing. I hope you understand."

She was quiet for a bit, then her eyes met with Hugh's for what felt like forever. Hugh dared not say anymore, as he didn't want to force her into wanting to continue their difficult adventure together. If she truly wouldn't be swayed to see their quest to the end, he would give it up as well, just so he could be with her

Finally, Sally moved. She reached over and pulled herself into a passionate embrace around Hugh. She leaned close to his body and moved completely off of her folding chair. She took a deep breath and began to speak. "Hugh," she said, "If this adventure really means this much to you, I will do my best to follow you to the end."

"Thank you, Sally. That means so much," said Hugh as he brought his lips to meet hers. They kissed for a few minutes, each drinking in the other's physical expression of affection. Hugh wanted that moment never to end, with he and she entangled in each other's arms, both so alive in that kiss. It was only when she pulled away that he could think clearly again.

Before going back to her chair, Sally inched her lips over to Hugh's ear and whispered so only he could hear. "Hughie," she said, "I love you so much, that I would follow you into a lion's den. I am surprised you hadn't realized this by now, after all the adventures we've had so far!"

"Ahem," said Bobby, getting the couple's attention. "You two lovebirds better not forget about me. I am not going to let you two go off into the unknown without me. This is possibly my only chance to find my father, be it alive or dead. So, as long as you two are still game, so am I."

"Thank you, Bobby. That means a lot," said Sally. Hugh nodded his head in agreement. Bobby might be a bit a jerk at times, but when it counted, he was a loyal friend.

"I, too, shall go with you, Hugh," said Icarus with a nod.

"You don't have to, Icarus," said Hugh. "You have gotten us this far already. You have a family of your own to watch out for. You should go to your mate, be with her, and protect her."

"Nay," said Icarus, as he turned his gaze to the ceiling, looking at something that Hugh couldn't see. "I, like you, am far too deep in all of this. Besides, we will never be truly safe until the Hawkers are all dead or transformed. I made a promise, and I shall keep it. As to my mate, she is the only other member of my flock as brave as I. She can take care of herself."

"Are you sure?" asked Hugh. "You told me she was getting ready to lay your eggs."

"I am sure," said Icarus with a slight grin. "She knows this city better than even I, and anyone who makes the mistake of underestimating her will be swiftly dealt with. I was the only one she ever paid attention to. To her, all other Sparrows just faded into the background."

"Pardon me," said Detective Catcher, just loud enough to interrupt the conversation between Hugh's crew. "It is good to hear that you're all in this together, but I'm afraid that it's simply too dangerous outside for you to go out into Nimbus."

"We've heard that one before," chuckled Sally.

"Well, whoever told you that was right," said Dannik, crossing his arms and legs. "My last flight outside was a day ago, and I had to do some seriously tricky things to lose the trio of Hawkers that found me irresistible."

"Why were you outside?" asked Icarus, his head tilting.

"Because I am simply too big to stay down here all the time," laughed Dannik, his voice sounding like a deep drum being pounded. "Don't you wish to get out and stretch your wings as well, hatchling?"

Icarus sighed and shook his head. "I'd rather keep my head down than attract unnecessary attention."

"That's a real shame."

"Look," said the detective, reaching behind his back with his good arm to scratch at something. "I highly doubt the higher-ups will send you out there, no matter how gung-ho you all are. At the end of the day, each and every one of you are only civilians, with the exception of Icarus. As the appointed members of Nimbus's finest, it's our duty to protect you."

Hugh began to think fast. He tried to think of any reason that the police would accept to allow them to go on the trip to Vulcan, but drew a blank. His desperate expression must have triggered something in the detective's face. Detective Catcher's features softened up.

"Tell me, Mr. Yeats," he started.

"Please call me Hugh," said Hugh.

"Hugh, how are you with those firearms you're carrying?" asked the detective as he shifted in his wheelchair, causing the leather to creak under his movements.

"I'm sad to say, I am terrible with these things," said Hugh.

"Oh, don't say that Hughie," said Sally. "You managed to take a Hawker down with one shot back at the park, and saved my life, remember?"

"That was just one hell of a lucky shot, Sally, but thanks for the vote of confidence," said Hugh with a shy smile.

"How about you, Miss Saltwater?" asked the Detective, "are you packing too, or only got that breastplate and your men for protection?"

"For your information," said Sally with a devious grin, "I do have a little gun of my own. I may not be as lucky as Hugh, but I have good aim."

Turning to face Bobby, the detective asked, "How about you, specks, are you good with that rifle, or are you as inexperienced as the rest of them?"

"I have fired a gun many times, Detective," said Bobby as he adjusted his glasses. "I used to shoot skeet with my father over at the Olympic Fields when we had free time."

"Finally, someone who knows what they are doing," said the Detective.

"However, I am more accustomed to using a shotgun, not a rifle," muttered Bobby, almost too quiet to be heard, but not silent enough to be missed by the detective's keen ears.

"Great," he groaned to himself, "and you three want to go out there with weapons you have no idea how to use?"

"It's better than nothing, right?" said Hugh, becoming a tad red in his face.

"Tell you what, kids," said Detective Catcher, looking up at Dannik beside him, the two sharing a quick and meaningful glance. "How about we do something to improve your firing skills?"

"How are we going to do that?" asked Hugh. "I don't think there are any shooting ranges around here."

"In that case, we'll have to make our own," said Dannik with a huge grin.

Hugh and the others watched as Dannik headed towards the wall with the remaining folding chairs. He reached out with one golden hand and grabbed one of the chairs, and with a flick of his wrist, spun the chair around to reveal a piece of paper taped to the front of it that featured a target. With the chair in hand, Dannik headed to the open area of the room and set it down. He headed back to the folding chairs and brought over a few more chairs, each featuring a similar target, though a couple had holes punched into the paper. With the chairs in place, the large white Sparrow headed over to the crates and brought a few of the boxes over to join the chairs. He then fetched several empty tin cans from a pile in the back of the room. With everything in place, he began to assemble from the miscellaneous objects an improvised firing range. He did it so quickly that it was clear that he had put this setup together several times before.

"Is that your idea of a shooting gallery?" asked Bobby, trying to act unimpressed and failing.

The detective chuckled and pulled from his injured arm's sling a police-issued handgun and a full ammunition clip, which he promptly slid home in the gun's stock with a satisfying click. He looked up to see everyone's surprised faces. "What?" he asked with a playful smirk. "I get bloody bored down here. I hate desk work and used to be one of the best shots on the force. I got to occupy my time somehow down here while the ones with good legs are up and about."

It did not take long for things to go into motion. Icarus and Detective Catcher were assigned the role of shooting instructors. When asked why Dannik wouldn't be helping the trio learn to handle their weapons better, he admitted he wasn't one of the special models that were designed to use firearms. His talent, as he showed them by shamelessly flexing his body like the strongman at the circus, was his muscles and physical prowess. In short, Dannik was better with his fists than with firearms.

The detective and Icarus took turns with who they were teaching. Icarus started with Sally while Detective Catcher took up station with Hugh. Bobby was left to wait his turn because he had more experience than the reporter or the photographer. Hugh was the first one up to bat, with the detective by his side. As it turned out, Hugh's time working his camera's view finder had aided greatly in helping him develop his aim. However, he had to re-learn how to aim with the sight of a rifle and a handgun, as they were not simple photo boxes he could bring right up to his eye. His first round of bullets went wide and punched holes in the wall around the targets and into the crate beneath them, leaving all of the cans standing undamaged.

"Okay," said the detective as he and Hugh moved away from the firing line and let Sally step up to bat with Icarus by her side. He talked with Hugh, giving him advice and telling him to relax and focus on the target. He told him that missing on the first shot can happen, but it should not be a wasted bullet. One can use that bullet as a benchmark for adjusting one's aim. He talked more with Hugh as Sally took her shots at the cans. Her bullets also went wide, but she managed to hit a few cans, causing them to fall off the back of the lowest chair.

"Tee-hee," she said teasingly. "Looks like I am the one who should be protecting you, Hughie!"

"Don't get over-confident," said Icarus in his emotionless voice.

"Oh hush, you," said Sally, lightly slapping the Sparrow on the arm. "I am only having a bit of fun."

Bobby then took his turn at bat, with the detective giving him advice. He did better than Sally with his new rifle, but when he brought out his magnum to fire with, Detective Catcher spoke up.

"Whoa, where'd you get that thing?" he asked, his eyebrows shooting up.

"Same place as we got most of our weapons," said Bobby, trying to be vague about it.

"From a weapons locker hidden under the streets of Galileo Plaza, in a place a lot like this one," said Hugh, bringing a scowl from Bobby. "What?" Hugh asked.

"Oh, I just didn't want them to know about where we got our guns, in case they might, you know, take them from us on the grounds we stole them from the city or something. That's all."

Detective Catcher simply shrugged at that. "I don't care where you got them. As I see it, they're yours, if you can use them properly."

"You're too paranoid, Bobby," said Sally as she shook her head.

"In times like these, one never can be too sure what will happen," muttered Bobby to himself as he brought the magnum up and took aim at the targets. However, each shot he fired caused him to wince in pain. Bobby was more used to firing his shotgun than a magnum, and he needed time to get used to the kick from the aptly named hand cannon. All said, Bobby managed to hit half of the cans. As he stepped away and reloaded his guns, the detective began to teach Bobby how to best hold the six-shooter so the kick wouldn't hurt nearly as much and to improve his aim. He also showed Bobby a few tricks with managing his rifle.

It was Hugh's turn again and he tried to take to heart what the detective told him. He relaxed and focused on the target. His first shot hit the crate dead center. He learned from this that he was aiming way too far to the left and too high relative to his intended target, a can of peas. Adjusting his sites, he missed again, the bullet flying too far to the right this time and hitting the wall. It took a few goes, but eventually he hit his target. Once both the rifle and handgun were empty, Icarus stepped up to give Hugh instructions on how to better manage the larger of the two guns.

Sally stepped up again for her turn, and fired off all her bullets, doing a little better than before. After her came Bobby, followed by Hugh and so on. They continued like this for hours till their hands hurt and shoulders ached from all the firing. During the time, improvement was made. Hugh got significantly better, and he felt his own self-confidence grow with each successful round fired. He didn't kid himself. He knew he was far from being as good as a professional, but he at least could hit a target now. Sally, too, had gotten a good deal better, but she was lagging behind Hugh now in skill. Bobby was the best of them all, quickly taking to his hand cannon and showing off skill with how fast he could draw the weapon, take aim, and fire it. He wasn't as skilled with the rifle, but he was told by the detective to try to use the rifle more than the magnum, since the larger ammunition clip of the rifle meant he had more chances to hit his target. The magnum was to be saved for emergencies only.

As they cleaned up the target range, it having fulfilled its purpose, there was a loud knock at the door to the room. The detective, being the one who could do the least to help clean up, wheeled himself over to answer the door. Upon seeing who was calling, he turned as far as his neck brace allowed and called out to the others to come. They were being summoned back to the boardroom to have another meeting with the Deputy Chief and his cabinet. Dannik, too, was expected to join the proceedings, although the officer sent to collect them didn't explain why, no matter how much they asked along the way back to the meeting room.

Their group received more curious stares than before due to having two Sparrows in the group instead of one. Hugh could only guess that this was because many of these people, if not most, probably had never seen more than one Sparrow before, as they had not interacted with a flock of the birdmen as he had. What's more, it was odd to see Icarus and Dannik walking side by side. One dressed in mere pants with a heavy duty backpack with a shotgun sticking out of one of the flaps and a sniper rifle slung over a shoulder. The other dressed up like Julius Caesar, standing a good foot taller than Icarus, his wing tips brushing against every ceiling of every room and hallway they walked through. Unlike elsewhere, the whispers that Hugh caught were not ill-spirited toward the Sparrows, simply questions as to how many Sparrows were in Nimbus and why another had appeared in the secret area.

Soon enough they were back in their seats around the long stainless steel table. Dannik, however, had to stand behind Detective Catcher. He did not look too pleased about having to stand, fidgeting about on his feet, but every time Hugh's gaze drifted over to the white Sparrow, the big bird cracked a smile and flexed a large bicep. Hugh found himself grateful that Icarus was not nearly as full of himself as Dannik. Hugh liked to think of himself as a pretty tolerant guy, but if there was one thing that annoyed him, it was people who were so into themselves that they couldn't spare a second thinking of anything else.

"Welcome back, Hugh and company," said the Deputy Chief, "I hope we did not keep you waiting too long while we got the results on the journal."

"Hardly," said Bobby as he pushed his glasses back up on his nose, "I am actually surprised that it required so little time. The book isn't a mere pamphlet."

"Be that as it may," said Deputy Chief Chapman. "But we hit a breakthrough half an hour ago, that the department and I believe will lead us to the Hawker's laboratory."

"What was it?" asked Sally.

"Trust me, it is something so incredible that we didn't even think it was legitimate at first," chuckled the Deputy Chief. "The techs had to run it through the city's system to see if it was real!"

27

"Come on, spit it out," Hugh begged, his curiosity burning. He was dying to finally get some answers, instead of more questions. Of course, the moment the words left his lips, he realized just how rude and disrespectful he sounded and his face visually colored in embarrassment. Sally looked taken aback by his sudden outburst. Bobby merely raised an eyebrow at his friend's unintentional sign of disrespect of the Deputy Chief.

"Chief, I think you better cut the dramatics," said Detective Catcher. "The kid is clearly chomping at the bit."

"Ahem, again, I am only the Deputy Chief, Detective Catcher," Chapman sighed as he reached down beside him and picked up a plastic resealable bag with the words "Evidence," written in black upon yellow tape. Hugh could not see what was in it from where he was sitting, but he suspected it held Dr. Crick's Journal. "Anyway," said Chapman after clearing his throat, "When the tech guys were looking over the journal, they found something stuck between two of its pages. It seems that when the journal took a dip in the sewer, it caused several pages to stick together.

"What did they find?"

The Deputy Chief did not answer. He simply slid the evidence bag down the table toward Hugh. Inside was indeed the journal, but there was also a piece of white plastic about two inches by three inches in size. Atop its slick surface was a black and white image of Dr. Frank Crick, and next to it were a few lines of small text with his name and a few snippets of information on the doctor, such as his height and weight. The bottom of the card had a circular logo consisting of a rectangular hammer with gears on either side of its handle. There were twin lightning bolts striking the top of the graphic mallet. Revolving around the hammer were the words "Mason Machines & Computers," and under the logo, was an address.

"We had suspected for some time that the Hawkers were being manufactured at that address," said Deputy Chief Chapman. "However, we didn't have anything solid to go on till now. The Hawkers are guarding several different buildings in that sector that could have just as easily been where they were being built. Now that we have something to go on, I can gather up a unit to try to investigate the property and see if we can't throw a monkey wrench into the works."

"I would like to be a part of the operation," said Hugh.

"As would I," said Sally, flashing a smile at Hugh.

"Count me in," said Icarus with a nod of his feathery head.

"Same here," said Bobby, his eyes seemingly glued to the tiny picture of his father on the plastic card.

"Oh no you don't!" said the Major who had bad mouthed them before. "The last thing we need in an operation this sensitive is three civilians and a birdman running around making a muck of things."

"We can protect ourselves," said Hugh, holding up his gun. "I promise we won't be a burden on the mission."

"I have had enough of this nonsense," said the Major, getting red in the face. "If McGullen was here, he wouldn't be putting up with this stupidity. He'd have these people with the other civilians, where they belong!"

"It's a good thing I am *NOT* the old Chief then," said Chapman as he stood up from his chair and glared at Major Felix. "Otherwise I would demote you to patrolman on the spot for being so disrespectful. You are just lucky we haven't had the time to hold the ceremony to have me instated as the official Chief." With that the Deputy Chief let out a deep breath and sat back down in his chair. "However," he said after he had a moment to compose himself, "I would normally agree with the Major in this type of situation. But, we're tight on men, with our people spread out all over the city and others watching over the survivors and others still trying to work on fixing this underground base's radio system so we can contact the surface. As things stand, I am willing to accept any and all volunteers on this mission."

"In that case, may I come along?" asked Dannik. "It has been as dull as marbles down here, and I am itching to go on an adventure."

"Normally I would say no, since the more Sparrows we have flying about, the more likely the Hawkers will become interested in our movements," said the Deputy Chief. "But we may need a Sparrow like you, who is familiar with the entrances to this part of the emergency area system of the city." Upon seeing Dannik's shocked face, the Deputy

Chief chuckled. "Come now wingman, did you really think we didn't know about your flights of fancy? This entire base is wired up with cameras. We have men who watch all the entrances and exits in case something nasty comes our way. Now," he said as he reached down and pulled out several folders filled with papers and passed them around, "I want to send a small team of fifteen good men out to Vulcan. With you four as volunteers, we can keep more of the NTAF here at home base in case the Hawkers try to attack us. What's more, it might be useful to have a reporter and a photographer around to help gather information on site. Not to mention having a Sparrow on the team would be very useful, given their ability to fly."

"The NTAF?" asked Sally. "Is that short for something?"

"I'm not surprised you haven't heard of NTAF," said another at the table, a man with grey sideburns and sandy blond hair. "We aren't supposed to go around talking about the NTAF unless there is an emergency. "

"Again, what does it stand for?" asked Hugh, his curiosity bubbling.

"It is an acronym for Nimbus Tactical Armed Forces," said another member of the congregation. "They're the best our city's police have to offer, and are trained to handle the most dangerous of situations. They have become very active in the past week, with all the Hawker attacks."

"How many members of NTAF are there?" asked Bobby, raising an eyebrow.

"We've got enough, but most of them are out in the field. They are searching for more survivors and Sparrow nests."

"Sparrow nests?" asked Icarus. "What do you want with others of my kind?"

"We have discussed this with Dannik," said the Deputy Chief as he slid a file over to Hugh. It was labeled as 'Read upon Arrival'. "The Hawkers have an advantage over most of us humans, as they can fly. The best we can do is to fight them from the ground or shoot one down when they get in the sights of our antiaircraft guns. The fighter planes the ground is sending up are helping matters, but they are nowhere nearly agile enough to take out enough Hawkers to even the playing field for us on the streets. We need the Sparrows. They are more than capable enough to go toe to toe with the robots. Heck, they once *were* the robots! They should know all the Hawkers' dirty tricks."

"I think you are forgetting the Sparrows are not invulnerable," said Bobby. "What's more, how will you get them to fight for you? I don't think all of them are as brave as Icarus or glory hungry as Dannik."

"Oi, Four-eyes," snarled Dannik, his gold eyes burning in the light of the room. "I told you, I am doing this because it's the right thing, not because I want to be held on a pedestal."

"Your attire says differently."

"Why, I ought to pound you into paste!"

"Calm down," said the Deputy Chief. "This is not a playground and you are not children! If you can't keep your temper, Dannik, you are off the team. Icarus could just as easily serve our purposes as you could."

Dannik grumbled to himself as he crossed his arms, his golden hands digging into his white feathered limbs, as he tried to suppress his rage. "Fine," he said, "I'll be good."

"Now that that bit of business is out of the way," said the Deputy Chief as he massaged his temple, "We can get back to planning out this mission. As I was saying, we need about fifteen men for this, and with our current volunteers, we only have ten slots open." Turning to his left, the Deputy Chief addressed the man with the grey sideburns. "Sergeant Maple, I want you to pick your best men for this mission."

"I got just the men for the job," said the Sergeant, as he pulled out a thick brown cigar and lit it with a silvery flip top lighter. "I'll round them up and send them your way. When do you want them?"

"As soon as possible," said the Deputy Chief. "We need time to plan a route through Vulcan. Dannik?"

"Yes, Chiefy?" asked the large white Sparrow, snapping instantly to attention.

"I want you to go out and scout out the situation over in Vulcan, to see if there is anything the mission team may need to be aware of. We already have some of our men stationed in Vulcan on the lookout, but I want your sharp eye in the sky. I need not tell you to avoid any Hawker contact or try to go in on the location by yourself, do I?"

"No worries, Chiefy," said Dannik. "Do you want me to bring a radio or just keep it to myself till I come back?"

"The radio," said the Deputy Chief. "In this situation, the more information our men have, and the faster they have it, the better we can be prepared for tomorrow."

"When do you want me to go out for my little fly by?"

"As soon as possible," said the Deputy Chief. Dannik gave a bow and walked out the door, having to duck to clear the top of the frame. After his white tail feathers disappeared from sight, the Deputy Chief turned to Sergeant Maple and gave him a nod. The Sergeant rose from his seat and headed out the door, carrying a folder of his own and leaving a wispy trail of cigar smoke floating in the air behind him. Once he too was gone, the meeting turned towards more mundane things, such as ration levels in the emergency area and the status of the scout teams in the field. Hugh could barely pay attention as the officers' voices droned on and on. He turned to look at Sally and saw that, as usual, she was taking everything down on her notepad, her pencil speeding across the paper pages.

After what felt like an hour of conversation, there was a sudden loud beep from overhead. It startled Hugh, causing him to jump a little in his seat. Sally gave a little start as well, but everyone else, including Bobby and Icarus, weren't surprised by the sound. However, the dialog being spouted by one of the other majors instantly stopped.

"Chief, we got an incoming message from Dannik," said a female voice over an intercom system that Hugh reasoned was built into the ceiling of the room, given how there was a speaker embedded in the ceiling tiles. It made him briefly wonder where the microphones were hidden in the room, as he hadn't seen any the first time he visited or even now.

"Excellent," said Chapman as he stood up and headed over to the woman at the machine. She had been there since their first visit, and was still working away at the device, which was similar to the one that they had seen in the other secret area in Galileo Plaza. Upon request, she reached down and pulled from somewhere before her knees a rolled up tube of paper, which she handed to the Deputy Chief.

"Would you like me to patch him through?" asked the female voice from the ceiling speakers.

"Yes, Martha," said the Deputy Chief as he unrolled the paper atop the table, revealing a large map of the Vulcan District. It wasn't a simple tourist's map, as it had every single building numbered and listed in the margins how many entrances each building had. The bigger buildings, such as the factories and manufacturing plants were color-coded by what type of goods they made. The ones that made furniture were pink, the ones that handled metal were grey, and the ones that made clothes were blue, and so on.

"Patch the big bird on through," said the Deputy Chief.

"Okay, you're live, Dannik," said the woman's voice before the transmission became significantly worse in quality. There were sharp bouts of static that made Hugh cringe, but over it Dannik's deep voice could easily be heard.

"This is the big white bird, can you hear me?"

"Yes, loud, but not completely clear," said the Deputy Chief as he went back to the woman at the machine and had her hand him a rolled up transparent plastic sheet, that he proceeded to roll out on top of the large map. Hugh watched as a couple officers stood up and used clips that were built into the table to hold down both the map and the plastic overlay. From the side of the table, the Deputy Chief pulled out a set of thick markers. "What do you see?" asked the Deputy Chief as he handed off the markers to the other men around the map, who leaned over the table and readied their hands.

"To start, there are Hawkers, but that isn't much of a surprise," said Dannik, his laugh getting cut short by a pop in the audio. "From what I can see, their patrols seem to be moving around the district in counterclockwise circuits, in groups of three to five."

As Dannik went on, the officers marked up the transparent sheet atop the map, writing red 'Hs', here and there, and having arrows lead away from the letters. A few black 'NFAs' and 'SHs' appeared as well on the plastic. Hugh assumed that 'SH' meant 'safe house.' He had seen enough crime shows on television to guess that much. The Deputy Chief frowned every now and then when Dannik reported a new cluster of Hawkers and they marked them down on the map. Eventually, the Deputy Chief interrupted Dannik's long string of speech.

"Dannik," said Deputy Chief Chapman, "You have been doing a great job. However, we need to check in with our men in the field. Can you stay up in the clouds and out of sight until we can correlate the situation with our men?"

"Roger that, Roger," said Dannik, with a static infused laugh. The interference went away almost instantly and the woman's voice returned. The Deputy Chief told her to place a call to one of the units stationed in Vulcan. Again, the static returned, and it seemed a bit worse than before. Hugh could barely make out voices over the interference. The Deputy Chief and his men began the process of confirming positions of Hawkers in Vulcan with the ground troops, making new marks on the board and erasing one or two. They drew a few red 'Xs' across streets on the map, and wrote down quick notes. Hugh turned to Sally to see what she was thinking of this, only to see that she was now pouting.

"What's wrong, Sally?" he asked her.

"I ran out of paper," she moaned. "Can you believe it? We've been through so much that I've used up three notepads!"

Hugh chuckled, "At least you will have one hell of a story when all of this is over."

"I sure hope so," said Sally, looking down at her pencil.

"Here, "said Hugh, reaching into his camera bag. With his right hand he pulled out a new notepad and handed it over to Sally. "I was saving this for you."

"Thank you, Hughie!" said Sally with a huge grin as she snapped up the notepad like a puppy gobbles up treats. Without missing a beat, she began writing away at the notepad.

Every now and then, they would have Dannik come back on the radio to see if he saw anything the ground troops had missed. Soon a new color was introduced to the transparent sheet, green, which was used to circle a building at the western end of the map. From the edge of the circle a line steadily grew outward like a winding emerald serpent of ink as it weaved in and out of buildings and avoided most of the 'Hs' on the map. There were a few times marked down on the map beside the line and next to the 'Hs', possibly representing the time that Hawkers would pass by the green path. The path did intersect with a few 'NTAFs' and 'SHs,' and when it did so, the high ranking offers contacted different units they had stationed in Vulcan, to check to see if the route was clear past their encampments.

Soon the green line reached an end. It spiraled around a single large building just south of the middle of the map. Hugh couldn't clearly see what the building was called, due to the green ink, but he did see it was colored grey on the map, indicating it had something to do with metal work, a likely place for the production of Hawkers. With the route devised, the Deputy Chief ordered Dannik to return to HQ. After Dannik signed off, Deputy Chief Chapman asked the woman, whose voice had returned when Dannik had left, to summon Major Maple. It was time to see who the man had chosen to be a part of the mission.

He soon arrived in the meeting room with the ten men. As each one entered the room, the major listed off their names. The first member of NTAF was named Jack Harper, who was of average height and was almost as young as Hugh himself. He had dark brown hair and held his weapon ready in his hands. Behind him followed Adam Regan, a much older man who had waves of grey intermixed with his black hair. He stood tall beside Jack, who had positioned himself in front of the wall across from where Hugh and Sally sat. Adam sported a backpack identical to the one that Icarus was wearing with the only difference being Adam's had dark stains upon its fabric.

Waddling in next was Samuel West, a fairly pudgy and short man who looked to be around his mid-forties. He wore a large smile on his red face as he went over to join the others of his unit, stopping only to give a friendly wave towards Hugh and Sally. Bobby, along with Icarus, had both turned around in their seats to take in the new arrivals. Soon another one walked in. He was introduced as Fredric Warren. He had a head of pure white hair and dark glasses covering his eyes, giving him a mysterious air. As he walked over to stand beside Samuel, Hugh thought he saw a quick glimpse of Fredric's eyes. They were a deep shade of red, a color that was eerily similar to the color of the eyes of an angry

Hawker. Filling in after the white-haired man, was Clark Gordon, who also gave Hugh a wave.

"It sure has been a long time hasn't it, Mr. Yeats?" said Officer Gordon.

"Eh?" asked Hugh in confusion.

"We met when you first came to see us at the warehouse," explained Clark. "You know, after the Transport Center exploded. Remember?"

Hugh thought back to then, trying to remember. He seemed to recall the name from somewhere but he couldn't put his finger on it. To be nice, he nodded his head saying that he did remember now, and it had taken him a moment to recognize Officer Gordon in the NTAF uniform. With a smile, the officer moved on to stand beside the others along the wall. After he was in place, the four remaining members of the squad walked in. They were Officer Jamie Walker, Edward Burton, and Terry and Owen Drew. The last two were identical twin brothers, who both had fair hair and identical freckles on their cheeks.

As soon as they were lined up, the Deputy Chief called them over to the table and showed them the marked-up map. He summarized the information that had been transmitted over the radio and outlined the path on the map, telling them about places that they could rest and times when it was safe to move out in the open. During the presentation, some of the men stole glances at Icarus. Their faces were unreadable for the most part. It was clear the one by the name of Adam didn't appear to like seeing a Sparrow at the meeting. Hugh hoped that there would be no trouble between the two while they were on the mission tomorrow. The last thing he wanted was another guy complaining and distrusting Icarus.

28

When the meeting finally ended, Hugh found himself nodding off. They ate a brief dinner with the other survivors who had managed to reach the protection of the police on the fourth level of the emergency area. The cafeteria they ate in was very large and filled with a dozen long tables whose seats were quickly filled. Hugh and his friends had to move fast to find a place to sit after they collected their meals on plastic trays. The food wasn't the best they ever had, beans with a side of canned fruit and a glass of powdered milk. They might as well have eaten from their own rations for all the difference it would make in taste, but they decided to eat with the other survivors and officers so they could save their rations for the days ahead. As they ate, Hugh looked around a few times at all the people eating together. He saw people of all ages, some with visible wounds and torn clothing, and others who looked as if they were stolen away from their normal lives. He thought he might recognize some of the survivors around him, but no one looked familiar.

After their meal, they were led by Detective Catcher back to his room to spend the night. Despite many of the other civilians being familiar with the idea of Sparrows through Dannik walking their halls, several of them still had a negative opinion of the large avian creatures. It was simply too hard for them to trust Sparrows after the terror Hawkers had brought down upon them. They were met by an officer at the door who had been given orders to give each of them a brand new sleeping bag to use for the night. They couldn't use one of the cots that were already in the room because they were actually Dannik's bed. He needed five because of his large size, as merely one of the small cots wasn't enough to hold his weight. As they unrolled the sleeping bags, the big white Sparrow returned.

"Did you have a fun flight, Dannik?" asked Detective Catcher as he wheeled himself over to his roommate with a smile upon his face.

"Oh, yeah," the large Sparrow chuckled, "Though the scenery leaves a lot to be desired out there, nothing but dead-looking mountains down below."

"Mountains?" gasped Sally. "Are we over the Rocky Mountains now? Just how far west are the Hawkers taking the city?"

"If we knew that, we'd be doing something about it, Miss Saltwater," said the detective.

There was nothing more they could do but turn in for the night. Hugh had another restless night, but he did his best to get some sleep, as he knew that they would be awakened the next day long before the sun peaked over the horizon. It had been explained to them at the end of the meeting that they would move out to Vulcan at roughly four in the morning in order to try to sneak past a Hawker patrol at their point of entry into the district. They would be using a similar cargo system as Hugh and his friends had used to get to the Warehouse District. They had a small window of time to enter Vulcan before a Hawker patrol passed by the receiving end of the cargo line, a factory that normally handled wooden materials.

When the call came to wake up, in the form of one of the members of the NTAF, Hugh struggled to clear the sleep from his eyes. He, along with Sally and Bobby, was not used to being up so early. Icarus on the other hand seemed perfectly fine with rising at four in the morning, and quickly gathered up all his gear. Dannik was already up, standing by the door with a backpack just as large as Icarus's slung over his shoulders, except his lacked any guns sticking out from under the sack's flap. In order to fully wake them up, Hugh and his fellow human friends were led to the shower room, where they were told to strip and go under the water. It was so cold that it felt like pure ice was being applied to their skin. Needless to say, the shock of the frigid water was more than enough to banish the last bit of drowsiness from Hugh's and his friends' bodies.

Once they were dry, they changed into uniforms provided by the NTAF. The shirts and pants were decorated in splotches of different shades of gray, a design that another member of their mission, Adam, informed them was called urban camouflage. It would make them harder to see amongst the buildings and concrete, thus making it harder for them to be spotted from the air. They were also given fresh ammunition for their weapons and their reserve pouches were filled to the brim. Once everything was set, the NTAF and Hugh's friends were escorted to another cargo hub, this time on the other end of the district.

It wasn't too far of a walk, given that the Warehouse District was a bit smaller than most sections of Nimbus since no one really lived there.

It was dark inside the cargo transport room when the leader of the NTAF unit escorting them, Adam, undid the bolts and pushed aside the hatch leading out from the secret staircase. They did not waste any time climbing out and entering into formation around a large platform hanging from the ceiling, a similar platform to the one Hugh and crew used a day before. Before they climbed on, or even fiddled with the console, Adam had the officer named Jamie use his radio to contact the officers on the other side of the abyss, and let them know they were preparing to cross. Hugh felt way out of his league among these professional men. It was as if he was a child among accomplished businessmen. The only one of the NTAF Hugh felt comfortable around was Jack, and that was only because they were roughly the same age.

Finally, the officer named Walt pressed the button on the controls that opened the massive door on the far wall of the room, exposing the pre-dawn sky and Vulcan floating in the distance. Even from here, and in this darkness, one could see trails of smoke leading up and away from the district, giving it a foreboding appearance. One might ask why some of the factories were up and running if there was no one to work them, but the truth of the matter was that several of the factories had been automated in the past few years, and were churning out goods even though there was no one to pick them up.

Once it was clear there weren't any Hawkers flying about, Adam nodded at Walt to send the message to the other side, stating that they were ready to travel. Unlike last time, a buzzer did not go off when the platform started to inch its way across the floor and toward the open hatch. No one questioned this, and Hugh assumed that there was a button on the console that switched the alarm off, and that the mall cop the day before simply hadn't found it.

No one said a word atop the platform. A few of the NTAF held strange binoculars and looked around the skies as the platform moved out into open air. Hugh wondered what the men were doing, since he could barely see anything but shadows at this hour. The sky was starting to lighten up, although very slowly. Turning to look at Liberty Estates off to the south-west, he saw that many of the lights were still on in the district, making it appear as a lonely island of light amid the darkness.

The sky was the light pink that heralded the dawn of a new day when they reached Vulcan. The platform hadn't even stopped moving before the NTAF officers started to hop down from it. Hugh, Sally and the others followed suit and followed the officers towards a large door at the other end of the room. There were wooden boards stacked everywhere, bound together by ropes. From behind one such stack emerged an officer with a hand radio. He waved the group over and talked in hushed voices with Adam. Hugh didn't catch much of what was said, and he could tell from Sally's pouting that she, too, couldn't hear the conversation. Once it was over, the unit reformed, with the twins in the lead, followed by Fredric and Sam, with Adam and Hugh's crew in the center. The other members of the NTAF gathered at their sides and rear, with their weapons at the ready. Before they could step out, Bobby voiced a question.

"Excuse me," he said, making everyone turn to look at him. Time was ticking and they couldn't spare a second. "Why don't we just use the underground passages?"

"Son," said Adam, glaring at Bobby, "the underground area here is compromised. If we could use it to travel, we would have. Now, are there any other questions you have before we lose our brief window to move out?"

"None, *sir.*"

With that out of the way, they moved out of the building and onto the street outside. There were strange smells in the air, lingering scents of the chemicals used in some of the factories nearby. The large billboards on the structures advertised paint brands and aerosol sprays. Wasting no time to take in any more of the sights, Adam gave the order for them to move out. Holding out a marked copy of the map from the meeting room, they followed the green line across the street and into a small personal warehouse filled with assorted paint buckets. They had once been stacked all the way up to the ceiling, but had long since toppled over and wobbled about on the floor as the city continued to vibrate as it sailed through the air.

They hurried through the store room and exited out into the mixing room where the paint's colors were made. The machines were still churning the mixtures in the vats, but since no one was there to take the cans off the conveyor belts, they were piling up in a mess of buckets and swirls of colors at the end of the line. Everyone stayed away from the mess, and headed deeper into the complex, past more machines and push carts. The only sound was the hum of the machines at work, mixing and pouring, and the occasional clunk of a can falling off the belt and spilling over the floor. Soon, they reached a door and one of the twins, Hugh wasn't sure which, stepped forward and cautiously opened it, revealing a beige hallway. It was lined with a few doors on either side, ending in a set of twin double doors at the end. They ignored the single doors and exited through the twin doors into the lobby of the factory.

Before they could exit back outside, Icarus's ears perked up and he told everyone to stop. Everyone backed away from the door leading out and waited, Adam giving the order to halt, despite the misgivings being clear upon the other NTAF officers' faces. Dannik's feathery ears also perked up, and he turned to look at Icarus with a silent question on his face. Icarus simply nodded, as from outside the sound of metal on rock began to ring out.

"What should we do, Sarge?" asked Jack in a whisper, looking nervously between the two Sparrows and the front door. "Move out or wait?"

"I say we move," said Jamie. "I think we have enough men to take them out. It sounds like only one or two of those Hawkers out there."

"I am more worried about what we can't hear," whispered Sally in Hugh's ear. Adam seemed to agree as he gave the order to wait. The sounds of footsteps outside grew louder and louder, and then started to fade away. Yet Adam still didn't give the order to move out, even after several minutes had passed. Just because they couldn't hear any footsteps did not mean that there weren't any Hawkers flying around outside. It was only when Icarus turned and nodded his head again that they started moving.

They hurried outside and made their way toward an alleyway across the street. It was extremely narrow so they had to traverse it in a formation of two columns. It was a very claustrophobic experience, with the windowless brick walls soaring four stories high on either side of the group. A perfect place for an ambush by robotic birds, but they made it through to the other side without any sign of danger.

They came out in a wide empty yard that they wasted no time in crossing, moving on down another narrow alley. They passed by smashed crates that held assorted bits and objects that none of them bothered to investigate. The alley had a metal gate blocking its entrance, but Dannik made quick work of the obstruction, tearing it off its hinges and placing it gingerly down on the ground next to the opening. There was a lot of loose trash scattered about this narrow passage, such as newspapers and flattened cardboard boxes. When they made it out onto the next street, they were greeted with the sight of several decaying human bodies that had once been workers in Vulcan. Flies buzzed about in the air and the stench was truly horrific. Sally turned pale and Bobby covered his face to block the flumes. The seasoned members of the NTAF around them hardly reacted, while the younger ones, such as Jack, turned green in the face.

There was nothing they could do for the poor souls lying in pools of their own blood, so they hurried along their route. They entered an office building mere seconds before Fredric, who was talking up the rear, noticed a Hawker flying overhead. It was close, but thankfully they managed to keep from being spotted by the robot and continued on their way, deeper into the industrial district. They only stopped moving when they entered a workers' lunchroom in one of the textile mills.

They were greeted by a few scout officers once they were inside. They were reassured that they had made it to a safe house of sorts, so the unit could rest before the next leg of their journey. By then it was roughly midmorning and they had been walking ever since they entered Vulcan. Hugh was grateful for a moment to sit down and rest his feet. The other members of the NTAF also took the chance to get off their feet, sitting down and chatting amongst themselves.

It was clear that the scouts weren't in the best of shape. Two of them had bloody bandages, while another was using what looked like the back of a broken chair as a crutch to walk around on. Needless to say, when they heard Bobby was a doctor, they instantly ushered him off to have him see to their injuries. Hugh took the opportunity to bring his camera to his eye and take a few pictures of the brave scouts as they were being treated by Bobby in the corner of the room. He also took a few of the NTAF officers as they chatted.

"So," said Samuel, one of the members of NTAF, as he slid over to sit next to Hugh, "are you this Yeats kid that the department has been abuzz about?"

"Yeah," said Hugh, blushing, "that'd be me."

"Nice to meet yah," said Samuel with a big smile, showing that he was missing a few teeth and offering out his plump hand for Hugh to shake. "Say," he said, "aren't you also that guy who takes the pictures for the paper?"

"Right again," Hugh mumbled as he started to blush and accepted the handshake. "Are you familiar with my work?"

"Not really," said Samuel with a shake of his head, causing the skin on his bald head to catch a glint of light from the overhead bulbs. "I was just curious, that's all."

"Oh," said Hugh, his blush disappearing as if someone had used a rag to wipe it away.

"The thing is," continued Samuel with a smirk, "when all of this is over, we will all be heroes of the city, right? That means there will be reporters and photos! I reckon that you'll want a few of my good side, right?"

"I am not sure that-" started Hugh before Samuel interrupted him.

"Oh relax, Yeats!" He said with a loud laugh, before slapping Hugh hard on the back. "I am only yanking your chain!"

"Hey," called out one of the NTAF, "Sam, leave the kid alone, we need you over here."

"Alright, I'm coming," said Samuel. He turned to Hugh and shrugged his shoulders before getting up and joining the rest of his unit. When Samuel left, Sally took his place beside Hugh. She looked small and fragile in the urban camouflage uniform. The greys made her face seem far paler than normal, as if it was made from smooth porcelain. She did not say a thing, and neither did Hugh. They simply sat together and enjoyed the moment of peace they had together before having to go back out in the dangerous streets. He gently stroked her neck, her golden locks flowing over the back of his hand. He could feel the rough fabric of her new backpack when his hand drifted down to the base of her neck. She looked tired, and hadn't bothered to apply makeup today. Such superficial commodities served no purpose in such trying times. That or she had simply run out of the products she used to make up her face.

"Hugh," she said, turning to face him, a question on her lips.

"What is it, Sal?" he asked, leaning close.

"I'm glad you've been taking photos."

"Thanks," said Hugh, looking down at his camera and back to her. "Someone had to."

"Don't get me wrong," she said bashfully as her face colored slightly. "I know that taking snapshots hasn't been high on our list of things to do with all the craziness going on, but I appreciate that you are taking the time to do it. It will make bringing the story of what happened here to the world all the easier. After all, a picture is worth a thousand words."

"You got that right, doll," said Hugh with a sly smile. "That's why we make such a great team."

Hugh turned to look over at Icarus and Dannik, realizing he hadn't taken a picture of them together yet. He quickly took one, lucking out on having them both facing each other in profile, showing the contrasting size between the two giant birds. Sally took in a breath and was about to say something more, when Adam stood up and loudly cleared his throat.

"Time's up people," he said in a gruff voice. "We need to get going. Dr. Crick?"

Bobby turned to look up from the man he was treating. He shrugged and looked back to the injured officer and tied off the bandage before standing and heading back to rejoin with the group. "Yes?" he asked.

"Thank you for tending to the scouts," said the head NTAF officer.

"It's what I do," said Bobby as he wiped his brow of sweat and accidently knocked his glasses off. He reached down to pick them up as Adam kept talking.

"However, I would appreciate it if you kept your meds to yourself, unless one of my men gets hurt. We may need them more than the scouts before the trip is over. Understand?"

Bobby grimaced as he reached for his cleaning rag and wiped grime off of the lenses. "Of course, officer," he said as he slid them back onto his nose.

"Now then, everyone into formation!" barked Adam. Everyone did a quick weapons check before saying their goodbyes to the scouts and heading out the back door of the cafeteria and into a packaging room. There were crates stacked all over the room. Most of the boxes had been piled up against the walls of the room, blocking the windows from prying Hawker eyes. They didn't stay long enough to take a good look at the boxes, as they were soon led out of a loading bay door and back outside.

They moved quickly through the lot outside the safe house, keeping up their guard and searching the skies for Hawkers. Hugh lost count of how many times they had to cut through a factory or some other building just to save time or take cover from a passing Hawker unit. He was getting more and more anxious, wondering just how much longer their luck would hold out. It was as if someone had placed a charm over them, protecting them all from danger. They made it to the second safe house without any issue, and only stayed for half as long as at the first one.

"I don't like this, sir," said one of the NTAF officers after they had left the second safe house and formed back up.

"What's not to like, Edward?" asked Adam.

"We have hardly had any contact with the enemy, sir," answered the officer.

"That's because we are right on schedule, Eddy," said Jack with a nervous laugh.

"I don't know," said Edward as he turned to look back at Hugh and his friends in the center of the unit. "I mean, we are heading to where these robot things are being made, right? Don't you think they'd have a heavier guard stationed?"

"Maybe they aren't as smart as we give them credit for," said Jack as he looked over at the other end of the street they were crossing.

"It would be a mistake to underestimate the enemy," said Adam in a matter-of-fact tone of voice. "That's when they swoop in and get you."

Finally, after what felt like an endless trek through a land of industry and a forest of smokestacks, the group reached the building that they had marked as the site of Dr. Mason's secret lab and where the Hawkers were being made. It was a large brick building with soot stains along its upper stones. It only stood one story tall, but that didn't keep it from it having a foreboding atmosphere. There wasn't a single sound or sign of life from the structure, no evidence that it was actively producing anything except dust mites. For some reason, the quiet did not reassure anyone in the group. Hugh could feel hairs rise on the back of his neck as he sensed the building anticipation of what was inside.

The front door of the building was held shut with a heavy padlock. Thankfully, the NTAF officers had anticipated this, and had brought along bolt cutters. The door was not a safe place to be, as there was no cover from the sky, so four officers watched over one of the twins, Owen, as he worked the tool's jaws against the thick metal ring holding the doors shut. While he worked, Dannik and Icarus flew over the building to keep watch for any Hawkers on the wing. Every second that it took for the cutters to dig into the thick iron of the lock, the tension in the air rose. Only Owen kept his eyes off the skies, for he was too busy focusing on breaking the padlock. Finally, with one last grunt of effort, the cutter's blades met and the lock fell off.

Wasting no time, everyone hurried inside the building, and only closed the door behind them when the Sparrows had made it through. That isn't to say that they could relax now, for they were literary in the lair of the beast, and none of them had any idea of what the inside of the building would be like. It was so dark that they had to turn on their flashlights to see.

The beams cut through the darkness and showed a long narrow hallway leading toward a thick metal door with a box built into the wall next to it. The hallway was so tight that some of the group couldn't even see the door past the cluster of bodies and feathers. Stepping cautiously forward, Adam pulled from his pocket the evidence bag holding Frank's identification card. With no visible handle or lock on the metal door, he slid the card into the box on the wall, which made a beeping sound. The metal door slid silently aside and they moved quickly inside the next room.

They no longer needed their flashlights as this part of the building was very well lit. It was an extremely small room that ended at a set of elevator doors. Without missing a beat, the NTAF officer reached forward and tapped the call button for the elevator. The stainless steel doors slid open with the lightest of hisses and revealed an elevator just large enough for all of them to fit inside. Before they stepped inside, Adam turned and issued a warning that they should expect some serious resistance at the other end of the elevator's tower.

They went in with guns at the ready and waited in silence as the metal room sank into the floor and traveled a few stories down into the building. Sounds that were previously inaudible suddenly made themselves known, as clicks and whirls filled the air. It was almost as if their mere presence had made the factory come to life, that they had awakened it from a dusty slumber.

Finally the doors slid open again, revealing a room just as small as the one at the top of the shaft. The walls were pure white and Dr. Mason's logo was on both of the double doors on the walls to the left and right of the elevator. Taking no chances, Adam ordered the unit to split into two to go at both doors. Adam, Samuel, Jack, Sally, Hugh, Icarus, Fredric, and Walt gathered before the right hand door, while the twins, Edward, Dannik, Clark, Bobby and Jamie braced against the left hand doors. Wordlessly, they readied their guns for any trouble on the other side. Hugh gripped his weapon tightly, sweat making his fingers feel unreliable on the mechanism's trigger, his hands shaking so much that he feared he wouldn't be able to shoot straight. Upon Adam's signal, both teams pushed through the doors into the room beyond.

They came out in a large rectangular room that soared all the way up to the top of the factory. Turning around they could see the metallic elevator shaft climbing five stories up. To their surprise, taking a few steps forward revealed that both doors leading away from the elevator opened out into this one room. The group instantly rejoined, but still there was no sign of any Hawkers. There were only the sounds of the factory working away at producing what could only be more of the flying robots.

Looking around more, Hugh saw that to the right of the room was a set of black iron stairs leading up to a catwalk, spanning the length of the wall across from the elevator shaft. He could just see a few doors leading deeper into the complex beyond the handrail of the catwalk. There were other exits on the ground level of the room, with signs affixed atop the door frames. From what could be seen, there were a total of seven doors, five on the first floor and two on the second.

After assessing the situation, Adam ordered that the group split into teams of five, and made sure their radios were functioning before sending them on their way. They named the groups team one, team two and team three. Hugh and Icarus were assigned to the first group, while Sally was put in team two, and Bobby in three. Hugh tried to argue that he should stay by Sally's side, but Adam wouldn't hear of it. At least she had Dannik in her group to protect her, or so Hugh told himself over and over, a frown on his face as his group, led by Samuel, headed up the stairs and through a set of double doors at the top. The other two groups headed off in different directions to see what information they could gather on the factory's inner workings.

On the other side was another catwalk, overlooking a long conveyor belt that ushered headless Hawker robots along their way from the left to the right side of the room. Every few minutes, the belt stopped and a dozen automated robotic arms jabbed at an unfinished machine, before the belt started up again. There was still no sign of the Hawker robots, but it did not make any of them feel any better. The only one to speak was Samuel, who relayed what they found to the other teams. As they moved through the facility, Hugh took pictures of their surroundings. He was nearly at the end of his roll, and was doing his best to pick and choose his snapshots so he wouldn't have to change the film in such a dangerous place.

Right now, their goal was to assess the situation inside the factory, not to do anything else that could draw unwanted attention. After all, they were on the enemy's home turf, and there could be Hawkers hiding in every nook and cranny. Yet, this didn't stop Hugh from fantasizing about using something, anything, to jam the belt or break the assembly robots. With a tap on his shoulder, he looked up from the moving Hawker parts to see Icarus. The Sparrow was just as enthralled by all of this as Hugh was, though for different reasons. Icarus could have been assembled in a place just like this, or had been activated after leaving the factory, for his eyes were filled to the edges with curiosity and wonder. Yet Icarus contained his feelings the best he could, and with a silver hand, led Hugh along the catwalk to join up with the others of their assigned team, who had moved on to a door on the right-hand wall.

Beyond this door was their first sighting of Hawkers. Samuel swore silently and pushed everyone back. He pulled out his radio and reported to Adam, who, as Hugh could overhear, had also encountered more Hawkers in what he called Assembly Room Five. Looking over the door frame, Samuel identified that there were more Hawkers in Assembly Room One.

"What do we do?" whispered Hugh, worried about Sally, hoping that she hadn't gotten into danger. The only good sign was that the air was filled only with the constant meticulous movements of the machines. Not a single bullet or scream had broken the monotony.

"Our orders are to move on, but keep it quiet," said Samuel, with a frown on his pudgy face. Gone was the good-natured man, and in his place now stood a man who was all business.

"Is that wise?" whispered back Hugh.

"Orders are orders," said Jack, who was also in Hugh's group. "Besides, the more info we have the more lives we save. It's a good thing you're taking photos," he added, as he nodded at Hugh's camera. "When we get back to HQ, we'll want that film developed so we can plan our next stage of attack."

"About that," said Hugh as he took the last photo on his roll of film. "I need a moment to change rolls."

"Alright, but make it fast," said Jack.

Hugh reached into his camera bag and pulled out a fresh roll of film. In a matter of seconds, he had the old roll swapped out and safely stowed in his bag, and the fresh roll in the camera. He breathed a small sigh of relief once the camera was ready to take more photos. He didn't know what he was expecting to happen, and found that he was chuckling softly under his breath at the thought of how silly he was acting. He had changed the film in his camera countless times before, and never had any trouble. With that out of the way, they moved on.

Silently, they headed back into Assembly Room One and inched across the catwalk. Every step against the iron grating made Hugh wince. At any moment, one of the Hawkers on the ground could look up from their carts or their posts at consoles and spot the four humans and one Sparrow and raise an alarm. Yet, this did not happen. They managed to sneak their way through a door at the other end of the catwalk and into a large room filled to the brim with Hawkers.

Before anyone could react, Icarus spoke up. "They aren't active," he said.

"How can you be sure?" demanded Terry, one of the twins.

"It's their eyes," said Icarus, pointing at the dark faces of the standing bird robots. "If they were active, we'd be seeing their eyes glowing either blue or red. What's more, they are all facing the stairs. If they were awake, we'd be dead already."

"Good point," said Samuel as he checked in with the other teams. Moving quietly down the stairs, so as not to alert the other Hawkers in the previous room, they soon found themselves surrounded by what felt like hundreds of the robots. Being so close to the stationary Hawkers was truly unnerving. As they crept deeper, Hugh took the opportunity to take a few photos of the mechanical birdmen up close. He also took a picture showing the rows upon rows of deactivated Hawkers, which made for a very foreboding image. As he looked around the large room, Hugh noticed something lying beside a set of stairs heading down near a set of double doors.

Breaking away from the group, Hugh drew closer to the mysterious object and discovered that it was several bits of broken glass. Looking up at the ceiling, there was no sign of broken windows above the shards, nor any on the walls above the stairs. He did not respond at first when

Samuel called out for him. The glass captivated him and stirred a memory that he could just not recall.

"Yeats, what the hell are you doing?" asked Samuel as he and the others gathered around Hugh to see what had caused him to break away. "Is that glass?"

"I feel we should go downstairs," Hugh said, surprising even himself with his words. What right did he have to command members of the NTAF who probably had infinitely more experience than he did in situations such as this?

"Alright," said Samuel. "We might as well check out the basement now, could be a trouble spot if things get heated."

With one last check of the large storeroom of silent, standing Hawkers, they gathered at the second set of stairs and made their way down, deeper into the bowels of the building. To their left from the stairs was a wall of thick glass through which they could see at least a dozen Hawkers moving about. Hugh could not tell what they were doing, but was glad that none of the robots seemed to have noticed the group's presence. Across from the bottom of the stairs was another set of double doors that the group, after Samuel again sent a message to Adam, headed through. On the other side was a long hallway leading off to the left, running along the expanse of the room that held all of the Hawkers. To the right was an open wall overlooking another set of stairs leading down, blocked off by thick iron bars. Looking through the grating, a room filled with work benches and scrawled notes could be seen, along with trays of strange slime and tangles of wires. Standing in the dead center of the lower room was a Hawker robot that was very much active, and staring right up at the team.

Everything seemed to happen in slow motion in the next few moments. The Hawker opened its metal beak and headed towards the set of stairs, surely in the process of sounding an alarm. Samuel's radio went off, beeping with the incoming transmission of one of the other teams, which he ignored as he started to give the order to fire. Hugh brought his gun up and tried to aim at the moving robot's bright red eyes, when suddenly they went out.

The Hawker let out what sounded like a sigh as it crumbled to the ground, as dead as a machine could be. From beyond the edge of the grate's opening hobbled an old man on a crutch, his other hand occupied by something Hugh couldn't make out.

"Hello?" he cried out in a dry voice. "Please, for the love of God, tell me you are human!"

Hugh knew that voice. He hadn't heard it for what may have been two weeks. It was none other than the long lost Dr. Frank Crick, very much alive.

30

"FRANK!" called out Hugh, unable to stop the word from escaping his lips.

"Hubert? Oh no, is that you?" asked Frank, hobbling into full view of the team in front of the iron window. "Why are you here? Who are those people... and LOOK OUT!"

Everyone turned in surprise at the doctor's sudden outburst and turned to see what had frightened him. There was nothing in the hallway, but five men and one Sparrow. A clicking sound could be heard, and Hugh turned to see his old friend franticly pressing a button on what looked similar to the handheld radio that the NTAF were using to communicate with.

"Damn it!" grumbled Frank as he kept pressing the button. "That one must be an older model. Everyone get out of there before it kills you!"

"Before what kills us?" asked Jack.

"The Hawker behind you!" cried Frank as he dove out of the way of the window. They turned again to see nothing in the hallway. After a few minutes, Samuel pulled out his radio and contacted the other teams, to let them know they had found Dr. Frank Crick. As he talked away, Frank came back into view, a confused expression upon his face. "Why are you still alive? Have you befriended a Hawker? Hacked it somehow?"

"Are you talking about me?" asked Icarus, stepping forward into the light so the scared doctor could see him.

"Yes I, oh," said Frank as he got a good look at the Sparrow. His entire body relaxed and he leaned heavily against his crutch. "I heard about ones like you from the monsters," he said in awe of Icarus. "I never imagined... are you... how?"

"Frank!" called out Hugh, pushing his way to be beside Icarus. "How do we get you out of here?"

"Out?" said Frank in a daze. He shook his head to clear the cobwebs. "The only way in and out is through Charles's private lab. It's the door to the left of that window, from your perspective."

"Are there any more guards?" asked Jack.

"Yes, but don't worry, I can deactivate them as easily as this fellow," said Frank as he kicked his good leg against the downed machine. "I just need a minute to get in range."

Suddenly, there was the sound of movement from the room that the doctor had indicated. Frank instantly became frightened and hurried toward the stairs. He moved as fast as his crippled leg could allow him, wincing as he went so far as to try to walk on the injured limb. Just as the doors flew open on both the NTAF side and Frank's side of the private laboratory, there was an audible click. The Hawker that barged out of the door near Hugh seemed to become instantly dizzy but stayed on its feet, while there was the sound of a garbage can filled with tin cans falling down a set of steps on Frank's side. Before the Hawker could get any closer to Hugh's group, Samuel stepped up and fired a shot point blank into the robot's eyes, killing it instantly. With that one quick, loud sound, many things went into motion. First, a loud alarm suddenly kicked up, and Samuel's radio began to beep angrily.

Upon answering it, one could clearly hear Adam swearing loudly. "WHAT THE HELL DID YOU DO, WEST?"

Before anything else could be said, Frank hobbled out through the door the Hawker had burst through. He looked terrible. His clothes were wrinkled and stained with strange fluids and blood. His leg that had been shot was wrapped in old bandages that looked like they were in desperate need of changing. His hair was a mess and his face showed signs of multiple bruises that made Hugh wince just to look at. "What are all of you waiting for? We need to get out of here now!"

As Samuel tried to calm Adam down, the sounds of bullets flying began to sound off from somewhere above their heads. Hugh turned pale and muttered Sally's name as the image of her being attacked blossomed in his mind like an evil flower.

Frank must had heard Hugh speak as his face took on a shocked expression. "Sally? As in Sally Saltwater? What is she doing here, Hugh?!"

"There's no time to explain," said Samuel as he turned away from his radio, the sounds of gunshots ringing out both through the small device and above their heads. "Doctor, you used to work here, right?"

"I... that is... Yes, I did," said Frank.

"We came in through a hallway on the first floor. Are there any other exits from this building? Our tactical map only showed one."

"I think there is the hatch in the ceiling of the store room, but you'd need wings to get out that way," mumbled Frank as he leaned against the wall of the hall, taking the weight off of his injured leg. "There are also the emergency stairs in the Spare Parts Room, but that is likely to be heavily guarded."

"Icarus?" asked Hugh, turning to the Sparrow.

"No, too many people, too little time," replied Icarus, a grim frown upon his face. "Even with Dannik, chances are we'd be torn to pieces before we are out of the building. What's more, those on the floor and the roof would have to fend for themselves while we are going up and down. There is also the possibility that both Dannik and I would tire quickly."

Samuel turned to the radio to ask Adam something when a set of doors at the other end of the hallway burst open and out came a Hawker. It yelled and pointed at them, shouting back into the room it came from. Several more of the vile machines hurried into the hall and ran at the team. Without missing a beat, the experienced officers brought their guns to the front and opened fire upon the approaching machines. Some of their shots missed, bouncing off the metal faces of the robots. Others managed to hit home, causing the Hawkers to fall over, tripping up the ones behind them.

Quickly, they turned and headed toward the double doors behind them. Icarus grabbed the doctor and carried him like he had Sally so long ago. Frank protested for a moment before the sound of a bullet flying over their head rang out.

"Since when did they have guns?" demanded Samuel as he fired back at the Hawker mass behind them.

"Well some do, some don't. S-classes are later models designed to use firearms," said Frank, as if giving a lecture.

"Not a good time, Frank," said Hugh, interrupting his old friend as they hurried past the glass wall and up the stairs into the store room. Taking the briefest of moments to look towards the room on the right, Hugh saw it was now empty, as the Hawkers were all behind them in the hall. Now he could see a grotesque display beyond the glass walls. There were roughly a dozen tables set up with Hawkers and Sparrows strapped down by bent metal and rope restraints. Hugh was grateful that Icarus had hurried on up the stairs without taking a glance at the disturbing display.

Once they were at the top of the stairs they were met by team three. The instant Bobby saw his father in the arms of Icarus, all color drained from his face. It was as if someone had punched him. His eyes welled up and tears began to drip down his cheeks.

"Robby?" asked Frank in a stunned voice. His whole body shivered in the feathered arms of Icarus. "Is that you, boy?"

"Father?" asked Bobby, moving towards his dad, finally reunited with him after so long.

Before they could say anymore, the sounds of Hawkers grew from both the stairs leading down, and from one of the doors in the wall besides the stairs, the one labeled Assembly Room One. Out from the doors labeled "Activation" ran Sally, Dannik, and Walt Roberts. Walt turned and shoved a spare rifle through the looping handles of the double doors, blocking them off from the inside. He turned and looked at those gathered, taking notice of who was not among them.

"Where's Regan?" demanded Samuel, as other members of the NTAF quickly moved some of the deactivated robots over to the stairs and pushed them over the railing, in hopes of stalling the Hawker's advance.

"He stayed behind," said Bobby, shaking his head clear of his emotions. "He gave his life so Owen, Jamie, and I, could make it out of the Assembly Room."

"That sounds like Regan," muttered Walt as he aimed down the stairs, taking pot shots at Hawkers trying to climb the steps as the twins, along with Dannik, worked to block the stairs leading down with more unactivated robots. "Always looking after his pups," he said with a sad smile.

"Sally!" Hugh exclaimed as he ran to hug her. "Are you alright?"

"Yes, thanks to Dannik," she said. "I think he took a bullet for me."

Looking over at the larger Sparrow, Hugh could see a trail of crimson running down the back of the bird as he worked with the twins. It seemed to spread as he went, making him wince every now and then.

"Remind me to thank him later," said Hugh as he looked toward the door marked Spare Parts. Samuel was clearly thinking the same thing, as he assumed control of the unit and directed them towards the doors and through them. On the other side were shelves upon shelves of scrap metal of all shapes and sizes. There were what seemed like hundreds of boxes of loose bits and ends, wires and bolts. At the other end of the room there was a long metal staircase that spiraled up to a door high up on the back wall. There were a few Hawkers waiting for them inside the room, and one got off a shot at Walt, who was saved from the bullet by the protection of his armored vest. They quickly took cover behind the shelves as Icarus brought out his sniper rifle and took aim at the robot at the other end of the room. With a pull of his trigger, the bullet flew out and hit home in the Hawker's eye, causing it to fall over, dead.

Cautiously moving out of cover, they weaved through the forest of shelves toward the spiraling set of stairs. From behind them came the sound of things falling over. Dannik and a few others broke free of the unit and hurried to the shelves nearest the doors and pushed with all their might against the metal frames. With the added effort of Hugh, they managed to topple the metal shelf, which fell heavily against the door, dumping its contents and completely blocking that entrance to the room.

Samuel quickly turned to Frank. "Are there any other entrances into this room?" he demanded.

"Yes," said Frank, pointing towards a far corner of the large room, "through Assembly Room Two."

As if on cue, a Hawker appeared from that direction. Upon seeing them, it ran at them, shrieking, with its eyes leaving a fiery trail of red behind it. Hugh raised his weapon to fire, but Terry pulled his trigger faster, giving the robot a dent under its left eye. Hugh fired his shot, which went right in the robot's open beak and out the other side. It only went down from a shot fired by Owen that hit it above the dent his brother put in the robot's face.

Without resting, they made a move on the stairs, turning to shoot at the Hawkers that emerged from the other doorway. The first one to the steps was Jack. He did not stop to call back. He simply started to ascend the metal stairs to freedom, with the others hot on his heels. The railings of the emergency stairs offered very little cover for those climbing it, and bullets were flying through the air in earnest now.

"Crap!" cried Samuel as a bullet caught him in the arm. "DOCTOR!"

"Yes?" called out both father and son.

"The old one," groaned Samuel as he tried to fire back with his good arm. "Can you use that doodad of yours to take those things out?"

"I wish I could," sighed Frank as a bullet flew past within inches of his nose, causing Icarus to flinch for a second. "It doesn't have a long enough range to reach them."

"How durable is it?" asked Hugh as a bullet barely missed getting his firing hand.

"Come again?" asked Frank

"Would it break if someone threw it?" asked Hugh as Fredric was shot in the head behind him, falling over the railing and all the way down to the floor. The last of him anyone saw was his white hair waving in the air as he fell.

"No, it should hold together... I think."

"Does anyone have tape or something?" demanded Hugh as he fired a shot off at a Hawker getting too close to the stairs.

"I do," said Sally, as she came up behind Hugh. She opened her purse and tossed him a role of tape.

"Thanks," he said as a bullet shot past the two, causing them to gasp. Wasting no time he handed the sticky stuff to Frank and told him to tape the button down. Dannik, who was just one step up from Icarus and Frank, seemed to get the message and took the strange device away from Frank and taped the button down, before throwing the machine like a quarterback at the gathered Hawkers by the door to Assembly Room Two. It whistled through the air as it sailed toward the mass of Hawkers firing at them and landed in the center of the gathering of robotic birds. Every single Hawker by that door dropped dead before the machine hit the ground. It bounced off of one of the downed robots before coming to a stop on the ground.

"That thing doesn't have the longest battery life," warned Frank as the group was finally free to hurry up and out of the spiral staircase. Any Hawker that tried to move past the device dropped dead on the spot. Hugh almost thought they were home free when shots rang out again. Looking down at where the strange device had landed, he could see it skid across the floor a tad. Another shot was fired, causing the box to skid a bit farther and bump into another dead Hawker. It wasn't quite clear if a Hawker on the other side of the room was firing and trying to destroy the device, but if it moved any farther away from the door, the robots would be able to walk around its signal's range and come at them again.

Thankfully, they made it to the emergency exit in record time. Not bothering to check if the coast outside was clear, Jack barged his way through the door, leaving it wide open with the others filing out behind him. However, they weren't safe yet, as from behind them could be heard the sounds of Hawkers shrieking as they flew out of the building through the hatch in the store room. The team hurried across the open expanse outside the back of the factory towards the nearest building. The only thing going for them was that the models of Hawkers chasing them were unarmed. They ran and fired at the skies, trying to take out as many Hawkers as possible. Neither of the Sparrows tried to fly up to fight the Hawkers. They both knew to do so would mean their deaths, so Icarus just fired back the best he could.

By the time they got inside the building, they had lost Jamie, who had been snatched up by a particularly agile Hawker. Once inside, they did not stop running, as the sounds of Hawkers raging behind them didn't let up. They wound through hallways and did everything they could to try to escape their pursuers. All too soon they were on the other side of the building and were welcomed with a rain of bullets from the sky. To turn back would have been just as bad as standing still, so they kept moving, running through the fatal downpour and going inside another factory.

Needless to say, everyone was starting to tire from all the running. Hugh was trying to keep up, but he was gradually falling behind the pack. He turned to look at Sally beside him, her face beet red from the exertion. Both were breathing very heavily and were starting to slow when suddenly they found themselves being swept off their feet. To their mutual surprise, Dannik, despite having been shot, had managed to lift the couple up and carry them as if they were sacks of potatoes. He did not say a word, simply flashing his golden grin with a hint of a wince of pain as he ran on.

They once again found their way out to the streets, just in front of a district train. Without a word, Samuel, showing more stamina than his weight suggested, put on an extra burst of speed and ran for the train, calling the others to follow.

"It's not fast enough," panted Hugh, remembering trying to use one to escape back in Valkyrie Park.

"That's because..." huffed the NTAF officer as he moved to the front of the car and tore at the engine compartment, "they weren't... on... full... speed!" Hugh could not see what the officer's hands were doing to the train's engine, as he was more interested in the large flock of Hawkers flying over the building they just ran out of.

Hugh asked Dannik to put him and Sally down so they could provide covering fire for Samuel as he fiddled with the train's engine. Hugh was still winded from all the running, but that didn't seem to affect his aim too badly, as he was able to nail at least one Hawker with his rifle. Sally also took up the fight, while the others used the train itself for cover from the Hawkers who had guns. As it turned out, it wasn't the best thing to take shelter behind, as the train had poles that supported its roof, leaving a lot of empty space between the seats for bullets to fly through.

"I got it!" shouted Samuel as a bullet caught him in the leg, making him crumble once it could no longer hold his weight. With time running out, Jack helped the officer into the conductor seat of the car and everyone piled in the empty seats. With a flick of a lever, the train started moving, slowly at first, but gradually building speed. They did their best to fend off the Hawkers, and to use what little cover the train provided to hide behind as bullets flew at them from the sky. Hugh let out a cry of pain as a bullet grazed his neck, opening a cut that started to bleed the instant the skin broke.

He quickly reached up to feel the cut but snapped back to the task at hand as a Hawker flew right up to his side of the train. He shot it in the face and it fell away, not dead but stunned. Soon the car was moving faster than any district train Hugh had ever been on before. The factories and buildings flashed by as the car rumbled along the tracks, slowly outpacing the Hawkers and leaving them in the dust. It was only when the sound of their screams died down that Hugh finally felt he could relax again and leaned back in the worn leather seat of the train. He turned to look at Sally, to see she had survived the attack with hardly a scratch on her. Sitting between them was Dannik, who now sported a few more splashes of crimson in his chest. He clearly was hurting, but was very much alive. He caught them both staring at his wounds and gave a pained smile.

"Don't worry about me, monkeys. It'll take a lot more than a few potshots to take this old bird down."

"We should get Bobby to look you over," said Hugh as he turned to where his friend was sitting. Somewhere along the way, he had lost his glasses and there were a few cuts on his body, possibly from near misses similar to what Hugh had experienced. Bobby was also holding his right leg, grimacing in pain as rivulets of red leaked out from between his fingers.

"Oh crap, they've hit Bobby!" cried Hugh, watching his friend suffer, and unsure of how to help. "Are you okay?"

"Damn it," swore Bobby. "It got me in the kneecap!"

"Robby?" asked Frank from the other side of the car, from where Icarus had placed the elder Crick. "What happened? Speak up boy!"

31

Out of the team that had set out on the mission to find and sabotage the secret laboratory and Hawker factory, only seven of the original ten NTAF officers walked out alive. Hugh dwelled on their deaths in his head, feeling responsible for them. If he hadn't seen the broken glass, and asked for his team to investigate the basement, there probably would be a good chance that Adam Regan, Fredric Warren, and Jamie Walker would still be alive. On the other hand, he told himself, as he shifted in his seat to look back at Frank as he worried over Bobby, there would also be the chance that they wouldn't have found the elder Dr. Crick. Frank was now safe, but did it have to come at such a high price?

Just as his thoughts turned to Sally, the train shook. There was a sudden loud snapping sound, followed by Samuel swearing, and a small puff of dark smoke from the front of the car. Hugh couldn't see exactly what was happening from his seat, but he could already feel dread rising inside of him. Samuel, the one closest to the problem, tried to fix it while the train started to lose speed.

"What happened?" called out Jack.

"Damn engine burned out," grunted Samuel as the car continued to gradually slow down despite his efforts.

"Are we going to be okay?" asked Sally as her face became so pale that Hugh could suddenly make out a shallow cut on her cheek, just under her right eye. It wasn't deep enough to be bleeding, a mere scrape really. However, it still stood out as plain as the nose on one's face when she turned ashen.

"I don't know. I really don't," said Samuel as he leaned forward and tried to get the engine working from where he sat. It didn't help at all, and only caused him to moan in pain as he shifted his wounded leg. All too soon the car came to a gradual stop, leaving them sitting near the end of the train's rail line. They were just before the station, where another train was stalled on the neighboring track.

"If we got anything going for us," said Walt as he looked at the barrier at the end of the rails, blocking off the track from the turntable that changed which rail the car traveled down. "At least we didn't jump the rail at high speed."

"One must count one's blessings," said Jack with a weak smile.

"We can't stay here," said Icarus. "They will follow the track to its end."

"Well bird-boy, take your pick," grumbled Samuel as he climbed painfully to his feet, gritting his teeth in pain at putting weight on his injured leg. "We certainly aren't spoiled for choice."

Looking around, there were a few buildings near where they stopped. They formed a partial ring around the train station, each building identical to its neighbor with the only real differences being the number of windows and the large billboards advertising the company that owned the properties. None of them were close enough for the group to hurry inside, due to several members of the group suffering from leg injuries. All of the potential shelters were surrounded by chain link fences with metal gates held firmly shut with chains and padlocks. They still had the bolt cutters from their forced entry into Mason's secret laboratory, but even if everyone was in perfect condition, it would take time to work the blades through the chains.

"What's the use," moaned Edward, not bothering to rise from his seat on the train. "Those Hawkers are going to find us long before we can hide. And if they don't, they'd find us soon enough."

"What other choice do we have?" asked Bobby, cringing from the pain as he tried to pull himself up and out of his seat. He let out a cry of agony as his leg gave out under his own weight. Bobby fell back into his seat, the wound fully exposed at last, showing the bullet had hit him in the kneecap. His father, who Bobby had reassured that the injury wasn't too bad, hobbled over to the other side of the train, with the aid of one of the officers. He covered his mouth in horror at the bloody mess on his child's leg.

"Bobby! I thought you said it wasn't that bad!" he cried.

"Oh, it really isn't," spat Bobby through gritted teeth as he forced himself back up, using one of the metal poles supporting the train's canopy as a support to keep him off his bad leg. "This is nothing compared to what will happen if we don't make ourselves scarce."

"Well, I don't think we have enough time to do anything, they'll be here any minute," moaned Edward from his seat.

"Will you please stop saying that?" asked Sally, still pale. "You are not helping our chances by stating the obvious here."

While the others were talking, one of the twins had hurried over to the nearest locked gate, pulled out the bolt cutters, and started to work on breaking the chain binding them shut. As he worked, Hugh began to think, looking at the broken train and back the way they came. No sign of the flying robots yet, but time was swiftly running out. Then Hugh looked at the other train, the one pointed in the opposite direction, and back toward the angry robots. An idea quickly formed in his head, one that he hurried over to Samuel to ask him to help with.

"Officer West?" asked Hugh.

"What now?" Samuel demanded, clearly at the end of his rope with the pain and the loss of his commanding officer and friends.

"I think I have a plan that'll buy us some time. Can you get the other train at the station moving as fast as ours did?"

Samuel considered the question for a moment, looking at Hugh and then over at the other train. It had a lot more structural damage than the one they had used, but it still had all four wheels affixed to the rails and its engine compartment looked undamaged. Limping over, Samuel opened up the compartment and looked inside, checking the motor for damage.

"You get what I am thinking, right?" asked Hugh, looking over the officer's shoulder.

"Yeah, a little bit of misdirection," smirked Samuel as he went to work on the engine. As his fingers pried at wires, the others had gradually gravitated towards Owen, the twin working the gate. Icarus and Dannik had both given out offers to fly the humans over the gate, but it soon became clear that the large Sparrow was hurting too badly from his bullet wounds to lift anyone with him over the gate. Icarus, on the other hand, had managed to escape major harm during the rain of bullets. However, flying back and forth over the gate to pick up and drop off the humans and Dannik would take too long and sap his energy.

Edward, who was still in his seat moaning about how they were all doomed, was the first one to notice what Hugh and Samuel were up to. Finally standing up, he shuffled over to the two men by the second train and watched the current leader of the NTAF team finish altering the car's engine. "What are you doing?" he asked. "Going back is not going to do any of us a lick of good you know."

"Oh, we're not going back," said Sam as he hobbled over to the driver's seat of the train. Hugh turned his head to look down the rail and saw in the sky tiny specks that grew larger the longer he looked at them. Their time was almost up. Thankfully, the train started to move down the tracks, with Samuel backing away from the front of the car with a big smile on his face, despite the pain of his injured leg. He turned to

Edward before grabbing one of the rifles that had been left on one of the seats of the broken train, and said, "That, Eddy, my boy, is what we call a distraction."

"Hopefully it'll buy us enough time to get moving to somewhere out of sight," said Hugh as he watched the train pick up speed as it roared down the rails toward the incoming flock of Hawkers. Meanwhile, Owen managed to finally make the bolt cutter's blades meet and the chain fell limp, allowing the gate to be opened at last. Everyone, with Frank being supported by Terry and Icarus carrying Bobby, hurried inside. Sally was the only one to bother to look back, and, when she saw Hugh and the other two officers, she called out to them.

"What are you doing?" she shouted at them, causing the others who had moved past the gate to turn to see what she was talking about.

"Just buying some time, Sal," said Hugh as he helped Samuel move towards the open gate, the officer leaning heavily on Hugh's shoulder, while his good arm used the rifle as a make-shift crutch. "Just go on inside, we'll be along in a minute."

"But what if they see you out here?" she asked, starting to head toward them.

"Well then, we've at least bought you and the others time to get to safety," was Hugh's answer. Turning to look after the speeding train, he could see that the specks that were their pursuers stopped coming and were floating about in the air like confused flies at the sight of the train speeding towards them. He only hoped that all of the Hawker flock would follow the decoy and that none of the robots would decide to continue down the track and discover their deception.

With the seconds ticking down, Hugh and the other two men made their way through the gate. Sally joined their small group just past the gate, coming to walk alongside Hugh, having stubbornly decided to wait for him to catch up. He flashed her a look that summed up both how much he hated that she had waited and how much he loved her for it, before they joined the other remaining members of their party outside a large metal shutter that Owen was again working the bolt cutters on.

Whoever had owned or run this particular factory seemed to think locks were something every door should have, which only meant that the group had to spend precious minutes waiting as the bolt cutters chewed through another padlock. Hugh asked why they didn't try any of the doors, and was told that Walt had checked all the ones available to them and found each one of them locked. Since none of them had any means to break the thick metal doors down, their only hope was the garage door. Thankfully, luck was with them this time, as the padlock on the accordion shutter was older and rusted, soon giving away to the efforts of Owen. Not missing a beat, he, along with Icarus, pushed the shutter up and open, allowing the others to hurry inside, with the ones with leg injuries going in first, with the aid of their able-bodied companions.

Hugh gave the skies one last look before heading inside. As far as he could see, it appeared that their trick had worked, and the Hawkers were now chasing an empty trolley. Either way, the sooner they were out of sight the better, and, after waiting for Samuel to duck in under the bottom of the shutter, Hugh turned and went inside. Icarus and Owen were the last ones in, lowering the folding door quietly behind them, just in case any of the Hawkers were in range or had hearing sharp enough to hear the metal impact on the bottom of its concrete frame.

Inside, they found themselves before a massive set of kilns, with crates of china dishware piled up beside their entry point. There were no bodies inside this abandoned place, no blood stains or any other hint of violence, except for shards of glass in the center of the room. The air smelled of dry clay and ash from the massive ovens used to bake the plates and bowls. As they moved deeper into the dim interior, the group passed by long tables and complex machines that were caked in dried clay. Most of the clay they saw was in plastic bags, keeping it protected from drying out when not in use, while some had hardened into useless bricks that would have to be broken down and recycled. Glancing upwards, Hugh could see that the pottery factory had once sported a large skylight overhead, but the glass had long been smashed out, possibly by the Hawkers when they took over the city.

As they moved into the next room, with the doors already unlocked for them, they soon found where the workers had gone. This room had also been a work room, and held its own set of large kilns. The only difference were the bodies, many lying by overturned chairs beside misshaped lumps of clay that only vaguely resembled table wear. There were maggots crawling around the floor near the bodies, and the smell was far worse than any they had yet experienced, possibly due to the bodies having died near still-burning kilns, causing their rate of decomposing to speed up. Upon the sight and smell, Sally, along with a few other members of the motley crew, drew out handkerchiefs to cover their noses from the stench. Frank, upon sight of the bodies, stopped in his tracks, almost tripping up the officer holding him up. The older doctor quickly crossed his chest and mumbled a prayer under his breath, before the other man nudged him to keep moving along, as they were nowhere near safety yet.

The next door took them into the building's offices, which were very unremarkable, aside from a few bodies of men in suits, possibly the managers of the factory. Once shrewd businessmen, these corpses were now little more than decaying obstacles that the group had to step over. This was hard for the ones with injured legs, especially Bobby, so once Icarus was across, he put Bobby down for a moment, before gingerly stepping over and carrying first Frank, and then Samuel, over the mortal remains. Once that was behind them, the bronze Sparrow picked Bobby back up and continued along with the others to the other end of the hall, which was locked from the other side.

Some of the NTAF cursed under their breath, clearly worried that at any moment, Hawkers would storm in behind them and either tear them to bits or shoot them full of more holes than Swiss cheese. As Jack stepped up to try to force the door open by ramming his shoulder into it, Hugh got an idea and went back to the bodies in the hall. They had fallen in such a way that the massive wounds that tore through their suits and skin were facing up for all to see. This made Hugh think that they might have been running for the door at the end of the hall, so he gingerly reached out to one of the bodies.

Frank, seeing what Hugh was doing, called out to him. "Hubert, leave the dead alone."

"Just give me a minute," said Hugh as he picked at the bodies, doing his best not to feel the rotting flesh through the thin fabric, a task that proved harder than he had hoped. His hand felt like it was brushing against what he imagined a sack full of spoiled meat would be like.

"Do you think they have any keys on them?" asked Terry as he walked over and watched Hugh try to coax a pocket out from under one of the bodies.

"Couldn't hurt to look," Hugh said as he finally managed to pull out the pocket, causing the body to shift with the movement of the fabric.

"The chances of either of them carrying the key we need is so slow," grunted Bobby as he turned to look over Icarus's shoulder at Hugh and Terry, "that if either of you find the right one, I'll kiss birdbrain here on the beak!"

As Terry stepped over to search the second body, Dannik, despite his injuries, pushed Jack out of the way and brought his considerably bigger bulk down on the door, yet it still wasn't enough. It held as strong as ever, not yielding even an inch or making any other sound but the dull thud of the impact upon its thick metal surface. However, it did cause Dannik's injury to bleed even more, and made the Sparrow grind his beak together in pain upon impact. Just as Hugh had given up searching his dead body, and was going to suggest searching those out in the work room, Terry stood up, triumphant, with a ring of keys clutched in his hand.

With the keys in hand, Terry hurried over to the stubborn metal door and began to test each key in the lock, until at last, one of them slid in and turned easily. The bolt moved and the door swung outward, open at last. With a shrug of his shoulders and gritting of teeth, Bobby suddenly leaned forward and pressed his lips to Icarus's grey beak. Needless to say, everyone, especially Icarus, was shocked by this. Upon pulling away, his face as bright as the blood still oozing from his bullet wound, Bobby said, "What? I always keep my word. Now stop looking at me and let's get inside before the Hawkers find us!"

32

Beyond the door lay a set of stairs leading down into a narrow tunnel. It wasn't part of the city's sewer system, nor the secret areas. It was a simple utility tunnel that was lined with pipes and wires, with plain concrete walls and exposed iron supports. The only light was provided by what leaked past the group through the open door, until Sally found a light switch and flicked it on. One by one, old light bulbs flickered to life, bringing sour yellow light to the gloomy passage. It seemed to stretch on for quite a distance, into a darkness that the light could barely penetrate.

One by one they descended the short flight of stairs and moved down the narrow hallway. The walls were so close together that they had to travel in single file, with the wounded having to lean on the backs of the healthy for support. Terry was the last one of the team to enter the utility tunnel, and locked the door behind him before rejoining with the others. They didn't speak as they moved cautiously along the dim tunnel. Dannik had to tuck his wings in as tight as he could so they wouldn't get smashed against the walls. However, that wasn't enough, and he had to walk sideways through the passage, just to fit inside it. It was so quiet that their footsteps echoed off the stone walls, and time seemed to lose all meaning. All there was were the cables and pipes, the supports and the walls, pressing in on their left and right. If the Hawkers found them now, there wouldn't be enough time to turn and defend against an attack.

Just when Hugh thought that they had entered some endless hell, the head of their pack stopped abruptly. "There's another locked door here!" yelled Jack from the front of the group. "Terry, somebody pass me the key ring!"

Like a game of telephone, only with the keys as the message, Terry passed the ring to Hugh, who gave it to Sally. She passed it to Edward who handed it to Walt. From him it went to Icarus and then to Bobby. Bobby handed it over to Clark who gave it to Samuel who gave it to Dannik. The large Sparrow passed it to Frank who gave it to Owen. And Owen, the one right behind Jack, handed the ring over to the man's impatient fingers.

"Alright," he said as he began to work his way through the ring of keys, "with any luck we'll be somewhere we can rest soon."

"I would love that," moaned Bobby. It was hard to tell if his leg was still bleeding due to his pants having turned mostly red from the wound.

"I know you are in pain, Doc," said Samuel with similar pain peeking out between his words, "Since this was only supposed to be a recon mission, we didn't bring any medics along with us. You're going to have to give us all... a once over..."

"I can help," said Frank. "Robby isn't the only physician here."

"Okay, got it!" called out Jack as the right key slid home into the lock and turned. This door opened into a medium-sized room that had all sorts of cleaning supplies stacked neatly on shelves that filled up every wall. Across from where they entered was another door, with a sign bolted to its sturdy surface. The center of the room was clear of furniture, with a bed, chairs and a table pushed into the only corners of the room that the shelves didn't cover. Despite this, the room was very cramped with all the people who had taken shelter inside it. Yet it felt like an open field compared to the tight hallway outside. Overhead, a single, weak light shone down upon them, casting crazy shadows upon the walls. There was a small sink attached to the wall opposite the small cot, its handles discolored from age. Judging by the room's layout, it was highly likely it had been a janitor's room before the Hawkers had disrupted the rhythm of normal life.

Once they were inside, Jack turned around and looked out into the long utility hallway, making sure nothing was following them, before turning off the lights from their end of the corridor and locking the door behind them. This door, too, bore a sign, stating the name and brand owner of the factory they had just come from. Now that they were finally someplace fairly safe from the Hawkers, everyone visibly relaxed. They wasted no time in getting the injured to the single cot and set up in the chairs. Bobby was the first to get examined, by demand of his father. They started by using a pair of scissors that they found atop the table in the room to cut away the fabric of Bobby's pants, revealing a truly gruesome mess.

The bullet had indeed gone through the knee, no question of that. As Frank hurried to clean his son's wound of blood with water from the sink and the aid of a rag provided by one of the NTAF men, the others began to take stock of what was left of their weapons and supplies. Many of them had left their rifles behind on the train in their hurry to find someplace to hide. Icarus still had his sniper rifle and Bobby's shotgun. Sally still had her weapon, but neither of the twins had their long range weapons. Jack had his, and Samuel had grabbed Clark's gun to use as a crutch. Bobby didn't have his magnum anymore, as he had dropped it in shock when he had been shot. Those of their group who had died in their escape had been left with their guns, and neither Dannik nor Frank had one to begin with.

Samuel washed himself up with a rag of his own, showing that his wound was higher on his leg than Bobby's was. There was a hole on the other side of his pants, indicating the bullet went right through his leg. Bobby on the other hand, as Frank soon discovered, still carried the bullet in his leg. Their tools were limited to what Bobby had brought in his backpack and the first aid kits that each of them had been given before leaving on the mission. They barely had enough supplies to bandage each other up. Bobby had to endure having one of the NTAF officers, under the guidance of Frank, dig out the round from his leg using tweezers from one of the health kits and the thinnest knife they had among them.

Hugh couldn't bear to watch his friend in such pain, so he went over to Samuel, who had been joined by Sally. She had been helping him clean his wounds, offering to stitch him up with the aid of her sewing kit, despite it not having the right kind of thread for the job. He asked her if there was anything he could do to help, but she had already threaded the needle and started to work it through the skin of the officer's leg, pulling the flesh together and sealing the wound. It was only once everyone had been looked over and patched up that they finally had a chance to find out what had happened to Frank Crick after he had been kidnapped from his hospital bed, and why he had been shot in the leg.

It was Hugh who got the conversation going, after the last bandage was wrapped around Dannik's chest, the bullet freshly removed from his body and his wounds sewn up by Sally's hand. "Frank," said Hugh, "A lot has been going on since I last saw you."

"Yes, there has, both to me and to the city at large," said Frank, as he absently rubbed his hand against his leg wound after finishing tying off Dannik's bandages. "I never should have become a part of Charles's operation. None of this would have ever happened."

"Hey, now," said Sally, who sat down beside Hugh in another chair. "Don't say that Dr. Crick. No one could have predicted how the Hawkers would turn out. They were originally designed to protect us, after all."

"Well, you know what they say about the best intentions," Frank sighed as he sat down in a chair of his own. He glanced over at Icarus, who was leaning against a far wall, talking with the other healthy members of the NTAF survivors.

"Frank," persisted Hugh, "What exactly happened to you after the exhibition? Last time we saw you, you were crawling across the floor with a bullet hole in your leg. Was it the Hawkers that got you? Or Dr. Mason?"

Sally glared at Hugh for a moment. Despite her inner reporter being just as demanding as Hugh's curiosity, she had a better handle on asking questions. However, she, too, was itching to hear what Frank had to say, so she let the old man speak uninterrupted.

"No place better to start a story than the beginning," said Frank as he leaned back in the old wooden chair. He took a breath and pinched the bridge of his nose. "Well," he said after a brief pause to collect his thoughts, "it all started after I returned to my home office after the demonstration in Liberty Estates. I received a phone call from Charles sometime after I had settled in. I don't remember the exact time, but he sounded worried, almost frantic, begging me to meet him as soon as I could. I, of course, suspected something was up. I couldn't say what for sure, but I had a very bad feeling from how insistent Charles was at seeing me. I didn't want to waste much time, but I did call my friend Matt McGullen to express my concerns." Frank paused for a moment to look at Hugh. "I guess you and he have already met, since how else would you have gotten tangled up with the NATF?"

"Yes, we've met," said Hugh, as he turned to avoid looking Frank in the eyes. He didn't have the heart to tell the old man that the Chief was dead. Since no one else said anything, Frank cleared his throat and continued his tale.

"As I was saying, I only talked to Matt long enough to let him know about my journal before I got ready to leave. I wouldn't have normally accepted Charles's summons, but it was clear in the man's voice that something had gone horribly wrong, so with my briefcase in hand I hurried out of the house and took the first district train I could find. His secretary met me at the door and let me right in."

"That's hard to believe," mumbled Sally, recalling how cold the Asian woman had been when they had tried to gain entry.

"Well, I was expected," sniffed Frank, making Sally blush. He knew how Sally could be when she was on the trail of a story. "Anyways, once inside I was shown right to Charles's office. He was at his desk, waiting for me. He greeted me in the usual fashion, offering a cigar, shaking my hand, and such. When I asked him why he had insisted on having me come, he paled and gave an order into his desktop intercom. From behind me, the door opened and in walked this horrific, wrangled monstrosity. It was just like the Hawker that was on stage at the exhibition, only it had clearly been affected by the transformation process that I had tried to warn Charles about. It was like someone had put a man and a bunch of scrap metal in a blender, resulting in something that was not quite fully alive. Of course, I knew what had happened the second I saw the abomination, and again tried to reason with Charles to stop what he was doing, to recall the Hawkers that he had let out onto the streets and have them either dismantled or put under observation to see what the Hawkers would become."

"I guess he didn't like either idea," said Hugh, thinking back to what Dr. Mason had been like when he had tried talking to him.

"That's correct. He told me that it was all my bio-brain's fault, because every case started with the head and worked its way down. I told him again that I had told him so months ago, but he wouldn't listen. That man's ego is big enough to hang Nimbus from! Anyway, he demanded that I find out what was happening and fix it. When I said that I had tried, but nothing would prevent the change, he began to act strangely."

"What do you mean, strangely?" asked Sally, her hands taking notes with a notepad that seemed to appear from nowhere.

"Well, if I remember correctly, he was pale, and shaking. He offered me money, obscene quantities of the stuff and even a full partnership in his company. I tried to tell him that there was nothing I could do, that something about the Hawker's bodies and the bio-brain's chemicals resulted in a full body transformation. He demanded that I give him all my research, so his men could use the information to try to solve the problem themselves. I told him that I had destroyed most of the notes, but he wouldn't believe me. It was then that he drew the gun. I tried to calm him down, to make him see reason, but he was too far gone by then. When he started firing at me, I knew I had to run. I am not as agile as I was during my college days, but given the situation, I found that I could still move pretty quickly. After shoving aside his secretary, I managed to get as far as the door, when he got me in the leg. At that point I was being fueled by adrenaline and didn't even feel the pain until I collapsed on a district train, heading towards the cable car station."

"Why did you come to us at the restaurant?" asked Hugh. "The hospital was probably a lot closer, and your house closer still."

"Once I realized he got me," said Frank as he looked down at this leg, "I knew that he would be looking for me at any place that would be qualified to properly treat me, including my own home. The train I caught was one of those new automated ones, without anyone piloting the engine. There was absolutely no one else on it, so I took the time I had during the ride to help myself the best I could. I made a tourniquet out of my necktie for my leg so I wouldn't lose too much blood, and let my pants serve as a bandage. I had already told Matt about my journal, but not where, or how, to find it. I was in no position to go to him, and the only key to my secret drawer was in my pocket. I had a feeling that if I tried to go to Robby's place, I'd find a Hawker there waiting for me. Besides, I wasn't even sure if he'd be home, given how late he often ended up working at the hospital. Given my situation, I thought my best option was to find you, Hugh. We have been friends for so long that I knew I could trust you with my journal. Given how popular the fireworks are, I had a feeling you'd be at that rooftop restaurant, possibly with young Miss Saltwater, so after arriving in Galileo, I made my way there. Luckily, the fireworks hadn't started yet, so the streets were fairly empty. The last thing I remember clearly was getting in the elevator for the restaurant. I am not even sure how I managed to get so far on my injured leg as I did. The last thing I remember before I passed out was giving you my keys." Frank paused and looked at Hugh before continuing. "Please tell me you were able to find it before the Hawkers did."

"Don't worry" said Hugh. "I got to it just in time. If I had been any later, it would have been gone."

"Is it safe? Do you have it with you?" asked Frank as he leaned forward.

"I had it for a couple of days," admitted Hugh. "I don't have it anymore. We left it with the police before coming here to investigate the Hawker's factory. Good thing you left that card in the book, or we would have never known to come here."

"Ah, thank God for small miracles," said Frank with a sigh as he relaxed in his chair. "You know," he said as he stared off into space, "I had wondered where that card had gone to. Anyway," he said, once he had recollected his thoughts, "When I regained my senses I was at the hospital and Matt had just arrived to see how I was doing. My only thoughts were of your safety, due to having given you my keys. I wasn't sure then if you had been able to collect the journal in time, but I didn't want to leave anything to chance. Once I got Matt's word he'd watch out for you, I relaxed and, I guess, passed out. Not unexpected, given how much blood I must have lost while making my way from one district to another. I am not sure what happened after that. The rest is a blur of sights and sounds. When I was able to think straight again, I was in that room you rescued me from, my hands tied behind my back and my good leg tied to the chair I was propped up in. I was fully expecting to see Charles, smirking in triumph or scowling in anger, but what leaned over me was a Hawker robot."

"So, Dr. Mason didn't order the robots to bring you back?"

"That was my first thought, that Charles was hiding in the shadows, waiting to make a big appearance. However, that changed when the monster spoke up, and told me why I was there. Charles was not in control of them, not completely. They had become self-aware."

"If that's true, then why didn't these things go to town on us humans sooner?" Samuel asked.

"We had originally programmed them not to kill unless given permission," replied Frank as he put his head in his hands. "Not even Charles was so proud as not to recognize there was a chance his robots might go too far in the name of the law, so he made sure that they couldn't kill unless he first gave the order. I still cannot believe he gave them that right in the end. There was always the chance that something would go wrong, and I didn't want blood on my hands. However, it's too late now, as so many have died because of our unholy work."

"And others have been born," said Icarus, who had drifted over to their little group, having left the NTAF officers to flock around Samuel. "Without you, my species would never have existed, and I would never have been born."

Frank took a moment to stare at Icarus, before letting out a soft sigh and a sad smile forming on his lips. "I suppose that's at least one good thing to come from all of this, but is it enough to justify all the death?"

"So, the Hawkers wanted you to fix their brains, right?" asked Hugh. It may have been sudden, but he wanted his friend to keep talking. Not just to satisfy his own curiosity of what had happened to Frank, but to also keep his mind off of the unexpected actions of the Hawkers.

"That's correct. They, like Charles, believed they could be cured of their transformations. They captured me, expecting that I would find some little trick to make them stay robots and therefore perfect in their eyes. They gave me raw bio-brains and tools to work with, and popped every altered bio-brain into the next batch of their kind by the hundreds. I-"

"Wait," interrupted Jack Harper, who had wandered over to hear Frank's story. "By the *hundreds?* Surely you are exaggerating, right? Nimbus is a city, not a country after all!"

"He's got a point," said Sally. "This is just a city, given, not your average city, but a city nonetheless. We've been running around so much that I hadn't wondered about this before, but why are there so many of these robotic birds flying around? Surely there wasn't a reason for so many to be made!"

Frank let out a tired sigh and turned to Jack and then Sally. "First," he said, "I am most certainly not exaggerating. The Hawkers run the machinery almost day and night, constantly increasing their numbers and replacing those who have either been destroyed or started to transform. As to Miss Saltwater's question," said Frank as he glanced at Icarus and Dannik, "I am not entirely sure. My best guess is that the Hawkers ran the plant after hours and increased their numbers in secret. I know from production records that I found in my prison that there were only supposed to be as many made as there were patrolmen on the force. I don't think even Charles knew how many there really were."

"Enough about the robots," said Bobby from the cot. "I want to know more about what happened to you, Dad. And how were you able to switch them off?"

Frank cleared his throat and muttered to himself for a bit, reviewing what he had already disclosed about his capture, until he was back to where he had left off. "As I was saying, I wasn't alone in the beginning. There were other members of the original project being forced to work along with me on the bio-brain's redesign. I will give the Hawkers one thing, they are fast. The second we had a new model ready they picked it up and entered its specifics into the machinery that reproduced it for their next 'generation'. As soon as they set me to work I had an idea, a possible means of escape from my prison. I was nowhere near strong enough to fight my way out, and neither were any of the others back when they were alive. So, we agreed to do our best to sabotage them. Since they kept trying to use the brains we worked on, I decided to see if I could work any weakness into their bodies from the inside. Not everyone was behind me on this decision, but those who were helped me at every turn. Together we tried to make them dumber, but that only resulted in more ferocious Hawkers. What's more, every day the altered bio-brains failed to do the trick, they killed off another member of the team. By the time you found me, I was the only one left."

"What about that machine that turned the Hawkers off?" Jack insisted. "That thing was pretty handy for getting us out of that hornets' nest."

"That device was little more than a glorified radio," said Frank. "It started out as something a previous worker in that hell had left behind when the Hawkers took over production. Since I was held in that little laboratory, I had it on, listening to what was happening in the city. I was working on one bio-brain with a few others. Mike-"

"Mad Mike?" asked Hugh in surprise, unable to hold back his surprise. "I thought he died at the asylum."

"No," said Frank with a sigh. "Don't get me wrong, poor Mike is dead, having been killed the day before yesterday in front of my very eyes. He was a brilliant man, and the world is a darker place without him. I only wish he had been a part of a different project, something where his intelligence would have been truly appreciated. He truly deserved better. The Hawkers brought him back due to his original position on the creation team."

"As I was saying, we had the radio on, listening to a music station as we tried to convince ourselves that things were still alright on the outside. Mike was supervising my work with the bio-brain on the table. At the time I was trying again to provide some means of weakness in the design, one that was subtle enough that the Hawkers wouldn't catch it, with suggestions given by Mike from over my shoulder. We were testing the wiring and the computing power of the bio-brain, using a special device to make sure that everything was working property."

"Suddenly, the bio-brain's readings instantaneously flat lined and the bio-brain died on the table before us. After some investigation, it turns out the bio-brain's OTM, Organic to Mechanical computer, had failed,"

"The OTM?" asked Hugh.

"The Hawkers are designed so that a small electronic computer, the OTM, works with the bio-brain," explained Frank. "It transfers the signals sent from the cameras, microphones and pressure sensors of the Hawkers' bodies into the artificially grown bio-brain. For the bio-brain to operate the body of the Hawker, signals are sent from the bio-brain into the OTM, which translates them from biological instructions to orders that the mechanical parts can understand. In other words, the OTM is crucial for the bio-brain to be able to control the Hawker's limbs. The OTM also regulates the temperature of the bio-brain, and provides it with everything the bio-brain needs to function."

Jack let out a loud whistle in amazement. "Gee, Doc, that's an awful lot for one little computer to do."

"Well, under normal circumstances, it would be impossible," admitted Frank. "However, Charles's advancements in the fields of robotics and computers paved the way to the OTM's creation. Without it, I doubt the Hawkers would have ever been able to function. Then again, they never would have functioned without my bio-brains either." He paused for a moment, his expression growing distant, before looking up and continuing. "Since the OTM is so important, if it is ever damaged, broken, removed, or ceases to function for any reason, the bio-brain becomes isolated from the Hawker's body and senses. It will quickly die without the OTM's monitoring."

"And that was exactly what had happened to the bio-brain we were working on," said Frank as he resumed his story. "I was confused by what happened, since computers aren't really my field, but Mike was able to figure it out. After explaining it to me, he came up with an idea. Mike suggested that we might be able to reprogram the OTM to shut down whenever it 'heard' a particular sound through the microphones in its 'ears', giving us a means to deactivate and kill a Hawker that was just covert enough that none of our guards were able to pick up on it. I have said it before in the past, but Mike had a truly creative mind. The world is a darker place without him."

"In order to prevent detection, I left the radio off while Mike, who used to fiddle about with radios before he was put in the asylum, worked with finding the perfect tone that we could use as a kill signal for the Hawkers' OTMs, while I used the one that died as a model to work from. To make sure it worked, we made two identical bio-brains, one that I left off so it wouldn't be affected when we tested the kill signal on it. It didn't work at first, but with some tweaking on my part, we finally were able to replicate the results so every time the tone was emitted and detected by the attached OTM, it would shut down, killing the test bio-brain. Mike started working on the radio itself, modifying it so it would emit a near constant note at that pitch as long as a button was pressed down. As you may remember from the brief time we had it, it was a hand-held radio, and we didn't want to risk burning out its batteries by having it on all the time. After all, we only had the ones inside the radio, and there weren't any spares in that little workshop."

"Before they killed Mike, he made sure that I knew what he had done to turn the handset into a Hawker death device, just in case something happened to the one we had with us. I was lucky that it still worked when all of you showed up. Neither I nor Mike had dared to test the device on any of the Hawkers, not even on the ones assigned to guard us. Despite knowing that the signal worked, we weren't sure if it would be strong enough to penetrate their metal bodies, or how their built-in speakers would react to the sound, since we were unable to get our hands on those parts."

"So," said Jack, "you had no idea if it would work when you used it. Talk about betting the farm."

"Pardon me," said Samuel, who had walked over while Frank was talking, with the other officers falling in behind him like sheep. He leaned heavily upon a spare chair, using it as a better crutch than the rifle. He was still in a lot of pain, but it was clear in his face that he had other things on his mind.

"Yes?" asked Frank.

"You said that machine was just an altered radio? Does that mean we can send that signal again with any other radio?"

"It is possible, yes," Frank mused, leaning back in his chair and bringing a hand under his chin to rub at the rough beard that had grown in during his captivity. "However, the range of the average radio isn't large enough to reach very many Hawkers."

"What if we could broadcast to every speaker and radio in Nimbus at once?" asked Samuel.

"That might work," said Frank, his hand moving upward, rubbing under his nose. "There may still be some of the early models of the Hawkers out there, ones without our particular bio-brain in their metal skulls, but most should by now. All Hawkers, or at the least the ones that I saw the designs for, had built in radio transmitters and receivers. If we were able to broadcast the tone, in a way that their radios could receive it, we could pipe it directly into their heads. That way we would be sure to get all of them, even the ones out of range of the sound of the tone emitting from normal radios."

"Wait," said Hugh, holding up his hand to stop Frank for a moment. "You say all Hawkers have radios? Are they able to hear what we are saying on the walkie-talkies? How have they not found the police in the warehouse's underground areas?"

"That's because they operate on a closed system," said Frank. "They can only hear what other Hawkers transmit, and like all things in the city, when there is an emergency broadcast going out, their radios will pick up that signal. Of course, they can hear like the rest of us, but this network is a private one that transmits directly from one Hawker to another." Turning back to Samuel, Frank asked what the officer had in mind.

"Well," smirked Samuel as he sat down in his chair, easing himself into it as if to minimize the pain in his leg. "I am sure you are aware of the city's emergency broadcast system. When that thing goes off, everything that can emit sound flicks on and sends out the message. If we can get ourselves to the broadcast station, where the signal goes out, we can set up the equipment to send the killing frequency all over Nimbus."

"That's... ingenious," marveled Frank, sitting back in his chair, his eyes wide. "Why hadn't I thought of that?"

"What does it matter?" moaned Edward, the only one who hadn't joined everyone in the center of the room, besides Bobby who had to keep his leg flat and straight on the cot. "We saw Liberty Estates on the way here. It has even more Hawkers flying over it than the damned factory had! We'd be dead the instant we set foot in there."

"Why are all the Hawkers flocking to the center of the city?" asked Frank, still dazed.

"Probably because the center of the city is where Nimbus's main control center is," said Samuel. "Each of the districts has an emergency control room that can move them around in case of an emergency such as an attack from hostile countries. However, all the minor control rooms can be overruled by the central controls in Liberty Estates."

"The city is moving?" asked Frank in shock. "What on Earth has been happening since I was kidnapped? Furthermore, why is my son with you people? Why are Hugh and Miss Saltwater here?"

Hugh let out a deep sigh, as he looked between his friends. He started their tale from the moment that they left the restaurant. He spoke of how he had witnessed the break-in at Frank's office and how he went to see his older friend at the hospital. He told Frank of what happened when he tried to confront Dr. Mason and how Sally had gotten involved. From that point on, Sally piped in every now and then to provide information that might have slipped Hugh's mind, often referring to her notes for things even she had forgotten. They told him about how they had tried to leave the city, only to watch as the Transport Center fell in an explosion. When they mentioned the Chief of Police, Frank smiled softly.

"That sounds like Matt. I am glad he listened to me when I talked to him at the hospital."

"Me, too," said Hugh as he reached over to hold Sally's hand. "Sally and I would have died long ago if it hadn't been for the Chief."

Frank's face drooped as he let out a deep sigh. "I am sorry that I got you mixed up in all of this, Hugh. I wouldn't have given that key to you if I had any other choice. I just knew if Charles or the Hawkers got a hold of it, and read all my notes, the Hawkers would become truly unstoppable killing machines."

"Strange," said Sally as she quickly flipped through her notes. "I don't remember hearing anything about improvements to the Hawkers when we read that book. Just that their transformation process was unstoppable."

Frank blinked at her in confusion. "That's odd," he said. "I know I wrote in there ways to maximize the brain's capacity, and so forth. Are you sure you didn't see anything about that?"

"Nope," said Hugh. "I guess that stuff was on the pages that turned to mush."

"Mush?" Frank asked in confusion. "What exactly happened to the book?"

"Well, it kind of took a dive into sewer water at one point, and the pages got soaked," admitted Hugh, blushing slightly.

"That might be for the best," said Frank with a sigh. "This way, the Hawkers will never know about how to improve upon their own design, even if they do manage to steal the journal."

"I don't get it," said Sally. "How did they even know about that notebook in the first place? For all they knew, it was Hugh's private diary."

"I don't think they did know about it, not exactly," mused Frank. "I think they were simply desperate for anything that could help them cure themselves. One of them probably saw Hugh leave my apartment after they had finished ransacking it. Maybe they thought he had found something they had missed and targeted him. I certainly didn't tell any of those beasts that the journal existed, so they must have assumed that I kept some notes."

With that out of the way, Hugh and his friends finished their story, ending with finding Frank's cell. Sally and Bobby, who had been in different groups, relayed what they had found as well. As it turned out, most of the Hawker production was automated, with several Hawkers watching over the manufacturing process, sometimes stopping the equipment to either pull off a defective body or to tinker with the bio-brains before they were installed at the end of the line. When the alarm had gone off, every Hawker in the building seemed to instantly know where the humans were and went on the attack. It was only through the use of heavy fire that they were able to make their escape and meet up with Hugh's team in the store room.

With the story over, they began to plan their next steps. Forging through to the center of Nimbus was clearly a very dangerous course of action, but the only plan they had. There were simply too many of the winged robots flying around for them to try to take them out with the limited range of their radios. This didn't stop Frank from being asked to do to the officers' handheld radios the same thing he had done to the radio from his little prison workshop. He had very limited supplies to work with in the janitor's closet, and was only able to prepare three radios to emit the special signal. The range wasn't much better than his original device, but would at least make it hard for Hawkers to get close to them without dying.

Samuel had used one of their remaining radios in an attempt to contact the warehouse headquarters with the intent to relay everything that had happened so far. However, he was unable to get through, either due to a poor signal or simply the distance. He had to make do with contacting the nearest scout troop. The scouts, after getting the message, promised they'd try to get word to the Deputy Chief so Hugh and his friends would have some backup during their move on to Liberty Estates, but it was uncertain if they'd get the help they would need in time. After signing off, Samuel turned towards the others and they continued to work out their plan.

33

"So, what do we do now?" asked Hugh. "What's the plan for getting to the broadcast station? Do we hitch a ride on a freight transport? Take a cable car?"

"It might be best if we just sit here and wait," said Samuel, putting away his hand set. "We are down to a handful of able men, and most of our weapons are back on the train."

"What's stopping us from going back there and getting them?" asked Hugh, starting to get irritated.

"For all we know, the Hawkers have figured out our little distraction by now," said Samuel, "and have found the train. We don't want to give them any more reasons to be snooping around for us out there. It would be best for us to wait this thing out. Besides," added Samuel, "according to what intelligence we were given before the mission, the only way in and out of this district is the cargo transport. The usual methods to Liberty Estates have been demolished. I highly doubt any of us would get very far on foot out there, even if we headed straight back to our point of entry."

"What if there was another way into Liberty Estates?" asked Icarus.

"Well, if we could get some people into the district," said Samuel, "it would almost certainly be a suicide mission with all the Hawkers flying around there. At best, only a few would make it back alive, and that's assuming one of these heroes was able to get the signal to broadcast at the station. Chances are high that they wouldn't even get that far." Turning to look directly at the bronze Sparrow, Samuel narrowed his eyes and asked, "Why do you ask?"

"I think I know how we could get into Liberty Estates, but it would involve us seeking some help," said Icarus. "As you know, we Sparrows are what Hawkers eventually turn into. Some of us are less aggressive, like my breed, while others are more like Dannik."

"Bigger, better, and stronger?" smirked Dannik before he grimaced in pain due to his chest wounds.

"That, and more willing to stick their necks out for a fight," said Icarus. "What we need to do is to find a nest of Sparrows like Dannik and try to convince them to help us in our quest to end the Hawkers' reign of terror once and for all."

"I highly doubt that would be enough," said Edward, "There are more than enough of those things out there to rip through you giant birds. It'd take an entire army for us to even stand a chance in Liberty Estates."

"What if we could raise an army?" said Hugh, getting an idea. "Couldn't we try to get all the Sparrows to come together to lend us a hand."

"It's possible, but it would take time for them to gather," said Icarus. "From what I have heard from my own flock, there is at least one nest of Sparrows in every district of the city. They usually try to avoid mixing with each other, and keep their flocks small to avoid being detected by the Hawkers. However, right before I met with you, Hugh, word had been going around that some of the different flocks were planning on joining up, due to the Hawkers beginning to come uncomfortably close to some of their nests. There is power in numbers, after all. However, I don't know if anything came of that. So far, Dannik is the only one of his variety of Sparrow that I have personally met."

"How would we go about finding these nests?" asked Samuel. "There must be a way. After all, your 'nest' had to form by Sparrows joining up with your flock. How would they know where to go?"

"In the beginning, at least in my flock, we had a few members who would occasionally fly out under the cover of the bottom of the district and watch for any changelings who may have either been thrown out or were flying on their own, looking for sanctuary."

"Well, that settles that," said Jack with a smile. "All we have to do is have you fly around under Vulcan and-"

"That probably wouldn't work now," said Icarus, interrupting the NTAF officer. "With all that has happened since the Hawkers made their true intentions known, it wouldn't surprise me if all Sparrows have decided to let the new fledglings fend for themselves, instead of exposing the nest by sending out experienced Sparrows to help."

"So we are back to square one. Wonderful," said Frank, slumping back in his chair.

"Maybe not," said Samuel, turning to Dannik, who was still sitting on the floor, little specks of red bleeding through his fresh bandages.

The dots appeared near his shoulders and around his abdomen. He had been extremely lucky that none of the bullets had hit any vital organs or arteries. "Dannik," said Samuel, addressing the large white Sparrow directly. "When you were doing a fly by over Vulcan to help plan out the route to the Hawker factory, did you see any signs of Sparrow activity?"

Dannik tilted his head in a way that was similar to how Icarus did when he was deep in thought. After a few minutes, his eyes lit up and he pounded a golden fist into a golden hand. "Of course," he said with a smile. "I remember now, I did see a few Sparrows gathered in the southern end of the district. I was going to say hello to them, but I didn't want to be late coming home to roost."

"What the hell were you doing down there?" demanded Samuel. "You were only supposed to check out the route from the entry point to the factory, nothing more or less. You could have been spotted!"

"Ah, but I wasn't," smirked the big bird. "Besides, it was such a nice evening for a flight! The sky was so beautiful, though the ground below was nothing special, just a whole lot of jagged mountains and dead rocks."

"Where exactly did you see the Sparrows?" insisted Hugh. "Were they near where we are now? Were they like you or like Icarus?"

"Well," thought Dannik, his face wincing for a moment as he pushed himself off the floor into a complete upright position. "I am pretty sure the Sparrow I saw was white like me, but where exactly, I can't quite say."

"Only one? Fat lot of good that will do ten of us," grumbled Bobby from his cot.

"At least it's a start!" yelled back Walt. "Maybe that Sparrow wasn't too far from its flock. And at worst it will at least give us an idea where to look!"

"Think, Dannik," said Sally, walking over to the big white bird. "Is there anything we could go on? Like a landmark or something?"

"Hmm," said the large Sparrow as he scratched the underside of his yellow beak. "I think there was a billboard with a cluster of large purple circles with a green stem spiraling out of the top around where I saw the Sparrow. But I have no idea what that would be."

"That sounds like a cluster of grapes," mused Hugh. Turning to Icarus, he asked, "That could be a winery. Do you think you could go outside and fly around and try to find the sign?"

"I can," said Icarus, looking toward the door at the other end of the room, the one that they hadn't entered through. "It has been long enough now that I doubt I would run into any Hawkers. However, in case there are some out there, it would be best if I go alone. The less people running around out there, the less likely they'll notice us."

"Be careful out there," said Sally as Icarus stood to go. As he passed Samuel, the officer held up his good hand to stop the Sparrow. He handed over his handheld radio so Icarus could let them know the instant he found the grape cluster sign, or if there was any trouble. Icarus accepted the device and clipped it to the waistband of his pants, his backpack having been left behind, beside the bed where Bobby had been set up. Hugh wished Icarus good luck and a safe flight as he headed toward the exit. Terry stepped forward and unlocked the door and opened it so Icarus could move out. Just in case there was a door locked at the other end of the second utility tunnel, Terry went along with Icarus, carrying the keys with him.

It wasn't too long before Terry returned, without Icarus. He locked the door behind him before turning around and telling the rest of the group that the other end of the hallway had exited out into some sort of textile factory. Now all they had left to do was wait for Icarus to radio in with either good or bad news. There wasn't a lot more they could do while they waited, other than talk and break out the food rations. According to their watches, it was just before sunset and they hadn't had a single bite since their quick breakfast before leaving the warehouse district. The NTAF officers ate from their own supply while Hugh, Sally, Bobby, Frank, and Dannik ate from what they had gathered. They were only half way through their meal when the radio started to beep.

It was Samuel who picked up the transmitter and brought it to his ears. "Tell me you aren't under attack," he said into the radio's microphone. Icarus's voice came through the speaker too quiet for anyone but Samuel to hear. The officer nodded his head as a large smile spread across his chubby face. "That's what I like to hear!" he said into the radio.

"I take it that he found the grapes?" asked Frank.

"Even better," said Samuel, still listening to the radio next to his ear. "He found the nest!"

"How far away is it?" asked Hugh, after he swallowed a mouthful of his sandwich.

Samuel held up his hand so they would all be quiet as he listened to what Icarus was saying. According to what Icarus was telling them over the radio, as relayed by Samuel, the building with the grapes sign was the same one that the Sparrow flock had taken up residence in.

It was indeed a winery, and had been vacant long before the Sparrows had moved in. It wasn't too far from where they were now, possibly a couple of blocks – close enough that they could make it on foot without having to rest along the way. However, according to Icarus, it was now dark outside. It was decided that since they had been through so much that day the group would spend the night where they were, and move out in the morning.

It was also decided that Icarus would spend the night with the other Sparrows, so he could get the chance to talk with them, and prepare them for what was coming. At dawn he would fly back to the textile plant and knock upon the utility door four times. This would be the signal that it was him, and not a Hawker. After signing off, Samuel got everyone to collect what sheets they could from the boxes on the shelves. There were not nearly enough to go around, and several of the group had to make do sleeping against the hard concrete floor. Others gathered up the chairs to form makeshift cots that were only slightly more comfortable to sleep on. Bobby remained where he was, under orders from his father. His leg had been injured so badly that any attempt to move him might result in causing his leg to heal poorly. As things were, Bobby would be lucky if he didn't need a cane in the future.

To say they had a peaceful sleep would be very far from the truth. Several of the small group of survivors woke up repeatedly during the night. It was cold down in the tiny room, so most of them had elected to keep on their heavy uniforms, which were lumpy and uncomfortable to sleep in. The only thing they could do to make sleeping easier was turn off the overhead light. The only one not sleeping in the janitor's room was Terry, who, after taking the key for the textile utility door, had left to spend the night alone down there, with only a loaded rifle and a flashlight to keep him company. The plan was that when Icarus arrived, Terry would knock four times on the door to the janitor's room. This would be the signal for them to get ready to leave and head for the Sparrow's nest.

There was no way of telling time down in that dark little room, other than when they shone light upon their wristwatches. Every time someone woke up, they would check the time before trying to get back to sleep. By the time morning finally did come, everyone was a little on edge, even Sally and Hugh. The four knocks upon the door, signaling Terry and Icarus's return, couldn't have come at a better time. Eagerly, the one who had been entrusted with the key ring, Owen, flipped on the light and opened the door, letting his brother and the Sparrow inside.

After an exchange of greetings, Icarus told them that the nest he had found was surprisingly made up of not just large snow-white Sparrows like Dannik, but also had a good number of the more agile bronze Sparrows like him. Not only that, they had welcomed Icarus with open arms, and were very interested in Hugh's plan, once Icarus had told them the summarized version. Now all that was left to do was to decide who was going, and who was staying.

"No way are you guys going without me," said Bobby, trying to get up from the dirty cot. His father, sitting beside him on the bed, pushed his son back down and shook his head.

"You need to stay here," said Frank. "At least until we can get some better equipment to look at your leg, Robby."

"I'll go mad being here, away from all the action," complained Bobby.

"Son," said Frank, his tone turning hard. "I would rather have you go crazy than dead. You are going nowhere on that leg. What's more, I don't see your glasses on your face, so chances are you can barely see anything beyond your nose."

"It won't be all that bad, Dr. Crick Jr," said Samuel, who was sitting in a chair beside the cot. "You'll have plenty of company with you. I won't be going anywhere either, not on a bum leg. Walt and Edward will be staying behind, along with Terry to make sure that there will be three able-bodied men to defend us in the small chance the Hawkers sniff us out."

"Alright," grumbled Bobby before turning to face Icarus. "Listen up, Icarus. You make sure that all of you stay alive, you hear me?"

"I shall do my best, Bobby," said Icarus with a nod.

"I hope you are staying behind too, Frank," said Hugh, his eyes drifting down to his friend's injury.

"I will be," said the old doctor, turning to look at his son on the cot. "With Robby the way he is, and my leg crippled, it would be for the best for me to stay behind. Besides, I'd only get in the way out there. I am not as fast as I used to be, even slower now. By making those alterations to your radios, I'm afraid I've done all I can for you. If only I could do more."

"You have done plenty," said Hugh as he held up one of the modified handsets. "All we need to do is hold one of these up to the microphone and that'll be that!"

"I want to come along," said Dannik, rising to his clawed feet, wincing a tad.

"It would be far better for you to stay here, Dannik," said Icarus, eyeing the red dots on the large white Sparrow's bandages. "I know your breed is not afraid of a fight, but you were shot, several times, in the chest. The last thing you need is to overexert yourself and pop your stitches."

"I don't care," grumbled Dannik, looking down briefly at his own chest. "I can't let something as little as a few bullets get me down. What would the others back home think? That I couldn't handle a few hits from a pea shooter?"

"Dannik," said Frank, rising from the cot and grabbing the larger bird's golden arm, pulling on it till the large Sparrow turned to face him. "I know how badly you want to be out there, to fight the good fight. I have seen men just like you go off to war, and come back in coffins. You have already survived one firefight, something very few men can say. Do the smart thing, stay here and heal up. Live to fight another day."

The white Sparrow looked at Frank, considering the old man's words. For a moment, it seemed that he might rebel, but then he let out a deep sigh and sat back down on the floor, looking down at his chest. "Fine," he huffed, the sound coming out like a deep whistle through his sharp beak. "I'll stay, but only until the bandages come off. Then I'm going to go out there and find the rest of you and lend a hand."

"Deal," said Jack Harper, who nodded his head. And with that, the group, down to only six members, packed up their things and reloaded their guns. Before they left the others, Hugh insisted that everyone stand together around Bobby's cot for a group photo. Bobby ended up in the middle of the image, sitting as straight as he could with his father next to him on the bed. The NTAF officers grouped together on either side of the father and son, some sitting and some standing, doing their best to fit into frame for the picture. The two tall Sparrows were assigned to stand in the very back, their height making them visible, despite having everyone else in front of them. Sally had to sit on her knees on the floor, as there was hardly any space left. Once Hugh had set up his camera on the sink across the room, focused it, and set its timer, he ran over to the gathering, and sat down beside Sally just seconds before the camera went off.

The purpose of the picture, as he had explained before everyone took their places, was to remember this moment, the moment before their group separated. He had a feeling that no matter what happened next, this one moment in time had to be remembered forever as the moment when mankind, and Sparrow kind, finally had a chance of defeating the Hawkers.

With the photo out of the way, Hugh's group said their final goodbyes and headed out the door and into the utility tunnel. This one was much shorter than the one leading to the china factory, and they soon came upon the next door. It yielded to them with a twist of a key.

34

With the door open, they stepped cautiously out into the textile factory proper. As before, they had to head down a hallway lined with a series of offices. Some had the doors broken off of their hinges, revealing trashed rooms and two dead workers. Hugh had seen so many dead bodies by now that they no longer carried the same impact upon him. It was still a terrible sight, but now he could glance at the dead without feeling squeamish. The beige passage they were walking down soon ended just beyond a sharp right turn. There were no doors separating the hallway from the rest of the factory, just hanging sheets of plastic that had bits of dried blood staining the semi-transparent material.

Icarus, at the front of the pack, led them past large looms that sat silent on the factory floor, their spindles not moving. Hugh glanced around at every loom they passed, taking brief notice of the patterns each machine had been set up to create. Some were simple plain colors, such as red, blue, white, and yellow. Others held incomplete patterns, from things as simple as polka dots to complex floral swirls. Above their heads was an iron catwalk that, before the Hawkers' attack, would have been where the factory overseers stood, leisurely watching over the looms as threads were woven together into fabric. They did not spend long in this central room of the factory, as Icarus brought them before another set of hanging plastic strips, and beyond.

The next room was a simple storage room, with large bolts of completed rolls of cloth stacked up, waiting for someone to come and collect them to be shipped out to either stores or other factories to be made into clothing or household goods. Several of the bolts had been knocked over, and they had to step over the thick rolls on their way to the exit of the textile factory.

The final door led them outside into a small loading area, where one of the city's specialized delivery trucks sat, its back doors left wide open and a trolley packed with bolts left unattended. Toward the front of the truck, with his back torn open, was the unlucky driver of the truck. His body hung limply out of the driver side of the truck, the seat belt the only thing keeping him from hitting the pavement. For a moment, Hugh considered suggesting that they take the key from the dead driver, but seeing how trying to use the vehicle to flee had worked out for its original owner, Hugh decided to keep his mouth shut. It might have made them move faster, but it probably would also cause enough noise to draw the Hawkers out again.

It was a gloomy day out, with rain sprinkling down in sporadic droplets. The wind hadn't died down in the least, meaning that the city was still moving to some unknown, westerly goal. Icarus completely ignored the truck, leading them toward the open gates and out into the back streets of the district. They had to risk traveling out in the open far more this time, as many of the doors and hatches of the factories lining the alley were locked. Every second they stayed exposed in the man-made canyon, the more uneasy they became of Hawkers swooping in and picking them off, one by one. The power of their firearms wasn't enough to ease the tension they all felt.

Icarus had been given a map of the district by Samuel before they left. Since he had only found the route to the Sparrow nest by flying over the buildings, they had to find a new route to reach their destination. Every now and then Icarus would have them stop as he compared the map to where they were and to his own memory. Every time he did, they first made sure they had a place to hide from anything flying by overhead. They took shelter under awnings and behind dumpsters, though their preferred rest stops were inside any factory that they found unlocked.

Whenever possible, Icarus led them through the factories, allowing them all to relax just a little bit, with the ceilings protecting them from the skies. It wasn't a moment too soon when they caught their first sight of the grape landmark. They had just exited a side street when the billboard with the purple cluster appeared, peeking out from beyond a row of two story buildings. They didn't let down their guard, as they crossed the open and empty street. The rain was falling a bit more steadily now, darkening the pavement beneath their feet as they moved forward.

"It sure would be nice if the Hawkers would rust in the rain like the Tin Man," said Hugh, being careful to keep his voice low enough that only the five others around him could hear.

"Wouldn't it though?" said Jack with a smirk, just as quietly as Hugh.

"All we'd have to do is sit under an umbrella and watch them become paralyzed."

"Rust does not affect metal that fast," pointed out Clark.

"Oh hush," scolded Jack, "leave us to our fantasies."

The buildings turned out to be a series of small brownstone apartments, pressed so close together that not even a piece of paper could be slid between them. The buildings seemed a little out of place, given how everything else they had passed up to this point were factories of one sort or another. They were fairly tall, at least six to seven stories each, and hid the grape billboard from sight. Thankfully, all the apartments' front doors had been smashed in, a little bit of luck granted by Hawkers on the prowl for human prey days ago. Picking the closest one, they stepped inside the open doorway and into a dirty hallway. There was a cheap colorless rug shoved up against the side wall, showing worn floor boards that were covered in terrible scratches. To the right was a set of stairs inside a protective metal cage, its gate wide open, with the body of a downed Hawker, a fire axe wedged in its head. Whoever had fought back and won was nowhere in sight, having either retreated up the stairs or left long ago. Going upstairs to check was impossible, as the Hawker took up most of the steps' entrance and the side was sealed off by the thick protective metal bars.

There were four doors lining the lower hallway that ran parallel to the stairs. Each door was smashed in. However, they also could see that some of the rooms had furniture piled up on the other side, in an attempt to barricade the doorway. As with the upper floor, there was no telling if there was anyone alive behind the blockades, the rooms too dark and the gaps too small to see past. The pools of blood near the pile of furniture suggested the worst. They did not stay long, making their way quickly along the dingy hallway and to a fire exit at the other end. It was locked, but thankfully the latch was on the inside, and moved easily aside under the touch of Icarus's silver-clawed hand.

Stepping back outside, they found themselves in a small yard enclosed by an eight-foot tall chain link fence. Just on the other side was the winery, so close and yet so far. There wasn't a single gate in the tall fence, and the yard was too small for Icarus to be able to get enough room to fly them over the top. Looking back and forth through the links into the other apartment's yards, it was clear that each one had the same fence. Their only option was to scale the metal mesh and hop down on the other side. Icarus went first, since his longer avian toes enabled him to grip the metal rings and move up the wall faster than the humans could. He jumped down on the other side, and waited for the others to go over, so he could help them down.

Jack went next, followed by Clark and Owen. They climbed considerably more slowly up the fence, since it was slick from the rain and their boots were just slightly too big to use the links as proper foot holds. When it was Hugh's turn to climb over, he stopped when he was at the top and offered a hand down to Sally. She gladly accepted it and with his help, she had an easier time scaling the fence. He let her go over first, and then jumped down himself.

With nothing more in their way, Icarus led the way to the winery. It was a fairly large building, made mostly of grey concrete with several large arched windows adorning its sides. Near it were parked a large crane and several trucks, suggesting that the building was either in the process of being built, renovated, or demolished. As they drew closer, movement could be seen beyond the glass. From a set of double doors stepped out a very large Sparrow, the biggest they had yet encountered. He was just as snowy white as Dannik was. He looked at Hugh and his friends as they drew closer, and scanned the skies overhead, watching for any trouble that the new arrivals might bring.

Once they had drawn close to the Sparrow, he nodded his feathered head, turned back towards the doors, and pushed them open. He held them open for Icarus, along with Hugh and the others, to enter through. Once inside, they were greeted with a fantastical sight. The large room they had stepped into was filled with Sparrows. Both of the two species were present, the bronze and the white. They were clustered into groups, as if they preferred to be with those of their own color and size. The NTAF members, along with Sally, could only stare at the gathered feathery ensemble, their eyes wide at the sight of so many Sparrows in one place. Hugh, however, was not as enthralled. After all, he first met Icarus among a similar flock of the giant birds. He thought he recognized a few of the Sparrows present before them from the Trash District, but he wasn't sure. Yet, he could not help but feel a sense of wonder looking at all of them. He brought his camera up and snapped a few photos of the gathered flock.

There were Sparrows atop the walkways bolted to the walls under the windows, and a few were sitting atop the wine presses, lined up in the middle of the room. Crates had been pushed right up against the wall to give the birdmen more room on the winery floor. Despite all of the Sparrows looking right at the human visitors, there were simply too many feathery heads to count. The birdmen wore all sorts of things over their bodies. From jumpsuits modified with holes in the back for their wings and tail feathers, to only pants and even no clothing at all. The big white Sparrow that had let them inside was wearing thick overalls, and seemed to be the leader of the gathered flock.

He stood tall over all of their heads, and appraised each of the humans. When he finished giving them the once over with his stunning blue eyes, he opened his beak and in a very deep voice, deeper than Dannik's, issued forth.

"So," his voice booming like a thunderstorm, "here you are. Icarus told us much about your plan. However, I wish to hear all of it, and from your mouths. Speak carefully humans, for if I feel that this plan of yours is flawed, if there is any chance that harm will come to my people, I will kick all six of you out."

"Alright," said Jack, holding his hands out palm first in the universal sign of trying to assure that things won't get violent. He turned to Hugh with a smirk and reached for him, pulling the photographer forward. "This is your story. Why don't you tell the big angry bird what the plan is?"

Hugh gulped uncomfortably as he looked at Jack's eager face and at Sally's scared one. This large Sparrow before him had to be at least a good foot taller than Dannik, meaning that Hugh had to crane his neck to look up at the massive Sparrow. For a moment, Hugh wondered where the Sparrow found overalls large enough to fit his massive frame, but his mere intimidating presence blew away all thoughts of mirth or unnecessary curiosity. Clearing his throat, Hugh thought over his plan and knew that despite their massive numbers, there was no way that all the Sparrows would be coming back, not unless they could suddenly move faster than lighting. Taking a deep breath, his brow sweating under the hard gaze of the leader of the nest of Sparrows, Hugh began to speak.

"Our plan," he said, doing his best not to stammer, "Is to shut down nearly all of the Hawkers in Nimbus. To do this, we need to get to the city's broadcast station in the center of Liberty Estates and use the equipment to broadcast a special tone so that every single radio and television connected to Nimbus's emergency broadcast system will play it. That tone will shut down nearly all of the Hawkers in one go."

"I see," said the leader of the nest. "I remember my time as one of the metal demons. We used to have our own radio system, connecting us together in thought. All of us Sparrows once did, though we rarely used it. So far your plan matches with what Icarus has told us. Now, tell me what part you want my flock to play, and speak well."

Hugh took a breath to steady his nerves and began to speak again. For the briefest of moments, he was upset with Jack putting him on the spot like this, but there was nothing to be done about it now. "First, we need to get into Liberty Estates in order to reach the broadcast station and send the signal. We know that the usual means of moving across the gap between districts, the sky bridges and cable cars, have been destroyed by the Hawkers. I still don't know how they took out the cable cars though…" Hugh glared at Icarus for a moment. The Sparrow could only shrug his shoulders in reply.

"I said they were hard to break, not invincible," said Icarus.

"Anyway," said Hugh, returning his attention to the largest creature in the room. "Since we humans aren't gifted with the ability to fly, we need some of your Sparrows to fly us across the gap."

"What is stopping you from using the one you have with you?" asked the leader.

"I could fly one across," admitted Icarus, "But flying back and forth to ferry five humans across would be impossible. I would tire out too soon, and might not be able to get the last one across. Waiting for me to recover will take too long, and risk whoever I have carried across, or those waiting to travel, being found by the Hawkers."

"And," added Jack, as he stepped forward, "We were also hoping that you'd be able to lend a few others to help us take the broadcast station, and distract the Hawkers in the sky."

The large Sparrow glared at Jack, who shrank away under its withering sapphire gaze. "So, this is what Icarus would not tell us, that you wish to send us to war?"

"It won't be for long," said Hugh, his heart pounding in worry. Any wrong word said now would most likely cause the alpha avian giant to turn them down, to withhold his forces.

"I do not care if it is for a minute or an hour," the big Sparrow huffed, turning his back on the humans. "Nor do I care how few you need. Any member of this flock being out there in Hawker territory puts our entire nest in danger of discovery. We have only survived for this long because we have kept to ourselves out of sight. As things are, they only think that a few of us Sparrows exist. With every Sparrow spotted, they become more and more aware of our presence."

"But that's part of the reason we need your help, and why you need to help us," said Hugh, taking a bold gambit.

"What's this?" demanded the massive white Sparrow as he wheeled around on the heel of one large clawed talon to stare down Hugh. The movement showed that the feathered giant was as nimble as a ballerina, for as he turned, he had also gotten down on one knee to bring his hawkish face mere inches away from Hugh's. "Do you dare speak for the good of my people? You are merely a human! Though we wouldn't exist without you and your understanding of technology, this does not mean that we still need you to dictate what we do, or what is best for our flocks."

"Let me explain," pleaded Hugh. "You have a lot of Sparrows here, right?"

"That is correct. When the day of death came, many flocks sought shelter among their own in this building," said the massive white Sparrow, standing up to his impressive full height. He spread out his arms and opened his wings wide, as if he was embracing every single Sparrow in the winery. "All of us here are the remains of several different nests over the city. This is all that remains of the northeastern flocks of Nimbus. Pray," said the Sparrow as he let his arms and wings relax, and looked back at Hugh, "why do you ask?"

"Well," said Hugh, "I imagine it takes a lot to feed all of you, right? I mean," he added with a shaky smile, gesturing his head over at Icarus, "I have seen Sparrows eat before. Icarus has put away more fish than I have ever seen any grown man eat in my entire life. Needless to say, all of your kind here would need massive amounts of food and water to survive, right?"

The leader looked at Hugh differently now, his anger fading into curiosity of where the human was trying to take the conversation. "This is true," said the leader of the Sparrows, glancing briefly at the wine presses. "When this was just one small flock, there was enough food in the crates stored here to feed all of us, but now we need to send out hunting parties. We can go for a few days without food, but eventually we must feed our hunger."

"Every time you send out a handful of Sparrows to bring back food for the flock," said Hugh, "You risk a Hawker finding them. Haven't you wondered about how we knew about you and your nest here in the winery?"

The giant Sparrow tilted its great head and glanced at Icarus and then at each of the humans in turn. When the leader didn't speak, Hugh supplied the answer.

"A few days ago, another friend of ours, Dannik, a Sparrow much like you, just not quite as... tall, was out surveying Vulcan for us. While he was flying by, he managed to see one of your birds returning to the nest."

Upon hearing this, the winged giant's head twisted to look at one of the white Sparrows above them, leaning over the railing of the catwalk. Upon realizing who the Sparrow's leader was staring at, it shrunk back from the rail and tried to disappear into the crowd around it. "I see," murmured the leader, almost too quietly to hear, before his voice returned to its booming volume. "It seems we got sloppy that time. I will make sure that that particular scavenger is punished properly."

"That's not what I am getting at here," said Hugh, getting back the giant's attention. "What I am trying to say is that, at some point, one of your Sparrows will be spotted by the Hawkers, just as that one was spotted by Dannik. When that happens, you can bet that the Hawkers will be determined to hunt all of you down. Then, seeing how many of you are gathered in one place, the Hawkers might realize that a lot more of their transformed buddies are hiding under their noses all over Nimbus, and go on a massive bird hunt."

The leader looked down at Hugh, his expression unreadable upon his snow-white face. It was only now that Hugh noticed that this Sparrow had light blue tints around the edges of every feather, giving the Sparrow leader an almost soothing feel about him. That is, it would be soothing if the Sparrow wasn't so massive. One good punch or kick from the winged behemoth would be more than enough to take Hugh out for good. He hoped not only for his own sake, but for that of Sally and the others there, that he hadn't overstepped any invisible boundaries. Deciding to take the leader's silence as an opportunity to finish his attempt to persuade the giant to let the Sparrows help Hugh and his friends put an end to all of this, Hugh took a deep breath and finished his line of reasoning.

"However," he said, forcing himself to keep eye contact with the intimidating creature, "there is still a chance that you, your flock, and all the Sparrows alive in Nimbus can come out of this. As things are, we humans are in the same boat as the Sparrows. We risk walking the streets, or even moving out of our own hidey-holes, with the Hawkers patrolling not just the ground, but the skies above. All it takes is one lapse in awareness, and then BAM, death from above! We need to work together here, to shut down the Hawkers once and for all. What we have with us is the exact signal to broadcast from the tower that will kill almost every Hawker in the city at once. The problem is that we have no way across the gap between here and the center of the city. Even if we did, and tried to go there on our own, we'd be heading to where most of the Hawkers are clustered, which would, on its own, be a death sentence. If you send just a few Sparrows to not only carry us over, but to help provide a distraction to the Hawkers, we may have a chance at getting to the controls for the tower and shutting them down for good. And if any of these things survive, they will be in far more manageable numbers. So what do say you? Will you lend a few Sparrows to help us out?"

Hugh shut his mouth, as there was nothing more he could say. He could only wait as the leader thought over his words. Sally gently took Hugh's hands in hers. He squeezed her soft hands, letting her know that he understood the gesture. They both watched, along with Jack, Owen and Clark, as the massive Sparrow looked down at them, and mused over what had been said. The giant Sparrow spoke the words "Wait here," as he turned away from the small gathering of six visitors and moved deeper into the massive flock of Sparrows. Once he was in the center of the room, the leader cleared his throat and spoke loudly, so every Sparrow in the winery could hear.

"Brothers and sisters," he said in a voice like a fog horn, "I, Tempest, your chosen leader, offer you all a decision. The humans wish for us to aid them in a battle that may rid all of us of the Hawker threat. Forget not that we were all once Hawkers, and to kill our metal brothers would be the same as butterflies killing caterpillars. However, we all know that they would just as easily slay us, and have tried to slay us from the moment we became flesh and blood! As we are, we are safe, hidden away from sight. But this may not last forever, as the human has reasoned. I wish for all of you to vote in this decision. Should we stay here where we are safe for the time being, keeping to the shadows and hoping that our hunters and scavengers are not spotted when they are doing their necessary rounds, or do we go out into the open, and take the fight to the robots? All in favor of helping the humans raise your wings! All against, keep them down!"

35

At first, there was no movement, only the sound of the aviary's Sparrows talking nervously amongst themselves. Then, a single pair of white wings rose up at the back of the room. Slowly, another pair rose from one of the catwalks, right before the massive windows. From atop one of the grape presses rose five more pair of wings, one of which was the bronze of the more timid breed. Slowly, wings went up all over the room. Outside, the skies began to clear up, causing the inside of the winery to brighten. Silver and bronze wings shone in the sunlight drifting in through the arched windows, making the field of upraised feathered limbs a truly magnificent scene. It was clear that all of the Sparrows present were tired of hiding, and were more than ready to finally take the fight to the Hawkers themselves. Needless to say, Hugh had to take several pictures of this fantastic sight.

Tempest pivoted around in the middle of the pressing room, taking in all the raised wings, counting them off with his eyes. About half way into his turn, he clearly gave up the count and simply nodded his head in understanding. He trotted back over to the gathered six visitors and took one last look over his shoulder at all the raised wings. "That's enough," he said to his flock and, as if on command, every Sparrow simultaneously let their wings drift down.

The giant turned back to the humans and Icarus and let out a mighty sigh. "It seems we are to go to war," he said without an ounce of emotion. "However, before we do anything else, I wish to talk to all of you, in private. Would you follow me?"

"Alright," said Hugh. "You've heard us out, time to hear you out. Lead the way, sir."

"Please, just call me Tempest."

And with that Tempest led them through his flock on the winery floor, to a small set of double doors that he had to duck under in order to pass through. Beyond lay a hallway that Hugh and his traveling companions had seen replicated in nearly every factory they had passed through in Vulcan. It was, of course, lined with doors and the walls were painted in a very neutral color, this time a muted olive green. Other than the wall color, the only difference between this place and the others they had seen was that between the doors were pasted several posters of famous wineries from around the world in places like Italy and Greece. Tempest did not travel too far down this hallway, stopping before a door set in the middle of the hall.

Following the massive Sparrow inside, they found themselves in an empty room. There were paint cans stacked up in one corner and a paint stained drop sheet spread out over every inch of the floor. Only one wall was covered in paint, a soothing light pink. The rest were naked walls of plaster and plywood. Once inside, Tempest moved to the very back of the room and sat down upon the cloth. He crossed his long muscular legs and rested his golden clawed hands upon his knees. With no chairs to be seen, the humans and Icarus had no choice but to follow suit and sit down upon the floor in a semi-circle before the white giant.

"My flock has made their decision," said Tempest, his voice still without any emotion. "I will not stand in their way."

"That's great!" said Owen, before shutting up when he saw the glare he was given by the leader of the Sparrows. "Right?" he added in a weak voice.

"It may be, it may not," said Tempest as he returned to addressing all six before him. "Only time will tell if this was the best decision for my flock. For all we know, we could have managed to stay safe and alive by doing as we have been, hiding and hunting. However, the choice has been made and we cannot turn back. This being the case, I want to know what you will be doing while we are risking our lives in the skies against our metal brothers."

"What do you mean?" asked Sally. "Hughie already told you, we'll be moving on the broadcast station, to send out the killing message to all the tin-heads."

"Aye," said the giant, nodding his head. "This is what you said you would be doing. However, what I ask is not what you, as in you before me, will be doing, but you, as in your species will be doing." Tempest paused for a moment to cross his arms and shift his feathery legs, before continuing. "In your speech out there, you said we Sparrows and you humans must fight together. I want to know that your kind will be just as willing to send theirs into battle as my Sparrows are."

"Of course we would," cried out Jack. "If we had a way into Liberty

Estates, there would be no stopping us. I can't count how many people want to pay back the Hawkers for what they did. Almost everyone on the force lost someone special when the Hawkers went berserk. You'd have to tie them up and lock them away just to keep them from the battle!"

"So what is stopping them?" asked Tempest

"Did you not hear what he just said, sir?" asked Clark. "There is no way for anyone to get into Liberty Estates. Every single cable car and sky bridge has been taken out. They can't even use the sewers like you can in some districts, because the damned machines have busted up the controls for the extending pipes on their side."

"I see," said the snow-white giant. "What if we were to supply these able-bodied men with Sparrows to fly them into the city's center? Would you guarantee that they won't mistake members of my flock for the enemy, as so many others of your kind have?"

"Well," considered Jack, looking back and forth between Owen and Clark before glancing over at Icarus. "Many of the NTAF have already been briefed on Dannik, so unless they missed the call out about Sparrows, there shouldn't be a problem with them mistaking feathers for metal."

"Dannik?" asked Tempest, cocking his head to the side.

"Oh, he's a big white Sparrow," supplied Hugh. "Although not nearly as big as you are," he mumbled under his breath.

"Well, I am a bit of an oddity among my own kind," said Tempest with a deep chuckle, so deep it could have been a series of sped up lion roars. "I used to be just a simple Hawker, no bigger than any other. When the change hit me, every part of my body simply felt too tight, and as I shed my metal cocoon, I found my body rising higher and higher. It is only for my height that the others have made me their leader. They think me strong enough to protect all of them, though I know better." Leaning over towards Hugh, the massive Sparrow winked at him. "I also, like all other Sparrows, have exceptional hearing. If you don't want us to hear you, best to just keep it in your head."

Hugh turned to look at Icarus, who merely nodded in confirmation of the giant's words.

"Anyway," said Jack, giving a sideways glance at Hugh, "as you can see, having your Sparrows meet up with our men shouldn't be a problem in the slightest."

"What about weapons?" Tempest asked. "Fists and claws can only do so much to the machines. We would be little more than an annoyance to our metal brothers. If we wish to really do some damage, we will need to put effective weapons in to my people's clawed hands."

"Not a problem," said Jack. "I'll just send the message through the

NTAF grapevine to not only be ready for feathered visitors, but to make sure that they get whatever gun they think is suitable for the job."

"How long will all of this take?" asked Sally, speaking up for the first time in quite a while.

"We Sparrows can fly pretty fast," said Tempest. "However, I cannot honestly say how soon we can go to war, without knowing where we are to fly first to meet up with the other humans."

"Let us just radio in first," said Jack as he pulled out one of their unmodified handsets to call Samuel. Through Samuel, the message was relayed to the scouts in Vulcan and from there all the way back to the police headquarters. There was a bit of a delay between the receiver and sender, but soon their plan was fully explained to the officers back at the Warehouse District. They arranged everything, places where the Sparrows could meet up with the best fighters of the NTAF, and locations where they could stock up on weapons. When everything had been worked out, Tempest thought over how long it would take for his birds to reach the rendezvous points. Most of them were in the Warehouse District, though there were others all over the city. It would take at least a day for everything to be ready for the attack on Liberty Estates.

Tempest, though not fond of humans, was not beyond offering to let them rest at the winery until everything was ready to go. Upon accepting his kind offer, the giant Sparrow bowed his head and rose to leave the room and tell his flock about the plan. He soon returned to the unfinished room, to inform them that already several of his flock had taken flight, once they had made sure the coast was clear, to meet up with the officers. As part of the agreement, every time a Sparrow reached its destination, the NTAF officer waiting for them radioed HQ, who in turn, sent word back through the grapevine of radios until it reached Jack's handset. Every now and then, Hugh or one of the others would get up and wander over to the central room of the winery to see how many Sparrows were left.

When the sun started to set below the horizon, there were only a handful of the birds left. The last of the Sparrows had flown out the door moments before and was steadily disappearing into the fading light over the smokestacks. As the sky faded from red to a deep purple, the entire district seemed to age with the light. Buildings darkened and the few lights that came on in Vulcan, mostly the street lights and a few blinking lights atop smokestacks, only seemed to highlight how tired the world was becoming. Looking out the open doorway, Hugh couldn't help but think things were coming to a close at last. Whatever happened tomorrow would seal the fate of Nimbus, be it salvation or ruin.

Hugh took a photo of the last Sparrow flying away before he closed the doors. With nothing left to do, he moved through the significantly quieter pressing room, past the remaining Sparrows. As he passed them, he glanced around at the few birdmen still cooped up inside. He hadn't noticed it before, due to how many had been at this nest when they had arrived with the others, but the Sparrows were not a uniform size. There were indeed many who stood taller than him, though none quite as large as Tempest. However, there were also some that were on the short side. A few were even shorter than Sally. It was very hard to believe that all of these avians had started out as mere machines, the last the same as the first. Perhaps it was some characteristic of the bio-brain that determined how tall they would become, just as with humans.

As he neared the doors leading back to the hallway with the offices, he noticed that there were one or two female Sparrows sitting atop rugs that were spread out atop the hard concrete floor. They were clearly pregnant, as their bellies were as swollen as Icarus's mate, way back in Xandir Square. This made him wonder what the children of the Sparrows would be like. Would they resemble baby birds, or be more human in shape? Would they be born in eggs ready to be hatched, or would the chicks come out like mammal infants? As with everything else that Hugh couldn't answer on his own, his curiosity bubbled away. He couldn't help but puzzle over these questions up to the moment that he rejoined the others.

Sally looked up and beamed him a smile upon his entry. At the back of the room sat Tempest, cross-legged like before, talking in private to Icarus, who sat in a similar position before the giant. Owen and Clark were talking to each other over a map of Liberty Estates. Jack was on his handset, waiting for word to make its way along the radio network concerning the arrival of Sparrows from HQ. Hugh stifled a yawn and walked over to Sally and sat down beside her. They talked just to pass the time before supper and bedtime. As with the night before, they had to sleep on the floor, with not a piece of furniture available in the building to use as makeshift cots, their bags having to serve once again as makeshift pillows.

For a brief moment, as they were settling in for the night, Hugh fantasized about sleeping atop Icarus, or using one of his wings as a blanket. However, he had a feeling that sleeping atop his friend would be frowned upon, so he simply lay down and hoped to get some rest before the big day ahead. In the middle of the night, he awoke with a start. He had been having a nightmare in which he had been shot through the heart and thrown off of the city into impossibly sharp mountains far below, when the sound of Jack's radio beeping woke him up.

Hugh rose to look in the dim light of a flashlight at the sleeping NTAF officer. Jack was sound asleep, his head tucked into his arms and his legs pulled close to his chest. The radio strapped to his belt had a little red light blinking away, and with each flicker it beeped, signaling someone on the other end wished to talk. Quietly, without wishing to disturb the others, Hugh crept his way past their sleeping bodies to the handset. Thankfully, Tempest wasn't sleeping in the room with them, preferring to be with the rest of his flock in the pressing room. If the giant had been on the floor with the others, Hugh would have had no chance of getting near Jack.

Upon reaching him, Hugh carefully unhitched the radio and brought it up to his own ear, pressing the listen button on the side with his index finger. "Hello?" he said into the device.

"Who is this?" asked the voice on the other end in surprise.

"Hugh Yeats," said Hugh. "Jack's asleep right now, who is this?"

"Hugh? I didn't recognize you at first. This is Samuel."

"You sound a lot different on the radio, Sam," said Hugh.

"I know, right?" chuckled the cop through the radio's speaker. "Anyway, I wanted to send Jack the message that the last Sparrow just landed in Xandir Square. If you can relay this to Jack, or the head bird, that would be great."

"No problem," said Hugh, trying his best not to yawn into the radio. His body was begging him to go back to sleep, but he didn't want to be rude to the NTAF officer. Besides, this was a very important message indeed. Before Tempest had left them for the night, he said that he would not let them fly to Liberty Estates until every Sparrow had been accounted for. "So," said Hugh, while he still had Samuel on the line, "how is everyone doing back at the camp? Is everyone still alive?"

"Yes," answered the voice. "Frank is doing pretty well given that he has a minor infection due to his leg not getting the proper treatment after being shot. It's nothing a bottle of penicillin can't fix. Bobby is still laid out on the only cot. That guy is such a jerk, you know that?"

"To be fair, he had his knee blown off," reasoned Hugh.

"True enough," admitted Samuel. "But, you'd think he'd at least be in somewhat better spirits with his old man back. As for myself, I'm taking the same pills as the doc. I am afraid that my pitching will never be the same again, but at least I can still hold my gun properly. Everything else has been quiet down here, save for Dannik."

"What happened?" asked Hugh. "Did he rip his stitches or did Bobby get under his skin again?"

"Naw," said Samuel with a deep sigh that was interlaced with a bit of static. "He just won't shut up about how he should be out there, flying free and fighting the good fight. We had to use some of our limited supply of sedatives just to calm him down."

"I guess you can't keep a good bird down," muttered Hugh to himself, glancing for a moment at Icarus, who had wrapped himself up in his large feathered wings. The Sparrow looked almost as if he had slipped inside a feather sleeping bag. Hugh found himself wondering how it was possible that Icarus's wings could bend in such a way without any bones breaking, before Samuel derailed his thoughts.

"Are you sure you are up to this, Hugh?" the NTAF officer asked.

"Excuse me?"

"It's just that, you are only a photographer, right? Don't get me wrong, you and your friends clearly have been through a lot. Heck," chucked Samuel, "your adventures are all Bobby talks about. However," he said as his voice suddenly became very serious, "that's part of my point. You and your little misses have been through enough. If it had been anyone else going through all the adventures you have, I bet they would have either been killed or given up long ago. You are the luckiest man I know. Heck, if you went to Las Vegas you'd probably leave with all of the casino's money."

"No one's that lucky," said Hugh as he rubbed at the cut on his neck, feeling the bandage under his fingertips.

"Exactly," agreed Samuel. "I really think you should sit this one out, let Jack and his men go to the broadcast station while you and Sally wait at the winery. They are professionally trained officers, after all."

"I wish I could, I really do," admitted Hugh to the handset. "Every day since the Hawker massacre, I have been wondering how much longer I could stay alive, could keep Sally safe. However, I'm in this far too deep just to get out of the pool now. I don't know if it's just my inner curiosity or my sense of duty egging me on to the battle tomorrow, but what I do know is that I have a part to play tomorrow, and, by God, I will do it."

"I see," said Samuel, after a moment of silence, "and what about Miss Saltwater?"

Hugh let out a sad little chuckle of his own. "Sally? As much as I would love to keep her safe, she'd hate me forever if I made her stay behind. The battle will be the biggest scoop of her career, and I know that she would rather stand by me than wait for what may come. If we are to die tomorrow, at least we'll die together."

"You have an interesting way of seeing things, Mr. Yeats," said Samuel before signing off, leaving Hugh alone in the sleeping room. Quietly, he replaced the radio on Jack's belt, and went back to his spot on the floor, right beside Sally. Using his camera bag as a pillow, he settled down and went back to sleep. The next day was only hours away.

36

The dawn of the next day, July the sixteenth, opened with overcast skies. They had all awoken around roughly the same time, about eight in the morning. Hugh wasted no time, once the last of his drowsiness had been shaken out of his system, to inform Jack of the message from the night before, which in turn the officer relayed to Tempest the moment the giant appeared in the doorway. They ate a hearty meal of what was left of their rations, sharing with the Sparrow king and the members of his flock who would be flying them into the center of Nimbus.

Once the meal was through, everyone did one last check of their equipment, making sure their weapons were functioning properly and that they had more than enough ammunition on hand for the battle to come. As they headed out of the double doors of the winery to the open lot in front of the building, Hugh turned for a moment to look at Sally, to ask her to wait for him. But he remembered his words to Samuel, and saw his thoughts confirmed in her dazzling eyes, set hard upon their dangerous mission ahead. Despite the clouds overhead, her golden hair shone as if each strand had been stolen from the sun.

Upon the direction of Tempest, the five humans lined up at one end of the lot, with five Sparrows assigned to line up in a parallel line behind them. Icarus, deciding to lend his services so that a few of the flock's original Sparrows could stay back in the nest, took up position behind Sally. Hugh turned his head to look at his feathered friend and knew, with a wink of the bird's eye, that his love was in good hands. He himself had been partnered up with one of the white Sparrows, by the name of Welch.

Welch reminded Hugh a lot of Samuel, for the bird was a tad overweight, and his beak seemed to be molded into a permanent mischievous smile. He was wearing overalls of his own, only instead of being blue and clean like Tempest's, Welch's pair were an unpleasant shade of brown and stained with oil and grease. Hugh could only hope that the Sparrow would be able to keep a strong grip on him long enough for them to make it to Liberty Estates, and that the slick stains on his clothes didn't get on the bird's golden clawed hands.

Before both lines, at the very end of the open lot, stood Tempest, his eyes scanning each human and Sparrow. He spoke a few words, giving the humans advice on what to do while being flown by their Sparrows, and he told the Sparrows what to do with the humans. Hugh briefly wondered how Tempest had become so proficient in flying humans around, but decided not to ask. Once Tempest was sure everything was ready, he raised his large right fist into the air and, like horses out of the gates, the five Sparrows, as one, ran for the humans, their wings beating, granting them lift. Right before they rammed head first into the humans, they reached out their arms and wrapped their target in a bear hug, right under the armpits. Upon contact, Hugh, Sally, Owen, Clark, and Jack jumped up, as Tempest had instructed them to, making it easier for their assigned Sparrows to gain altitude. Hugh watched as the ground slipped away beneath his feet, his stomach doing flips in every direction.

As they headed off to the west toward their destination, each of the humans did their best to curve their backs, and bring their legs up so their ankles could be gripped by the Sparrows's clawed feet. This made it infinitely easier for the Sparrows to fly, as having dangling passengers made it harder for them to be aerodynamic. This had all been explained to them in great detail by Tempest before they were cleared for takeoff. They flew all the way up into the clouds, so as to keep their flight as secret as possible from the Hawkers.

It was very cold that far up in the sky, and Hugh couldn't help but shiver, wishing he had brought his heavy jacket along when he had gone to Valkyrie Park all those days ago. It would have been very strange for him to be wearing a thick coat, but at least he'd probably be warm now. He pressed himself into the body of the Sparrow above him, in hopes of being able to at least keep warm through the body heat of the bird. It worked to an extent, as his back soon felt some much needed heat, but the rest of him remained as chilly as ever. Worse, since they were flying through the clouds themselves, the precipitation they gathered caused Hugh, and he assumed the others, to soon become soaking wet. He could only hope that he wouldn't catch a cold, as being sick would be simply unbearable on top of everything else.

Hugh couldn't see the others, as the clouds were simply too thick. All he could get was brief glances of murky shadows darting in and out of the wisps. None of them talked, as the air was thin this high up, and they needed every breath just to remain conscious. There was no way to tell how fast they were going, or if they were moving at all in the clouds. The only landmark to go by in this mysterious white world was the diffused glow of the sun at their backs. Everything felt so unreal up in the clouds. Nothing was solid, and the ebbs of the clouds played tricks on Hugh's eyes. Only the Sparrow holding him up knew where they were going, and if they were still on track for, like most birds, the Sparrows appeared to have internal compasses and a truly amazing sense of direction.

Finally, after what felt like years, but could have been a matter of minutes, Welch descended out of the clouds. Suddenly, Hugh could see again, and before him was Liberty Estates, the center of Nimbus and the richest part of the city. He turned around to see Icarus and Sally, along with the others, burst out of the grey clouds behind them. Bringing up the rear was Tempest himself, whose massive wings brought with them chunks of the fluffy clouds. As they dropped lower and lower, Hugh could hear the sounds of distant shots being fired, and saw that the battle had already begun. Already a few Hawkers were flying towards their small flock, having spotted them the instant they broke cloud cover.

Tempest went into a dive that brought him to the front of the flock, and raised his fists with a shriek that sounded eerily similar to the battle cry of the Hawkers. In his large golden hands he held a sledgehammer and brought the large hammer down against one of the robots, sending it spiraling out of control to whatever part of North America the city was currently floating over. There was some green below them, and the mountains had given way to foothills while the city had been moving ever westward. It was because the city itself was moving that the flight from Vulcan had taken so long.

With the Hawkers distracted by the giant, the Sparrows weaved around in the aerial fight and headed for a landing at a viewing platform at the edge of the district, just a block south of the cable car station that normally linked Liberty Estates and Vulcan together. The instant they were low enough, the Sparrows let go of the humans' ankles and let them dangle for a moment, before releasing their hold around their bodies. Hugh, Sally, and the NTAF officers fell about a foot onto the fancy brickwork of the viewing platform, as the Sparrows came to a proper landing a little ways away. It turned out that the lookout point opened up into a large park, with several trees that had grown a tad wild without the constant care of gardeners. Many of the flower bushes in the park had been trampled upon by careless feet, though if it had been when the Hawkers attacked the humans, or by the Hawkers themselves on patrol, one couldn't say.

Lining the edges of the park were rows of five-story apartments, far fancier than anything elsewhere in the city. Each building was built in art deco style, with nods to European architecture. They had tall windows with shutters held open by iron hooks, and several windows sported flower baskets. Turning to look up upon landing, it was clear that the skies were quickly filling with the flying forms of Sparrows and Hawkers, tangling up in a battle that could only be replicated by angels. Wasting no more time, the NTAF officers, along with Sally and Hugh, ran off of the exposed viewing platform and past smashed benches until they were under the cover of the trees. The less visible they were, the better their chances for survival.

Once they were under a tall oak, Hugh turned and watched as, with a wave, each of the Sparrows took off at a run and flew into the skies overhead to join the fray. Icarus was the last one to go, hefting Bobby's shotgun before joining his winged brothers. Both Hugh and Sally called out to their companion, wishing him good luck as he flew into the sky.

It took a few minutes for Jack and Owen to orient themselves with their map. According to it, they were currently in Zephyr Park, which had three exits. One would take them down Wright Avenue, right to the broadcast tower. Another, Windward Lane, led off to the south and the other one to a winding street by the name of Serpent Corridor. Had it been any other ordinary day in Nimbus, they would have simply taken the avenue, but at the moment there was a crashed airplane blocking the gate along with rubble from one of the apartments that it had hit when it went down. It would be too dangerous to climb over the rubble, so, after checking the map, with Jack in the lead, followed closely by Hugh and Sally, with Owen and Clark bringing up the rear, they made their way to the north and followed the wide but twisting Serpent Corridor.

As they hurried along, they passed by other NTAF members and regular police officers who were firing long range weapons at the metal monsters overhead, helping out the Sparrows in their fight. At the end of the second sharp turn in the street, a tall white building appeared. It was easily identifiable as the original headquarters of Nimbus's finest, the police department building. It was built in the neo-classical style that made it look more like a massive ancient Greek temple than a specialized office building for the city's workers.

As they hurried closer to the imposing building, they had to ready their weapons as several Hawkers burst up from manhole covers in the road before them. It stood to reason that there would be robotic birds down there, given the location of the hidden areas of other districts, but it still took them by surprise. Thankfully, Jack and Owen were unfazed enough to open fire on the robots before they could shoot. Their bullets flew and hit home in each Hawker's eye, and they fell back into the hole they had crawled out of. With that out of the way, they continued on their way, stopping just in front of the old police department.

Checking the map again, Jack led the group up the granite steps of the building and kicked open the doors leading into the structure. They hurried into a large round lobby with a massive mosaic covering most of the floor. If viewed from some of the upper offices, the thousands of tiny tiles would form a perfect picture of a police badge, with the coat of arms of the city emblazed upon it. However, no one had time to take in the floor art, as they hustled across the hall and through a set of steel double doors. After moving down a thin hallway, they exited into a large room.

This was the city's bull pen, with office spaces set up in neat rows of four by four. Normally, there would be detectives sitting in these open topped offices, working away on their assigned cases, but now this open space was more of a ghost town. From above their heads came the cry of angry Hawkers, so Hugh and the others dove for cover inside one of the wooden walled offices as one of the robots dove at them from a walkway that ran along the top of the large room. It crashed into the floor tiles just outside the small office, having not enough room to pull up from its dive. To make sure it wouldn't get up, Owen turned around and quickly fired a shot into its eye as it glared angrily at them.

"Coming in here sure was a dumb idea!" cried Sally as she stumbled out of the way of another Hawker, this one smart enough to glide down from the balcony.

"How about we focus on getting out of here?" shouted back Jack as he fired point blank into the face of a Hawker that was seconds away from ramming into him. He had just enough time to duck out of the way as the Hawker crashed through an office wall, taking out a free-standing bulletin board and knocking over a series of filing cabinets like metal dominoes.

"The prison, we can get out through the 'special entrance'," said Owen as he fired up at the balcony, trying to disrupt the Hawkers stationed up there, with little to no success.

"Which way is it?" demanded Hugh as he managed to hit the sweet spot on a Hawker who was moments from clawing his chest open, the lessons Detective Catcher had given him clearly paying off.

"Just follow us," commanded Jack as he took off at a run towards a couple of vending machines. With their guns firing, keeping the Hawkers at a distance, they followed Jack through the bull pen, taking cover whenever a Hawker lunged at them from above. When they were halfway across the room, shots began to come down from above.

"DAMN IT," swore Clark as a bullet caught him in his shoulder. "Guess the smart ones have joined the party!"

"Clark!" shouted Jack, turning his head to look over his shoulder.

"I'm fine, it's only a scratch."

"Like hell it is," said Hugh, coming up behind the wounded officer.

"If we don't keep moving," growled Clark, "it will be the least of my worries. I tell you, the armor got the worst of it! We need to keep moving!"

Thankfully, there only seemed to be two Hawkers with firearms, as they were able to weave in and out of the fire with only minor injuries before they reached the vending machines. Jack ran behind them, and upon following him, a thick metal door with a bolt was revealed. Atop it was a sign that said "Penitentiary, official business only." In one fast fluid motion, Jack slid aside the bolt and pushed the doors wide open.

The prison of Nimbus was an ugly grey addition to the police department. It had been built when it became too costly to send criminals down from the city to the state prison in Kansas. They had to pass through a small guard post that was empty, before pushing forward into the cells themselves. Once everyone was inside, Jack stopped to smash a glass box beside the entrance, which caused a siren to go off. Swiftly, strong steel shutters slid down in front of the doors leading back into the department, and bars slid into place from the left.

"That should buy us some time," gasped Jack, turning back to the others.

"What's happening?" asked Hugh, a bit stunned by the loud and shrill noise.

"He just activated the lockdown system," replied Owen, who had let his gun rest on its strap so he could use his hands to examine Clark's wound. "It's only for emergencies, such as prisoner riots. I guess having murderous robots on one's tail counts as such an emergency."

"I would believe... SO!" said Clark as he let out a little yelp of pain as Owen pulled down Clark's shirt's collar to get a better look at his injury. It was bleeding profusely, but they had enough supplies to bandage up the officer and plenty of painkillers to keep his head focused on things far more important than his wounded shoulder. As they were treating his wound, a pounding began on the security door behind them. At first, it was only the sound of metal hitting metal, but then fist-sized dents began to bulge through the metal shutter. Seeing the barrier beginning to give, they hurried up with treating Clark and picked up the pace.

The city's prison wasn't all that big, and they were able to reach the other end of it without wasting too much time. As they ran, Hugh looked at each cell they passed. None of them had anyone inside, and he was thankful for that. He highly doubted that if there were any prisoners in the city's jail they would have been spared by the Hawkers once they had taken over the city's police department. After passing through a gate set into thick metal bars, they found their path blocked by another security shutter, with a similar glass box beside it.

Without hesitation, Jack used the butt of his gun to smash this box too, revealing a key pad on the inside. With nimble fingers, he keyed in a code that Hugh could not see, and the lockdown lifted. The sirens stopped and the bars and shutter slid out of the way of the exit. Now that the exit was clear, they wasted no time barging out into the back lot where there was a special district train station. This one was used only by the police for quick travel through Liberty Estates, and for the transportation of criminals. It was currently useless as one of the specialized trains had, at some point, been knocked over and now blocked all the rails leading away.

Before them in the street were the downed bodies of a few Hawkers, their heads crushed upon impact, or their eyes shot out. There were also dead Sparrows and a few wounded and dead NTAF Officers too. The ones that still drew breath took shelter in doorways and inside buildings that had their doors smashed in for extra cover from the skies. A few manholes had been popped open from the inside, with claw marks in the pavement around them. Thankfully, not a single Hawker popped out from the smelly openings as Hugh's group moved deeper into Liberty Estates. Every step they took brought them deeper into danger, but also closer to their goal.

After running down the gently curving street behind the jail, they passed through a security gate and back into the public parts of the district. The apartments on either side of the narrow street were a tad rundown, due to their location near the prison, but still were far fancier places than what Hugh had been living in. They managed to find a way into one of the buildings on the west side of the street, which brought them inside a rather seedy pawn shop. There was a little fire burning beside a smashed counter, possibly caused by a Hawker that had crashed head first into an electrical panel. An NTAF officer, who was dealing with the fire with an extinguisher, turned to wave the group on and pointed them toward a door leading deeper into the apartment, located between a display cabinet that was leaking jewelry and beads through its broken glass front, and a very gaudy coat rack.

The door led the group of five to a small back room with a staircase leading up to the second level, and another door that they headed right for. This brought them back outside, in a small backyard that was ringed with a brick fence topped with iron spikes. The wall was low enough for them to easily hop over and continue on their way into the next building, which was clearly much better kept than the one they just left. They entered into a room that was identical to the back room of the pawn shop, yet extremely different. There was the same set of stairs and the same doors as the last building, only the floor was spotless here, and two large ovens dominated the space under the stairs leading up. There were a few stainless steel carts filled with loaves of forgotten bread that had gone stale and had bits of mold growing on them.

They moved through to the next room, which was a kitchen set up for the sole purpose of making pastries and loaves. In the middle of the black and white tiled floor were the remains of a body that had become food for a different kind of customer. They didn't even bother with the corpse as they pushed forward, through a set of swinging double doors into a space behind a long colorful counter. It was just a bit too tall to jump over, due to the tall glass display shelves holding baked sweets that were no longer fit for anything but rodents or a dumpster. There was another body on the floor right behind the cash register that they had to step over in order to pass through a small gate and into the bakery proper. The front of the store was made up of large plate glass windows that looked out to the street. Before them was another set of apartments, but peeking out from behind the row, much like the billboard with grapes before, was the broadcast tower. It was so close now, but not nearly close enough.

Suddenly a Hawker dove in through the same window that had briefly captivated them. It crashed into Jack, knocking him back into the pastry display, shattering the glass and sending spoiled baked goods rolling. Owen and Clark were too busy fending off more Hawkers, who tried to follow the first Hawker's example. Hugh turned to see Sally was holding her gun, trying to aim at the metal monster's eyes, but couldn't get a straight shot because it was moving about as Jack struggled. Hugh, acting on pure instinct, swung his rifle like a bat at the robot's head, stunning it just long enough for Sally to lock on and shoot it dead.

With the robot down, Jack pushed it aside and snatched up his gun, which had been knocked free when he hit the counter. He flashed Sally a winning smile, which made Hugh fume a little on the inside, before he dusted the glass shards off and joined the other three men at the window. Just when it began to look like they were going to be pinned down in the bakery, an explosion rang out, knocking the advancing Hawkers senseless and startling the humans.

From across the street, in one of the upper apartments, gleamed the barrel of a grenade launcher. Hugh turned to Jack and asked "Geez, why haven't you brought those things out sooner?"

Jack turned to Hugh, his mouth hanging open in bewilderment. "We don't have weapons like that. In fact, they are illegal in Nimbus because they would cause too much damage, even in the most experienced of hands."

"Whoever fired that, under normal circumstances, would be put under arrest on the spot," added Owen. "However, given how things are now, that man may come out of this as a hero instead of a crook."

"He won't come out of this period if we just stand here talking about it," growled Clark. His words snapped the others out of their stupor, and they proceeded to reload their weapons before heading out. Sally was doing pretty well on her supply of ammunition, as were the NTAF officers. Hugh, on the other hand, had gone through half of his supply. His shots, though better than when he had started almost a week ago, were still prone to flying wide of the mark. Sally, he reminded himself, only had so many bullets left because she didn't use her gun all that much. Instead, she chose to stay back and only shoot when it was a sure thing.

Once they were ready, they hurried outside past a few small tables that had been knocked over when the Hawkers broke in. The wind was really starting to kick up by now, and rain was starting to pour down upon their heads. As the storm picked up, the battle between flesh and machine continued, with a few casualties falling out of the sky here and there. They moved as fast as they could, avoiding the battle's fallen as they smashed their way inside another apartment, this one whose front hall was littered with toys and suitcases.

"We're almost there," muttered Hugh under his breath as they moved quickly through the hallway, passing by a body too small for him to dare look at. They passed through an open doorway and entered a fancy dining room with a crystal chandelier hanging crookedly from the cracked ceiling. The oval table in the center of the room was a mess of dishes and moldy food. The table's soft pink silk table cloth had been pulled almost completely off of the table, bringing most of the dishes to teetering on the very edge, while a few plates had already fallen to the floor. There was the body of a middle aged woman on the floor beside a fallen chair, a carving knife held tightly in one cold hand, in the other a corner of the table cloth.

As they moved past her, Hugh took a moment to notice that she had fallen, not away from the front of the house, but from the back, suggesting that the Hawker that killed her had come from the kitchen, not the front hall. She had died while trying to give her child a chance to escape, but had not been able to hold off the robot for nearly long enough. With a sigh, Hugh turned to see that the others had already moved on without him. With a start, he hurried over to the door to the kitchen. It was one of those doors that swung both in and out, and was painted a soft yellow color, that was only interrupted by clashing dried blood near the decorative handle.

Hurrying through the door, Hugh saw the others looking at him, expectantly. He blushed, realizing he held them up when time was of the essence. He followed them out the door and into a yard enclosed with a chain link fence. Before them, standing just a few yards away, was the Nimbus broadcast station. Red lights flashed along the length of the tower, from its base to the very top of the massive metal antenna. Closer than the tower stood the building in which the equipment that broadcast the information was held. And just beyond the tower, Hugh could see the office building where the city's paper was written up and printed.

He briefly reminisced about how things were. He would travel to that very same building, and take the elevator up to visit Sally and turn in his photos at his boss's office. Now, the building was dark, and chances were that the big boss was either in hiding or long dead. Such a different world he lived in now, despite the environment being roughly the same as it had been before.

Thankfully, as with the previous fence they had encountered, this one was also short enough for the group to climb over without too much hassle. The second their feet touched the grass on the other side, they set off running for the broadcast station. The Hawkers were at their thickest in the skies here, nearly blocking out the very rain itself from falling. As such, they had to fight most of the way there. Half the time, it felt to Hugh like he was just taking a step forward to sidestep three back just to avoid getting killed by Hawkers from the air. It did not help matters that bullets were being fired every which way from the sky. Some were aimed at him and his companions, while others were intended to hit the Sparrows. There were even some stray shots that were fired by the bronze Sparrows in the sky above their heads that went so wide that they almost hit the humans on the ground.

Clark was clearly hurting, as his shots began to get sloppy. Hugh was about to run back to help him when a Hawker came out of nowhere and pounded the officer into the grass, mere feet from the pavement in front of the broadcast station. Sally cried out and Jack swore. Owen, who was the closest to their fallen companion, had to deal with his own monster first. He quickly turned and fired at the Hawker, killing it instantly. By some stroke of fate, Clark was still alive, but only just. His chest had become misshapen from the impact and blood was pouring out of the corners of his mouth.

"Crap," he moaned through spurts of crimson.

"Hang on, we'll get you out of here," said Hugh before Owen stood up and pushed him aside.

"No, it's too late for him," he said.

"But he's still talking!" cried Hugh.

"He's got maybe a minute left with his entire chest smashed in," said Owen, glancing back at Clark, who was starting to spasm in the grass, sending droplets of blood flying from his lips, his eyes rolling back into his head. "The last thing we need is to make him hurt even more by moving him. He would want us to succeed."

Hugh turned to look down at the ruined man, his chest creaking disturbingly as he tried to breathe. Owen didn't wait any longer, and ran on ahead to join Jack at the doors to the station. Sally hung back, watching Hugh while also glancing nervously at the sky, preparing to yell out in case another Hawker broke free from the melee above their heads. It was only when Clark gasped his last that Hugh finally moved. Just in time, too, as the Hawkers had noticed them again and a pack of the machines had broken free and were on course for the humans.

By the time he and Sally had rejoined with Jack and Owen, they had forced the doors of the broadcast station open and were waiting inside. Once the two passed through the doorway, both officers slammed the double doors shut. Owen, who had taken Clark's rifle, slid it between the handles of the doors from the inside in an attempt to try to stall the Hawkers.

"Wouldn't Clark have wanted us to use that?" asked Sally. "Not a bullet wasted, right?"

"Doesn't matter, the clip's empty anyway," Owen assured her as they looked over the doors before them. There was no way the door would hold for long, but it would buy them some much needed time.

37

With the doors shut and the lights on inside the broadcast station, one could pretend that things were normal. There wasn't any blood anywhere inside, not on the walls, the doors or even the windows. There wasn't a single dead body, just fluorescent lights shining down upon them, the slightly dusty plain floor tiles under their feet and the white walls on either side. To their left and right were offices. One had a tag next to its frame with the words *"Waiting Room"* on it. To the right was a security office, which the remaining officers hurried inside, to see if they could possibly restock their ammunition. Alas, the best they found in the meager weapon locker was a hand gun, one box of small rounds, and a night stick.

Despite the poor pickings, they did find the locker itself very useful. It was light enough that they could lift it and sturdy enough that it could hold up under some serous punishment. Together, Hugh, Jack, Owen, and Sally carried the metal weapons locker out of the security office and wedged it in front of the entrance doors. It was placed down on one side, with the back against the weaker double doors. It was just tall enough to stick in the hallway and support the doors, preventing them from swinging inward. As an extra precaution, they busied about the offices, piling up furniture in front of the lockers. As they got started, the doors began to shake violently as a Hawker on the other side tried to beat them down. Every time the doors shook from the impact on the other side, the hinges groaned alarmingly.

However, the locker provided just enough support to keep the doors in place for the time being. It didn't budge under the onslaught. The hinges, however, were slowly working their way free of the door's frame. The doors themselves were showing the strain of the attack, as they cracked and splintered with every blow. With the time bought by the locker, Hugh and the others hurried to pile up other pieces of furniture in front of the door, ensuring that if the doors ever broke, the Hawkers would have to dig their way through to reach them.

With this out of the way, they turned and headed down the hallway, passing by old posters of famous lounge singers and popular bands. None of them, not even Sally, who worked the closest to the broadcast station, was familiar with the building's layout, so they had to go exploring. It wasn't a very big building, only one story high with a handful of rooms. All the windows they came across were small enough that a Hawker would be unable to squeeze through, which brought them all some piece of mind. Hugh wasn't sure if even the prototype Hawkers would have been able to fit their scrawny bodies through the narrow slits. The central hallway was in the shape of a letter T, with the left branch being longer than the right. They found an empty broadcast room, which held only a card table and a microphone connected to some recording equipment. Unfortunately, the room seemed to be without power, either by the Hawker's interference, or due to some technical gremlin. They still had the modified radios with them, and nothing would have been simpler than turning on the microphone, and holding the radio up.

Turning around, they explored more, finding a small bathroom and beside it a supply closet. When they reached the top of the T-shaped hallway, they saw, to the right, there was an emergency fire door. For a moment, there was the worry that the Hawkers would try to get in that way, and indeed, a pounding could be heard from that direction. However, the door was strong, and locked up tight. It looked like it could handle a herd of rampaging elephants, let alone a furious machine. From behind them there was the sound of splintering wood as the entrance doors finally gave in to the onslaught of metal fists.

Hugh and the others hurried to the other arm of the hall, as bullets flew through the air from the door, burying deep into the wall behind where they were standing. The humor of how the shots hit a poster for a gangster radio drama was not lost on Hugh, but now was not the time for cheap laughs. From the entrance the sounds of metal ripping metal could be heard, as the relentless Hawkers clawed at the barricade of the weapon locker and stacked furniture, signaling that their time was running out. As they hurried inside the one door on this side of the hallway, Hugh turned to see that there was a window looking into the broadcast room.

Upon entering the room, Hugh was greeted with a beautiful sight. In front of him and the others was a rack of machines and equipment. Lights were blinking on and off, and there were wires everywhere. At the very back of the room was a large console with slide bars and plenty of buttons and dials. Among it all were a pair of microphones hooked up to the console. This was clearly where they needed to be to send the message.

Behind the equipment was a normal-sized glass window that faced out towards the broadcast tower itself. The glass looked strong enough, but Hugh doubted it would hold up for long under attack. Wasting no more time, he ran toward the equipment and realized he had no idea what he was doing. After all, he was just a photographer, not a radio operator! The only experience he had with this sort of thing was from the time he spent playing with his father's ham set back when he was still living with his parents, but that thing was a toy compared to this setup.

"Here, try this, Hughie," said Sally from the left. Hugh turned to see her with a sly grin plastered upon her face, and in her hand a navy blue binder with the words *Operator's Manual* gracing its cover.

"Sally, you've saved the day!" said Hugh as he took the binder and flipped it open, his eyes scanning the diagrams and notes on the pages inside.

"No problem," she said with a smile. "Where would you be without me?"

"Dead, most likely," said Hugh as he skipped irrelevant pages and turned back to the table of contents so he could find the page number for the controls themselves.

"Owen," said Jack, looking at the only other remaining NTAF officer among them, "We are going to have to make sure trouble doesn't come in through the back or the window. You stay in here with the civilians. I'll go back out and give those Hawker bastards something to think about."

"Roger that, Jack," said Owen, nodding his head as he turned to face the window behind the console. He slid a fresh clip into the weapon's chamber and raised the barrel so whatever tried to jump them would get a face full of lead on its way in. Sally, too, had her weapon at the ready, though it was not as big as Owen's. It was clear that she was ready to shoot, and wouldn't hold back. Hugh, meanwhile, was turning knobs on the machine, following the illustrated start-up directions in the blue binder. Jack, after taking one last look around the equipment room, turned and exited back into the hall, where the sounds of breaking furniture could be heard. In his hand he held one of the three modified radios, a last ditch resort. The other two were in the hands of Sally and in the pocket of Hugh's pants. They had saved them for this crucial moment, as they would need all the time they could get.

Hugh took his modified radio out of his pocket and held it tightly in his left hand. Sally saw this and took out her own. Since she was still using the handgun they had found days ago when they had first spent a night with Icarus together, she was able to wield the weaponized handset and the gun at the same time. Hugh, who was holding the binder with one hand, and working with the console with the other, put his radio down atop the broadcast console. As a precaution, he switched it on so that if any Hawkers did try to get in through the window, they'd have to contend with the radio's kill radius before getting very far inside.

The sounds of the battle in the air outside, and the growing storm, made Hugh nervous. His fingers slipped and tumbled about the keys, and he had to restart the whole process again after he made a disastrous mistake. Owen swore at him, but Hugh ignored it. He had far more to deal with in his own head at the moment than to listen to unhelpful remarks. When he was midway through, a Hawker suddenly appeared in the window, only to drop dead before it could punch through the glass. This didn't stop Owen from firing at the robot, or from Hugh flinching and backing away from the console in surprise. Sally too let loose a bullet of her own, that punched a hole in the wall right above the window itself.

Owen's ill-timed shot hit the window dead on and sent a spider web of cracks shooting out from where it impacted the glass. Somehow, the glass did not completely shatter, and stayed inside the window frame. However, now they couldn't see clearly what was happening outside, which only served to raise everyone's anxiety. From out in the hall, gunshots could be heard, a sign that Jack was giving it his all to delay the Hawkers from his end of the broadcast station.

Hugh had gotten back to the console, and was keying in the sequence for activating the city-wide emergency broadcast system, when a dark shadow appeared before the window. As before, it fell over dead on the other side, but not as quickly as the first had. Hugh for a brief moment feared that the Hawkers had somehow developed immunity to the kill signal, until he noticed that there was a light blinking on the handset. Looking over at it, he saw a little stylized symbol of a battery on the black plastic beside the blinking light.

"What's wrong, Hugh?" asked Owen, still aiming at the now cracked window.

"I think the battery may be going on this," he called back as he backed away and finished keying in the emergency code.

"Do you want to use mine?" asked Sally, holding up her own radio.

"No," said Hugh, waiting for the code to be accepted by the machine. "I'd rather you keep ahold of that Sal. You may need it more than I do if things go belly up here."

"I think it would make more sense if you took it, hero," said Owen. "You're the one sending out the signal."

"Be that as it may," said Hugh as a red light turned green on the console. "But she's my gal. I would gladly sacrifice myself to keep her safe any day of the week!"

"That is very romantic of you, Hughie," said Sally as she walked up behind Hugh at the console. "But a world without you would be no world that I want to be a part of."

"Sally," started Hugh before the light turned red again.

"Damn it! I must have hit a wrong key!" he said as he consulted the manual again. He typed in the key code again, and this time the light stayed green.

"There we go!" said Sally with a smile, as she looked over his shoulder to watch him work. Hugh smiled just as widely back. He had become giddy with how close they were to victory. They were literally minutes, if not seconds, away from bringing the terror of the Hawkers to an end. Now, everything was all set to go, all he had to do now was bring one of the two modified radios up to the microphone and press one more button to start the broadcast and send it out to every single receiving speaker in Nimbus. He glanced at his radio, still sitting atop the console, the battery's light glowing a weak red. Sally was about to hand Hugh her radio, as Hugh's own was too weak now to be picked up by the broadcasting equipment. Hugh was moving his hand out to accept the radio from her, when suddenly he found himself being pulled back from the console, broken glass flying past him as cold metal arms wrapped themselves around his body.

Sally screamed as a Hawker dove inside, and tried to use her own device to stop it. But the Hawker managed to swat it out of her hands with one claw while the other was still wrapped around Hugh's torso. He heard the sounds of twigs snapping and felt pain in his chest. Owen, of course, aimed his rifle to fire on the mechanical beast. But before he could get a shot off, it stood up and held Hugh before it like a shield, making sure the photographer's head was right in front of its own.

"WEAPONS DOWN!" it shrieked. "OR THE MAN DIES."

Sally, having been shaken up by the sudden invasion, quickly shook the cobwebs free from her head and looked around for the fallen handheld. It was nowhere in sight, having been sent flying out the same window that the Hawker had burst through. However, she somehow had managed to turn it on, as there weren't any more Hawkers coming in through the breach.

As they stared at the robot holding Hugh hostage, it became clear that this machine wasn't working properly. It shifted from foot to foot and its head twitched every now and then atop its neck, as if it had to fight to keep looking in one direction. There were signs of damage from the battle over its body, in the form of dents and scratches. At some point, it had been shot in one of its eyes, leaving a broken hole in which sparks danced and a thin waft of smoke rose out of. Despite having been hit in its weak spot, its bio-brain hadn't been damaged enough to kill it. However, something important had broken, leaving its actions erratic, and whatever mind it had, in shambles.

"Let him GO!" cried Sally, all her pent up rage let out in one word.

"YOU DIE ALL DIE MONKEYS DIE," was all it could say, its speech breaking down from the damage to its bio-brain. This wasn't to say it wasn't still very much capable of ending Hugh's life then and there. It had him not only by the waist, but also by his neck, and its grip was barely loose enough for Hugh to draw breath into his lungs. Owen yelled at the Hawker, trying to get its attention, while Sally inched her way to the control panel, but it was to no avail. The robot tightened its grip on Hugh's throat and screamed for the humans not to move.

"BACK UP HELP KILL ERROR!" it yelled out, its eyes flipping between blue and red as its bio-brain struggled against the effects of the signal of Sally's handset. With Hugh as a hostage, neither Sally nor Owen could make a move against it.

Suddenly, Hugh found himself flung to the floor, his nose breaking upon impact on the hard floor tiles. The Hawker that had been holding him had released its grip in surprise as a bronze bolt of lightning shot through the broken window and plowed into the machine.

"ICARUS!" cried out Sally in surprise, too stunned to move. She then realized Hugh was free and hurried over to him, helping him up off the floor as large globs of blood dropped out from his bent nose. "Oh my God, Hugh! Are you okay? SPEAK TO ME!"

"I'm fine, Sal," wheezed Hugh, his speech slightly slurred due to his nose. It hurt like hell, but at least he could breathe again, be it more through his mouth. He shook his head and let out a few coughs before looking over at his savior. Icarus was on the back of the Hawker, struggling to grapple with it. The bronze Sparrow was bleeding from his wings, where they had grazed the broken glass of the window when he dived through. His muscles strained as he tried to hold back the arms of the Hawker, who was screaming gibberish interlaced with death threats. It tried to tear at Icarus's flesh, but the birdman kept moving, dodging the robot's claws.

"Nice save, Icarus!" said Hugh as he watched Owen join the Sparrow in attempting to hold it down. The officer had pulled out a smaller hand gun that he was currently trying to get lined up with the eyes of the robot, but having no success with it thrashing about in Icarus's arms.

"DO IT NOW," yelled Icarus, looking over his shoulder at Hugh and Sally.

"I can't!" Hugh shouted back. "We lost Sally's and my battery's dead!"

"Here," said Sally as she held her hand out to Hugh. At first he didn't understand what she was giving him, as he was still reeling from getting bear hugged by a Hawker and getting his nose broken. Once the cobwebs cleared, he saw she was holding out a pair of batteries. "These are from my flashlight," she said. "I don't know if they will work in your radio, but it's probably our only shot now, wouldn't you say?"

Without even a word of acknowledgement, Hugh gingerly took the batteries from Sally's outstretched hand and moved away from his twice savior and dashed back to the console. The panel was covered in shards of broken glass and rain water from the skies outside, and there were some claw marks and dents in it from when the Hawker burst through the window, but everything still seemed to be lit up and working. His radio had been knocked off the console and was lying on the floor among the shards of broken glass. Being careful not to cut himself, he reached down and picked up the handset and worked as fast as he could to get the battery flap open on the back of the device. Glancing briefly at Icarus and Owen struggling to hold down the Hawker, Hugh saw that Sally had taken up a stand on the other side of the Hawker and had her own weapon out, trying to aim just like Owen, at the monster's fluctuating, glowing eyes.

Looking back at the radio's battery chamber, Hugh felt a massive wave of relief flow over him, as the batteries Sally gave him and the dead ones in the handset were the same type. Wasting no more time, he quickly swapped them out with the fresh ones and turned the radio on. It came to life instantaneously in Hugh's hands, and the Hawker on the floor stopped moving, allowing Icarus to finally relax his hold on the machine. However, it was clear from the sounds from the hallway outside that they were far from being in the clear yet. Hugh, with one last look at the prone Hawker on the floor and at his friends, took a deep breath, and pressed the button labeled *"Live Broadcast."*

There was the sound of the emergency broadcast system's introductory siren in the air. It was repeated everywhere in the city. Hugh prayed this would work and took another deep breath to calm down as he prepared to send the signal out. He held the modified handset tightly as he brought it up to the microphone.

"This ends now," he said calmly into the microphone. And with that, he pressed the button that let his little radio be heard throughout the flying city.

At first, there was nothing but a second or two of silence. Then the tone from the modified handset emitted from every speaker in the city. From the hallway, the sounds of gunfire and the shrieks of enraged Hawkers suddenly stopped. Outside, the battle in the sky came to an instant standstill, as if in a photograph. Then, first one by one, and then in growing numbers, Hawkers began to fall from the sky, their wings and jetpacks no longer responding, their minds dead and eyes dark. They fell like giant pieces of metallic hail, impacting the ground around the station and the tower hard enough to bury their shells into the dirt and crack concrete.

As the Hawkers rained down from on high, Hugh counted the seconds as he held the small handset to the microphone, wanting for at least a minute before he deemed it safe to leave the microphone. He didn't want to risk stopping the broadcast until he was sure it had had enough time to reach every single one of the metal birds that had the reprogrammed OTM and bio-brain in their heads. After two minutes, he finally backed away from the microphone, and let the hand holding the handset fall to his side. He couldn't help but jump a little as a few Hawkers crashed down before the broken window, slamming into the other robot bodies piled up outside the window. Behind him, Jack barged back in to the room, a huge smile on his face.

"It's over! It's all OVER!" he cheered.

Hugh smiled back and brought a hand up to his face, to feel his broken nose. He watched as Owen and Jack approached each other and shook hands, both with wide grins on their faces. He realized then that Sally wasn't speaking and turned to look at her. She was down on the floor, having fainted in relief at the danger finally being over. He went to her, and sat down beside her on the floor. He gently picked up her head and placed it in his lap, the blood from his nose now slowing down to trickle. She roused in his hands and looked up at him through heavy eyelids draped with thick lashes.

"Hey, hero," she whispered, reaching out to touch his face.

"Hey, Sally," he said back, his heart fluttering like a bird let free of the cage for the first time.

"Did we win?" she asked, as her eyelids drooped.

"Yeah, everything is going to be okay now," said Hugh as he leaned in close to kiss her on the lips, leaving a bit of his blood on her face by accident.

"Good," she said with a sigh as she passed out again.

All over the city, Hawkers were falling from the sky amongst cheers of the survivors. The NTAF officers on the streets had to hurry to take cover from the rain of metal bodies, as they fell with enough force to crack pavement. Some officers weren't quick enough, and were struck by the dead machines, but most managed to move in time. The robots fell everywhere, from the battle over Liberty Estates, to the secret areas of the outer districts. The Hawkers manning the factory in Vulcan slouched over and fell onto the conveyor belts. Their bodies jammed the machinery, causing production to stop. What Hawkers that were left alive, the models without the altered bio-brain inside their heads, were easily dealt with by the Sparrows. Several even surrendered, saying that they were actually in the early stages of becoming Sparrows themselves, claiming that they had only fought back so the Hawkers wouldn't find out.

The wind outside died down as the Hawkers controlling the city's flight died in the hidden control room deep inside the city of Nimbus. It wasn't long after that that the Sparrows all came down for a landing all over the city. This caused a bit of a scare to surviving residents, many of whom had never seen a Sparrow before. Thankfully by now, Jack, thinking about this, had taken over the emergency broadcast system and, with the help of the blue binder, restored most of the panel's default settings so his voice could ring out loud and clear.

"Attention citizens of Nimbus. The terror of the Hawkers is OVER! I repeat. The danger has passed! The giant birds you see before you are NOT Hawkers. They are called SPARROWS and they are on OUR SIDE. I repeat..."

While he gave out the announcement, Hugh stayed with Sally on the floor, his hand stroking her hair as she slept. He was glad she was able to rest. After everything they had been through together, she deserved that much, perhaps more than anyone else in the entire city. Hugh looked up from her and out the broken window, watching the dead robots falling outside. He dared not leave her side in this moment of victory, but words she had spoken only a few days ago came back to him. He reached down to his old camera bag and pulled out his camera. He had no idea if it still worked, given everything it had gone through in the fight to the radio station, but knew in his heart that Sally would have wanted him to capture this moment. He reached back into the bag and pulled out his long range lens and attached it to his camera. He aimed the view finder through the broken window, up at the mass in the sky and the falling metal bodies. He took several pictures in rapid succession. When he had almost finished the roll, he turned the camera away from the window and disconnected the long range lens. He looked over to Icarus with a smile and said, "Say cheese..."

Epilogue

It had taken a while for the Sparrows to become accepted among the humans. Many of the people who had survived the battle and the Hawkers' terror still had trouble adjusting to these new winged creatures taking up residence in their city. It was even harder to convince the Air Force, whose connection had been immediately reestablished. After a while, and many broadcasts between the city and the rest of the nation explaining the situation and how the danger was over, a new squadron of rescue aircraft was sent to Nimbus to retrieve the survivors. This time, there was no resistance to prevent the pilots from landing in the city. Due to the normal landing strips having been destroyed long ago with the Transport Center, such places as Valkyrie Park, Olympic Fields, and Vulcan had to be turned into temporary airports, due to the flatness of the districts and the space available for a plane to land.

With the aid of the Sparrows, many of the sky bridges were repaired, once again connecting the districts together, so as to provide a means for survivors to travel to the evacuation points. Everyone was to leave Nimbus until the government could come in with professionals to assess the total damages done to the city and the price tag of repairs.

Everyone who stepped inside the planes was flown down to Salt Lake City International Airport. They were greeted by men in suits who checked off their names from a long list of known residents of Nimbus. The Sparrows rode down to the surface in these planes and had their names written down in a separate series of papers. This was to help document the newest species on planet Earth and make it easier for the officials to keep track of the Sparrows and discover how many Sparrows there were. To make sure everyone was found, rescue teams were sent out into the city to search high and low for anyone left behind.

They found Bobby, Dannik, Frank, and the others in that little janitor's room and brought in stretchers to carry out Bobby and Samuel. Samuel protested that he could walk just fine, but they wouldn't listen, saying that it would be best if they carried him out. Bobby tried hard not to laugh as he watched the experienced officer squirm about as he was carried out of the dark room on the shoulders of their rescuers. Dannik walked out on his own two clawed feet, having made an unbelievably fast recovery from his bullet wounds. He helped Frank walk out of the room and out into the daylight, where a repaired district train was waiting to carry them to the plane waiting to take them down from Nimbus.

The officers stationed in the Warehouse District and those they had sheltered, upon hearing the Hawkers had all been defeated, rose out of their underground lair and helped out the rescuers in locating places where survivors could have held up. With full control of the city's broadcast system, they were finally able to contact all the NTAF officers around Nimbus, who in turn set out to help. Though the toll on Nimbus's finest had been heavy, far more officers emerged alive than anyone had dared to hope for.

Everyone who had been hiding in the employee hallways of Full Moon Plaza had made it out alive. Even Andrew, who after seeing Hugh and his friends off, had been attacked by a Hawker who flew in through the open cargo bay hatch. He didn't know how to shut it, and by the time he had figured out the console, one of the monsters had managed to spot it and flew in. Thankfully, he had his pistol and was able to stop it before it could kill him, or alert its friends to his location.

As for those they left behind in the basement of Angel of Mercy Hospital, they were in slightly worse shape. After Hugh and the others had left, Dr. Craven had had a bit of a meltdown, and had ordered that everyone remain in the sick room, under constant surveillance. He wasn't sure how Amy had managed to slip out of the building, but he was determined it was not going to happen again. Of course, none of the doctors or patients would stand for this, and many rebelled against his orders. By the time the rescue crew found them, the survivors had split into two groups, a large one that was under the advice of Nurse Rogers, and the smaller one that had the guns and followed Dr. Craven's orders with a blind loyalty. It wasn't easy, but they managed to get everyone out in the end, despite Dr. Craven's best attempts to keep them inside and "safe."

Once those who had survived the ordeal of the Hawkers were safely out of Nimbus and on the ground at Salt Lake City International, an inquiry was held. Everyone was put through an interview with an assigned handler to give their side of the story of what had happened and what went wrong up in the flying city. Everyone had their turn, even the Sparrows. It was a very lengthy process that took up the remainder of July and most of August to complete. During this time, the survivors were given free board at hotels across Salt Lake City, and were pestered by news crews from across the nation.

Sally, of course, with the aid of her notes, was able to write up the best story of the lot, having lived through most of the excitement. She was given a temporary job at *The Salt Lake City Tribune*, where her story made front page news. Her story was accompanied by photos taken by Hugh. The picture he had taken of Icarus had been reprinted in papers across the country, along with the ones of the Sparrows with their wings up in the winery, the devastation in Galileo plaza, and the skirmish outside of Bobby's apartment. It was Sally who had the film developed, as Hugh had become indisposed upon leaving the city.

Hugh, like Bobby and the others who had been harmed by Hawker claws and lived to tell about it, was put up in the best hospital available. Thankfully, Hugh's injuries were not too serious, though he did have to wear a special brace around his chest like a girdle so his ribs would set properly. His nose would never be as straight as it used to be, but he took that in stride, joking that it added to his God-given good looks. Bobby, whose leg justified that he was given more hospital time than Hugh, had been given a room with his father, who had his leg looked at again. Bobby would have to use a cane to walk for the rest of his life, but at least he was alive. Other survivors weren't nearly as lucky, having suffered far worse.

Time passed, and seasons changed. Bobby was released from the hospital, sporting a new leg brace and a wooden cane. Sally won a Pulitzer for her article and Hugh's photos worked their way around the globe, along with before-and-after pictures of the devastation in the floating city, many of which were taken by government officials. Hugh found an apartment to rent until he and Sally could put together enough money to travel back east to Boston. Hugh's parents were more than willing to have their son and his fiancé stay with them until they could get back on their feet. The place wasn't the best Utah had to offer, being a one bedroom flat, but it was enough for now, and Hugh and Sally were more than happy with the view. From their windows they could see a busy street, bustling with life and cars zipping by, a reminder that they were no longer high in the sky, but safe with both feet on the ground.

Eventually, with Sally's help, Hugh sent out letters to all of their friends to invite them to dinner at an expensive local steakhouse. He had finally managed to gather enough money to give Sally an engagement ring and it seemed like the perfect reason to get the gang back together. The restaurant was designed to look like a Wild West saloon on the outside, with matching hitching posts standing at attention beside the front door.

The inside was decorated with cowboy hats, horseshoes, and pictures of famous western movie stars. The food was advertised as the best beef in Salt Lake City, and it easily met the couple's expectations. They booked a large private table in the back of the restaurant, which quickly filled up as the guests arrived.

The first to show up was Bobby, with his father helping him walk. They congratulated Hugh and Sally on their engagement and shook their hands. The next to arrive were Samuel and a few members of the NTAF, including Jack with a big smile and a little present for the lovers. Following on their heels was Dannik, who was dressed up in a pair of simple blue jeans and sporting a white tee-shirt with buttons on the back and holes in it for his wings. The tall white Sparrow was an oddity among the other patrons, but after a public address from Dwight D. Eisenhower, the President of the United States, introducing Sparrows into world society a few weeks earlier, people were starting to adjust to seeing the giant manlike birds in everyday life. Currently, talks were being held between Tempest, who had survived the battle, and the country's government as to where the Sparrows would end up staying. Several of the birds had flown back up to Nimbus, as it was the only home they had ever known, despite access to the flying city being forbidden until the damage had been fully assessed. Others had been allowed to take up residence in apartments much like the one Hugh and Sally were staying in. Several Sparrows had taken on simple jobs in Salt Lake City to pay for their room and board.

Dannik still got a few odd looks as he sat down in a chair at the end of the table, his large muscled body and long wings making sitting anywhere else a challenge. The last guest to arrive was Icarus, who was late because he was bringing a few unexpected guests of his own.

Upon sight of the bronze bird, now dressed up in a proper pair of pants and a specialized sports jacket that had slots for his wings to poke out of, everyone at the table turned and waved him over. Behind him strolled a tall and elegant female Sparrow dressed in a simple but stylish blue dress. Hugh instantly recognized the female Sparrow from the brief moments they met back when he first teamed up with Icarus.

In her arms she carried two babies covered in down feathers with tiny little beaks instead of lips and noses. Their hands looked human, save for the black fingernails, and they had only three toes on their little feet. Both were wrapped in fuzzy blankets, one blue and the other pink. Hugh stood up and called out to the restaurant's management, calling for an extra chair and two high chairs for the young children. Icarus, upon reaching the table, turned and introduced everyone to his mate, and to his children.